The Arrest of Scotland Yard

In 1877, a third of Scotland Yard's Detective Division appeared at the Central Criminal Court on charges of taking bribes. As a result of this scandal, the CID was founded and the first Director of Public Prosecutions was appointed. This is the real-life background to Inspector Swain's gripping new case.

Inspector Swain is hired by the family of John Posthumous Lerici, decadent poet, black magician, and unacknowledged son of Lord Byron. His investigations into the murder of Lerici in the sinister surroundings of Agamemnon's Mycenae lead Swain back to England and the familiar hunting grounds of Victorian Brighton and Pimlico. But as the truth of Lerici's criminal associations comes to light, it reveals the corruption of Scotland Yard officers by two of the century's most skilful international swindlers and blackmailers, Harry Benson and Billy Kurr.

As threads of extortion and murder ensnare the operations of Scotland Yard, Swain can trust no one and no one trusts him.

But the inspector is beginning to find himself more troubled by the strange beauty of Amalia de Brahami and the darkest crime of the ancient world coming to new life in Victorian England . . .

THE ARREST OF SCOTLAND YARD

Donald Thomas

**MACMILLAN
LONDON**

MC

First published 1993 by Macmillan London Limited

a division of Pan Macmillan Publishers Limited
Cavaye Place London SW10 9PG
and Basingstoke

Associated companies throughout the world

ISBN 0–333–60506–3

9 8 7 6 5 4 3 2 1

A CIP catalogue record for this book is available from
the British Library

Phototypeset by Intype, London
Printed by Mackays of Chatham, PLC, Chatham, Kent

The action of this novel takes place against a general background of historical events in the 1870s. These culminated in the 'Trial of the Detectives' at the Central Criminal Court and the creation of the CID, the first appointment of a Director of Public Prosecution and the passing of the Bills of Exchange Act (1882).

He is borne away who bears away:
And the killer has all to pay.

Robert Browning, *The Agamemnon of Aeschylus*
(1877)

1

INSPECTOR SWAIN AND THE GREEK KEY

1

Petrides, 'The Wolf of the Argoloid', as his people now called him, sat expressionless on the grey wooden gun-carriage with his two escorts. A length of chain connected his ankles, and his wrists were strapped behind his back. Four of the soldiers with an officer in command had taken him from his cell at daybreak. Now he listened with half his attention to the first lines of his own burial service. Fiercely moustached and with his hair bound in a kerchief, Petrides glanced once at the sergeant beside him. There would be no escape. On every side of him the early light rippled in a quicksilver glimmering on the massed blades of the fixed bayonets and the officers' drawn swords.

The gun-carriage, drawn by a team of four greys with riders on the left-hand horse of each pair, rattled between two long ranks of grey-uniformed infantry with long bayonets on their rifles, scarlet scabbard-tabs at the rear of their black belts. A few yards ahead of Petrides, a plain cart bumped over the stones. It carried an open oblong box, painted white, matching the condemned man's height. The murderer's coffin was to stand beside him as he died, a warning to any of his followers or admirers behind the shuttered windows.

The procession was in the square of the town by this time, red-tiled domes of the old mosque rising at one end and the arcading of a Venetian warehouse at the other. As Petrides looked round him, the white and caramel wash of the houses warmed to the yellow dawn sunlight, their shutters bare of paint as if it had been scrubbed from them. He glanced up at the windows on either side, trying to make out if the thin pale Englishman had come to see him die.

The bearded priest, in his tall Orthodox hat and black robe, walked on beside the gun-carriage, intoning the liturgy of the dead. Petrides again assured himself that he had no wish to die – would have leapt at the least chance of escape. If he must die, then he would show them how the thing should be done. He would be the Wolf of the Argoloid, the robber of Agamemnon's gold. If they believed that, he might still conceal the truth from them. It was easier to die when there was something to accomplish. On the previous day, as he was told, a cut-throat, Teodoro, had wept as the gun-carriage bore him across the square, had knelt with clasped hands and pleaded at the firing-post for the sake of his wife and children. It did no good. They raised him up, bound him, and shot him as he sobbed. Anything was better than that. Petrides was not an educated man. He understood, of course, that he was to die for murdering his master. Or perhaps he was to die because the signore's death had angered the powerful queen of England in her far-off island. And, of course, he was to die so that someone whom he treasured more than himself should live. He cleared his throat, turned his head, and spat in the slow foot-steps of the priest.

The gun-carriage stopped and they helped him down. He was to be shot with his back to the warehouse and his face to the rising sun. The sun was above the hill now, over the long crenel-lated ridge of the high Venetian fortress of the Palamidi. Petrides looked down either side of the long square towards the abandoned mosque to see if the Englishman had come after all. Now that time was so short, it mattered more to him that the Englishman should hear what he had to say than whether he died on this day or the next.

A wooden screen, left in place since the execution of Teodoro on the previous morning, stood behind the firing-post. It was about six feet high and ten feet long, made of thick deck-planking, pitted and splintered in a dozen places by bullets, splashed here and there by dark spots of dried blood. Petrides let them fasten his wrists to the post behind him and tighten two straps round his waist and ankles. When they tried to put a blindfold over his eyes, he shook his head impatiently. How should he see the Englishman if he was blindfolded? The officer made a sign and the soldier put the cloth away.

The priest approached the condemned bandit and applied a moist touch to his forehead. Petrides smelt fish on the old man's breath and shook his head again, dismissing him. Almost all the shutters had been closed at the windows of the square but Petrides was not such a fool as to suppose the windows were unoccupied. There were eyes at every chink and crevice, some of them his friends. But half a regiment of the King's army still stood with rifles and bayonets between him and any hope of rescue. The Englishman. Petrides spoke little of the language. His murdered master had always used Italian to him when orders were necessary, even in England. Now Petrides felt the injustice of dying for a man who, in his own way, was as depraved as the murderer.

An officer in blue with his French pill-box hat was standing in front of him now, reading from a paper to the effect that he had been tried and condemned in the King's name for the crimes of robbery and murder. The reading ended. The officer pinned a pocket-sized square of white cloth to the breast of Petrides' tunic, just above the heart.

The morning was still and calm in the seconds before the first order was given to the riflemen. The woman was sobbing and he avoided looking in her direction. The chief of police and the Prefect of Nauplia were standing with the commander of the troops but without their English guest. Petrides knew he would have to call out. He had not wanted to do that, knowing that some of the swine who came to watch him die would think he was crying like an animal for mercy of some kind. 'May your women all be unfaithful and infect you with a shameful disease,' he said to the onlookers under his breath. Faster and faster he scanned the closed shutters of the square.

'Mis-ter Swa-in!'

It was a wild cry but he saw a shutter move. Of course, it was the house of the English Consul, half-way down one side of the square. Petrides strained for a glimpse of the fair thin-faced man with the look of an intelligent horse.

'Mister Swain!'

The shutter moved a little more. At the officer's command, the

3

dozen riflemen had lifted their weapons to their shoulders. Petrides, who should have been mesmerized by terror of the twelve black muzzles, gaping like dark iron wounds, looked past them and above them. For the first and only time, he was free to tell the Englishman what the interference of his interrogators had made impossible before.

'Iphigenia, Mr Swain...! Iph-i-gen-ia...! Find her! In her lies the truth...! She is the weapon of your enemies that will destroy you...'

The cobbled square echoed to a ragged crash of detonations. A torn veil of smoke drifted on the cool morning air. Petrides slid in a crumpled genuflection down the firing-post. As the detail grounded arms, the captain in his dark blue uniform stepped forward with a pistol drawn. He almost touched it to the nape of the crumpled figure, then drew back. A *coup de grâce* was unnecessary. The squad of riflemen had been well chosen. All life was extinct in the shattered breast of the Wolf of the Argoloid.

The screams of a woman scarcely more than a shape huddled in black by the body burst from the wails with which she had awaited the death of Petrides. The onlookers stared at her as a stranger, knowing her only as the woman who is always present on such occasions, the wife, the mistress, the mother... They paused a moment to watch her weep and then began to walk away into the little streets on either side. At the first-floor window, John Munro, Her Britannic Majesty's Consul in the port of Nauplia, drew the shutter closed and fastened it. He was a substantially built man, a subaltern grown old without promotion, showing a fresh complexion, tarnished fair hair and a carefully waxed moustache. When his companion made no movement, standing at the shutter but no longer seeing what was beyond it, Munro crossed the room to a marble-topped sideboard.

'It can't be, Mr Swain. It can't be the first time you've ever seen a man put to death. Not in your occupation.'

'Once or twice before,' Alfred Swain said dully, still staring at the closed shutter.

'Once or twice!' Munro laughed as the spirit splashed into a glass. 'When I was a young fellow, we used to make up parties to see them do the rope-dance bright and early on a Monday morning outside Newgate Gaol. In public in those days. All done away

4

with now, of course. They do it in the prison grounds nowadays. Here. Drink this down, You look as though you could do with it.' Swain said nothing but Munro jollied him along. 'Greeks shoot well, you know. Mind you, they use our rifles. Snider back-loaders with that extra couple of inches of barrel beyond the stock. Deadly accurate. Good thing the Prefect got his way. Determined to do the thing in public as a lesson to the rest of that rabble. *Encourager les autres* and so on.'

Inspector Swain took his glass from the consul, without turning from the shutter and without drinking.

'What did he mean? Iphigenia? Why find her? Who is she?'

Munro swallowed his brandy and laughed. 'Who knows and who cares? His woman probably. Or some nonsense or other. One thing sure. That rogue Petrides can't tell you any more. By God, he died game, though. Didn't he? Not like yesterday's namby-pamby.' Munro's tone suggested that he might clap the policeman on the back for encouragement.

'Yes,' Swain said, turning from the shutter but ignoring his glass. 'And men who die game generally do it for a reason. Everything happens for a reason. When a man's come to his last gasp and he's going to have even that blasted from him in a second, he doesn't waste it on nonsense – damned or otherwise. And I doubt somehow that he ever had a woman called Iphigenia.'

Munro let out a long, tolerant breath, smiled and gestured at the glass in his companion's hand. 'Get that down, old fellow, and you'll feel better for it. It's the shock, even when you're prepared for the scoundrel's death. Bound to be. Takes getting used to.'

Swain crossed the room and put his glass down, untasted, on the sideboard. The tall thin figure, neatly but plainly suited, turned its intelligent equine profile and gentle eyes on the consul. A good many men and a few women had miscalculated what lay behind the gentleness of that glance.

'I've seen men die, Mr Munro,' he said quietly, 'I've seen the bodies of men, and women, and even children, after they've died in ways far worse than this. I'm used to it, thank you, so far as a man can ever be. I won't waste your brandy. I've never found much help from it on these occasions. Poetry sometimes, remembering lines of it. And verses from the Bible. Great things that have been said. Sometimes they make it better. Not always.'

5

'Poetry?' Munro's florid cheeks seemed to expand a little at the unfathomable idea. 'School-book lessons? Draw it mild, old fellow!'

'I generally do,' Swain said, unconcerned.

The consul crossed to the window. This time, he unfastened the slide-bolt of the shutters and pushed them wide, flooding the room with warm light from the April sun. His tone lost its clubman's affability and he took no pains to disguise the fact that Swain had begun to bore him.

'I don't suppose I can do much more for you; then. The *Marchioness of Lorne* should berth three days from now, out of Alexandria, bound for Gravesend. I've arranged for you to collect the body of the victim. John Posthumous Lerici – bastard son of Lord Byron, if you believe such rot – was taken to the custom house last night. The town surgeon bandaged him top to toe, like an Egyptian mummy, two days after he was killed. He was lowered into his cask of rum and nailed down. When old Bonaparte's nephew was killed in the fighting here, they kept him for two years like that before they sent him back to France. By the time you get Lerici home, he should be well pickled. Where's he being buried, by the way?'

'In his own grounds in Sussex,' Swain said, 'at Mondragon, the house he built on Folly Ridge outside Brighton.'

Munro nodded. 'The town surgeon's advice is to coffin him as he is. Don't unbandage him. There's been a full identification and inquest here, in my presence as British consul. The *Marchioness of Lorne* is an old tub with more rust than water in her boilers. Been trading to the Levant ever since I can recall. You won't see England for three weeks. So keep Lerici nailed down. What he'll look like when you get him back is anyone's guess. Anything else for you to do, is there?'

'I must make two reports,' Swain said thoughtfully. 'One for the family lawyer, Mr Abrahams of King's Bench Walk, and one for the Metropolitan Police – or rather for the Metropolitan Police to forward to the Foreign Office. I shall need to see the place where he died. There hasn't been time yet.'

'Chuck it,' Munro said.

Swain held the Consul's gaze. 'Why?'

Munro picked up a paper and looked at it, as if to avoid Swain's eyes while he spoke. 'Don't be a fool, man. Petrides killed him and he's died for it. But Lerici was as big a scoundrel as Petrides in his way. That's why he employed the fellow. Petrides killed Lerici out at Mykenos, the devil knows why. Out at the site. The police here think it was in a quarrel about gold ornaments which Lerici had stolen from the tombs out there. Or, rather, he bribed some of the workmen to steal them. The villain Petrides wanted his share and that's all about that. There's nothing to see there but bushes and rocks. And, of course, Herr Schliemann with his eternal excavations. Where's the use?'

'I'll tell you when I've been there,' Swain said with gentle stubbornness. 'I don't understand why everyone tries to stop me going. You don't want me to go. I asked the Commandant yesterday. It seems that the Greeks don't want me to go. Why?'

Munro sat down in an armchair and shook his head. 'I dare say they don't want you wandering off the beaten track,' he said with a shrug. 'Those hills are full of Petrides and his kind. There's nothing out there for you. Nothing but Herr Schliemann – and he's drier than the dust itself. Avoid him if you can. The place is a heap of stones, nothing more. You won't discover anything there.'

'Perhaps,' Swain said, 'but I can't help feeling that Petrides would make a poor bandit. I don't mind the journey and I've never before found it a waste of time to visit the scene of a murder. As for Herr Schliemann, I've read something of his work. I should like to meet him. How do I get there?'

Munro put down the paper and stood up. 'If you must go, there's a narrow-gauge railway up to Argos. A train first thing in the morning. After Argos, there's a halt at Mykenos – what you call Mycenae. Then you walk about three miles into the hills on a rough track. Don't bother.'

'I'd like to bother,' Swain said reassuringly.

The Consul shrugged and gave him up. 'I wouldn't put too much on it, if I were you,' he said again. 'Just because a fellow shouts out nonsense the minute before they shoot him.'

'No,' Swain said noncommittally, 'I suppose not.'

'Look,' Munro said, 'I don't mean to be personal.'

'I don't think I should mind if you were.'

'You haven't been abroad before, they tell me. A man behaves

7

differently abroad. This isn't England. Less formal. More easy-going.'

'Ah!' Swain appeared to see the point at last. 'You think I should drink brandy at dawn and have a few of the local women?'

'No!' Munro spoke as if something had stung him through his clothes. 'I mean that a man is more easily taken here for a prig.'

'Thank you,' Swain said kindly, 'I'm sure you're right. I'll try to remember that.'

The spectators had gone and the square was deserted. He crossed it with the sun already hot on his back. There was a little street leading from the square to the quayside, an alleyway overhung by cascades of yellow jasmine and mauve wistaria. The houses, washed in yellow and pink, were the homes of a merchant class near the port. He came out again into full sunlight. The water that slapped along the quay was calm as an inland lake. Across the few miles of the Gulf of Argos the sunlight patterned the mountain slopes of Arcadia with veined snowfields round their peaks and the deep shadow of long descending valleys. Swain chose a table at the Hotel Mycenae and waited for his coffee.

Consul Munro had been correctly informed, of course. A mission on behalf of the Lerici family was the first time that Alfred Swain had left England. A railway ticket, 'To Brighton and Back for Three-and-Six', a fish dinner, and a stroll on the Marine Parade had been his nearest approach to continental travel. But the new world of the Peloponnese, its unremitting sun, bright colours, and strange chatter, left him undaunted. It seemed as unreal to him as a theatrical set he had once seen for *The Corsican Brothers* at the Britannia Theatre in Hoxton. Yet he felt no worse than a boy thrown in a river for the first time and finding he could swim after all. There was nothing to it.

The scrap of paper which he took from his notecase and unfolded had been cut from the obituary column of the *Literary Monitor*, a day or two before leaving England. He read it through again.

LERICI, John Posthumous. News of the violent death of this man of letters at the hand of his Greek servant must deprive the literary world of one of its most curious figures. If John Posthumous Lerici means little to the rising generation, it is because he belonged to that of the earlier Romantics, as much in the scandals as in the attainments of his life. If his constant claim is to be believed, both his existence and his middle name were the gift of Lord Byron. The late gentleman had always claimed to be the posthumous son of the great poet by Giovanna Lerici, the daughter of a Venetian notary. Lord Byron's liaison with this lady must, then, have occupied him in the days immediately before he sailed from Italy or Zante to assist Greece in throwing off the yoke of Turkish dominion. Unhappily, by the time that Signorina Lerici was brought to bed of the boy, the lamented author of CHILDE HAROLD and DON JUAN had already paid his tribute to mortality at Missolonghi for the freedom of his adopted country.

Swain sipped his coffee, stared across the placid gulf to the snow-tipped peaks and turned the paper over.

Certain it is that Mr Lerici counted Captain Edward Trelawny, companion of Byron and Shelley in their last days in Italy, among his supporters in his claim. Certain it is, too, that the fortune upon which he subsisted in England was the inheritance from his Venetian grandfather.

The world knows what became of that inheritance. Mr Lerici was renowned as hermit and voluptuary, in a manner peculiar to that age of romance. His Gothic extravagance, the house of Mondragon, gave the name 'Folly Ridge' to its location and stands yet as his monument. There he was attended by an entourage of dwarfs and mutes, catamites and ladies not of the nicest kind. There, among the richness of his furnishings, his paintings, manuscripts, and books, such revels were held as added by rumour the titles of orgie and even murder. (Let us say here that we ourselves were courteously received by Mr Lerici several years since and found an amiable gentleman with the twinkle of a joker, rather than a diabolist or a necromancer.)

Now that he is gone, who cannot grieve at so much talent foolishly misapplied? Here was a man who might have added nobly to the literature of Romanticism, perhaps in the manner of Edgar Poe or Miss Brontë. But see the result! A volume of poems in 1860, SOULS OF THE DAMNED, is best passed over in Dryden's line as 'Scenes of lewd loves and of polluted joys'. It was a young man's wilful assault upon the drawing-rooms and deaneries of England, written in Italy while Mr Lerici was living near the Campo Santo of Pisa. There he numbered the late Mrs Browning and her husband among his acquaintances. Messrs. Moxon, fearing demands for a criminal prosecution, withdrew the edition. It appeared, almost *sub rosa*, from the press of the old pirate, John Camden Hotten. Yet even this denizen of the liberary bordello could not bring himself to set in type Mr Lerici's *magnum opus*. Of this novel, SATURN'S KINGDOM: OR, THE FEAST OF BLOOD, the best that can be said is that few innocent eyes of the present day have seen so much as the title, let alone the contents. Its extreme mingling of voluptuous incident with profane ambition was beyond anything that an English printer would adventure. It appeared, in 1868, printed in Pisa 'For the Author', in four volumes. Even in that less scrupulous moral climate, it could not be issued until its creator had emended the title. For it was at first to be called not SATURN'S KINGDOM but SATAN'S KINGDOM.

We have said enough in condemnation. Let us, in charity, suppose that Mr Lerici was a jester rather than the worshipper of dark powers. Let us concede that his passing breaks the last link with an illustrious age and with one of its most famous names. To be sure, even in his extravagance and his rebellion, Mr Lerici was the posthumous child of that age of show and revolution. So let it be. The line is ended. The world will not look upon his like again. Some may lament that the world will be the poorer and the plainer.

Alfred Swain folded the cutting away, frowned and sipped his coffee again. He had not asked to be sent to Greece as the homeward escort for the body of the murdered man of letters. The executors of Mr Lerici's will had insisted upon hiring a 'Scotland Yard man' for the purpose. What purpose, Swain wondered? To write a report of the details of the crime? Or to prevent a greater crime from being investigated? The life of John Post-humous Lerici had been so peppered with indiscretions and scandals that it scarcely seemed worth the money to conceal another. But apparently the Foreign Office was also sensitive to the case of an eminent Englishman murdered in foreign parts. Lerici had always insisted upon his Englishness.

So the day after tomorrow Swain would take the little train to Argos and Mycenae. He would draw up his report, for what good that would do. Consul Munro was right. The journey to the hills was a waste of time. Except for one thing, which those who commanded the report had not bargained for. Iphigenia. Who the devil was she and who might she destroy?

Swain glared at the tranquil harbour, the romantic mountain range and the port whose first Italian masters had called it wistfully the Naples of the Peloponnese. Petrides might yet be more trouble dead than he had been alive. So, indeed, might his victim. Families that hired a Scotland Yard man on the death of one of their members usually did so to silence scandal or deter blackmail. Swain slid his hand into the pocket of his brown jacket and drew out an octavo volume in good condition. It was an odd volume, from a set of four, bound in dark olive-green cloth and with the title neatly gilt at the top of the spine. He had found it for sale on a barrow in Holywell Street, outside a dusty little shop whose window offered *The Voluptuarian Journal* and *Stereoscopic Views*. At any other time, such notices might have provoked his professional interest in the premises. On that spring afternoon in London, three days before his journey, the discovery of the volume had seemed like a favourable omen. He now opened it and looked critically at the title page, the paper still crisp and the print clear.

John Posthumous Lerici

SATURN'S KINGDOM:
OR, THE FEAST OF BLOOD

Volume the First

PISA: PRINTED FOR THE AUTHOR
MDCCCLXVIII

He drew his thumb across the edges of the closed pages. They had been opened neatly by a paperknife but not trimmed. The paper was clean and the type unblemished. Someone had taken good care of it. A sensible fellow, perhaps, who had picked it up out of curiosity during his European travels, in the market at Florence or from a bookstall by the Seine. A man sensible enough to decide that one volume of Lerici's vapourings would be enough. Swain had dipped into it on the voyage out. Before he left Nauplia, he would read it through. Something to occupy him on the little train that ran from the Gulf of Argos up to Corinth.

2

On the following morning, with the pages of Lerici's gothic horror firmly closed, Alfred Swain sat on a wooden seat at the end of the little carriage and stared out at the passing landscape. The narrow-gauge railway followed the coastal plain at the head of the Gulf of Argos. Swain studied the nearer hills, the scooped humps of their receding mountain crests, peaks, and dunes shaped by giant hands. A race of Titans, older even than the ancient gods of Greece, had created these ranges.

After half an hour, the great Homeric name of Argos on a station sign-board revealed only a dusty little town below another fortified hill. The toy train ran through the streets like a tram-car. There were shabby children in white nightshirts and black-scarved women. Swain thought of his long-dead schoolmaster father and the childhood tales of Troy. Was it really from this collection of chicken yards and tinkers' shanties that the great King Agamemnon had led a thousand black ships and the world's most powerful army across the seas to destroy Priam's city?

The little engine and its old-fashioned carriages lurched forward again. To either side of the track were orchards of orange trees and, on the foothills, a distant terracing of olives. The undulating slopes were steeper now and the peaks showed bare rock. Death had chosen a hard and bitter place for its encounter with Lord Byron's bastard son.

It was less than half an hour when the train stopped again. A sudden halt, the engine panting as if for breath in the noon heat. Someone opened the carriage door for him. Swain got out in his

English suit and narrow-brimmed hat, blinking in the unshaded light of the noon sun. There was a sign proclaiming 'Mykenos', which he now knew stood for the Golden Mycenae of his volume of Homer as translated by Butcher and Lang.

He looked about him. Nothing but a few orange orchards, bare earth, and a scattering of rough stone buildings that might have been English cow-sheds had they been larger. He turned to ask advice from the guard of the train. As he did so, the engine gave a ribald snort and the carriages pulled forward again with an uneven jangle of buffers on the line to Corinth. Swain stood on the little platform, alone except for a small and rather wizened man in a black hat who seemed as puzzled by the new arrival as the policeman was by him. There was nothing for it. Swain approached. The man smiled nervously rather than in greeting.

'Mykenos?' Swain asked hopefully.

The weather-beaten little man smiled more intensely, as if to please him, and pointed emphatically at the ground on which they stood. Swain shook his head.

'Mykenos?'

Nothing. The man looked puzzled. Swain gestured across the landscape, taking in both plain and hills.

'Mykenos?' Then in a moment of inspired recollection he found a word from his schoolboy vocabulary. 'Archaios Mykenos?'

'Old Mycenae' did the trick. To his relief, the old man beamed at him and nodded, pleased to be of help at last. He beckoned Swain and led him from the station platform to the dusty stone-filled track that ran beside it. With an emphatic scything gesture of the hand straight ahead, the man indicated the direction that ran towards the majestic hills. Swain smiled and inclined his head politely. The old man bowed and backed away. Presently there was no one in sight. The stony track shimmered in the heat. How many miles? There was nothing to be seen of Herr Schliemann or his encampment. Swain acknowledged that Consul Munro had been right. He had far better have stayed in Nauplia and abandoned his visit to the scene of the crime.

The sun was high and very hot. As he strode forward Swain ruefully watched the pale dust gathering on his polished boots and saw their leather grazed by the sharp stones of the track. The rubble slid and jabbed underfoot. Swain encouraged himself by thinking that he trod now the same path as the great warrior king of Mycenae on his road to Troy, the same way that had led him back ten years later to death at the hands of a faithless queen. At the foot of the escarpments ahead of him, Agamemnon had lain writhing and bleeding in the net while Clytemnestra and her lover axed him to death like a sacrificial steer.

Perhaps it was in keeping with such dramas of the past that John Posthumous Lerici had been struck down by a murderer's hand almost on the very spot where the great king had died three thousand years before. Brooding on this, Swain strode ahead. The wide verges of the road were dazzling with yellow mustard flowers and white blossom crowned the cherry trees, thick as a snowfall. The air was alive with the sound of bees. Swain took out his watch and saw that he had walked for half an hour. The hills seemed as far away as ever. The half-hour became an hour, then an hour and a half. The few small scattered buildings of dun-coloured stone were not shelters for animals but farmhouses as well. They were built on two levels, the sheep or goats living below and the family cramped in an upper room, reached by an outside stairway.

Ahead of him, Swain saw a village of some sort, a clutter of small buildings along the track. The narrow road climbed steeply between rough stone walls and porches made of overhanging thatch with chairs and tables beneath. Of Agamemnon's palace or Herr Schliemann's excavations there was not the least sign. He walked slowly between the walls, aware that eyes were upon him from every angle. He came to the end of the walls and the road divided. There was no means of choosing which direction to take. He turned back and saw a girl of nine or ten standing in the dusty track and watching him go. She was brown as a Romany, unkempt, wearing a dress of dark colours which dragged in the powdery earth.

Swain turned cautiously, smiling and trying not to alarm her. 'Mykenos,' he said quietly, 'Archaios Mykenos?'

The child looked doubtfully at him, the edge of her hand to her mouth. Then she ran ahead to the division of the road and pointed to the right. Swain felt in his pocket and found a coin. He smiled again and held it out to her. The little girl took it with extended hand, closed her fingers on it and ran as fast as she could towards the houses again.

14

Swain walked uphill. There was nothing but the sound of the bees. Across the great plain of Argos, as far as the sea and the mountain-barrier of Arcadia, the world was lost in heat and silence. For the first time his impatience and doubt were subdued by a sense of awe. It was unlike anything that he had ever imagined. Surely nothing had changed here since the age of the Mycenaean kings. Like the sons of Atreus, he looked upon the morning of the world. Somewhere in the harsh dry hills ahead of him lay the palace of his childhood reading, mythical to him then as Aladdin's Cave.

He turned another corner and saw a house, a proper house this time. It was squarely built, plain but substantial, of the same dun-coloured stone as the little shelters in the field. Indeed there were several of them just behind it. The big house had shutters at its windows and an air of comfort. It was the only building of its kind for miles around. Swain knew that this must be 'Schliemann's House', as it was called, the visible evidence of the great archaeologist's commitment to his quest.

He drew level with it. The house stood silent and, perhaps, unoccupied. A man was coming down the track beside it, possibly from one of the smaller buildings at the rear.

'Herr Schliemann?' Swain asked expectantly.

Yet again, the answer was pointed out, uphill and further on.

'At the site,' the man said with the careful accuracy of one using a foreign vocabulary. 'He works.'

'Excellent,' Swain said. 'Thank you.'

He was in the foothills now, or nearly so, about three miles on from the little station where the train had set him down. The road turned and he saw at last the destination of his journey. The Golden Mycenae of Homer's story. Divided from the lower slopes of a great hill by a steep valley, Agamemnon's citadel was a massive stone-lined mound, quite large enough for a fortified palace, perhaps even a small town. There was no palace any longer, only a few lower walls which Swain made out as he came closer. It was not at all the graceful and columned retreat which he had pictured during his childhood daydreams. More like a Bronze Age hill fort. But it was golden, after all. Homer had told the truth about that. It was not the brash gold of the Bond Street jeweller's window but a pale sandy tone that stood out against the darker hills behind it, as if it had been illuminated by a stage spotlight. Swain's pulse quickened. What little time he had for such reading in his adult life assured him that clever men now believed Homer's account to be nothing but myth or legend. Let them stand where he did now. Mycenae in its golden stone climbed the spring hillside. It was no myth. Swain knew in his heart that the ancient tale was true.

There were men working on part of the site, for all the world like gardeners in dark jackets and trousers. He approached by a flight of shallow marble steps, uneven and ill matched. There was no Athenian elegance here. Then he turned a corner and confronted the great Lion Gate.

It was magnificent, colossal and barbaric, a place that made Lerici's death seem like a trivial incident in the greater struggle of Mycenaean history. The way led between two high walls whose massive stone blocks might have lined the shaft approaching a pharaoh's tomb. The monumental gateway, its square opening through which Agamemnon and his legions had marched for Troy, was crowned by the arch of stone with two rampant and headless lions carved in relief upon it. There was nothing of classical elegance here. It was the gate of a war-lord who flourished centuries before Athenian perfection. Indeed, the lions had been here, as Swain was told, a thousand years before Agamemnon. The great king himself, let alone the other heroes, had looked upon the very stones at which Alfred Swain stared in wonder on a spring afternoon of the railway age.

Then, with a shock, he remembered murder. Not Lerici's death but something more portentous. Before the Lion Gate, he stood upon the very stones where Queen Clytemnestra had revealed the bloodied corpses of her royal husband Agamemnon and his slave-girl prophetess Cassandra. Three thousand years ago. More than two thousand years ago Aeschylus had written of the crime in his great play. Orestes, Electra, even Menelaus and Helen had passed across the threshold that now held an English 'private-clothes' policeman in such awe.

Alfred Swain, the boy whose father had been master of a little school in Dorset, was left an orphan at ten years old. That father's stories and the childhood books had opened a door into a world of learning and romance. That door had been shut again by his

16

guardians, who thought only of useful employment for the boy and some means of getting the nonsense out of his head. Now he would have stood all day before the great Mycenaean gate in utter contentment. When he was dying, when there was time to remember only one moment of his life, it would be this. Surely, it was this for which he had been born.

'The lions have lost their heads, I fear. Pausanias tells us that they were intact when he saw the gate in the second century after Christ. And then, who knows?'

Alfred Swain came to the surface of consciousness again, as if from the ocean depths of a powerful dream.

'Mr Swain?' the stranger asked.

When Swain turned, there was a middle-aged man standing behind him, a rather short wiry figure dressed in a black suit with a white hat. The face was kindly, if sceptical, adorned by a rather luxuriant dark moustache like a hotel waiter's. From a broad forehead, the face diminished to a narrow chin, disconcertingly close to the shape of an uncovered skull.

'Herr Schliemann?'

The archaeologist smiled and shook the policeman's hand. 'Mr Munro sent a railway telegraph message yesterday, promising that you would be here today. One of the men saw you walking up the road from the village. I hope it will not be a wasted journey for you.'

'Oh no,' Swain said thoughtfully, 'it won't be wasted. Whatever happens, it won't be wasted.'

The eyes, Swain thought. Dark as they were, they were at the same time humorous and ecstatic. They never let one alone, following each word and movement of the face. Heinrich Schliemann looked not much like a scholar, nor the businessman that he had been before. He reminded Swain at once of an itinerant preacher he had observed years before at Salisbury Horse Fair. There was something in such a face and voice that compelled you, made you long to be one with him and never in your life to be separated. It was good humour and faith. With such a companion, you knew that anything was possible. At that Whitsun fair, it had taken all Swain's adolescent rationality to prevent himself from stepping forward with half a dozen other men and women to volunteer for Salvation. That preacher's power was in Schliemann now. It did not surprise him much that the romance of the past had beguiled so many lesser men through Schliemann's advocacy. It surprised him even less that the middle-aged businessman had arrived in Greece and promptly won the heart of an eighteen-year-old beauty who became his bride. As with the Whitsun preacher, so with Schliemann. You longed to be on his side, to join his cause and be one with him.

'First let me show you what you came to see,' Schliemann said amiably, 'the place where the tragedy happened. You shall see the rest afterwards.'

'If you please,' Swain suggested courteously.

He did not call him 'sir'. For all his authority in the matter of Mycenae, Schliemann was a man who commanded enthusiasm and comradeship rather than mere deference.

'It happened outside the palace, Mr Swain, near the grave-circle below. The palace itself has never been lost. The ruined walls have been a landmark here for centuries. It is the graves of royalty and warriors which our diggings have brought to light. The gold death-masks and ornaments, of which you have perhaps read, were discovered among the treasures of the tombs.'

Swain had read something of the discoveries. It was Consul Munro, however, who had told him the ghostly story of Schliemann unearthing the bodies of Agamemnon's court, preserved by clay and the thin gold face-masks. In the air of a new century, the features of kings and heroes had crumbled to dust in a few hours while the searchers looked on helplessly. The loss had not prevented Schliemann's sonorous telegram to the King of Greece. 'Today I have looked upon the face of Agamemnon.' Even that was wrong, Munro said jovially. The king whom they dug up was a thousand years older than Agamemnon. But the romance of the story had quickened Swain's heart.

Schliemann used a walking-stick to assist him on the rough slopes. Swain followed down towards a wide hollow overgrown by scrub and gorse. The wild grass brushed at waist height, bright with poppies, purple vetch, and yellow mustard.

The rough path downwards, strewn with stones, followed the edge of a deeply excavated trench. They reached the lower level, where the heat and the stillness of the remote site gathered with greater intensity. Swain turned and saw that the trench was yet another shaft lined with monumental stone. At the end was a pointed arch, an entrance some twenty feet high, leading into darkness.

He followed his guide. It was not quite dark inside the underground structure. Swain found himself standing on the earth floor of a vast hive-shaped chamber, lined with stone. The air was alive with a swarming hum of bees. Sparrows chirped high up in the dim roof.

'What is this place?'

'This is where we believe Mr Lerici and his servant were before the crime. They came here without my authority and entered the site unobserved, so far as I can tell,' Schliemann said. 'The man was no doubt carrying a lamp for his master. This is the tomb of Clytemnestra.'

He spoke as casually as if he had been giving Swain the name of the nearest post office. The inspector never doubted the truth of it. Yet, to Schliemann, the events of so many centuries past were as real as if they had happened yesterday.

Swain followed him into the sunlight from the bee-laden air of the royal tomb.

'They had no right to be here on that day, of course,' Schliemann said. 'The week before I had allowed Mr Lerici and his companions to visit the site. I was away at the time he returned with Petrides and can only tell you the story at second hand. It seems they came out and walked away from the grave-shaft. So I was told by one of the workmen. The Greek authorities questioned him as they did the others. There was no sound of a quarrel. Petrides had probably laid his plans by then. He was seen later – alone. We knew nothing of Mr Lerici, of course. No one knew he was here. Soon after that he was missed but it was not thought he had been killed. A week later, by chance, his body was found just ahead of where we stand now, deep in the grass.'

He allowed Swain to go forward alone. Away from the stone-lined shaft, the lower ground opened out in a wide distant view towards Argos and the sea. Swain knew from the Greek police report where the body had been found in the following week. But that had been a matter of a workman chasing off a dog. Petrides had reason enough to think that the cover would be undisturbed by the digging until long after he had been forgotten.

Standing there with the massive foundations of Mycenae above him and the hills rising to either side, Swain confronted the tangled wilderness of tall grass and waist-high mustard. Gorse bushes and half-covered mounds of rubble blocked his way. John Posthumous Lerici need only have lain dead until his black velvet jacket and the fair well-tended flesh beneath had been eaten away. The heat and fauna of a single Argive summer might have reduced him to bone.

'Will it help you?' Schliemann asked anxiously. 'Now that you have seen the place, will it help you?'

Swain turned round. 'Oh, yes. My duty is not to investigate the crime. That has been done and justice carried out. My task is simply to write a report on the death of Mr Lerici for my superiors and the representatives of his family. And, of course, to see that his body is returned to England. To see where it happened will help me to report how it happened.'

'The poor fellow.' Schliemann began to lead the way back. 'I knew very little of him, of course. It seems he had an interest, of a rather curious kind, in ancient sites.'

'I have his obituary here.'

Swain took out the cutting from the *Literary Monitor*. He handed it to Schliemann and stood by courteously while the archaeologist read it. Across the terraced olive slopes and the plain of Argos, snowfields still shone on the upper peaks of the mountains guarding Arcadia. Schliemann handed the cutting back.

'Poor man. A life wasted, indeed. And to learn so little of mankind! To take such a scoundrel as Petrides for a servant! Mr Lerici came here two or three times before the fatal day, the only one when he was here alone with his murderer. As to "ladies not of the nicest kind", that seems to be the case. There were three of them with him when I was here. Soft yet perverse, the morals of cats, sly and depraved. He had them with him in his apartments at Nauplia, I suppose. I know nothing of dwarfs or mutes. So far as I could see, he travelled with three young women, four or five servants, and the man who killed him.'

'Was it possible that he found gold coins or ornaments here and that Petrides killed him for it? That was what Petrides said.'

Schliemann shrugged. 'Then Petrides may be right, Mr Swain. There are thefts from all such sites as this. They are difficult to prevent. A workman may find a coin or a ring and keep it to himself. If Mr Lerici had corrupted such men by money, he or Petrides might lay their hands on such things. There is much still to be excavated, of course. Among the treasure of the grave-circle there has as yet been no lion-head ring of the kind I had hoped for. You may be sure that rings of that pattern are lying here somewhere. Perhaps Mr Lerici was killed for the contents of his purse on the one occasion when Petrides found himself alone with his master in a deserted spot. I suspect, however, that he had stolen such treasure as he could lay hands on here and that it precipitated the attack. Petrides considered he had not had his share of plunder.'

'He confessed as much but no objects from Mycenae could be found.'

They walked back up the path above the shaft.

'Is that all, Mr Swain? You do your duty most diligently to come so far for so little.'

The laughter was back in Schliemann's eyes. Swain smiled at his own foolishness.

'I could not bear the thought of being so close to Mycenae and never seeing it. My father was a schoolmaster. He told me stories of so much that is here.'

Schliemann nodded, as if this satisfied him. 'And you read Greek, Mr Swain?'

'No,' Swain said hastily, 'no. My father taught me a little Latin when I was a child. Enough to dip into Caesar and Virgil. I tried Greek on my own. I couldn't do it. Reduplication in past tenses was beyond me.'

Schliemann's eyes gleamed with sympathetic amusement. 'I have done it alone, Mr Swain. So might you. Perseverance is all that it takes. But what would your friends at Scotland Yard say?'

Swain laughed. 'They would think I was mad.'

Schliemann nodded, still smiling. 'I have known that too, my friend. You must pay the world no attention in such things.'

They walked up towards the Lion Gate again. Schliemann led the way through it and began to climb the uneven patchwork of marble steps which led to the top of the mound and the foundations of walls which had once sustained the royal apartments. At the top, the ground was covered by a soft lawn, bright with scarlet anemones and stars of Bethlehem. The view on every side was of deep valleys, stony hillsides, the misty coastal plain in a silence of utter isolation.

Schliemann paused. 'Aeschylus places his watchman here at the beginning of his play. After ten years of waiting, the poor fellow sees, from the Arachnaean height, the last of the chain of beacon fires signalling the fall of Troy.'

'Really?' said Swain politely.

'But look, Mr Swain. He must have had remarkable vision. You cannot see that height they now call Arna. The hill is in the way. Take that home with you and puzzle your scholars with it.'

Swain smiled and changed the subject. 'I came also to ask you a question. You might answer it better than any man I know.'

'Surely not about Mr Lerici's murder?'

'Yes,' Swain said. 'A moment before Petrides died, he shouted out a name, as if it meant everything in the world to him – or perhaps to me. There may be nothing in it but I should like to know. The name was Iphigenia. Tell me, Herr Schliemann. Who is Iphigenia?'

Schliemann looked across the plain towards the distant sparkle of the sea near Argos and the jagged ridges of Arcadia.

'Do you not know already? Iphigenia, Mr Swain, was the daughter of King Agamemnon. When the great expedition first set out for Troy, it was delayed at Aulis to the north-east for lack of a favourable wind. In order to obtain that favourable wind, Agamemnon sent for his daughter. She was sacrificed there at Aulis in the Temple of Artemis. The King's prayer was granted and the fleet sailed to Troy. When he returned here, ten years later, Clytemnestra took her revenge upon her husband for the murder of their daughter.'

Swain concealed his impatience. 'I know that, though perhaps Petrides did not. It cannot be what he meant, surely.'

Schliemann shook his head. 'There are variants of the tale, in the plays of Euripides. According to one of them, Iphigenia was a willing sacrifice to the goddess for the sake of her country. In another version, the goddess Artemis spirited her away to become a priestess. But I do not imagine Petrides had either of those in mind.'

'And how may she harm us, as Petrides warns?' Swain asked.

'Is there anyone alive today who bears the name?'

Schliemann hunched his shoulders and shook his head again. 'I very much doubt it, Mr Swain. Modern Greeks sometimes name their children after heroes and heroines of the past. Andromache, for example. But they are superstitious enough not to use the name Iphigenia, a daughter put to death by her own father.'

'Perhaps one of the women who followed Lerici had that name.'

'I think it unlikely, Mr Swain, for the same reasons. The three I saw were not Greek and had still less reason to adopt such a name.'

'Then what does it mean?'

'A wild-goose chase, Mr Swain. Perhaps at the end he was invoking a curse on you all by using a name he had heard once but never understood.'

'No,' Swain said, 'how he shouted was almost more important than what he shouted. He was warning, not cursing. And he was warning me. He had no cause to hate me. I did him no harm. The Greeks took him prisoner, questioned him, tried him, and put him to death. I spoke to him once. Or, rather, he spoke to me through an interpreter, telling me that it was a dreadful tragedy. Mr Lerici had tried to corrupt him in stealing treasure from the tombs. I know liars, Herr Schliemann. Petrides was one. I did not even have to speak his own language to see it. However, I said that if he had spoken the truth, I would do what I could. Of course, it was hopeless. The man was guilty.'

'They found Mr Lerici's purse in his pocket, I understand.'

'Then why should he tell me of Iphigenia and her threat?'

Schliemann lifted his head and laughed. 'If you take such things seriously, Mr Swain, you have too much imagination for a policeman. Too much imagination for any rational man.'

Swain looked about him and then down at the carefully uncovered foundations of the first grave-circle. 'Had you been a rational man, Herr Schliemann, devoid of too vivid an imagination, would not all this still be covered by the dust of centuries?'

Schliemann smiled again. 'Perhaps, Mr Swain. But, unlike you, I am not a detective.'

Swain looked at the great man thoughtfully. He became, at last, both accusing and deferential. 'Are you not, sir, one of the greatest detectives that has ever lived?'

23

Schliemann saw the point and conceded it with a laugh. 'I underestimated you, Mr Swain. You checkmate me there.'

They walked down together. Where the stone track began below the Lion Gate there was a donkey-cart waiting.

'This will take you back to your train, Mr Swain.'

'There is no need,' Swain said hastily.

'There is every need, Mr Swain. There are still bandits of one sort and another in these hills. Petrides was one of them. The authorities execute them as they are caught but you were not well advised to walk alone as you did this morning. Even I would not. See.'

Schliemann pulled back the flap of his black jacket and Swain, with some surprise, saw the shape of a pistol in his belt.

'The man who drives you now, Mr Swain, has just such another in his pocket. Now I wish you good fortune in your quest.'

'And you in yours, sir.' Swain heaved himself up beside the saturnine driver.

'And persist with your Greek, Mr Swain. It will come right suddenly, much sooner than you expect.'

'I mean to try again,' Swain said.

As Schliemann turned away, the cart lurched forward. Had there been a Greek grammar aboard, Swain would have fallen upon it. His heart had beat faster since the moment he had set foot on the stones of Mycenae. It would run faster for the rest of his life. He had stood upon the Golden Mycenae of Homer's poem, walked through the Lion Gate with heroes of legend. How could he return to 'A' Division, Metropolitan Police, as though nothing had happened? How spend his life among the drunk and disorderly, pickpockets and card-sharps, private-clothes sergeants with their talk of beer or Saturday-night carnality?

On the little train to Nauplia, he sighed and opened Lerici's gothic romance.

In a turret-chamber of the Black Penitents held the Horned Demon his court. A single window, narrowly arched in Caen stone, admitted the moon's rays high in the lofty walls. Their ghostly lustre lay upon the midnight sacrifice. Incense-grains scattered on brazier coals rose with a serpent-hiss in snakes

24

of blue and green flame. No draught stirred the black silk hangings of wanton and arcane embroidery. The air was heavy with odours of tainted passion . . .

In a circle of flamelight before him stood the dark-eyed mistress, Venus Syriaca, his worshipper at Thebes and Carnac . . . Lamplight flickered on the golden contours of her naked form. She wore none but the bronze adornments of collar and cincture, bracelets at graceful wrists and ankles . . .

Swain was not quick to condemn literature for indecency. His greater scorn was for the claptrap that Lerici thrust upon thin-blooded drawing-room virgins. Closing the book, he indulged in a fantasy, whereby he offered himself for the humblest labour at Mycenae. He toiled among gods and scholars, cherishing each stone on which Agamemnon had trodden. He needed only a simple lodging, the food of the country. Bread and olives, goat cheese and wine. He would drink the cheap local wine every day. He would have some reputation among the local inhabitants. Less than Schliemann but something at least. As with the master, so for the servant. One day there might be a Greek girl, a simple Venus of the hills, warm skinned and dark eyed—

Iphigenia!

Oh, damn her!

3

And then the adventure was over, almost before he could savour its beginning. Two days after his visit to Mycenae, Swain stood at the taff-rail of the *Marchioness of Lorne*. The placid surface of the gulf churned as the ship went astern, swinging away from the quayside and the waterfront of Nauplia. He looked back across the quiet sea to the white and caramel wash of the Italianate houses, the customs office, the Venetian arches of the warehouse and the Hotel Mycenae with its windows lamplit.

Alfred Swain, a pocket volume of *Homer Translated* in his hand, tried to imagine King Agamemnon and his black ships sailing this way for Troy. Ten years later, how few had returned – and to what disaster!

25

'Mr Swain?' It was the purser. 'I think you'll find everything in order. The berth you are to share is with Mr Steer. The gentleman is an army chaplain going home on furlough from Egypt. We thought it would be a good match. You don't mind?'

'Not in the least,' Swain said humbly, appalled at the thought of having to share his bedroom with a perfect stranger, something he had not done for years.

'Good,' said the purser cheerfully. 'I'll wish you good-night then, Mr Swain.'

Swain turned, determined to stick at the taff-rail until the latest possible moment before surrendering his privacy to the Reverend Mr Steer. To either side, the bare Argive hills ran sculpted in long mountain crests, their deep ravines filled by misty sun and gargantuan shadows. The ship passed closer to the precipitous shoreline than Swain would have thought possible. It was a sheer and inhospitable coast, high cliffs of ochre-coloured rock dropping straight to the deep and quiet water. They were below the two bastion-like headlands where the gulf narrowed outside Nauplia. Alfred Swain indulged the pleasant reverie that he looked upon a scene unchanged since Agamemnon's eyes surveyed it last three thousand years before.

Iphigenia. What of her? He pulled himself together with a sense of duty. John Posthumous Lerici's absurd novel contained no mention of such a name. The scoundrel's natural daughter, Amalia de Brahami, far from being butchered on a pagan altar, was travelling with nurse and grandmother overland to England by rail from Venice to dispose of her father's estate. A sensible man would forget Iphigenia and Alfred Swain was a sensible man. But he had heard again Petrides' last cry. He heard it as he lay down to sleep and sometimes he heard it while he slept and it woke him up. None of that was evidence, however, none of it could be reported to the Commander of the Detective Division. Swain winced as he anticipated a howl of scorn from the belligerent gnome-like figure of Superintendent Toplady. The inspector's attachment to what Toplady called 'school-miss poetry books' was already marked against him. Best to leave it alone.

As for Lerici's family and companions, they would be home long before Alfred Swain. While the *Marchioness of Lorne* wallowed and rolled the length of the Mediterranean and across the

Biscay swell on her three-week journey, Lerici's menagerie would be borne by express train across Switzerland and France in a few days.

He was still standing at the rail as the ship reached the mouth of the little gulf, the thickly wooded shore of Spetse to one side with its tall juniper trees and the last of the little islets rising like smooth humps of pumice stone. There was no possibility that he would ever come back, no likelihood that he would leave England again in the thirty years or so of life that might remain to him. There was a melancholy in this departure from Agamemnon's kingdom. He turned and saw a school of dolphins, four or five of them, breaking the calm sea in their rhythmic curve, keeping a constant distance from the ship. A mist veiled the Argive hills but through it there was sun enough to dance in a fierce cut-glass glitter on the wavelets of the western sea. Swain watched until the winking lamp of the lighthouse on the last rock of Spetse was too faint to make out. Now it was open sea.

He went down to the cabin, among the smells of hot oil and damp wood. The Reverend Mr Steer was not at prayer. He was in his bunk asleep, half snoring and half blowing. A slight but discernible whiff of spirits touched Swain's nostrils. It was hard to know whether this was better or worse than what he had expected. He lay down, thought of the bandaged Lerici washing about in his cask of rum, and then went to sleep. One way or another, the great adventure was over.

4

Spider McBride hung splayed and taut on his midnight perch. From the ground he might have seemed to be dangling at the end of a dropped thread. His fingers were hooked on the brittle baking of grey stucco on Mondragon's gimcrack masterpiece. The slender eight-sided tower in Portuguese gothic rose above him fifty feet to the railed lantern and fell away fifty feet below. In the thin star-flush of a spring night the little man moved as if upon an invisible web. The lesser turrets and the arched vault of the entrance hall were below him now. No policeman with his bull's-eye lantern nor any guardian of the house itself would look for him at such a height. Everything was exactly as the spiderman had expected. The Lord of Mondragon, creator of strange gothic fictions which were nothing but 'slum-gulleon' to McBride, had withdrawn in darkness to the secret and silent world of death. As for his lordship's household, if half of what McBride heard was true, sighs of pleasure and murmurs of desire, opium smoke, and a thick stupor of pagan incense would be enough to deaden the occupants of the shuttered rooms.

The ascent was long, but straightforward to a climber of McBride's experience. There was no easy way into the house at the lower level. If his information was correct, the womenfolk posted a guard at night. There had even been talk of a hired jack from Scotland Yard. There was none yet that McBride could find. In any case, a jack would find himself a kitchen corner and doze the night through. McBride knew the breed. His route was by the tall lantern tower, then down inside to the desk for papers and information. It had to be done fast. For reasons unknown to McBride, the Lord Lerici had ordered his lawyer to hire a police-man to list his papers in the event of his violent death. Those who employed the spiderman expected the jack's arrival any day.

The men who were paying him for his skill were anxious to have the business done in short order. McBride pulled himself up to another foothold and grinned. Someone, he guessed, had been blackmailing the Lord Lerici. But now his lordship was dead, the evidence might come to light. And very likely it would turn to evidence against the blackmailers themselves. He shook his head philosophically. The biter had been bit! Spider McBride was not opposed to blackmail on principle. It was only a tax on the pleasures of the 'harristocrats'. But he thought it a double-edged blade, liable to cut the hand that used it. And when it cut, it cut deep. To the white of the bone.

He stopped and drew a gasp of breath and grinned again. The masters and mistresses of Mondragon would hardly expect some clever fellow to enter from the top of their octagon tower, a hundred feet above the ground. Sixty feet above the paved terrace, a cold condensation on the plaster surface soaked his thin woollen gloves and froze his narrow fingers. McBride shifted his foot and felt a loose finger of stucco break away. He held still, as if a wrong step now might bring down the entire tower. After a pause, he heard the biscuit-snap of a plaster fragment bursting far below. No one else would notice that. Silence again. To one side of the trees, a stable clock chimed the quarter after midnight. Below him, the carriage drive to the lodge and the garden walks were deep and still as mountain canyons. The lead roof and dome of the conservatory lay rutted by the heat of summers past. The girl was down there, of course, hiding for the moment among the trees, waiting to unhook each item from the line as he lowered it. Ellen with her thin features pasty-white from six months' moral reformation in Millbank penitentiary. A foolish tongue but a brave heart.

He reached for the upper ledge of the embrasure and, as he did so, an acid draught of smoke teased his lungs. He caught the spasm of air without opening his mouth and controlled the explosion that seemed to be bursting from his throat. He did not think anyone in the house could have heard it.

Pressing his face down to his chest, Spider McBride cleared the stickiness from his throat as quietly as he could. The higher embrasure ledge was under the spiderman's fingers now, then under his elbows, then with a chest-aching effort it was under his knees and his feet. The worst was over. Above him, the pinnacles and battlements on the tower platform seemed to fly like wind-blown gothic pastry against the starlit cloud drifts.

McBride had done his training early, in a group of child acrobats who tumbled for pennies in the city streets. He worked his way up patiently on a surface of stucco between an angle buttress and the arch of the nearest window in the final set with its leaded panes of coloured glass. When he had got as far as he could, he drew from his black jersey a spiderman's hook, attached to his length of rope. Long practice and instinct ensured that he seldom had to make a throw twice. Lobbing upwards, he heard the faint clink of metal and felt from the tension of the rope that he had caught the ledge of the next gutter-entry, fair and square.

'So if this should be the worst barrikin we ever come upon,' he said to himself firmly, as if he were leading a whole army of valiant spidermen, 'we shan't have cause to complain.'

Swinging across, the rope slipping an inch between his fingers, he got his first foot on the ledge of the highest band of tall mullioned windows and found it firm. Then a toe-hold for the boot that still hung over seventy feet of space. The tight boot bumped a little on the sheer facing of biscuit-coloured stone. A man must climb with method in his movements. No jumps. No cleverness. So McBride held his breath and delicately swung clear to try again. At this height, every movement was like adding the final ace of spades to a gamester's trembling pagoda built of an entire pack of cards.

He perched a moment, like a bird. Then, with a ripple of the slack rope, he dislodged his hook and slung higher. Another pull upwards. The girl below would see that there was nothing now beneath his feet but a fall more than a church tower to the terrace with the cold air shrieking at his ears and the pressure forcing air from his lungs in a hollow scream. But McBride knew better than anyone that he would not fall. The spider hung as safely by his fingers as if he were home in bed. Even though he felt the pain of it in his arms, he knew that he could bear this and more for the rest of the night, if need be. It was his trade.

'And what's a man without his trade?' he asked himself quietly for encouragement.

The vertical gaps between the gothic windows were smaller in the final set and the going was getting easier. Spreadeagled against the coloured glass of the mullions, McBride took his right hand down from its hold above him and tightened the grip of his left. He felt for the steel hook and rope. First he locked the hook round the loop of pipe and then began to pay out the rope a little more. He gave it a tug for luck. Deftly as a monkey in a tree, he swung himself up to the last and narrowest window-niche.

The curtains were open and the moon through the opposite glass of the octagon showed something of the interior. This was his first target. The so-called tower room. The walls were hung with yellow damask and the ceiling carved in flowered rondels. In McBride's opinion, the furniture was too heavy. There was nothing for him in a carved ebony armoire more than six feet in height, matched by an inlaid ebony table. Across the room was a table of carved oriental alabaster on which stood a vase cut from a single Hungarian topaz. Several cabinets and stands of ebony or ivory displayed their individual collections of Persian miniatures, Japanese carving, and Cantonese vases. The remaining alcoves of the octagon were filled by ottomans patterned in gold and purple velvet. On the far wall, with gold-tasselled curtains of red velvet drawn back from it as if in a theatre, a large painting hung in the further alcove. The moonlight caught it squarely. The colours were bright but the subject sombre. A young woman leant naked over a page of text on a lectern.

McBride knew just enough for the purposes of his profession about the way 'the harristocrats hooks it'. In this case, it seemed that the Lord Lerici had hooked it pretty well. But the picture troubled the spiderman. The girl was good enough for the stage of a gaff in Lambeth or Hoxton but the picture, with its place of honour and velvet curtains, intrigued and repelled him simultaneously. It had an air of the satanic. A man who stole such an article might steal the curse that went with it.

Eight tall pinnacles with vertical gaps in the surrounding masonry gave the lantern platform the look of a coronet. Taking the rope taut in his hands again, McBride swung gently aside in a pendulum arc, pulling up until his feet touched the last stone band that ran round the tower and he could just see over it on to the flat surface of the lantern itself. The little door that led down to the tower staircase was shut and, no doubt, locked by this time. But McBride carried two slim steel jemmies and a chisel that would have it open on its hinge side, if necessary.

He hoisted himself over the rail and at last looked down. The lantern was so high above the ground that even the tops of the tallest trees seemed like toys below him. But there was enough thin cord coiled round him to lower the papers and booty to the girl now concealed in the trees below.

A cloud obscured the starlight and McBride had just time enough to remember that there had been no clouds. That was what had made the spring night so chill. Curiosity rather than fear was uppermost in his mind as he turned slowly from the parapet. With a speed that caught him even before he could ask his question, a heavy walking-stick struck hard the side of McBride's skull with its short crop of dark hair. The spiderman let out a strange animal cry that came from deep in his throat. He went down with the blow, motionless on the platform of the octagon. The stick caught a faint reflection of the moon as it struck twice more with savage force at the wounded head. Then the assailant prodded the victim with the toe of a boot as if to test for some reaction or sign of life. There was none.

The coil of rope and the hook were tossed over the rail of the

31

octagon. They fell, the rope uncoiling in snakelike patterns as it sank to the path far below. There was a soft impact and the clink of the hook as it landed.

In the quiet moonlit grounds, there was no movement for a moment or two. Then a figure in a bonnet and a cloak came out of the shadows and walked a little way towards the rope lying on the ground. She stood, hesitating, as if summoning up the strength to go further and look. She knelt for a moment. Then, turning, she walked quickly away along the carriage drive between the trees. She would be child's play if she ever caused annoyance and she knew it.

2

AN INSULT TO CONFIDENCE

1

A thousand miles from Mondragon and Folly Ridge, in a city that Spider McBride could never have imagined, a slightly built man in black biretta and soutane, its cape edged by scarlet, sat on the bench of the public *passeio* and read a newspaper. It was printed twice a week for the English merchant community in Lisbon and he had taken great care in buying a copy. The story which held his attention was printed on the third page, the account of an 'insult to confidence', as it was now called.

Mr Wise, an English jeweller in the Rua Augusta, one of the narrow commercial streets between the Rossio and the quayside, had received a visit. His customer was a captain of the 24th Regiment of Foot, returning to England from the Cape. The brave fellow had been badly injured in one of the earlier skirmishes of Sir Theophilus Shepstone's campaign that spring. He had escaped the general massacre that had been threatened, only to fall victim to severe injuries in a close engagement which followed. Though he was too modest to say so, it seemed he must have been one of the small band of heroes who had defended an isolated Dutch mission station against a savage army of tribesmen. Many Victoria Crosses had been earned in a couple of days but the heroes had paid a price. This young officer's right arm was still in a sling and the hand was quite useless. Now that his health had improved, he was making his way to England by stages. During his stay in Lisbon he proposed a reception at the yacht club for certain brother officers and required silver plate on hire. Hence his visit to Mr Wise the jeweller of the Rua Augusta.

By a happy chance, the jeweller and the gallant captain shared

33

the name of 'Wise'. There was much talk of the ladies of Leeds Castle and possible family connections. Mr Wise the jeweller, who had such no connections, felt his heart warmed at being regarded as part of the household of Leeds Castle. Silver plate to a value of £500 was chosen. The captain, whose wife had come to Lisbon to supervise his convalescence, insisted that he would pay the £500 deposit for the silver that day. He would not hear of the jeweller being kept waiting. There were ample funds at home. If Mr Wise would be kind enough to write a note at his dictation, he would send his servant for the money at once. He moved his injured arm a little to recall the impossibility of penning a message himself.

Mr Wise the jeweller, seeing the £500 almost in his grasp, penned the note as instructed. 'My dear— Do not be alarmed by this. I have been offered a fine display of silver plate for our own use but must put down cash to secure it. Please therefore entrust to the servant a sum of £500, plainly wrapped, or such funds as are at present in the safe.' Mr Wise wrote on behalf of the injured hero. Though Captain Wise could not add his signature, he made a mark with his seal-ring at the foot of the paper. Mr Wise slipped it into an envelope for him and sealed it down. Turning to the door, the captain handed the note to his servant.

'Here, fellow. Take this to your mistress and be quick about it.'

Conversation was resumed pleasantly in the jeweller's shop of the Rua Augusta. Tea was taken in its shrine of pale polished oak and heavy doors with carved panels. After a while, the captain became impatient with his servant, whose laziness he swore was a trial to him. He apologized to Mr Wise and promised to give the servant a piece of his mind when he found him. Then he slipped out into the Rua Augusta to see if there might be some sign of the idle fellow. Neither the captain nor his servant was ever seen again.

The little man in the biretta and soutane reached this point in the newspaper report and nodded. They had it right so far. Better had they got it wrong. The report added that Mr Wise the jeweller waited in vain for the return of his customer or the servant. That evening, he returned home to Belém along the shore of the Tagus, irritated at the loss of custom. In a garden fringed by olive, eucalyptus and palm stood the pink-washed house that he had bought ten years before. Evening sun cast a peach-coloured light on the white gothic tracery of the nearby Jerónimos monastery.

Mrs Wise was there to greet her husband. A moment or two passed before she asked him gently about the day's business and whether he had acquired the silver, which had made him send for so much money. Mr Wise, his heart cold as a stone, was about to say that he had sent for no money. But just then he felt too sick to speak. He saw in her hand the note in his own writing and the envelope printed with the insignia of the shop in the Rua Augusta.

'My dear— Do not be alarmed by this. I have been offered a fine display of silver plate for our own use but must put down cash to secure it. Please therefore entrust to the servant a sum of £500, plainly wrapped, or such funds as are at present in the safe.'

The end of the paper, bearing the seal of 'Captain Wise', had been trimmed away. Under the message was what might plausibly be the jeweller's own signature. The message was plainly in his own handwriting. After a day of agony, torn between vengeance and seeming a fool, he had gone to the authorities. By then, it was much too late.

The little man in the biretta and soutane closed the newspaper and folded it. He was sitting on a wooden bench at the lower end of the public *paseio*, where it began to slope upwards from the Tagus to the rotunda at the top.

He looked thoughtfully at the ornate bandstand in olive green and sighed. It had been pleasant sitting there under the palms and chestnuts of the wide paving, grass and trees with café tables grouped at intervals. Lisbon was a city he could easily come to like, though it was out of the question to cultivate it now. Among the trees and pools of the central reservations were the green octagonal kiosks of the tea gardens. He sat down and ordered tea, while he looked quickly at the morning's *Diário de Notícias*. Not a word of the story appeared in the Portuguese press, so far as he could see, though he did not speak nor read the language very well. For the past two days, he had been careful to speak nothing but French, in which he was fluent enough, having been born in Paris.

As he sipped his tea, the mild spring air hung stagnant by the Rossio railway terminus, a stucco monster of statues, abbey windows and cathedral pillars in pseudo-Manueline style. The stillness of the warm afternoon held a roasted smell of Brazilian tobacco, a hint of perfume and whisper of silk which stirred his desires. Old men dozed on the benches and artists sketched at their easels here and there along the *paseio* paving of black and white marble lozenges.

At last the little priest got up and shuffled down to the open pink-washed square of the Praça do Commercio with its quayside and colonnades that would have suited Venice as easily as Lisbon. With his leather bag like a doctor's, he seemed a figure of quaint amiability as he followed the quayside street to the station of Santa Apolónia, where the express for Madrid and Paris would be ready in twenty minutes. He paused to make a vague sign of benevolence towards a beggar who was cooking his fish on the pavement by the aid of firewood from a broken orange-box. Entering the station, he ignored the marble temple of the booking hall, having provided himself with a ticket the day before.

Where the lines of carriages stood at their platforms, he sat down again. Presently, among the passers-by, there appeared a powerfully built fellow in tweeds. Their eyes met and the gaze endured. The quaint figure in the soutane stood up and looked about him. Then he walked away towards the trains. The larger man sat down and saw that a newspaper had been left behind. He opened it and found the story he was looking for. At the foot of the page there was a note in pencil. *Bon voyage, Mr K.* Harry Benson had been tempted to write *A bientôt!* but had decided that it would have been rather beyond Billy Kurr's linguistic abilities. It would be taking the 'French priest' charade a bit too far. *Bon voyage* seemed good enough, however. The big man read it and smiled, as though it had been his birthday.

The Paris express pulled out below the cliff of square houses washed in pink or lime green, walls tiled here and there with white and blue azulejo. Lines of washing spanned the slope where the white dome of Madre de Deus rose above the skyline. In the corner of the carriage, ignored by its other two occupants, the little priest in soutane and biretta pulled out his breviary and settled down to the devotions of his journey. He opened the volume in its black calf binding, glancing at the first page, which he knew almost by heart.

The tall flames of the candelabra rose in slender brilliance. Venus Syriaca stood close behind her victim, deep bronze of Arabian beauty against the whiteness of the sacrifice. She unclipped the gold brooch of the maiden's cloak, permitting it to fall and reveal her nakedness to the horned idol. Her hands wandered at will . . .

Whatever might be said about the vices of John Posthumous Lerici of Folly Ridge, he certainly knew how to give a fellow a good read. The 'read' occupied the quaint little priest for a day and a night until the express lay panting in the dusty afternoon of the Spanish plains at the junction of Medina del Campo. Bare earth stretched to a shimmering horizon-line. By then the other passengers had left and the cassocked figure was sitting alone. The door of the carriage opened and the large man who had met his gaze at Lisbon's Santa Apolónia railway terminus got in and sat down opposite him. He handed the priest a note and the priest read it.

'Tip from our friends, Mr Benson,' the large man said. 'Seems that Spider McBride come to grief in a very unfortunate place. Fell off Lerici's tower.'

'Had he done the trick yet?' the man in the soutane asked. 'Got anything of use in his pockets p'raps? If he had, there'll be interest from the jacks.'

The big man shook his head.

'Not that our friends found. But where's there another chance of getting our hands on Lerici's stuff before they put some jack on the job? Told you he'd be no use.'

The priest stared from the window at the dust, the heat, and the vast horizons of the plain.

'Policeman Swain was sent out to bring the body back,' he said thoughtfully, 'I had a note from our friends about it. He's very likely to be the jack that's sent down to Folly Ridge. I think he could be made to sit up and beg all right, Mr Kurr. He's a good dog.'

'Is he? You sure he is, Mr B.?'

'Oh, yes,' the priest said in the same thoughtful tone, 'and if he isn't now, he soon will be. And Spider McBride always was a stupid little bugger. Lucky for him he had a good long fall. He won't be talking, so he won't be getting into trouble. Only his ghost might whistle in the dark.'

And this last comment, not obviously amusing in itself, caused the two companions a good deal of chuckling.

2

At St.-Jean-de-Luz the high clouds in an azure sky reflected the freshness of a summer ocean. Major Hugh Montgomery, a dapper figure in his cream linen suit, stepped off the train followed by his servant, a heavy fellow with the baggage. It was a relief to get into cream linen after the stuffy black soutone of his priestly impersonation. The major crossed the road to the Café de la Gare, in whose dark and austere depths travellers and gypsies, soldiers and whores gathered for the arrival of the Sud Express from Lisbon and Madrid. Even by mid-afternoon, the café interior was lamplit, a warm light reflected from the marble floor and wall-mirrors, timbered ceiling and brown distemper. There were a dozen little tables with chairs in bentwood and red leather. An ancient clock ticked time away with its brass pendulum.

The major booked a room in fluent French. He enquired after a bureau de change. A few minutes later, leaving his valet with the baggage, he set out for Perret et Cie in the Place de la Pergole. The major walked with a jaunty step and just managed to restrain himself from a swing of his cane. He crossed the Place Louis XIV by the cathedral, the house-fronts of timbered baroque above the little shops and cafés. Square white pavilion towers with their Roman-tiled roofs, the long shutters behind wrought-iron balconies overhung with lilac-blue wistaria were a reminder of Aragon and Spain as the warm breeze blew across the Biddasoa.

Half an hour later, Major Montgomery walked back towards the railway. The spring of his step was still more evident. He reached the Café de la Gare, retiring to his shabby and airless little room with its patched and dusty carpet. Sitting on one of the little chairs, he spread before him the five bills of exchange purchased by a substantial bundle of Portuguese escudi. Each of these bills was drawn upon Perret et Cie in favour of Major Hugh Montgomery to the sum of two thousand five hundred francs.

The major studied the bills. Perret et Cie was not a bank and these were not printed bills. They were inscribed on authorized forms which might be bought in any town, rather as men and women bought forms for drawing up their wills. The major noticed, however, that these bills of exchange were not to be honoured unless countersigned and stamped by the correspondent of Perret et Cie at Bayonne, Biarritz, or Paris. The major nodded. It was just as he had expected.

Getting up from his chair, he opened a leather bag and took out a wooden box containing two rows of ink-bottles in every colour. There were half a dozen pens whose nibs varied in thickness. From an attaché case he took a folder of blank forms for bills of exchange and spent an hour in profound concentration. At last he sat back and held a bill of exchange from Perret et Cie in one hand and his own creation in the other. Without being a braggart, he thought that few people would be able to see the difference between them, except that one had been drawn to the sum of two thousand five hundred francs and the other to the sum of five thousand.

'So far so good,' the major said to the dusty room. With great care, he put away the tools of his trade and went downstairs to join his servant, who was drinking brandy at one of the little tables.

3

On the following morning, with his servant four paces behind him, Major Montgomery crossed the long span of the bridge over the Adour at Bayonne to the colonnaded elegance of the Hôtel de Ville. Crossing a smaller bridge over the Nive, he stopped at the Banque de Bordeaux.

The high-vaulted banking hall was quiet as a church and almost as deserted. Its marble floor was inlaid with a pentagram design. To the head clerk who approached him, the major presented his letter of introduction from the London and Westminster Bank of Leadenhall Street in the City of London. Then he presented a bill of exchange drawn on Perret et Cie. The clerk read it, letter by letter, figure by figure. It was a scrutiny the like of which the major had never known in a provincial bank. He admired the fellow for it. Even the other clerks at their desks had stopped work and were staring at the visitors. Then the examination ended.

'M'sieu.' The clerk's intonation was flutingly nasal and monotonous, like a priest invoking a blessing. 'For Perret, you may change the bills at Perret Frères in the Place d'Armes.'

The major nodded and smiled, understanding but disagreeing. 'Unfortunately, Monsieur, Perret Frères change only into francs. I shall need specie – or a draft at least – in English money.'

The clerk intoned again: 'Yes, but, Monsieur, the bill must first be countersigned and stamped by Perret.'

'Absolutely,' the major said. 'My servant shall take it there. Your messenger shall accompany him, of course, if that is necessary.'

'That will be necessary, Monsieur.'

The major made himself comfortable. In half an hour his servant and the messenger returned. The clerk withdrew to an inner office and returned with a draft made out to Major Montgomery for one hundred pounds.

That night, in a well-appointed suite of the Hôtel Panier-Fleuri, the major studied a second bill which his servant had presented to Perret Frères for signature and stamp but had never shown at the Banque de Bordeaux. The major spent two hours reproducing the signature and an impression of the stamp on half a dozen bills of his own creation. Next day he returned to the Banque de Bordeaux. He again pleaded his case for English pounds and presented the remaining four bills of exchange purchased from Perret et Cie in St.-Jean-de-Luz. Again there was scrutiny. Again his servant and the messenger set out for Perret Frères. Countersigned and stamped, the bills were returned to the major's servant who, slipping them into the folder, replaced them by those the major had exercised his craft upon the night before.

At the Banque de Bordeaux, the clerk thought that he saw only the same bills to which he had given such scrutiny half an hour earlier, now countersigned and stamped. Leaving the major in the cathedral silence of the banking hall, the clerk withdrew to the counting-house. Time passed. Major Montgomery wondered if something might be amiss. The great outer doors of the bank were shut with a groan and a crash, as if to prevent an escape. In the twilight of the marble hall, the major felt a twinge of panic in his entrails. He could not see, by any means, how he had gone wrong. Why had they shut the doors and locked him in? Then he

40

remembered that even in south-west France there was a feeble imitation of the siesta, the banks closing for an hour or two at noon.

The head clerk reappeared alone. He walked across to the major and, with a slight bow, handed him four bills drawn upon the Banque de Bordeaux for a total of ten thousand francs.

With his servant at his heels, the major marched smartly back across the Nive bridge and along the quay to the little steam-tram which left from the Hôtel de Ville for Biarritz. Breakers glittered in the sun, the gaudy strips of bathing canvas fluttered like trapped butterflies. There was a healthy breeze along the Plage de l'Impératrice. The Hôtel du Palais at the northern edge stood like a chateau of the Bourbon monarchy.

Major Montgomery felt that he could have spent all summer here, among the elegant and knowing women with their pious little girls of sixteen. Such amusements would not do, of course. There would be ample time for them soon enough. With his servant following at the distance prescribed by etiquette, he walked from the terminus of the steam-tram above the Casino and entered the British and International Bank in the Place de la Mairie. He was at home here. Four entirely genuine bills of exchange, drawn upon Perret et Cie in St.-Jean-de-Luz, countersigned and stamped by Perret Frères in the Place d'Armes at Bayonne, were exchanged for English banknotes.

Major Montgomery, who had begun his journey with nothing to his credit a week before, had come to St.-Jean-de-Luz from Lisbon and Medina del Campo the day before with five hundred pounds. Having given his address as the Hôtel du Palais, and made a little joke about the Casino as his reason for needing funds, he now left Biarritz with a thousand pounds to warm his pocketbook, less the modest expense of railway travel.

At the Hôtel Panier-Fleuri, as the major paid his bill, the clerk handed him a blue pre-paid telegraph reply form. The major slit the thin paper with his thumbnail and read the contents. As soon as the hotel servants had stowed the baggage in the cab for the station, he turned to Billy Kurr.

'Our friend Mr Palmer asks to be remembered. Seems Lerici got the wind up. Left a provision in his will that in the event he died in mysterious circumstances, his papers were to be subject to inventory by a Scotland Yard man hired by his attorney. I must say, I never bargained for that, not thinking he'd pass to higher things so soon.'

Billy Kurr swore and tightened his fist.

'That's all right, Mr Kurr,' said Benson reassuringly. 'Our friends got more to lose than we have. And they picked a lovely one.'

'Which of 'em was picked?'

'Policeman Swain!' Benson said, rolling his eyes humorously.

'Oh my, oh my!' Kurr said and they both sniggered.

'He can't be bought, Mr Kurr.'

'He certainly can't, Mr Benson.'

'But then, Mr Kurr. He ain't worth buying either!'

That evening, in a first-class carriage of the Chemin-de-Fer d'Orléans et du Midi, the major turned to his companion.

'Our friends were sure, I suppose, that little fool McBride never laid hands on anything before tragedy overtook him?'

The larger man in his check suit grinned and shook his head.

'Not 'im! Just fell off the bloody tower.'

'Not digging for himself, was he?'

'Not 'im, Mr Benson! Wouldn't know where to look.'

'Silly little tyke!' the major said savagely. Then he softened a little as he stared through the dark window at the passing meadows and finally pulled down the blind. 'That young woman of his. Ellen or whatever she was. Strapping great ox, she'd make three of him. You reckon he ever got the saddle on her, Mr Kurr?'

This caught the fancy of the large man so acutely that he laughed until he coughed, eyes bulging and watering with humour and constriction, the tears running down his cheeks. Nothing would stop it but a pull from his silver flask.

4

In the warm spring evening, Inspector William Palmer sat in his basement office below the area railings of Whitehall Place. He perched on his high stool and leant his elbows on the counting-house desk. A crash of iron-rimmed wheels on cobbles and a faint odour of horse dung came through the window above him. He got up and closed the catch.

The paper in his hand was giving him some concern. The telegraphic strips of print pasted on the form were simple enough in their meaning.

RE: INCIDENT OF CAPTAIN WISE LISBON 24TH INST CHECK IDENTITY AS MAJOR HUGH MONT-GOMERY.

It had been dispatched by the British Consulate. Inspector Palmer stood a moment in thought. He had the immaculate air of a waxwork, hair parted scrupulously in the centre, moustache-tips waxed, wing-collar geometrically precise. Then he went out and turned down the corridor to the Document Room where the day books were kept. Opening the ledger, he ran his finger down to see if the telegraph had yet been entered. There was no entry.

Palmer turned away again. He did not believe that what he must now do was safe or sensible in itself. Yet it was easy to do because there was no alternative. He was like an acrobat on the high wire, had been so for two years past. If he kept his head and kept his nerve, there need be no danger. There were colleagues in whom he could have confided but he thought it best to say nothing. What they did not know, they could not betray, either to save their skins or by some accidental glance or gesture.

One thing was sure, the matter could not be left. A British Consul had the right to arrest a British citizen abroad and even to put him on trial before a consular court.

The gas was already burning white on the gauze of the mantle. Palmer read the sender's address once more and committed it to memory. He reached up, touched the telegraph message to the flame and watched the paper catch light. Holding it carefully, he walked over to the black-leaded grate, dropped the burning paper, and stood there until it crumbled into ash.

He told himself that it was done of his own free will. Behind him stood the figures of a wife and three children. He was easier in the knowledge that he had done it for them, never for himself. Yet the daring and the exhilaration of the plan was over now, only the bitter consequence remained. They had been jolly fellows to begin with and had paid him well, making it seem so much like a practical joke that there was almost no harm in it. Now they could have him for nothing because he must defend them to defend himself. With a heavy heart, he walked out into the evening sun, crossing Westminster Bridge into Lambeth. It was safer to send a reply from outside the building. Moreover, the post office was busy enough in the few minutes before closing to make him inconspicuous. At least, Palmer thought, it was beyond anyone's power to prove that he rather than another had sent the reply.

MONTGOMERY IN ENGLAND SINCE JANUARY STOP NO CONNECTION WISE STOP TOPLADY SUPERINTENDENT WHITEHALL PLACE.

Knowing that he had acted for the best and the safest, Palmer handed the form to the clerk, waited while the words were counted and then paid for the dispatch of the message. As he walked away, he was struck by a thought that would have astonished him a year before. Instinctively, he hated the men who were not part of what had happened to him, who seemed to him now smug and dangerous in their honesty. He hated them even more than those into whose hands he had fallen and who, playfully and amiably, showed him from time to time how impossible it was that they should ever let him go.

5

Alfred Swain stood in the approved posture for a private-clothes man reporting to his superior officer. He was at ease with his hands clasped lightly behind his back. Superintendent Toplady glanced at him, sniffed, and then glared at the papers of the inspector's report, which he held in his hand. Through the window behind Toplady's desk, Swain could see the river, moving sluggishly under a pearl-grey sky from Westminster Bridge down to Blackfriars. Penny steamers with tall black funnels scurried and puffed among the rust-coloured sails of slow collier barges. On the slime of the Surrey foreshore, the juvenile shapes of male and female mudlarks scavenged under the overhanging hulls of barges, beached to await cargo. The children waded thigh-deep in the ooze, picking coals from among the broken crockery and dead cats left by the morning tide.

Superintendent Toplady looked up from the papers again. A spry bow-legged gnome, he seemed about to dance round from behind his desk and box the inspector, man to man. Alfred Swain could never encounter Toplady without wondering what freak of genealogy had given a name suggesting feminine elegance to so incongruous a figure. Montague Toplady was the great-nephew of a more famous namesake who had fought for Calvinism against free will and written one of the most famous lines in the English hymnal, 'Rock of Ages cleft for me'. His great-nephew slapped the pages of Swain's report with the back of his hand.

'A pretty story here, mister! A pretty story y'have here, by God! Y'are hired by a noble family to complete a simple investigation. Y'are fed by 'em, shipped abroad, given every facility, fetched back again in comfort. And what do we have? A school-miss romance of Iphigenia and then nastiness done by harlots in a ruined castle. Are y'mad, sir, to think that I can offer such trumpery to them as a report?'

'With respect, sir . . .'

Toplady gave him a terrible grin, which Swain knew was not a grin at all, merely an agitation of the facial muscles.

'Be silent when I speak, mister!' the superintendent said curtly. 'Have the goodness to listen when I talk! With respect, sir! With respect, indeed.'

He returned to his glaring perusal of the pages. The size of the superintendent's head, by comparison with the stunted body, was of pantomine disproportion. The grizzled hair was cut short as a 'Newgate fringe'. It stood stiff and upright with an appearance of comic fright. Indeed, Toplady seemed determined to improve upon his naturally grotesque appearance. He favoured old-fashioned collars that were high and starched in exaggerated points. At every turn of his head they scraped his cheeks in a slight razoring sound. Swain looked on with an apprehension that a sudden downward glance by Toplady would cause the cruelly starched collar-point to pierce the superintendent's eyeball.

Toplady threw the report down and slapped one hand into the other behind his back. He paced up and down before the broad windows which looked out across the embankment and the chopping wavelets of the breezy Thames towards the huddled streets of Lambeth.

'This is what comes, mister, of an officer that goes skulking from

45

duty to bury his head in romantic fiction with a German dilettante.'

'I ask permission to speak, sir . . .'

'Do you, indeed?' Toplady swung back again. 'Then speak, damn you.'

'The manner in which Petrides shouted out the moment before he was shot ought not to be ignored. I went to Mycenae as instructed to view the scene of the murder. While there, I took certain evidence from Herr Schliemann and asked for any meaning of the name that he might know.'

'Did you, mister?' Toplady turned away on his sentry-go before the window, rolling the contempt round his tongue like a rare vintage. 'Did you indeed? And what good of it? What good, mister?'

'If it should prove that I have been negligent, sir, I would prefer to seek my discharge from the force and offer my services to Herr Schliemann in his digging at Mycenae.'

Toplady stopped, turned, and faced Swain, leaning towards him and supported by his fist on the desk. The grin was back.

'Mister! Y'shall put your papers in this minute for what I care. As for digging – I would not trust you to dig horse-dung into a rose bed.'

He turned and marched again. In that moment, Swain had no idea whether he still held a commission in the Metropolitan Police or not. Toplady swung back in his slow march.

'Unhappily, mister . . . Unhappily, I say, those who have hired you have chosen your services. I dare say it is intended that the old lady Lerici may be spared whatever nastiness her son left behind – so that she may not have to deal with the events of his death. Their lawyers have seen fit to hire you. Under the supervision of the family you are to break the seals, unlock the desk, and list what may be there. You must spend what time is necessary at the house of Mondragon, making an inventory of the private documents. You shall account direct to Mr Abrahams of King's Beach Walk in the Temple. When that is done and your hire is over, you may put your papers in and leave the force next day. Is that plain enough?'

'Yes, sir,' Swain said coldly.

'Yes, sir!' Toplady echoed contemptuously. 'For what I care then you may spend your life with school-miss nonsense and Mary-

Ann poetry books, mister! What sort of pastime is that for an inspector of constabulary?'

'By then I shall hold no such rank, sir.'

'By God, you shall not, mister! By God you shall not in this division!'

The awful grin of triumph returned. Toplady walked up and down a few minutes more.

Alfred Swain waited and watched. In the Crimean campaign, Montague Toplady had been Lieutenant of Horse Artillery at Inkerman. In the blind and bloody skirmish of that battle, the position had been overrun. Toplady had fought hand to hand with the advancing Russian troops in the terrible hour of mist and mud that followed. Now he continued to seek, in his constabulary role, the exuberance he had found in the slaughterhouse of war.

'And is anything more known about the rascal Petrides?' he asked suddenly.

'Not that I am aware of, sir,' Swain said calmly.

'Not that you are aware of, mister!' The superintendent rolled the saliva round his mouth as if he might expel it in a jet upon Inspector Swain. 'I'll be damned if y'ever are aware of much, sir! And without my boot behind you, y'd be content to remain so. Would you not?'

Swain stared at him.

'Answer when spoke to, mister! Where the devil d'you think y'are?'

'I will stand by what I reported, sir.'

'Oh, will you, mister? I'm sure we shall all be obliged to you for that!'

The sneer that accompanied the exclamation was not reserved exclusively for Swain. The superintendent treated him better, in general, than the rest of his subordinates.

'Very well,' Toplady said at last, 'then y'may take yourself to Mondragon by the shortest route. Make all the speed y'can to finish your commission there. Return here at the earliest convenience of those who hire you. Then put your papers in and let us be shot of you. I doubt that you will relish the consequence, mister. Look at yourself! Y'have soft hands, Mr Swain. A man that fancies governess stories and poetry books soon whimpers at

47

the blisters of the spade when he begins to dig. Howsomever, mister, we shall be well shot of you here!'

'Sir,' said Swain noncommittally.

Toplady handed back the pages of the report. 'Write it up fair, mister. Then get yourself to Mondragon. Mr Abrahams the attorney expects your answers forthwith. And you may take advantage of the presence of Inspector Palmer or Sergeant Lumley.'

'Sir?'

'Sergeant Lumley and Mr Palmer!' said Toplady with scornful irony. 'Are you so green, mister, that you do not know a policeman must not search unaccompanied? And since Palmer and Lumley must be there in any case, they may chaperon you.'

'In any case, sir?'

Toplady, spike-haired and sharp-collared, stared at him as if suspecting Swain of a joke. He saw no joke. 'Do you care so little for your employment here, mister, that you do not enquire of events at the scene of your investigation?'

'With respect, sir, I have been back in England less than a week, and so have been on overseas privilege leave. I believe Mr Abrahams thought it unfitting that any investigation should begin until after the late gentleman's obsequies.'

'Why, you fool,' said the superintendent helplessly, 'do you not know there is a body to be dealt with by Lumley and Palmer and an inquest to be attended at the coroner's court? A sly little devil, Joseph McBride, fell from the top of the tower at Mondragon a fortnight since.'

'Spider McBride?'

Toplady grew a little calmer as his energy flagged. But he was content with the assurance of having won a battle against insubordination.

'On terms of acquaintance with him, mister? Well, you have drunk his ale the last time. Sergeant Lumley is to examine the scene and report to the inquest. Mr Palmer was the officer called when the body was found. Lumley is also to see if one of the servants may not have had a hand in the plan for robbery. Who more likely than a servant?'

The superintendent worried this round his mouth for a moment or two, staring out across the river scene under the bright sky of the cool spring day.

48

'And now, mister,' he said softly, 'have the goodness to take yourself off. Have your report in two fair copies. Then make the best of your way with Lumley to Mondragon. Y'shan't waste the time of those who hire you by going back to your lodgings. Send word to Pimlico that Mrs Beresford may expect to see you when you have done your duty. Your duty, mister! Understand that?'

'Sir,' Swain said in respectful acknowledgement.

Toplady had an afterthought. 'And see that you leave your desk tidy for your return, mister. A man that puts his papers in must be away sharply when the time comes. Y'should not want to keep Herr Schliemann waiting, I dare say.'

As he closed the door behind him, Alfred Swain had the impression that Superintendent Toplady's slow march had quickened to a dance.

6

Half an hour later, Alfred Swain sat on the high counting-house stool and stared across his desk at Sergeant Lumley's round florid face with its dark moustache and flattened hair.

'I think I've lost my job, Mr Lumley,' he said quietly.

Lumley ignored him.

'You was lucky, you was, Mr Swain. Bein' in foreign parts the last few weeks. It's been more than a man could bear in this division. Old Toplady, sour as vinegar and mean as a stoat – even for 'im. And then the general inspection. Every moth-hole in a uniform to be stopped out of wages.'

'I think I've sacked myself,' Swain said gloomily.

Sergeant Lumley was too far gone in the depths of his own grievances to notice what had been said. He took another consoling bite from the pork pie that he held in a cabbage leaf and chewed with a slow well-fed movement.

'You was lucky, you was,' he said indistinctly.

It was hopeless. Swain dipped his pen in the china ink-well again and finished two fair copies of the report, one for the division and one for Mr Abrahams, attorney for the Lerici estate to whom the division had hired him. Then, in company with the private-clothes sergeant, he set off for Charing Cross and the train that would take them to the coast.

As the bell rang and the engine snorted, Swain said, 'I never knew about Spider McBride. How should I? They wanted me out of the way while the funeral was held. I was put straight on overseas privilege leave for five days and came back off it yesterday. I never gave a thought to McBride.'

Lumley shrugged. 'Old Spider got too clever for his own good, Mr Swain. The burglaries there's been in that area, Brighton mostly. King's Parade. Brunswick Square. Royal York Hotel. Albion. You think that wasn't McBride? Not 'alf it wasn't! Mr Palmer been down there a month on his track. And he was minding Mondragon while he was there till you got back from foreign parts. When they found Spider dead on the terrace, they called Handsome Palmer.'

Conversation dwindled and died as the engine panted and laboured past wide glimpses of fields and gardens. The trees gave way to expanses of the Sussex downs interspersed with spring copses in flower. Lumley showed disappointingly little interest in Swain's travels, as the inspector recounted them. Even Petrides and the firing-squad evoked only a murmur of surprise. It was when the train rattled over yet another river bridge that Swain said again, 'You don't cry out like that the moment before they shoot you, Mr Lumley. Not unless it's something important. But Mr Toplady cares nothing about it at all. And the only man who knew who Iphigenia was is dead.'

A herd of brown and white cows in a field slid past them.

'Gammon,' Lumley said.

'What do you mean?'

A farmhouse and a barn slipped by.

'Gammon,' Lumley said again, 'everyone knows who Iphigenia is – or was.'

Swain felt a profound apprehension at what lay ahead. Sergeant Lumley was not the type to waste time on Greek mythology.

'I don't know who Iphigenia was,' he said meekly.

Sergeant Lumley sniffed and agreed. 'No, course you don't. But any man that doesn't spend his life with his head in a book knows who Iphigenia is.'

Swain stared at him. 'But surely a book is where you would expect to find her.'

Lumley glanced out of the window and shrugged off a laugh.

'One book, I dare say. You could try the old *Calendar*.'

Swain knew what was coming and yet hoped he was wrong. 'The *Calendar*?'

'The *Racing Calendar*,' Lumley said with quiet patience. 'Strike me, Mr Swain, the whole world knows it!'

'Knows the *Racing Calendar*?'

Lumley leant forward, his face glowing with simple zeal. 'The whole world knows it, Mr Swain! A horse, in other words! A horse that wins races! Iphigenia was the name of a horse!'

7

The carriage shook as the wheels went over the points where another track curved in from Hastings and the east. Alfred Swain tried to curb the incredulity, self-pity, and resentment in his voice.

'But how can Iphigenia be a horse?'

Sergeant Lumley looked puzzled. 'Horses has names like that. They often get called funny things when they're bred to race.'

'What happened to the animal?'

Lumley sniggered. 'It made me and the sergeants' room a few bob richer. Won the Portland Plate at Goodwood three summers ago. Hundred to eight, Mr Swain. Hardly been out before and it came in by lengths. Several of us had five bob on that.'

'You bet five shillings on a horse?'

'Good thing I did,' Lumley said self-righteously. 'I had a week at Margate on that when my summer leave came round. I never forgot it.'

'A week at Margate? Just from that? What made you choose this horse?'

Lumley shrugged. 'Something that somebody must have said. I don't recollect what. I must have been tipped somehow.'

Swain sighed and looked from the window at the long wooded valley above the sea. 'It can't be what Petrides meant. How could a Greek bandit know about an English racehorse? And what became of this horse? Does it still run races?'

Lumley frowned. 'It died, like horses do.'

'But the race at Goodwood was only three years ago.'

Lumley's frown grew deeper with the effort of recollection. 'It hadn't won a race before, not to speak of. After the Portland Plate, it had a fall. Broke a leg training. Had to be shot, I suppose. Poor devil.'

'Who owned it?'

But Lumley stared at him. 'That's a bit hard, Mr Swain. I forgot that long ago, if ever I knew it. Some funny sort of name, I think. Tell you who the jockey was, though. Little Dicky Dash. Real champion. Never such.'

'Lerici,' Swain said, 'John Posthumous Lerici.'

Lumley's face brightened. 'It could have been, Mr Swain.'

'Mr Lerici also owned Mondragon! He had the house built, for God's sake! I'd bet more than five shillings it was his horse.'

Lumley shrugged again. 'All I know about Mondragon was Spider McBride falling off the tower. Poor little swine. Me and Handsome Palmer got to see his inquest straight and keep our eyes open for any stolen property that Spider's girl might have. Nothing said to me about any Lerici until you started on.'

'That's the only Iphigenia,' Swain said thoughtfully. 'But it's ridiculous. Petrides couldn't mean a racehorse. What happened after it died?'

Lumley looked at Swain as if the inspector had gone stupid. 'I dunno. What does happen to horses when they're put down? Most gets turned into cat's meat or glue. Some get buried. Some get sent to the butcher's. Who knows what happened to it?'

'Someone knows,' Swain said ominously. 'For a start, why call a horse Iphigenia? What's the Trojan War got to do with race-horses?'

Lumley stared at him. 'Since you come back from being in Greece, Mr Swain, you been acting different. And I'm not the only one that thinks so. You want a bit less Trojan War and bit more about the twining dodge that's ruining the Haymarket with wooden sovereigns.'

Swain ignored the bait. The more he heard about the story, the madder it got. Yet Lumley's revelation made sense in its way. Petrides' last cry could hardly refer to the daughter of Agamemnon. And Schliemann was right. No modern Greek, nor anyone else, would name a daughter after the ill-fated heroine of Aeschylus and Euripides. A racehorse was another matter, Swain supposed. Lerici had evidently owned this horse, an outsider, an unexpected winner of the Portland Plate that had fallen and been put down. Swain was not a racing man. It was an odd story but not outrageous. It would have to be looked into, if the remains of the horse could still be found. But how the devil – and why the devil – was such a chain of events going to destroy anyone?

There was a dog-cart at the station to take them up the hill of elegant Georgian houses with their green canopies and striped awnings, across the flat and windswept uplands to the gate of Mondragon. The sun, which had been playing fox-and-geese with the torn clouds in the spring sky, now vanished behind a sullen bank of grey and it began to rain. Swain, however, kept to his purpose. He called the driver to a halt where the stone pillars marked the driveway and the two officers got down with their Gladstone bags. As the senior of the pair, Swain felt in his pocket and handed the driver a pair of coins.

A stormy east wind strained at the yellow-green of the trees in their young foliage where the broad gravelled carriageway passed between weathered limestone pillars. Spruce trees arched overhead, the vaulting of their branches almost obscuring the low sky. The rain clouds had the darkness of a drawing in Indian ink.

Swain had dismissed the station dog-cart as soon as they reached the gate so that he might arrive at the house unnoticed and in his own time. The terrace and the crenellated outline of the house were still hidden from him by the intervening woodland. All the same, Mondragon was much what he had expected. There were copses and spinneys, a carefully landscaped view of the sort that a retired East India merchant might have laid out for himself in the 1850s and then allowed to run riot. The dark alleys and bridlepaths where only the faintest dappling of sunlight would ever penetrate might have been the paradise of a hunter with dog and gun.

Swain was no countryman and he saw too late that they had taken the wrong path. The driveway dwindled to a track with dark leaf mould underfoot. The trees on either side were dank and leafless as they might have been in winter, the spring delayed by the cool depth of the woods. All about him he heard the measured dripping of rain as it ran through the tangle of twigs and fronds, soaking slow and deep into this arboreal cavern.

'You sure?' asked Lumley again. 'You sure this is right?'

'Yes,' said Swain gently, 'yes, Mr Lumley. I'm sure it is.'

Just before he spoke, he saw that the path opened out again into a wide green space, open to the clouds. It was a curious enclosure, the trees on every side broken only by a carriageway running through it. They had regained the driveway. Beyond the gravelled path rose the newly built mausoleum. The greater part of it was above ground, though steps of York stone led down to the iron latticework of its gates. Swain shook his head.

'He built it for himself, Mr Lumley. A few years ago. Wouldn't trust anyone else. You only need look at it. It isn't new. All ready for him, except the date on the inscription. Even Lerici couldn't put a date to his own death.'

He stared at it. In general appearance, Lerici's mausoleum looked like a large and ornate hearse, modelled in stone and set down in this dank Sussex parkland. Iron posts and chain surrounded it, a pair of stone lions sat timelessly at the head of the steps. The tomb-house itself was topped by an octagonal gothic column. The setting of it, in the centre of the path with dark trees either side, strengthened the impression of a monument in a ruined abbey of Lerici's imagination.

Lumley became confidential. 'They reckon, in the village, that there used to be goings-on here at nights, Mr Swain.'

'Goings-on? Of what sort?'

'After dark,' Lumley said. 'According to one or two of the poaching fraternity, there was lights seen in the tomb. They reckon he used to take two or three young persons in there and the lights used to burn till dawn. And sometimes he'd take three in and only two would come out. And once he took one on her own and came out alone. If he's in there now – and they ain't all agreed as to that – then he's got company. That's what's said.'

Swain sniffed derisively. 'Tap-room gossip, Mr Lumley! Tittle-tattle for old wives who can't be satisfied until they've frightened themselves stupid with tales of some bugaboo. I've seen Mr Lerici bandaged in his shroud, and I expect he looked much the same as any corpse in the Lambeth mortuary.'

'It's what they say.'

Swain stared more critically at the mausoleum. 'In that case, Mr Lumley, either set about substantiating charges under the Offences Against the Person Act 1861 or else leave well alone. That's my advice to you.'

Lumley sniggered at his own cleverness. 'Bit late for that now, Mr Swain. There won't be goings-on in there now. Not so far as your Lerici's concerned.'

Swain ignored him. He gave his attention to the inscription which was cut light and sharp into the free stone on which mosses and lichen had already grown.

Within this mausoleum are deposited
the mortal remains of
JOHN POSTHUMOUS LERICI
Born 24 March 1824
Died 12 February 1877

'My task is done – my song has ceased – my theme
Has died into an echo; it is fit
The spell should break of this protracted dream.'

'I dare say he wrote that for himself too,' Lumley said scornfully.

Swain stared at the lines again. 'No, Mr Lumley. Those words were written for him by his father. From *Childe Harold.*'

'Child?'

'For God's sake, Mr Lumley! The man in that mausoleum – the man who caused us and the rest of the world so much trouble – is the bastard son of Lord George Byron. His lordship wrote those lines.'

'I've got better things to do than read school-books,' Lumley said self-righteously.

'And have you better things to do than read police reports too? Lerici's history was set out in full for you there.'

Lumley scuffed at the grass with his shoe. 'I'm not here for that, Mr Swain. How that stupid little bugger Spider McBride come to fall off the roof. That's all. Once we've got that tidied away, we can be off home.'

But Swain was not listening. He read the inscription again. 'And the irony of it all, Mr Lumley, is that the man proves himself a liar, even on his own tombstone. Look at that!'

Lumley looked and shrugged. Swain pointed to the dates. '24 March 1824, Mr Lumley, and he the posthumous son of Lord Byron! He can't be. Lord Byron was still alive in March 1824. He died in Greece a month later, when the heat and the fever began. Not in March.'

Lumley smiled. 'P'raps they didn't know exactly.'

'Oh, come on, Mr Lumley! The first thing they do with a child in those countries is baptize it, for fear it should die, and go to hell. And you don't call a child 'Posthumous' when you think its father is still alive.'

Lumley shrugged again. 'Whether he was or not, Mr Swain, it can't make any odds to Spider McBride.'

Swain scowled to himself as they began to walk along the wider path towards the house. Perhaps it was the idyll of Mycenae, the finer things he had glimpsed. Whatever the reason, his return to duty made him wonder how he had ever tolerated Lumley so long. The well-fed self-importance and the impertinent ripostes were almost unendurable. How could he not have noticed before? Was he to work ten years, twenty, the rest of his life with this flea-biting voice beside him?

The inspector was roused from his sullen reverie by the rattle of wheels on the gravel drive behind him. He stepped clear and turned round. It was a little garden carriage driven by a girl of eighteen or nineteen with an elderly woman sitting beside her and another woman, a servant of some kind, walking behind. Lumley stood at attention and Swain tipped his hat, forward and back, with grave precision.

The old woman was plainly dressed in a tea-gown of black velvet with white lace at collar and cuffs. She held a parasol to keep the worst of the thin rain from her. Neither she nor the dark-haired girl wore clothes that were suited to walking or riding. Swain judged that they had come out in a hurry.

'Mr Swain?' the old woman asked quietly. 'We missed you on the path. I believe you have come the wrong way. The drive and *porte-cochère* stand on the other side. I dare say your driver left you at the far entrance to the grounds.'

The voice was odd, odder because the English was near perfect, until she said '*porte-cochère*' with continental correctness. Swain stared at her. The skin was fair, or rather pale with age. There was a length and elegance to the neck which he had seen before only in the style of certain painters and had thought artificial. Now it was part of a grace that the woman had had in youth and whose

56

lineaments shone through the ruin of mere beauty. The hair was still dark, coiffeured and piled with elegance upon her head. Women in England did not grow old as she had done. He knew what she would say before she spoke.

'I am Giovanna Lerici, Mr Swain. You have come to see me, I think.'

From her perch, she extended a hand downwards to him. Swain lifted off his hat with his left hand. With his right, he took the old woman's hand, bowed his head, and kissed it. Their respective heights made it impossible to offer any other acknowledgement. Alfred Swain had never done such a thing in his life before and was not quite sure why he did it now. His brain was alive with the thought that his lips touched the same hand as Lord Byron's, that his kiss fell in imitation of the greatest romantic of all time.

He drew back and saw Sergeant Lumley, still at attention, eyes wide and face colouring with suppressed astonishment.

'You will follow us,' Giovanna Lerici said and then turned to the woman who was walking behind the little carriage. 'We will go to the house, Basileia, if you please. This is Miss Brahami, Mr Swain. My granddaughter, Amalia.'

After so much formality, the old woman performed the second introduction when the little carriage had almost moved past and its occupants had their backs to Alfred Swain. It was as if even the servant Basileia took precedence over Amalia de Brahami. But as they passed him it was the servant who turned upon Alfred Swain a look of distaste that Superintendent Toplady might have envied. She was a strongly built woman of forty with the complexion of Greece or Italy. In her youth, Swain suspected, she might have been beautiful or at least handsome. Now her expression was one of powerful plainness. She looked away from him and followed the carriage.

Swain gestured to Lumley and the two officers fell into step at a little distance behind the vehicle. Despite the cool formality of their meeting, Giovanna Lerici might yet unbend. Swain conjured in his mind the questions he would ask her, if ever he was given the chance. To hear, from one who had known him, the last glorious days of Byron, something perhaps of Shelley... The world that opened before Inspector Swain, a thinking man of the modern age, made him oblivious of Lumley until he realized that the sergeant was directing a muttered comment from the corner of his mouth.

'What?' Swain asked impatiently.

'I said, "Here's a rum go," ' Lumley said in the same constricted tones. 'That one walking behind the cart looked as if she could stick a knife in you. P'raps she was the one going to help McBride rob the house. And the old girl in the cart didn't look pleased to see us. Mind you, there's the young 'un. I could be partial to what I might get there.'

Alfred Swain turned away with a suggestion of scorn and thought of *Childe Harold*.

8

At the head of a broad flight of steps within the great west door, the hall of Mondragon was unlike anything that Swain had imagined. It was a series of alcoved salons, grandly proportioned, its wall hung everywhere with damask of the deepest crimson. The hall and reception rooms were furnished with heavy elbow-chairs covered in the same material. Even the tables were draped in cut-velvet flounces. There was no glass, no gilding, no pictures except keepsake miniatures and photographs standing on the available surfaces, the very frames covered by velvet. At the far end of the hall rose the leaded lights of an oriel window in its recess. The whole place was like a page of Lerici's fiction. The air was still and confined, impregnated with a scent of burnt lavender. It was as if some medieval extravagance of Sicily or Spain had been enfolded within the damp Sussex stone and stucco.

That afternoon, in the presence of Sergeant Lumley and Giovanna Lerici, Alfred Swain broke the seals on the lock of the heavy gothic desk. John Posthumous Lerici's study was plain as a monk's cell, the walls plastered and whitewashed, the floor of polished pine. There was no furniture but three chairs and the mahogany desk itself, its panels inset with reliefs copied from Plantagenet window tracery.

Swain dismissed Lumley with a perfunctory nod. Giovanna Lerici chose a chair by the far wall. She behaved, it seemed to Swain, as if this was none of her business. England had been her son's home but never hers. The legal process belonged to a culture that was alien to her and her self-confidence wilted. The old woman sat like a little girl on her chair, waiting to be told what to do. Swain performed a half-bow in her direction and felt foolish even as he did so.

'If you will allow me, Signora, I will begin the inventory.'

'Do whatever must be done,' she said wearily.

Swain sat down and broke the wax seal holding the stout wire. He broke the wax carefully, putting the pieces into a little tin that had once held menthol pastilles for chest complaints, slipping the tin into his pocket so that he might inspect them again later. At a glance, they had been made with a seal-ring of Mycenaean design. Perhaps an item of Lerici's booty from the grave-circle.

He turned to the desk again, its very knee-hole shaped like an ecclesiastical arch from the example of Wyattville, Pugin and High Church fashion half a century before. The key that Giovanna Lerici had given him turned easily and he slid open the deep drawer above the knee-hole.

There was a soft leather cover, folded over a collection of papers and a manuscript book. Swain drew the book out first. By touching it, he knew that it belonged to an earlier age, like so much else in the house. Soft rag paper of this sort had been little used after the American Civil War had created a cotton shortage. He set the quarto manuscript before him. The paper had darkened to yellow-grey and the black ink was rusty as a bloodstain. Six words crossed the cover of the book in a bold and impatient italic script.

DON JUAN IN THE NEW WORLD

Swain's heart stopped beating as it seemed to him. Before him lay a treasure the world had never seen, except perhaps Giovanna Lerici and her son. He opened the cover and saw the familiar Byronic stanza form, the scornful, laconic, rebellious wit of the greatest romantic of the modern world. It was surely the story of Don Juan in America – the lost gold of English poetry.

> Upon the Virgin land was Juan set,
> A place of beauteous slaves and tropic morals.
> (I don't much wonder that Bob Southey funked it

Or that his women found a score of quarrels.)
Juan lay fast in Venus' toils, whose jet
And agile limbs wore little else but corals.
Pillowed he lay on skin as dark as Hades,
Treasured by these who sported like true ladies.

Sing, Muse, of Coleridge and the Susquehanna,
(I won't sing Southey, since he came in first).
Who knows, from Philadelphia to Savannah,
Which of Juan's conquests would have pleased 'em worst?
Both Senate's wives and maiden queen Susannah
Juan's nocturnal catalogue rehearsed.
O Lords of Golden Horn, stand ye in wonder
To see our hero steal your Sultan's thunder.

In his excitement, Alfred Swain could scarcely speak. It was all there. Four cantos of it! The masterpiece that even the poet's friends like Moore and Hobhouse thought was lost or burnt or never written. He wanted to run into the streets and shout it to the world.

'Signora,' he said gently, 'there is a poem here, *Don Juan* . . .'

'I know,' the old woman said quietly, meek in its presence as a child again, 'my lord would go to Greece or America. He wrote those verses on the island of Cephelonia before he went to Greece and died there. He admired the hope of a new world and the greatness of George Washington.'

'The Cincinnatus of the West,' Swain quoted eagerly. 'But this . . .'

'It was my lord's,' she said simply and Swain realized from the reverence in her voice that she had probably never read it – nor had she cherished it for any reason but that it had been written by a man who loved her when she was eighteen. Swain had read in fiction of those whose hearts were said to burst with excitement. He had never known until now what that cliché meant.

'There is much here which my son collected,' said Giovanna Lerici. 'Nothing else of his father's, I think.'

Swain was looking at another page of verse, incomplete. *Savonarola to the Signoria 1498*. At the corner of the page, someone had pencilled the letters 'RB'.

'This was your son's?' he asked, holding it out to her.

She shook her head. 'He took it from a café table, I believe. When he was at Pisa in 1859, Mrs Browning was at Bagni di Lucca for her health. It was the summer and the city was too heavy for her. They were not friends, my son and Mrs Browning. With her husband, it was different. Mr Browning had a taste for the macabre. They had a wager one evening. Each was to write the last speech of Savonarola before he was put to death for heresy in the great square at Florence. My son wrote something which he later copied into his novel. He also kept what Mr Browning had written that evening. The friendship was not long. The husband and the wife could not approve that novel of my son's. He had betrayed himself, they thought.'

Swain glanced at the paper, the last defiance of the fanatic, the gallows high and the bonfire built beneath to face the palace of the Signoria.

> I drink the cup, returning thanks.
> (The rack that turns one cripple in an hour,
> Draws a man's throat to nothing with the pain.)
> So let them hear me, first and last,
> The Florentines that keep death's holiday.
>
> Ah, sirs, if God might show some sign,
> The very least, to be God's own,
> The certainty of bliss with hell beneath,
> What man stands here who'd not endure my flame?
> Or buy my place in pain with all he has?
>
> But God being not, not in that sense, I say,
> Let such unworthy flesh His proxy stand . . .

'So much in my son's life, Mr Swain, was destroyed by that foolish book of his. As to poetry, I cannot tell you. I am not a poet and I cannot make much of it. I have seen little of my son since he was a child. My life was lived in those few months, before my lord went to join Mavrocordatos, to fight that Greece might still be free. You understand? To know such a man is never to live again when he dies. I am a ghost, Mr Swain. I have died more than fifty

61

years ago in a little port on the island of Cephelonia, the moment that I heard the news they brought from Greece. To me, my son was my lord's son. But he was not my lord. You see?'

Swain nodded. 'But what is in this drawer, Signora, is treasure beyond description.'

He held in his hand a dozen pages of orchestral score, something abandoned by its creator and picked up or stolen by Lerici in his Italian travels. For Lerici was surely a thief, Swain thought, among many other things. The manuscript score consisted of an overture, a chorus of soldiers, musical dialogue, and a bass aria against which someone had pencilled, 'We shall express our darker purpose.' At the head of the score, in the same ink as the composition itself, was written 'Il Ré Lear' and beside it, in pencil, 'By the composer of Macbeth.' Swain was no musician but the sweeping and soaring of the music in the manuscript conveyed powerfully the drama and the sound, the great opera house of Milan or Naples or Paris with the packed rows of balconies seen dimly in the limelight of the stage and orchestra. Several years before, when the Pimlico Debating Society to which he had belonged discussed 'Unwritten Masterpieces', Swain had invented a description of Shakespeare's *Tragical Historie of Mary Queen of Scots*, suppressed at the time for fear of offending the great Elizabeth. The prize, however, had gone to a musical amateur who held forth on the imagined grandeur of Verdi's *King Lear*. What if it were reality, after all?

'To me,' said Giovanna Lerici simply, 'there is no treasure but my lord. I am sorry, Mr Swain. I care nothing for other men's works, not my son's. My son was not worthy of him. He was my son but I know the truth. He was my son but he was a stranger to me after he was ten years old. Now, if you do not mind, I shall leave you to your task.'

Swain got up hastily. 'I should prefer that there was someone present, Signora. A witness should be here, as much for my protection as your own.'

The old woman shrugged. 'You are not a man to steal the spoons, Mr Swain. One can read your face too easily. Basileia is not free to sit here at this moment and it would not be right to impose such a duty on a servant. You have your sergeant at the door. You may call him in if you wish.'

She went out and Swain sat down again, struggling with thoughts

62

and emotions. Beyond the pointed arches of the leaded windows, the marble balustrade of the terrace was streaked rusty by years of rain and frost. The terrace had been laid out in oblong compartments of marble containing geraniums, aloes, and China roses. As the thin rain fell, they looked to Swain like the burial plots of a cemetery.

He turned through the papers and pages, the letters still in their envelopes. There was a ledger in dark blue boards, its spine bound in sandy leather. This was far more recent, evidently a purchase made by the late John Posthumous Lerici, whose own mother thought he was not worthy of his father. Curious, Swain thought. Had Signora Lerici still been sitting behind him, he would have thought it intrusive to pry into the murdered man's finances. Under the present circumstances, it would surely be a wise precaution to do so. Alfred Swain opened the book. There were columns of figures for money paid out and columns for money paid in. But there was no clear statement of why the money had been paid or received.

Swain frowned and began a closer inspection. There was no need to call Lumley in. It was best to be alone. Just until he understood what all the figures referred to. These were not regular accounts but seemed to relate to particular occasions or events. His fingers skimmed down lists of names. The sums were sometimes large but seldom very large. Fifty or a hundred pounds at the most. Most of the names meant nothing. His finger passed Clarke . . . Palmer . . . Meiklejohn . . . Druscovich . . .

For the second time that afternoon, Alfred Swain experienced the truth of a cliché from popular fiction. The hairs on the nape of his neck seemed to bristle as the skin tightened. Clarke, Palmer, and Meiklejohn might have been common enough names. Druscovich was not. They were together in a list of a dozen. The others meant nothing to him. But Clarke, Palmer, Meiklejohn, and Druscovich, who were grouped together in the column, were four of the fifteen officers in the Detective Division of Scotland Yard.

Swain looked at the head of the page. There was a date. 12 May 1873. There were no dates beside the individual entries down the column. So whatever these entries were, they all presumably referred to a single transaction on 12 May 1873. But why should four Scotland Yard officers pay money to Lerici or he to them?

Why? After the elation and excitement of so many literary treasures, Swain felt the chill of reality all the more keenly. He turned the page. The next one was headed 18 June 1874. Had there been no transactions for more than a year? What sort of accounts were these?

He ran his finger down again, noting the names and the sums. Clarke £13 10s. Several other names and then Druscovich £6 15s. Meiklejohn £3 7s. 6d. It was still not clear whether the money had been paid or received. He felt a sense of relief. If it was the worst, money paid to police officers for dishonest purposes, this made no sense. Someone might pay £5 or £10 but surely not an odd sum like £3 7s. 6d. Swain returned to the column, ran his finger down and stopped with a feeling of dread. Lumley £3 7s. 6d. Thank God he was in the room alone.

But what the devil did it mean? He flipped through the pages. There were later entries for May and June 1874. But Lerici was not in England during the spring of 1874. Swain had cause to know the dead man's movements in some detail. Lerici and his menagerie had descended upon the wooded hills and royal palaces of Sintra. There had been misconduct of some kind and the outraged Portuguese had threatened charges of debauchery which, in turn, brought the British consul into the scandal. Lerici could neither have paid nor received these sums in 1874. Swain turned back to the column with Lumley's name in it for 18 June 1874. In his mind, he heard again the conversation with Lumley in the train about a horse called Iphigenia.

'It made me and the sergeants' room a few bob richer. Won the Portland Plate at Goodwood three summers ago. Hundred to eight, Mr Swain. Hardly been out before and it came in by lengths. Several of us had five bob on that . . . I had a week at Margate on it when my summer leave came round . . . I must have been tipped somehow . . . It died, like horses do . . .'

Swain did a little calculation. Suppose this was the occasion when Lumley had bet five shillings on Iphigenia and won. Five shillings times 100–8 was five shillings times twelve and a half. And that would be £3 2s. 6d. Then there would be the return of the stake that Lumley had wagered. Five shillings. And that made exactly £3 7s. 6d. With a sense of relief, Swain thought that it was only a betting book after all. But why was it locked in Lerici's desk with the treasures of Lord Byron and Robert Browning? The man was surely not a bookmaker. And if Lerici was deep in dishonesty of some kind, why would he have put a provision in his will that his executors should employ a detective officer to open the desk? It was surely the last thing he would have done.

Had the ledger been left in the desk by someone wanting to impugn Lerici's honesty? No. It would have been so easy to do it by conventional means. Swain had found few people, not even Giovanna Lerici, who believed in the dead man's honesty. Surely the ledger had been left there by Lerici who wished to impugn the honesty of someone else after his death. That made sense. Lerici had information and he had written it down. In this case, he had somehow discovered the sums of money placed on Iphigenia for the Portland Plate at a King Street bookmakers by officers of the Detective Division. But how? And why?

He looked at the foot of the page and frowned. Across the columns in larger letters and in Lerici's hand were the words 'Running Rein'. What the devil was that? The name of a horse but nothing like Iphigenia.

Swain turned to the back of the ledger and found a different section. It was divided into individual columns with the name and address of a client at the head of each page. These were personal accounts of a rudimentary kind. Swain turned these pages and felt as if the sun had fallen from the sky. There were thirty or forty names. With two exceptions, they included every officer in the Detective Division of Scotland Yard.

He glanced at the page with Lumley's name at the top, recognizing the entry for £3 7s. 6d. on 18 June 1874. Very well, so these were payments made to the names on the pages. Presumably they had been paid such winnings after the races. There followed Inspector George Clarke, his address in Great College Street, Westminster, and several payments made. But Clarke had been more than twenty years in the Metropolitan Police. Surely, these were nothing more than bona fide winnings. Although a man addicted to gambling would endanger his position in the detective police, a police officer was not forbidden to bet on horse races.

He turned another page and stared at the name. Toplady. Montague Augustus Toplady, Superintendent of Detective Police, had won almost £40 in May 1873. Swain tried to think of Toplady as a betting man and failed. But what was the point of leaving such a ledger to be found if the bets had not been placed? How had Lerici discovered these details from a bookmaker? Was the whole thing a monstrous post-mortem hoax of some kind? Was the clause in Lerici's will a final sardonic joke or trick?

The next two pages had the names of strangers at the top. Then Swain saw his own, complete with his address. How had such information come to Lerici or his confederates, if not from other officers at Scotland Yard? There was a single entry of £50 with a question-mark and no date. But Alfred Swain had never bet on a horse in his life. Nor had he ever received money from John Posthumous Lerici. Even his hiring by Lerici's executors was a matter between them and the Commissioners of Metropolitan Police.

What the devil did it all mean?

In search of an answer, Swain sifted through the remaining papers in the drawer. There was nothing relating to horse racing or betting except a printed circular with a page of newsprint folded into it. In its way, it was the most bizarre item of them all.

SOCIETY FOR INSURING AGAINST LOSSES ON THE TURF

Swain snorted at the cheap trickery of the title. It stank of fraud. A man might as well set up a society for insuring against death. The page of newsprint appeared to be an editorial from the *Sporting Times*. It protested against the decision of the Jockey Club that certified bookmakers should be prohibited from accepting any further bets placed by Major Hugh Montmorency. If Major Montmorency backed a horse, it always won. Unless stopped, he was in danger of bankrupting the bookies and single-handedly destroying the Sport of Kings by his unerring foresight. Henceforth, his bets were to be refused. Bets placed by anyone in England on his behalf would also be void.

Accompanying this denunciation of the Jockey Club in the *Sporting Times* was a letter addressed by Major Montmorency to correspondents abroad. He asked only that they should accept money which he would send them and place it on a horse whose name he would give them. All they need do was to forward the cheque to a firm of 'certified bookmakers' in London. An address in Northumberland Avenue was given. If the horse lost, so did Montmorency but not the 'friend' who forwarded the cheque. If it won, then ten per cent of the winnings would be forwarded to the 'friend' in France or Germany who had placed the bet.

Swain stared out of the window as the thin rain drifted across the sombre parkland in the spring afternoon. He began to recall something of the case of the Turf Insurance swindle, though he had not been involved in the investigation himself. It was at least two or three years ago, in March 1874 as he recalled. Major Montmorency had sent money to his dupes and the name of the horse to be backed. The money was in the form of cheques drawn on 'the Royal Bank of London'. The dupes heard that the horses had won. They received cheques and letters of thanks from the major, though in accordance with the 'Betting Act of 1856' the cheques must be held by them until the result of the race had been 'Validated by the Jockey Club' a fortnight later. Like the first cheques, those which paid the commission on the winnings were drawn on the Royal Bank of London.

Human greed and gullibility prevailed in several cases. A dozen of the dupes begged Major Montmorency to let them wager money of their own on the horses that always won. The major demurred, unwilling to lead them into bad ways. At last he agreed. On receiving his cheque, the dupes added money of their own and forwarded it to 'Archer, Certified Bookmakers, Northumberland Avenue, London W.' The Comtesse de Goncourt had placed a total of some £5,000 of her own funds on four occasions.

No sooner was the money forwarded than Major Montmorency fell silent. No further news was heard of the horses or the race. The Comtesse de Goncourt tried to cash the cheques for her 'winnings' and discovered that the Royal Bank of London did not exist. She hastened to the Sûreté in Paris. The Sûreté communicated with Scotland Yard. The offices of the 'certified bookmakers' in Northumberland Avenue were in the next street to Scotland Yard. When visited by officers of the detective police, they were deserted. As Swain recalled, there were signs that the occupants had left no more than a few hours before. The page of the *Sporting Times* which complained of the ill-treatment of 'Major Montmorency' was proved to be a forgery. Beyond that, the inquiry revealed nothing.

In May 1875, there had been a swindle in reverse. It was the launching of the 'City of Paris Guaranteed Loan' from offices in the Rue Réaumur with an appeal to English investors. So great was the need for a sewerage system in the French capital that its government had guaranteed a premium of fifteen per cent annually on the investment so long as the work should last with repayment in full at the end of the period. The English recipients of the offer were supplied with pages from the French financial press, which praised the scheme as an investment without parallel in modern European finance. A statement of the guarantee by the Minister of Finance and a confirmation of forecasts by the Governor of the Bank of France were enclosed. By the time that this farrago of forgery and imposture had been investigated, the greedy and the gullible in England had paid the price of experience as surely as their fellow sufferers in France at the hands of Major Montmorency. And, once again, the officials of the Sûreté had found only a bare and deserted office in the Rue Réaumur.

Swain gazed at the dripping parkland, thinking how simple it would have been for a Scotland Yard officer, knowing of the complaint from the Sûreté, to have walked to Northumberland Avenue and warned 'Major Montmorency'. How simple too, when the complaint was received from English dupes, to have wired a warning to the office in the Rue Réaumur before the Sûreté heard of it.

But Lerici's name had never been connected as a suspect with either of the two swindles. It brought Swain back to the same question.

Were the documents in the desk evidence against Lerici? Or had they been collected by Lerici as evidence against someone else? Was this what Spider McBride had been sent for? If Lerici had been blackmailed, his death with such documents in his possession would have turned the weapons against the blackmailers themselves.

Even that was not the worst of it. Whoever was at the bottom of this web of fraud could not have succeeded alone. It now seemed that he could not have succeeded at all without the connivance of at least some of the fifteen officers of the Detective Division.

And that, Swain thought, was where the problem became dangerous. If the ledger before him was to be believed, there were only two officers apart from himself who not been paid money by Lerici or those known to him. Sergeant Bennett and Inspector Shaw, both recent appointments to the division. Some of the payments might have been innocent, the result of bets placed on horses. But how to tell which were innocent and which were not? At that moment it was impossible.

Swain stood up and walked to the window. If there was any truth in this at all, men he had worked with for years – Clarke, Palmer, Meiklejohn, and Druscovich – men to whom he had entrusted his life at certain moments, were practising deceit and corruption on a system. If this were only true of some of his colleagues, how could he tell which? If the evidence had any truth in it, there was not a single colleague whom he dared trust. Not Toplady. Not Lumley.

Like any other innocent man, Alfred Swain was trapped by the evidence. Of the fourteen other officers, twelve were named in the ledger. They might be innocent but that was a risk he could not take.

The plot had been so contrived that it was impossible for Swain to discuss the matter with anyone. He could not speak of it to his commander, nor to his closest colleague, Lumley, posted at that moment outside the door. Both their names were listed in Lerici's columns. Swain felt that he had been caught as neatly as the dupes of the City of Paris Loan or the Society for Insuring Against Losses on the Turf.

Swain sat down at the desk and studied the three fragments of red wax which had once formed the seal. Almost absent-mindedly, he pushed the wafer scraps together, searching for the right pattern. Presently he had it. The image was unmistakable. A sun and crescent moon rose above the god behind his double-lozenged shield. Two griffins stood guard. Surely it must be a Mycenaean ring, one of the items looted from the treasure of Agamemnon's city. Where was the ring itself? If justice prevailed, it had returned to the dust of Argos as Lerici fell under the blows of Petrides' knife.

One thing was certain, Swain knew he could not take the ledger with him. It would require authorization and there was no one he could safely ask. If it was found to be missing and his name was known to be in it, he would be inextricably incriminated, as it seemed to him. He drew a notebook from his pocket. For half an hour, he wrote down names, dates, and sums of money. Then he closed and locked the desk and went out.

'Anything of interest?' Lumley asked.

'Poetry,' said Swain, 'nothing to concern us. May we go back to our conversation of this morning about horses? Iphigenia, Mr Lumley. What made you back that horse?'

Lumley looked puzzled but not self-conscious. 'Tip, Mr Swain. News round the department that morning was that it was likely to win the Portland Plate. Long odds.'

'Where did you back it? Where and how?'

Lumley frowned as if attempting recollection. 'Betting office. The one in King Street, Covent Garden, most like.'

'Did you go there and place the bet yourself? Did someone do it for you? Did you collect the winnings yourself?'

'Hang on,' said Lumley impatiently. 'Hang on, Mr Swain! It was a few years ago. I've backed a horse or two in that time and not always the same way. I can't remember every time how I did it. What's it matter?'

'I'll tell you, Mr Lumley, when I've found that horse and had it dug up.'

'I thought we was supposed to deal with Mr Lerici's will and tidy up Spider McBride for his inquest. What's a horse matter?'

Swain, in his neat suiting and with his long patient features, studied the plump sergeant. 'Suppose, Mr Lumley, the two should come to the same thing? Tidy McBride as best you can tomorrow. I shall make a report on the horse.'

Lumley shrugged, as if it were all beyond him.

9

Superintendent Toplady grinned horribly at Alfred Swain.

'Poetry books again, mister? Tell me that the fellow had nothing but such drivel? And he would hire Scotland Yard for that, would he?'

He skipped round the desk and stared malevolently up at the inspector.

'Take us all for fools, mister? Eh?'

'There were household accounts, sir,' Swain said evasively, 'I judged those to be the business of Mr Abrahams or Signora Lerici.'

'Si-gnor-a Lerici!' Toplady rolled it derisively round his tongue. 'Mrs Lerici not good enough for her? Eh?'

'The lady is not married, sir.'

The large head rolled round and Swain winced on the superintendent's behalf as a cruelly pointed collar narrowly missed the eyeball again.

'Why the devil should I care, mister, if she's married or not? Are y'paid to go down there and come back with such trumpery as this? Drivelling inanity and an old wench that had a bastard? Eh?'

'No, sir.'

Swain stared straight ahead again at the view of the sparkling river and the penny steamers beyond the window. The gloom that he felt had little to do with Toplady's insane rages. He was well used to those. But it was out of the question to discuss the ledger with such a man, let alone ask Toplady if he had ever backed a racehorse called Iphigenia.

'I should like authority, sir, to exhume . . .'

'You should what, mister? You should want what?'

'Authority to exhume the remains of a horse.'

Toplady stared at him, clenching his fist a little as if to shake it at the inspector. Then he seemed to get control of himself with difficulty, relaxing the fingers and breathing hard a moment.

'A horse,' he said, tight-chinned. 'A horse? What has a horse to do with any of this?'

'It was a horse that belonged to the late John Posthumous Lerici, sir. Iphigenia. A three-year-old that won the Portland Plate at Goodwood Races in 1874. On 18 June.'

'If you knew better, mister,' grumbled Toplady, 'you would call that day Waterloo Day. What should it matter to anyone if it won the Portland Plate or not?'

'It might matter a good deal, sir, to a man who had placed money on it.'

As he spoke, Swain watched Toplady with great care for any sign that might betray his interest. He saw none.

'Iphigenia!' the superintendent said scornfully. 'No, mister. You shall not have authority to waste the time of this police office

71

searching for dead horse-flesh. There is a job to be done. Oblige me by seein' to it!'

Before Swain could reply, there was a knock at the handsome white-painted panels of the superintendent's office door. Toplady let off an interrogatory squawk and the door opened. A uniformed sergeant appeared with a paper in his hand.

'Mr Abrahams, sir. By appointment, Mr Abrahams says.'

'Ah!' said the superintendent sharply. 'To be sure. Mr Abrahams. By all means, sergeant.'

The sergeant stood back and a tall dark-haired man entered the room. The face was one of amused intelligence, the profile that of an actor or a born politician. The dark suiting was immaculately cut and the old-fashioned leather stock was buttoned up to the chin.

Toplady shook the lawyer's hand, grinning quickly. Abrahams turned to Swain with a look of enquiry.

'Perhaps I intrude?'

'No y'don't, sir,' said Toplady quickly. 'This is your man, Mr Abrahams. The hired officer. Swain.'

The lawyer's face relaxed and he stepped forward, hand held out.

'Mr Swain! How very fortunate.'

'His report shall be made this week,' Toplady said, before Swain could answer.

'Indeed,' Swain said, shaking hands with Abrahams and seeing his chance. 'However, there are certain matters which I should like to clarify with Mr Abrahams, if I might have a private interview. It would expedite the report.'

Behind the lawyer's back, Toplady directed a glare in Swain's direction.

'I'm sure there is no reason to prevent that,' Abrahams said, collecting his thoughts. 'I shall be engaged at court most of the day, Mr Swain, but if you can come to my chambers at five this afternoon, I shall be free for half an hour.'

'I should be most grateful,' Swain said, avoiding the rage in Toplady's eyes as the superintendent saw himself cut out of the arrangement by the inspector.

'Perhaps, in that case, I should withdraw now,' Swain suggested.

'Don't presume to dismiss yourself!' Toplady snapped. 'Wait the command!'

Mr Abrahams turned meekly to the superintendent. 'There is no business of mine that need detain Mr Swain at the present.'

'Very well,' said Toplady, half to himself, making a gesture of dispatch towards Swain. 'Return to your duties, mister. See your diary written up and the report made.'

Swain bowed his head towards Abrahams and withdrew. He walked down the stairs slowly towards the inspectors' office. How the devil could he perform any duties here? Almost every man he encountered appeared to him as a conspirator. On a high counting-house stool at one desk sat George Clarke, white haired with the round rubicund face of a jolly sailor. He turned his head as Swain came in.

'Blessed!' he said. 'You got your money's worth from old "Tops" this morning!' And Clarke began a warbling chuckle at Swain's discomfiture.

'It's the war wound the Rhoosians gave him,' Meiklejohn said, the grizzled hair on the large head cropped almost as short as a convict's. 'Plays old Toplady up on damp mornings.'

'There are times,' Swain said, 'when a man can neither do right without affliction nor wrong without being ruined. Junius says so in one of his letters. I think of that every time I try to hold a conversation with Mr Toplady.'

He watched them as he spoke but the old phrase provoked nothing from them. Swain was a reading man and so they gave him up.

'Blessed,' said Clarke again, shaking his head at the mystery of it all. Alfred Swain edged his rump on to the hard little oval of the high stool and attended to his immediate task. He opened his inspector's diary, wrote the date at the top of the page, took the round wooden ruler in his fist like a truncheon and drew a line across the page.

Clarke? Meiklejohn? If Lerici's accounts were to be believed these were two of the men who had been bought and sold. Swain looked up furtively. George Clarke's jovial red face was relaxed as he copied details from one page on to another. Swain could not imagine a man who looked more content in what he was doing. Meiklejohn was reading from a notebook, his face drawn in a slight frown of scepticism. These were his colleagues, Swain thought, men he had worked with, eaten with, and sometimes drunk with. Were there secret patterns of corruption and criminality hidden beneath their plain and decent exteriors?

And Toplady? Surely it was impossible. Yet Alfred Swain now understood the true evil of such suspicions which spread a malignant growth of doubt and distrust. There was not a single man in the division, from Superintendent Toplady to Constable Dooley, to whom he could confide his troubles. Shaw and Bennett were the only two names not in the ledger. Why? Perhaps because they were the men behind the plot. With a glum resolve he began his diary entry, recounting the inventory of 'family papers' in Lerici's desk.

What was he to say of the ledger? Either he would include it, in which case he must accuse the entire Detective Division of corruption – or he must omit it. If it was subsequently found with his own name listed, then he would be first among those called to account at the Central Criminal Court.

Swain omitted it. However, he left a space in which he could enter it later on, in contravention of police regulations. Why the devil had he not stolen it while he had the chance and burned it? But he had not burned it. Swain glanced up at the other two inspectors and knew that he had left himself with only one way forward. There was nothing for it but to confront them.

'Mr Clarke . . . Mr Clarke! Did you happen to bet on a horse called Iphigenia in the Portland Plate at Goodwood a few years ago?'

This time Clarke did not say 'Blessed!' in his genial manner. He looked at Swain without speaking, his features immobile. In that rubicund mask, Swain thought he saw geniality replaced by apprehension, hostility, a shabbiness of soul.

'I might, Mr Swain. I might. Can't exactly say.'

'I only ask, Mr Clarke, because it proves that the gentleman whose executor has hired me was the owner of Iphigenia. Mr Lumley tells me that most of the division bet on that horse for the Portland Plate.'

Confidence returned to Clarke's face. Now he knew where he was. 'Then you tell Mr Lumley with my compliments that my business is none of his.' He returned to his careful transcription of the evidence in a petty larceny.

'And you, Mr Meiklejohn?' Swain enquired. 'Did Iphigenia make you a few sovereigns richer?'

Meiklejohn grinned. Swain the reading man was nothing to him and he took no pains to conceal it. 'Iffy what, Swain? Draw it mild, old fellow. I wouldn't back anything with a name like that.'

'What's the interest, then?' Clarke took the offensive now.

'Just interest,' Swain said. 'I'm not a betting man myself.'

'No,' Meiklejohn said casually, 'not a betting man. I should say you was altogether too good for this world, Mr Swain. Altogether too good for us.'

'And you being on foreign duty, Swain,' Clarke said indifferently, 'I suppose that must have give your landlady Mrs Beresford time to heal up. There's half the street knows of you, old fellow, and most of the division too. Just needs someone that wishes you harm to drop a word to old Tops. Misbehaviour in lodgings – that's an outer from the force, that is. You need to remember that next time you're in the mood for exercise.'

Anger, disgust, humiliation, and despair blocked Swain's reply. He turned his back on Clarke and tried to work. But he had touched a nerve. Clarke's reply left him in no doubt. There was more to the Portland Plate and far more to Iphigenia than he had thought at first. Even as the three men worked at their desks, the sense of hostility from the other two quickened Swain's heart. When the time for their duty break came, Meiklejohn said quietly and pointedly, 'You coming, Mr Clarke?'

They went out, leaving Swain to his bitter thoughts.

10

At quarter to five, Swain turned out of Whitehall Place for the river. The sky was pale blue and chill in the last of the sun. At the corner came a clout of ice and a razoring wind. He lengthened his stride towards the pier by Westminster Bridge. A bell was ringing as he ran to the toll-gate, paid his penny, and stepped on board the little steam-boat. The broad plank over which the passengers had passed was drawn ashore. A cable was cast off and the paddle wash frothed against the wooden piles.

A shower of smuts fell from the tall black funnel as the bows turned into the stream. Swain stood in the shelter of the canvas staring at the late sunlight as it painted wavelets with glancing flames. Churches, warehouses, steam-chimneys, shot-towers, wharves, bridges swept by on a rushing tide. The little boat battled the current under the arches of the iron bridge, and revealed another, and another, spanning the river down to the docks. The wharves on the Westminster side were still busy and the foundries and glass-houses and printing-works on the Surrey shore poured dark feathery smoke skywards.

At the Temple Gardens, Swain was first off, entering a collegiate calm of lawyers' courtyards, Georgian buildings tall on every side. The trees of King's Bench Walk stirred in the wash of air as light faded from the sky. By a doorway of the elegant terrace, a discreet inscription announced Abrahams and Abrahams.

A disembodied hand painted on the wall directed him to the upper floor. Abrahams himself stood in the clerk's office, the door open to the landing.

'Come in, Mr Swain. Tell me what it was that you preferred not to say in Mr Toplady's presence. Dear me! I see I have hit the target at the first shot!'

Swain passed through an outer room leading to chambers built for a portly and bewigged counsel of King's Bench in the reign of the first King George. If he thought much of heaven, he would have imagined it as a room like this. Tall, elegantly proportioned, the mahogany break-front bookcases of regency design rising high on every side glowed with the coloured leather of volumes of wisdom. The turkey carpet in blue and red was soft as snow. The polished walnut of tables and the leather padded chairs shone in the late sunlight.

'Sit down, Mr Swain.' Abrahams faced him across the desk. 'Tell me what you have discovered about my late client and do not wish Mr Toplady to hear.'

Uncharacteristically, Swain fumbled for an answer. 'I said nothing ... nothing about Mr Toplady ...'

'Oh, come now, Mr Swain. I have been a lawyer long enough to know when a man would speak but can't. John Posthumous Lerici was my client and I owed him a duty as such. But a lawyer is not obliged to like his clients, Mr Swain. Thank God for that! You will not shock me by telling me what I have long known. John Posthumous Lerici was a liar, a fornicator, an adulterer, very probably a thief, possibly a sodomite. And what is far worse, he was the author of the most banal housemaid's novelettes. The Miss Brontës and their deplorable example in literature have much to answer for, Mr Swain.'

'There are manuscripts of incomparable value in his desk, sir. A lost work of Lord Byron's, written at Zante. *Don Juan in the New World*. A monologue of Mr Browning's on the execution of Savonarola. A musical score of *King Lear* ...'

The lawyer held up his hand, interrupting the inspector with a smile. 'Forgive me, Mr Swain. He was my client but I was not obliged to accept his claims without examination. He often boasted of such treasures. But he was a joker, Mr Swain. I will believe these treasures genuine, rather than his own creation, when they have passed the scrutiny of experts.'

'His mother believes them so.'

'And she, poor lady, has been put upon more than most.'

Swain made no attempt to return the lawyer's smile. 'Then I have something far worse to tell you, sir.'

'What worse, Mr Swain? His mother's family gave him up in the end. John Posthumous Lerici was taken on at ten or eleven by his father's people. He was educated in England by tutors. Never at school. He was allowed what money he wished. He had a certain literary flair for which he never found a proper outlet – and a mania for collecting which would have brought a less fortunate man to the door of the bankruptcy court. He went around with a rag-tag and bob-tail of degenerates – men and women alike. The wonder is he was not murdered years ago. He believed he could have built another Strawberry Hill or Fonthill Abbey, I dare say. But instead he built Mondragon. What worse have you to tell me? Did he murder others before someone murdered him?'

'I believe he stole, sir, from the site at Mycenae. Rather, I believe he or his minion corrupted workmen at the site and they stole for him. The wax seal on the desk, Mr Abrahams, was made by a ring. A Mycenaean design, I believe.'

'Is that your worst, Mr Swain?' Abrahams laughed at it. 'It would not go far at Old Bailey Sessions. I doubt Lerici thought such things a crime at all.'

Swain shook his head. 'The worst is among the papers in the desk. There is also a ledger.'

'Ah,' said Mr Abrahams, 'a certain whiff of fraud.'

'A betting book,' Swain said, 'records of bets received and winnings paid on races during the past five years.'

This time it was the lawyer who shook his head. 'Gaming was among his vices, Mr Swain, but it was not much with him. His greater aberrations were matters involving women. And when he gambled it was at cards, among friends. He may well have mixed with racing-men and their kind but that was not his first choice of company. And I cannot think he would have taken bets on horses.'

'I believe these are his records of other men's wagers, sir,' Swain said gently, 'I believe also that there is evidence of gross fraud. I believe I can prove it.'

Mr Abrahams met him, eye to eye. 'Then had you not best take your belief to Superintendent Toplady at Scotland Yard, Mr Swain? Had you not?'

'No, sir,' Swain said. 'That is the very thing I cannot do. I am not here to blacken John Posthumous Lerici's reputation. I am here to ask your help.'

'Well, Mr Swain! You are the policeman, not I. And Lerici was my client. Whatever my feelings, I owe a certain duty there.'

'Was he your only client?' Swain asked gently. 'I have spent a little while reading files in the records office of the Detective Division this afternoon. Were you not asked to act for the Comtesse de Goncourt, following money obtained from her by means of a fraud three years ago? The Society for the Insurance Against Losses on the Turf? Did you not also act for James Arthur de Savin of Manor Park, Hawkhurst, Kent, following the City of Paris Guaranteed Loan swindle a year later? There are papers in Lerici's desk which associate him with both those swindles.'

Abrahams had lowered his head and was staring at the backs of his hands spread out upon the desk.

'And what else, Mr Swain? Why have you brought this to me and not to Mr Toplady?'

'Mr Toplady's name and those of twelve of the fourteen other officers of the Detective Division are in the betting ledger as men in the pay of the swindlers. My own name is among them.'

'Really, Mr Swain! If your own name is there – and if you are innocent – how can you accuse a single officer of the division?'

Swain had anticipated this. 'With respect, sir, I don't. But I have

78

tried to put the case to two of them. They closed ranks, sir, and in their way threatened me. I know that most of the officers in the division are honest and loyal. But I do not know which. I cannot go to Sergeant Lumley, with whom I work. I cannot go to Mr Toplady . . .'

Abrahams spread his hands out, appealing to reason. 'You cannot believe that Mr Toplady . . .'

'No, sir. But I cannot take this to him. He would have none of it. And his name is in the ledger as having been paid a large sum of money when Iphigenia won the Portland Plate at Goodwood three years ago. If he did not make a bet on that horse – Iphigenia – in that race, and if the money was none the less paid to him, what can the conclusion be?'

Abrahams thought about it and sighed. 'I do not suppose you are right, Mr Swain. Not for one moment. But say you were – put it that corruption had gone so wide and so high. Then I do not well know how it could be dealt with. It would be well nigh beyond dealing with.'

'I will make a start,' Swain said, 'if you will help me. I have trusted you with everything, Mr Abrahams, and you may very easily destroy me if you wish. But I know of no one else who can assist me.'

Abrahams got up and walked across to the window, staring out as the twilight gathered in the Temple Gardens, his back to Swain and his hands clasped behind him. He spoke without looking round.

'And how are you to start, Mr Swain, or I to help you?'

'Mr Lerici, sir. Did he insure his property?'

'Of course, Mr Swain. The matter was dealt with here, on his behalf. There was a policy at Lloyd's.'

'And a race-horse would be insured?'

Abrahams turned to him. 'It would have to be insured, Mr Swain. Not only the rules of the Jockey Club but those of any race course would require it. A horse that falls may fall on someone. It may collide and injure another jockey in the race. It could not be admitted to a race without insurance.'

'Then Iphigenia was insured?'

'If the animal was entered for the Portland Plate at Goodwood, Mr Swain, it was thoroughly insured.'

'And when it met with an accident which caused its death, the insurers must pay a claim?'

'Unless the insured made no claim. That sometimes happens, even in cases of an accident. A claim may lead to an increase in premium, after all.'

'But a man would scarcely neglect to claim in respect of a horse which had lately won the Portland Plate. A valuable animal, I would imagine.'

'And yet, Mr Swain, I never recall such a claim.'

'Precisely,' the inspector said, 'and that is what seems curious. A man has a valuable item, well insured. Its value is publicly demonstrated a few weeks before. He loses it. And though he is nearly bankrupt, he never claims the money to which he would surely be entitled.'

'One moment,' Abrahams said. He went through a communicating door and Swain heard the rattle of keys. It was several minutes before the lawyer returned with a black metal deed-box. Swain made out the white-painted lettering and numbering. 'LERICI 1874.'

'We had best have this plain,' Abrahams said, unlocking the metal box and taking out a folder of documents. 'I dealt with major transactions myself but an insurance claim on a horse might easily be agreed between the two parties without a lawyer's intervention. Ah, Mr Swain. Here we have it. Iphigenia. There was no claim by Mr Lerici because he sold the horse – a week or two before its death, I imagine – to Mr Henry Benson and Mr William Kurr. The horse to remain at Mondragon for stabling and training.'

' "Poodle" Benson and Billy Kurr!' Swain pronounced the names as if swearing an oath.

'Yes, Mr Swain?'

'They were two names that came close to the City of Paris Guaranteed Loan swindle and that other business of losses on the turf. Benson was in Newgate from 1871 until 1872 after fraudulently taking a cheque for £1,000 off the Lord Mayor of London for so-called orphans of the Franco-Prussian War. Harry Benson, otherwise known as Poodle Benson. All silk and soap. He's got a gift of the gab that could sell water to a drowning man. Billy Kurr's rougher, though they work together. Started with a moneylender's office. God help those that didn't pay back with interest. Then he changed to bookmaking.'

80

'I see,' said Abrahams thoughtfully, though Swain doubted that he did.

'I came here, Mr Abrahams, to ask for your authority to exhume the remains of this horse, Iphigenia. If the animal remained at Mondragon and died there, presumably it was buried there.'

Abrahams stared at him. 'Will it really help you, Mr Swain, if you discover who killed a horse?'

Swain shook his head. 'No, sir,' he said gently, 'I'm interested in who killed a man. What do you know of Running Rein, Mr Abrahams?'

Abrahams looked at him, smiled and shook his head. 'Not your case, Mr Swain. I dare say you weren't even born when Running Rein won the Derby at Epsom in 1844. The trouble was that the losers alleged that it was the same horse with a slightly different appearance which had won the St Leger the year before as Judas Maccabeus. Its age was beyond the limit for the Derby. A very nasty lawsuit followed between two very unsavoury parties. The Lord Chief Justice presided. At one point he threatened to commit everyone concerned to prison.'

'And the horse?'

'It died, Mr Swain, before it could be evidence. Very well, you shall have an exhumation if you can find the spot. I believe you may be wasting your time. I assure you that neither force of circumstances nor his creditors would have caused John Post-humous Lerici to indulge in such expedients.'

Swain stood up. 'I wasn't thinking of force of circumstances nor creditors, Mr Abrahams. A man can be blackmailed when he can't be bought.'

'He thrived on notoriety, Mr Swain,' the lawyer said gently. 'What can you blackmail such a man for?'

'Something a lot worse than gothic horrors.' Swain watched Abrahams' pen cross the paper. 'Something that might destroy him – as indeed he was destroyed. What he left for us was his assurance that the truth might come out. Running Rein was the clue to anyone who knew how to use it. Why else write it across the bottom of the page?'

He left the chambers with a written authority in his pocket for the exhumation of Iphigenia and made his way up Middle Temple Lane to Fleet Street. At the corner a barrel-organ was playing in the dusk, 'I couldn't help laughing it tickled me so'. Swain crossed the street between the hansom cabs and twopenny buses. At 52 Fleet Street, a steep and narrow staircase led up to the offices of the *Sporting Times*, above a tailor's shop. Swain went up and tapped on the small ground-glass window of the enquiry cubicle. Someone opened the window a little and said, 'Evenin', Mr Swain.'

'Evening, Mr Charles. I'm here for a favour. Mr Corlett home, is he?'

'Not exactly, Mr Swain. Anything I can do?'

'The Portland Plate of 1874, Mr Charles. Won by a horse called Iphigenia that upped and died soon afterwards. You recall it?'

'Yes, Mr Swain, I recall it. Why?'

'Was it favourite to win?'

Mr Charles blew out his plump cheeks with the difficulty of it. 'Became favourite very late. Almost on the day. Consequence of a lot of money being put on.'

'Is that unusual?'

'No, Mr Swain. Not the least. Often a rush of money at the last. There was some other favourite that was scratched. So this horse takes its place in the betting. Very common occurrence.'

'Forgive me, Mr Charles. I'm not a racing man.'

'I'll say you're not, sir!'

'What was the horse that was scratched?'

Mr Charles looked at him. 'Step inside a minute, Mr Swain.'

He reached from his stool and pulled a string. A door at the side of the window swung open and Swain walked into the 'Pink 'un' office, a low, square room of painted wooden panels with a long window over the street, the lower half was papered over to conceal the view from the tops of buses. Swain stood in the gaslit office among the smells of paper and hot ink.

'The Portland Plate 1876,' Swain said helpfully, 'won by a horse called Iphigenia. Owned by John Posthumous Lerici and ridden by Dicky Dash.'

'Why, Mr Swain, you know it all! And you want the name of a horse that was scratched?' Mr Charles walked across with a limp towards the tall shelves on the far wall. Volumes of the *Racing Calendar* for the past fifty years were bound in pillar-box red and lettered in gold. 'Now, Mr Swain, the Portland Plate is just a race for three-year-olds. Not the fastest nor the strongest race in the world.' He took down a red-leather volume. 'As I recall, the favourite that was scratched had outings at Ascot or Epsom and impressed. Nothing here about it being scratched at Goodwood. Let's try Epsom. Here we are. And that's neat as apple-pie, Mr Swain. It was Dicky Dash riding again and the horse was Lady Luck. Won at Epsom, scratched at Goodwood. Damaged a tendon training at some stables out near Lambourne.'

'Who was the owner? Not Lerici?'

'No,' said Mr Charles, 'Harry Benson, that's called Poodle Benson. Only man in London, they say, that can go in a revolving door behind you and come out in front.'

Swain's heart beat faster. 'I still don't see why Iphigenia became favourite to win.'

'Money, Mr Swain. Before Lady Luck was scratched, Iphigenia was long odds, 100–8 or so. Even when Lady Luck went, odds on Iphigenia were still long. Never won a race before. Then someone starts piling the money on. By the morning of the race, it shortened right down at 7–2.'

'And after the race it died,' Swain said thoughtfully.

'That's right, Mr Swain. Horses do have falls when training. Not uncommon. Lady Luck came back into the business, though. Mr Benson sold it when he disposed of the racing interests a couple of years back.'

Swain nodded. 'And if a horse had to be put down, Mr Charles, where would that happen?'

A man in a swivel chair turned towards them and Swain recognized by sight Colonel Newnham-Davis, editor-in-charge of the paper.

'The nearest place they could dig a thumping hole big enough,' the colonel said. 'Lead the poor brute to the edge, shoot it, and let it fall. Unless they sold the carcass.'

'Thank you,' Swain said, 'I don't think this one would have been sold.'

'Which poor brute do you want, Mr Swain?' Charles asked. 'Lady Luck or Iphigenia?'

Swain gave a tolerant laugh. 'I don't want any horse in particular, Mr Charles. Just the principle of the thing.'

'You, Mr Swain?' Charles shook his head. 'There was never a

time when you didn't want something particular.'

Swain took his leave and came out into the evening bustle of Fleet Street and the Strand. As he walked down Villiers Street towards the river, the open doors of the Hungerford music hall filled the early darkness with sounds of the chorus, girls as pretty as pictures and like as peas in a pod.

> My father is a barber, and he's unkind to me
> And I'd be glad if my old dad would go to Barbary,
> I'd rather lather Father – with that he won't agree;
> Yes, I'd rather lather Father than Father lathered me ...

Alfred Swain pressed through the crowd, the scarlet tunic'd troopers and the clerks in caps or tall hats, the young women with their bonnets and feathers, towards the pier, the homeward steamer for Vauxhall Bridge and Pimlico. It was nine o'clock by the time that he came to the little street near St George's Square, the shops that sold boiled sweets or tobacco, the houses in their raw-coloured brick. Here he had his lodgings, in two rooms rented by the week from Mrs Beresford, widow of PC Beresford who had kept afloat an intended suicide off London Bridge wharf until rescue came, and had then been caught by the current himself before he could be pulled to safety.

Only now, as their reunion grew nearer, did Alfred Swain promise himself how much he had missed the young woman's pretty face and kindly manner, her warmth and willingness. The thought that others would use her to defeat him, to gain their own ends, filled him with a greater sense of outrage than any form of dishonesty that might be laid to their charge. He lengthened his stride in the gathering dusk.

11

'The old girl's took to her bed, the one they call Signora Lerici,' Lumley said. 'Not that there's much wrong with her so far as anyone knows. So that leaves Miss Amalia in charge. Least said about her the better. Very peculiar sort of young person, if you ask me.'

They stood in the cool morning air, witnesses at the exhumation of Iphigenia. Swain said nothing as the stable-clock chimed eight through a thin mist.

'What about the servant?' Swain asked. 'The Greek woman they call Basileia?'

Lumley pulled a face. 'They got servants all right. There's two men and an English maid. The Greek woman looks like she could turn us all to stone. Never a word to no one. Is it that she don't understand? She listens all right but never says a word. You don't think she's a mute, Mr Swain?'

'No, Mr Lumley, I shouldn't think she's anything of the kind.'

Swain turned his collar up a little against the morning chill. He was uncomfortably caught between Lumley on one side of him and Inspector Palmer on the other.

'You'll be all right with me, Mr Swain. Anything you want to know, you just ask me,' Palmer said in the reassuring voice of a young baritone hero. 'I was born and brought up to horses. Trained 'em, rode 'em, and sometimes ate 'em, when times were bad. One thing I never did was bet money on them. Mug's game, that is.'

'Really?' Swain said without interest. 'I'm sure I shall be much obliged for your advice, Mr Palmer.' He turned aside to Lumley. Before he could speak, the spades of the two estate hands digging in the nettle-bed behind the stable-block struck stones.

'That's it!' Palmer chuckled encouragingly, 'Always weight 'em down with a bit of stone. They blow up with the gas otherwise, just like people.'

'Careful!' Swain shouted at the diggers. 'If there's any bone in there, I want it in one piece.'

'Anyway,' Lumley said as the spades of the farm-hands sought the last resting-place of Iphigenia. 'The old girl took to her bed and Miss Amalia didn't seem to know Christmas from Easter about the way things were done. It was Chaffey, the boots down the Cavendish Arms, that let it out. After the horse died, Chaffey and the other little boys used to come and play on the mound that covered it. Seems all the other nags that were put down went for cat's meat and glue. This one, being special, got buried here.'

The sun was turning pale gold through the vaporous morning, glinting on the hands of the stable-clock and the cream shingle-boarding of its little tower. The screen of spruce trees and young beech concealing the stables from the house was now plainly visible.

'Handsome' Palmer hoisted his operatic bulk a little and grinned at them.

'Speaking of dismemberment, they're going to top Moll O'Dowd at Wandsworth on Wednesday. That was my case. I was witness on her statement with Mr Pearman. Strapping young wench Moll O'Dowd is. Took three of them to take her in. Did the old lady with the back of an axe. Boiled the body.'

'Yes,' said Swain, trying to forestall the rest.

'Did the torso up in a hat-box and dropped it in the river. Washed up on the foreshore at Barnes. They found a foot at Twickenham and that was all. The girl scooped the fat from the boiler, put it in two basins, and sold it round the neighbours as dripping. Imagine eating that, eh, Mr Swain? But people did and only found out afterwards.'

'Quite,' said Swain irritably.

'Pity they don't hang 'em in public any more,' Palmer said wistfully, 'I'd like to see how she steps off. Havin' had so much to do with the business. Nice to see it through to the end.'

The diggers had stopped and one of the two uniformed constables standing by the rim of the excavation held up his hand.

'Mr Swain, sir!'

Swain took a linen handkerchief from his pocket and held it over his nose and mouth as he went forward. Behind him he sensed Inspector Palmer hot with excitement, eager for his meat. It was only a horse, Swain thought. Why such foreboding?

He stood on the rim of earth. The two diggers in kerchiefs and shirtsleeves were waist-deep in the excavation. Plain in the brick-red soil showed the whiteness of bone. One of the men was laying aside the soil now with the tip of his spade, the other brushing fragments clear. Little by little they revealed what might have been an inlaid paving. Oddly, as it seemed to Swain, the skeleton of the horse was at a gallop. Had someone arranged the dead limbs in this attitude as a final tribute to the winner of the Portland Plate, a sign to future ages that here lay a champion? A bridle had been left by the bones.

'That's the horse all right,' said the first uniformed constable sadly, 'and there's its bridle.'

Like a true Mycenaean princess, Iphigenia's treasure had been buried in the grave.

Swain stared at the phantom outline of bone. He knew little of equine anatomy but he knew sufficient in this case.

'There's no lower jaw-bone,' he said quietly. 'That's why the animal was done away with secretly.'

'Sift the earth a bit,' Palmer suggested, 'see if it hasn't just worked down below.'

'It hasn't worked down, Mr Palmer,' Swain said impatiently. 'See for yourself. It's not there. The lower jaw would still have been attached to the rest. In other words, the very thing that would have told us the horse's age is missing.'

'Well then, so it is,' said Palmer, a little sulkily.

Swain turned round. 'Mr Lumley, if you please! Your opinion as a racing man. Iphigenia won a race for three-year-olds, the Portland Plate. What would happen if a four-year-old horse was entered?'

'Stand a good chance of winning,' Lumley said. 'But they look at horses, Mr Swain. They don't just let 'em run. There's rules.'

'And there's also switching horses,' Swain said. 'As I recall, the animal broke a leg in training and had to be put down. Kindly tell me which of those legs is broken.'

Lumley scowled at the patterned bones in concentration. 'Couldn't tell you, Mr Swain.'

Palmer chuckled again. 'None of them is broken. You were quite right, Mr Swain. There was some mischief here. The poor creature was shot, I have no doubt. The bone is incomplete at the forehead. But there has been fraud and worse.'

'Much worse,' Swain said. 'A great deal worse.'

'Only,' said Palmer, 'with Mr Lerici dead, you'll never prove it now. He's the one that must have pulled the trick. Chuck it, Swain.'

'I beg your pardon, Mr Palmer, but with Lerici alive or dead, I mean to prove it.'

Lumley shook his head. 'There was a lot of money made on that horse, Mr Swain. Anyone that backed it for the Portland Plate was a bit richer. As for the bookies, it's up the spout and Charley Wag for them. I can't see that being put right three years later.'

'Of course it can't be put right,' said Swain sharply. 'Any man that deals in racing and betting probably deserves what he gets. I'd like to know the reason for this, though. Why was it done, when he had this estate and all the money that went with it?'

'Clever,' said Palmer soothingly, 'Mr Lerici was one to think himself clever from what I've heard. And then he went to Greece with that riff-raff of his and found that he'd got too clever for his own good. Still, Mr Swain, you'd know a lot more about that than I would.'

Swain turned to the uniformed constables. 'I want two men here to make sure nothing is disturbed until I have an answer from Scotland Yard. Nothing to be touched. I'll want them here day and night until I give orders to the contrary.'

The first constable looked doubtfully at the outline of the dead horse. 'With this, sir? Day and night?'

'Yes,' Swain said unsympathetically. 'Good God, man! It's not going to jump up and bite you, is it?'

As they walked to the house, Palmer drew Lumley back, out of Swain's hearing. 'How long are you down here for, Lumley?'

'As long as I'm told, Mr Palmer,' Lumley said philosophically. 'At least until there's a verdict in the inquest on Spider McBride.'

'Yes,' Palmer said. 'Well, let's hope it's not a long do.'

Lumley made a sympathetic murmur but Palmer had not yet finished.

'Lumley, old fellow, does he always call you "Mr Lumley"? When I was a skipper, my governors always called me just "Palmer" or "sergeant", never "Mr Palmer".'

'It's his way,' Lumley said helpfully. 'Mr Swain tries to have educated manners, like a gentleman.'

Palmer stared at the inspector's back.

'But the question is whether a man in our Mr Swain's situation isn't asking for trouble, behaving like that. A man needs a sense of authority, if he's to deal with man, woman, or beast. I found that out a long time ago.'

12

Beyond the leaded lights of the oriel window, the sky of the summer afternoon was smoke-grey with rain clouds, giving added lustre to the pale green majesty of the elm trees. Alfred Swain sat at a little sofa-table among the deep crimson velvet of the main hall at Mondragon. He drew the splayed and useless nib from the wooden stem of his pen and fitted a new brass-coloured one from the packet. Its label assured him that 'They come as a boon and a blessing to men, the Swallow, the Owl, and the Waverley pen.' He dipped the nib into the cut-glass ink-well, scraped off the excess, and resumed his inventory.

Musical manuscript, incomplete, inscribed 'Il Ré Lear', twelve pages . . .

'Mr Swain!'

He looked up. Amalia de Brahami was sitting in a low nursing-chair, on her knee an embroidery hoop with her needlework stretched upon it. The design of acanthus leaves had progressed little, if at all, since he had first seen it several days before. She was not looking up at him but staring at the needlework. Swain caught only a sidelong view of the Arabian gold of her profile, the demure chin, the sharp nose and tall forehead, the hair piled and coiffeured to add to her appearance of height. The tight-lidded ellipse of her dark eyes avoided him. Motionless though she was now, her lithe young body suggested to Swain the untamed energy of a wild goat.

Behind her, stiff-backed and arms folded, stood the servant Basileia with the air of the girl's chaperone. The face was strong and square-jawed, the waist thickened. She was the sort of woman in Nauplia or Argos who would look the same from forty until the day she died. Swain guessed she was about forty now. She stood with the absolute control of a sentry, effortlessly still. Lerici had been attended by dwarfs and mutes, according to rumour. Could this one be a mute, after all?

It was the girl who broke in upon his meditation. 'Mr Swain,' she said thoughtfully. 'Do you like me, Mr Swain?'

Swain smiled at her, and she lowered her face in response. 'Of course I like you.'

'Do you like me very much?' Amalia moved a little and the gold of her skin against the crimson glow of velvet teased the inspector with a pang of sensuality. She posed upon the chair rather than sat upon it. Swain was uneasily aware that the black dress had been drawn to Amalia's figure so that it suggested the narrow waist and slender thighs, the slight backward jut of the hips and the flatness of the abdomen. Despite the languid attitude, it was a body that exuded energy and agility.

Swain was conscious only of the silent and expressionless figure of Basileia behind her young mistress. Was she mute? Was she deaf? Did she merely not understand the language? Surely it was one of these for Amalia to talk so freely.

'Do you like me very much, Mr Swain?' The question was repeated with impatience.

'Very well,' Swain said, in the voice of an adult agreeing to please a child, 'I like you very much. But it is not considered polite in England to ask people whether they like you and how much. The thing should speak for itself.'

'I have spent long enough in England to know that,' she said, 'I do not care much for English manners, Mr Swain. They are cold and, I think, often insincere.'

Swain left it at that and turned again to the problem of the inventory. Why the devil could Lerici not have deputed his solicitor to undertake the matter? Was it truly possible that Mr Abrahams might have found himself compromised by the evidence of the ledger?

The girl twisted round and said something to the woman behind her in their own language. Her sweep of the hand across the sofa suggested that there was a part of her embroidery set missing. Basileia responded with a low noncommittal phrase. Amalia de Brahami stamped her foot and spoke again. The woman unfolded her arms and walked away with a final sullen glance in Swain's direction. A moment or two passed.

'Would you die for me, Mr Swain?'

She was looking directly at him now. The tight-lidded almond ellipse of the dark eyes was expressionless and yet he felt the intensity behind her gaze. Swain, the practical man, turned the demand aside.

'The question does not arise.'

'If it did, Mr Swain, would you die for me? Am I the sort of person you would die for?'

Swain put down his pen and sighed. 'A policeman may sometimes die in the course of his duty, as a soldier may die. He does not die for a particular sort of person but for whoever may be in peril. He dies, like a soldier, in the service of his country.'

Amalia looked sadly down at her embroidery hoop. 'That was not what I meant,' she said. 'That was not what I meant, Mr Swain, and I am sure that you know it.'

Swain, rebuked, picked up his pen again.

'Do you love me, Mr Swain?'

He put the pen down.

'Do you, Mr Swain?'

'Questions of that sort are only asked by people who have known one another for a long time and are in a certain situation. It is not considered . . .'

'Good manners!' Amalia de Brahami spoke the words with contempt. 'I do not care about English manners, Mr Swain. I ask you if you like me and you say you do. I ask you if you like me very much and you do not deny it. Well then, I ask you if you love me. It is the sort of question that your first two answers may invite. And you are frightened to tell me that you do or that you do not.'

'I do not know you,' Swain said, 'and I think you are playing a game because it is raining and you cannot go out – and because you are bored by your needlework. But it is a game for little girls and not for young ladies.'

Amalia's eyes did not waver. 'You do not know me, Mr Swain! You love only those whom you have known for a long time? My father told me of Petrarch who saw the woman he loved only once, in church. He never saw her again nor ever spoke to her. Yet he devoted the rest of his life to her in his poetry. Does such a thing mean nothing to you?'

'Yes,' said Swain grimly, 'Petrarch, however, had the advantage of not being an officer of the Metropolitan Police with duties to perform.'

The irony was lost on her.

'Very well, Mr Swain. We will not talk of love. But you think I am attractive, do you not? In the secret places of your policeman's heart, you think I am attractive?'

'Of course you are attractive,' Swain said. 'There is no secret about it. I am quite sure you think it for yourself.'

'Touché, Mr Swain,' she said softly, 'and because I am attractive and because you like me very much, you would like to be my lover?'

'No!'

It was intolerable. Swain began to gather up the papers on the table. To his dismay, he heard Amalia begin to weep, her hands over her face. Though her conduct on previous occasions had seemed to him odd and even disturbed, he had never suspected anything like this.

'You are a coward, Mr Swain!' Amalia de Brahami said loudly, checking her sobs for the moment. 'You are a coward!'

Swain, thoroughly alarmed, saw Lumley and Palmer at the top of the steps, staring at the strange tête-à-tête upon which they had intruded. Swain stood up and Amalia de Brahami, uncovering her face, saw the two sergeants.

'He is a coward,' she said, defending the remark which they had evidently overheard. 'He makes love and then he denies it.'

In the space of a few minutes, Alfred Swain found himself compromised without ever having got up from the table. Before he could explain what had happened, Palmer walked up to the chair where Amalia sat. His face was set hard as judgement.

'Stand up!' he said sharply and for an instant Swain thought Palmer was about to hit the girl. But it was the force and menace of his voice that subdued her. She stood up, prepared to draw back if he tried to strike her. The embroidery hoop lay on the chair.

'Pick up your sewing!' There was anger as well as command in Palmer's voice. Amalia, without taking her eyes from his face, reached down and took the embroidery hoop.

'Now, kindly withdraw to your room and remain there until you are sent for.'

'This is my house!' she cried. 'Everything was left to me! Not to grandmama! It is mine!'

'Then if a police investigation is obstructed,' Palmer said firmly, 'you shall be the one to answer in court and in prison if necessary.'

She stared at him a moment, then turned and half ran, stumbling once, towards the stairs.

92

'Mr Palmer,' Swain said gently, 'there really was no need for that.'

Palmer, smooth and well built, flushed a little. 'Beg pardon, Mr Swain, but that young person is touched, I'd say. Keep a firm hold on her, sir, or you don't know what she'll do nor say.'

Swain let the point pass. He stood in awe of Handsome Palmer. The cutting down of Amalia de Brahami was something he simply could not have done. And Palmer was certainly right. There was no knowing what she might do or say.

Lumley stepped forward. 'It's adjourned till Thursday, Mr Swain. The inquest on Spider McBride. Misadventure, they think it might be. I thought an open verdict myself, seeing that there was no witnesses. But it seems the stupid little fool went and fell off the tower, like everyone thought.'

'Spider McBride.' Swain said thoughtfully, 'Everyone hadn't met him, had they? He wasn't one for falling as a rule.'

'Drink, perhaps,' Lumley said, 'or perhaps he had hold of something that came away. A lot of it's only stucco up there.'

Swain nodded. 'I dare say you're right, Mr Lumley. All the same, the rain's stopped and I'd like a breath of air. Perhaps we might go and have a look at the tower. Mr Palmer! Perhaps you wouldn't mind keeping an eye on matters here for a moment.'

Palmer nodded and turned to the little sofa-table. The look on his face suggested that he felt he had deserved something better than being cut out by his two companions.

13

With Lumley walking beside him and a pair of chipped opera-glasses in a small leather case, Alfred Swain crossed the terrace of Mondragon with its flowers in their marble compartments. The opera-glasses had been purchased from a barrow of bric-à-brac in the Farrington Road market some years before.

'Handsome Palmer,' Lumley said cheerfully, 'bit of a caution.'

'Yes,' said Swain doubtfully, 'I can't say it's a manner I admire.'

'Comes from training animals, I dare say.' Lumley chuckled at the thought. 'Sort of instinct for command. Still, Mr Swain, he certainly give that young person something to chew on. You got to allow him that.'

'Have I?' said Swain sceptically, unbuttoning the case of the little opera-glasses. 'Have I indeed? Did you notice how he never once considered that what the young lady said might have been right? The moment she spoke, he saw her off. I hadn't even the chance to deny it.'

'Authority, Mr Swain. Mr Palmer puts a lot of faith in authority and rank.'

'Does he, Mr Lumley? Well, let's hope that's it.'

The lantern tower was at the rear of the house on the south-west corner. It rose one hundred feet precisely above the terraces, its octagonal form derived from the Portuguese gothic of the monastery of Batalha. Swain scanned upwards with his glasses. The pearl-grey stucco was rough and slapdash under the closer scrutiny of the glasses.

'In case I should be asked, Mr Lumley, just how does the inquest suppose that Spider McBride came to grief?'

Lumley was at his elbow, as if trying to follow Swain's view with the glasses. 'They couldn't say exactly on the evidence so far, Mr Swain. He hadn't been into the house so he must've fallen on his way up or at the top. At least, he wasn't carrying stolen goods, there's nothing reported missing, and there's no sign of a forced entry.'

'So he fell on this side, did he? And since he was stone-cold dead, he must have fallen almost the entire height of the tower? That it, Mr Lumley?'

'Something of that, Mr Swain. While you was still on that boat coming from Greece with Mr Lerici's remains, I examined old Spider's clothes. Nothing like a moleskin jacket for showing up bits. There was fragments of stucco, Mr Swain. Now, you look up there. It's stonework below. That stucco don't begin until about twenty-five feet up. So he must have been above that. And then there's a broken line of bitumen or tar that never set properly, not far below the parapet. He'd have had his head almost level with the parapet by then. However, there was a smudge of tar and grit on one knee of his trousers, as if he'd pressed against it or sort of knelt against it. He must have been just pulling himself up the last bit, almost on the parapet, when something gave way and he fell.'

Swain nodded. 'That's very good, Mr Lumley. Very good. And that's the story from the inquest, is it?'

'More or less,' Lumley said uneasily. 'So far as they'd got this morning before they adjourned. Mind you, it was Mr Palmer from the Detective Division that was sent for. The old woman, it seems, sent straight for a man from the division. Mr Palmer was down here most of the time with all the burglaries round Brighton. He was at the house in no time at all.'

'Good,' said Swain encouragingly. 'Now you just take the glasses, Mr Lumley. Have a look up there and tell me where it was that something gave way or came away.'

Lumley took the chipped glasses and squinted up awkwardly.

'I'm not actually saying, Mr Swain, that I can see anything exactly.'

'Of course not, Mr Lumley. Touch the focus a little. Having any better luck now, are you?'

'Not exactly.' Lumley sounded breathless. 'I'm not really used to these glasses, Mr Swain.'

'No sign, though, of anything broken away or having given way? And, of course, no fragments found on the ground down here?'

'Now look, Mr Swain. I told you what the witnesses said, not what they imagined or saw through funny glasses like something at a fairground. Just because there aren't any bits broken off on this side doesn't mean he didn't fall. He must have fallen or he wouldn't have been down here, would he?'

'Very good, Mr Lumley. I expect he must have fallen from the parapet itself, perhaps while he was standing on it. Shall we go up and have a look?'

They climbed the enclosed stairway, narrow as a coffin, that wound to the top of the octagon. Lumley, heaving for breath, said nothing on the ascent. At the top, the wooden door was secured by a bar on the inside.

'Well,' said Lumley, 'he never got through here. See that for yourself.'

They stepped out on to the octagonal platform with a view across miles of summer trees and parkland that seemed like a child's toy-farm far below them. The platform itself had been coated with bitumen and scattered with gravel to retain a protective moisture against summer heat.

95

'Well now,' Swain said in the same quiet voice of encouragement, 'I expect Spider McBride must have fallen while he had hold of the parapet – or was standing on it, or at least leaning over it. As you say, Mr Lumley, something must have given way. Whereabouts would you say it was?'

Lumley looked about him. 'Who the devil knows?'

'I thought the inquest knew,' Swain said. 'Shoddy stuff, this stone. Look, the scratch of a fingernail turns it raw. Don't you think a man sliding to his death, clinging for dear life, or his feet slipping, would make a bigger mark than that?'

'All right,' Lumley said at last. 'What's the game?'

Swain stared across the billows of green trees below them to a grey line of marine light over the expanse of the Channel.

'I don't know, Mr Lumley. What about his boots? Did they have any flecks of this grit caught in them?'

Lumley was getting red in the face. 'What does it matter if they did or didn't? Either he fell before, or he got up here, found the door closed and barred, then tried to get back down.'

Swain shook his head. 'No, Mr Lumley. That certainly didn't happen. Spider McBride knew better than anyone about doors and how to get in. He never climbed to this height unless he could either open that door . . .'

'He couldn't kick through it with a bar like that behind.'

'Or someone had opened it for him. Nice and quiet up here, Mr Lumley. Much the easiest way into the house if someone wanted to help him in.'

'What for?'

'I don't know, Mr Lumley. Suppose McBride was sent by someone to get to Mr Lerici's private papers before I did. How did he die, by the way?'

'Head injury,' Lumley said. 'Hit the terrace head first, broke the back of his skull.'

'Broke the back of his skull, Mr Lumley?'

'Yes,' said Lumley defiantly, 'broke the back of his skull. Kills people in case you hadn't heard.'

Swain ignored the insubordination. 'Mr Lumley, do you have any idea of the speed at which McBride was travelling when he hit the terrace?'

'I wasn't here, was I?'

'No, Mr Lumley, but I dare say you were once at school. The speed of falling bodies. Thirty-two feet per second at the end of the first second, sixty-four at the end of the next, ninety-six feet at the end of the third. About three seconds to fall from here.' Swain paused and the brain behind the mild intelligent horse face did its calculations. 'McBride would have been travelling at sixty-six miles an hour when he went head first into solid marble. Good God, man! That wouldn't just fracture his skull. His entire head would explode. You wouldn't recognize him.'

'All right,' Lumley conceded, 'so he fell off lower down.'

'That's what worries me, Mr Lumley. McBride was one of the best spidermen in the business. You can see for yourself there's nothing that gave way or came away lower down. As for falling off, McBride was less likely to fall from this tower than you'd be likely to fall over while standing still. Where is he, by the way?'

'Who?'

'McBride, of course. The cadaver. They'd hardly have it at the inquest.'

Lumley sniggered. 'Spider's gone up in the world. He's at Surgeons' Hall or one of them places where a man ends up in a row of jars. He won't do a bunk from there in a hurry.'

14

That night, as the stable-clock chimed twelve, Alfred Swain sat on a bedroom chair at the plain little table in the servant's room which he had been allotted. It was just under the leads of Mondragon and even with the little window open the heat from the kitchen chimney and the warmth of the roof made the air oppressive. Lumley, whose stay was shorter, had been quartered with Palmer, lodging with the landlord of the Cavendish Arms.

As though afraid that he might be isolated from the world of his thoughts, Swain had brought with him most of the dozen volumes which were his library in the rented rooms of Pimlico. There was Lyell's *Geology*, Mr Swinburne's *Poems and Ballads*, the Poet Laureate's *Idylls of the King*, Tait's *Recent Advances in Physical Science*, and Laing's *Modern Science and Modern*

Thought. Pride of place, however, went to his latest acquisition. Like the opera-glasses it had come secondhand from the market. It lay, yet unopened, on the table beside him, bound in dark green and lettered in gold, a little rubbed but the paper crisp and clean: *The Agamemnon of Aeschylus*, transcribed by Robert Browning, published by Messrs. Smith, Elder of Waterloo Place. It was enough merely to look at the unopened volume in order to see in the mind's eye the Golden Mycenae of Homer's legend and Heinrich Schliemann's passion, the Lion Gate before which Alfred Swain had stood on that hot April day.

Swain put the image resolutely from his mind. The reward of an hour in the company of such a book had yet to be earned. He turned again to the sheet of paper in front of him and added a few lines to a chronicle of misgivings, for the eyes of Mr Abrahams, Attorney of King's Bench Walk.

15

Two days later Swain stood, like a Christian awaiting the gladiators, on the little podium of Surgeons' Hall. Like a Roman arena, the tiers of empty seats behind their balustrading rose above him, empty in the watery light that filtered through the cloudy glass of the dome. His audience consisted of a dozen skeletons, each braced upright in its Georgian niche, at the level of the highest seats. Beside him stood the gravely bearded figure of Dr Thomas Stevenson, pathologist.

'That one up there, Mr Swain. Mrs Brownrigg. Hanged in 1767 for flogging to death one Mary Clifford, her female apprentice. Mrs B. is our oldest resident. That's the poet Dr Dodd up there, hanged for forgery in 1777. When he was cut down, his family was ready with a pair of bellows filled with a mixture of air and sal volatile. They pumped up his lungs with it, massaged his spine and his oesophagus. They pumped white steam of balsam up his posterior, they used horseradish, peppermint, and turpentine. But all to no effect, Mr Swain.'

'So he came to you?'

'He came to us, Mr Swain. Three days on this table the autopsy would last – and every seat up there filled by a ticket-holder. They cut 'em small in those days. The best people bought their way in to watch. At the end of each murderer's three days on the table, a banquet was held next door for the ticket-holders. Just to mark the occasion.'

'Really?' Swain said with just a suggestion of distaste. 'I had no idea.'

'A carnival of mortality, Mr Swain.'

The inspector clutched in his hand a scrap of pasteboard like a large railway ticket. Issued by the masters of Surgeons' Hall and handed to him by Mr Abrahams, it carried the simple inscription, 'Admit Mr Alfred Swain.'

'Now then,' said Stevenson cheerfully, 'I expect you'd like to see your friend. Through here, if you please.'

Swain followed the pathologist beyond a panelled door at the side of the dais. They entered a gaslit corridor with deep racks on either side, the shelves occupied by lumps and hunks of veal-white human flesh in bell-jars and limb-sized tanks of spirit. Swain tried to put from his mind the harsh spirituous air of the place.

'Here we have him,' Dr Stevenson said cheerfully, 'the late Mr McBride.'

Swain turned, almost expecting to see MrBride in his entirety. He found himself looking at half a face in a jar of fluid. One eye, one nostril, half a mouth, the scrub of cropped dark hair floating upwards in the spirit with a suggestion of prolonged astonishment at his mutilation. The lid of the eye was not quite closed so that on this half of his face Spider McBride appeared to favour Inspector Swain with a long and confidential wink.

'There's your friend, then, from the neck upwards,' Stevenson said optimistically. 'Mr Abrahams asked me to take a look at him and I will tell you what I have found. Let me turn him round for you.'

Dr Stevenson manoeuvred the heavy jar, the spirit sloshing and slapping a little against the glass, until the section of Spider McBride's brain was towards them. Swain stared glumly at the enfolded layers of cortex which had assumed the brown colour of meat that is cooked one day and served cold the next. He felt only the oppression of mortality. The meat-like object had once been the intelligence of Spider McBride, guiding the little man upon his infallible acrobatic way across rooftops and up drainpipes, down walls and over hazardous chasms.

'Alas, poor Yorick,' he said quietly.

'Very good, Mr Swain! Very good!' Dr Stevenson chuckled and tapped the bell-jar with a pencil. 'Now, see here, Mr Swain. So far as death was caused by injuries to his head, it was here, at the rear. You see? The bone is chipped, the skull is damaged. But down here there is darkening of the skin. Evidence of a haemorrhage in the brain. It was not noticed at first because, of course, the poor fellow's hair concealed it. That is where the blood seeped under the skull, after the injury. The blow was a severe one. Enough to lay him unconscious and probably enough to kill him. It would not kill at once. The evidence of injury, the extent to which the blood had spread among the brain membranes, suggests that he lived for about five minutes after the injury was sustained.'

Swain looked up at the pathologist. 'Are you sure of that?'

'Quite sure, Mr Swain. You could not tell from external appearances, I dare say, but on dissection, there is the mark of bleeding into these cavities of the brain. Bleeding to that extent would not have been completed in less than five minutes, shall we say. It could have been longer, depending on the position of the body and other factors. The bleeding would, of course, stop when he died. He would not have bled like that if the blow had killed him instantly.'

Swain stared at the darker outline in the rear of Spider McBride's brain. The gaslight hissed in a pale glare on the mortal remains of London's criminal class. He chose his words with care.

'But he fell about a hundred feet on to marble paving, Dr Stevenson. Surely he would have been killed outright?'

Stevenson looked at him a little doubtfully. 'You are the detective, Mr Swain, not I. One cannot always say what the result of a fall will be. People sometimes fall from considerable heights and sustain relatively light injuries. Again, the surface on to which a body falls will make a difference. Again, it may be that the fall is broken temporarily by, let us say, the slope of a roof. Though the body slides down this and falls further, it will not land with such force as in a direct drop. All the same, I cannot imagine Mr McBride falling on to marble paving from a hundred feet and not being worse injured. There are no reports of other injuries to the trunk or the limbs. I notice one to the face, however. There is a mark on the forehead. Nothing much. If you or I were to fall over, as we stand here now, we might sustain something of the sort. But if that was caused by impact with marble paving from the height of a tower, I would expect it to have shattered the frontal bone, barring a freak of nature.'

'You mean to say he can't have fallen?'

Stevenson shook his head. 'No, Mr Swain. Only you can decide that. Falling is not a precise science. The one scientific truth in this case is that, however he came by this fatal injury, he lived for several minutes at least after sustaining it. He was not conscious, I feel sure, but he was alive. If he fell on to marble paving, it is incredible that he was not killed outright. I cannot say, however, that it is impossible.'

'He was a spiderman,' Swain said. 'Spidermen don't fall.'

'Not so, Mr Swain. Even spiders fall to their deaths on occasion.'

Alfred Swain thought about this. 'Would it be possible that he fell to earth and then crawled a little distance to the place where he was found?'

Dr Stevenson smiled his sympathy at the inspector's predicament. He shook his head. 'No, Mr Swain. Once that blow was struck to the back of his head, Mr McBride neither crawled nor moved in any other way. On its own, it was a fatal injury and must have knocked him unconscious at once.'

With a proprietorial gesture, Dr Stevenson turned the bell-jar so that Spider McBride once again showed his half face to the world with his long and preposterous post-mortem wink. The pathologist and the inspector walked back down the corridor.

'Tell me,' Swain asked, 'what power would be needed to inflict such injury to the skull?'

'That would depend on the implement,' Stevenson said philosophically. 'With something of weight, a stone or a bludgeon, a relatively light blow might suffice. The wound was not examined at the time for fragments left by any implement?'

'No,' Swain said dourly, 'the coroner's inquest saw no reason for that. They assumed that he must have fallen off the tower.'

'Which he may well have done.' Dr Stevenson raised a warning finger in farewell. 'Which he may well have done, Mr Swain. The obvious answer, though sometimes tedious, is most frequently the right one.'

16

Evening sunlight, reflected from sky and river, lay across the Temple Gardens again as Alfred Swain kept his appointment with Mr Abrahams. On the far wall, eminent legal figures in gilt-framed caricature posed, pranced, and grimaced in the inspector's direction. As they sat across the desk from one another, Mr Abrahams' questions fenced from behind the mask of handsome amiability.

'I have done as you asked, Mr Swain, both in the matter of the horse and the late Mr McBride. I cannot see quite how Mr McBride concerns us, other than that he met with a fatal accident while trespassing on the late Mr Lerici's property.'

Abrahams leant forward and placed three photographic prints on the desk in front of Swain. One showed a huddle of clothing which eventually resolved itself into the figure of McBride lying dead on the terrace of Mondragon. The second was a general view of the terrace and tower. The third showed a section of the terrace paving about ten feet square.

'There's no sign of blood on this.' Swain offered the photograph of the paving to Mr Abrahams. 'If he bled from any wound for several minutes, you'd see it on marble like chalk on a blackboard.'

'It seems from the other photograph, Mr Swain, that he lay face down. I understand the majority of people do when they fall. There were no wounds to the front of the body, I believe, and the injury to the brain was internal.'

'The impact, sir,' Swain said gently, 'was the injury to the back of his head.'

Mr Abrahams looked at him sympathetically. 'I'm told, Mr Swain, that a man may fall head first, like a diver. When he hits his head on the ground, the body will naturally turn as it comes to rest. It will very probably turn on to its face. A matter of the disposition of weight in the human frame, Mr Swain. As for the mark on his face, he may have got it after his head had hit the paving. After he had more or less come to rest.'

'Without breaking another bone in his body, sir?'

'If he fell head first, Mr Swain, that may indeed be so. I too have done a little medical investigation and had the advice of Dr Stevenson. There is nothing in your theories so far that would alter the evidence of the inquest. If he lay face down and the bleeding was deep, contained within the skull, there really is no reason that the paving should be marked.'

Evening sun through the Venetian arch of the Georgian windows lit the room with golden fire.

'I have my reservations, sir,' Swain said mildly.

'So you have, Mr Swain.' Abrahams sat back and looked at him thoughtfully. 'I hope you will not mind, however, if we deal with our second cadaver. It is what my clients require me to do. The horse, Iphigenia. Whoever removed the lower jaw of the skeleton knew too little about horses, Mr Swain.'

'Surely the teeth of the lower jaw are the indicators of the animal's age?'

Abrahams shook his head. 'Only when that age is needed precisely. In this case, we need only ask whether the horse is more than three years old. If so, then the Portland Plate of 1874, being a race for three-year-olds, was won by dishonest means. A good deal of money was also wagered dishonestly. On my instructions, two veterinary surgeons have examined the upper jaw and, indeed, the rest of the skeleton. The horse was four years old at least and possibly somewhat more. It had suffered no previous injury, though it had been put down by means of a bullet fired into the head. Without question, the bridle buried with the animal has the name "Iphigenia" marked upon it. The name Running Rein, written by Mr Lerici in his ledger, indicates a fraud of some kind. The suggestion of the surgeons is that it was a horse which ran well in the previous year's Portland Plate under the name of Bellevue, owned by Lord Lynton. I believe it came in a good second. Mr Lerici's accounts confirm the purchase of the animal in November last year. He then renamed it Iphigenia, both horses having a common black coat with white markings, altered the appearance of it as little as necessary, and entered it illegally in a race where it was over-age. Not surprisingly it won. To make it easier, the favourite was scratched by its owner, Mr Benson. And Mr Benson subsequently became part-owner of Iphigenia.'

'With a criminal of Harry Benson's stamp,' Swain said gently, 'Mr Lerici might well be blackmailed into using the animal for this deception. There is not a man nor a woman in the world, Mr Abrahams, who cannot be blackmailed in one way or another. Not you, not I, not anyone.'

The two men sat in silence for a moment.

'Sir,' said Swain hesitantly, 'nothing can make any difference to Mr Lerici. All the same, the evidence of his accounts is that a number of officers in the Detective Division benefited from this fraud. If there is corruption in the division, it may go very deep. One of its threads leads to these two men, Harry Benson and Billy Kurr. There is reason to suppose that they defrauded Madame de Goncourt and another of your clients through the Turf Insurance swindle and the City of Paris Loan.'

'Neither can that be proved,' said Abrahams slowly, 'it has been tried and the proof is lacking.'

'But the reason it has not been proved, Mr Abrahams, is that Benson and Kurr have had friends at Scotland Yard. Someone has protected them. It cannot be less than two officers who are involved and more likely three or four. If it is only three or four out of fifteen, then the division is too deeply corrupted to survive. Benson and Kurr were warned of the police interest in their activities by men in the division. Mr Lerici's ledger may be proof that the informants were well rewarded for those warnings. I do not say, for one minute, that every officer whose name appears in that ledger has been corrupted or even approached. But I am as sure as I sit here that several of them have been. There is no other conclusion.'

'And what will you do, Mr Swain? Report the matter to Mr Toplady?'

Swain shook his head. 'No, Mr Abrahams. I propose to deal with Benson and Kurr directly. I cannot conclude the business of Mr Lerici's estate without confronting them. All I ask is that you shall be a witness. A witness that I do this honestly and that whatever may be later alleged against me to destroy me is done for precisely that purpose.'

Abrahams stood up. 'You ask very little, Mr Swain. Let me warn you, though. The sort of men you would deal with are those who will destroy you by the means you least expect. You have taken no bribes. You have given no favours. You are an honest man and I will, of course, vouch for you. But suppose, Mr Swain, that they arrange matters so that I shall not be believed?'

Even as the lawyer mentioned the possibility, Swain tried to see how it might happen.

17

As Alfred Swain walked down to the river, past the trains and Hungerford Music Hall, the song that the whole world seemed to be singing that summer had reached its chorus.

> Up in a balloon, boys, up in a balloon,
> All among the little stars, sailing round the moon . . .

He had no doubt that the lawyer's warning was well timed. Yet he only half believed it. If a man took care and if he was honest, how could he be compromised by scoundrels? And if he had taken the precaution of sharing his intentions with a man like Mr Abrahams of King's Bench Walk, that was surely his safeguard. In any case, it seemed to Swain as he crossed the plank on to the penny steamer, he had very little choice. Until justice was done, his position at Scotland Yard was intolerable. And until justice was done all round, there could be no solution to the mystery of John Lerici nor to the enigma of Spider McBride.

With one night at home before he must return to the old lady and the young girl in their lath-and-stucco fantasy of Mondragon, he would put the whole business from his mind. But Swain tried and, like a jealous lover, it would not be excluded from his thoughts.

At the best of times, there were few people in the world with whom he could share those thoughts. On this occasion, there were fewer still. Not Sergeant Lumley, because Lumley's name appeared in Lerici's accounts. Not Handsome Palmer, the stern figure of authority, about whom he knew too little. Not Superintendent Toplady, above all. There was Mr Abrahams, of course, and there was Mrs Beresford, widow of Police Constable Beresford and landlady of Swain's lodgings in Pimlico.

Later that evening, Swain occupied a blue velvet chair in Mrs Beresford's sitting-room. The last of the daylight still lingered over the chimney-pots in the little street of brick houses with their stucco ornaments and twiddlings. Below the first-floor window, children hopped and shouted among the chalked games on the paving-stones. Further off, a barrel-organ in St George's Square was playing a final chorus of 'My Flo from Pimlico'.

Mrs Beresford emptied the last of the kettle into the blue china teapot. The plain red dress with its narrow waist suited the fair curls and the face which Swain always thought of as having a high-boned prettiness. From an accidental glimpse of a document in the division, he knew that she was now twenty-four and had no living relatives. They were united in that bereavement. The entry also told him that she had been twenty-one when Constable Beresford had died in the cold and fetid current off London Bridge wharf while a child was pulled to safety. The couple had been married almost a year. A small pension had been awarded to the widow under the auspices of the Royal Humane Society. The Police Commissioners added Mrs Beresford's name to those of police wives and widows who kept lodgings for officers of the Metropolitan force.

The barrel-organ fell silent. The children's voices in the street dwindled in the distance while they loitered home. Mrs Beresford reached up and put a match to the mantle as the gas came on. The sleeve fell back, revealing an arm that was slim and sun-browned with a lightish down. Swain had heard something of the seaside childhood in Sussex, the open air and the infant acrobatics, before Mr Beresford brought her to London.

'What was your father, Mrs Beresford? In the way of business, that is.'

She watched the flame burn up and then turned the jet a little lower, blowing out the match and adjusting her sleeve.

'Likenesses, Mr Swain. He was a likeness man.' She turned and smiled at the inspector with the pleasure of recollection. 'He cut from black paper or card while they waited. Just a stool he had, by the pier-gates, a pile of black paper and a nice sharp scissors. He had a chair for the customer to sit on and he'd do 'em while they sat there. Only a couple of minutes. He'd do 'em for a penny or a couple, one profile on another, for twopence.'

'What happened in the winter?' Swain asked, knowing that it was his professional failing to ask too many questions.

'He stayed home,' she said, surprised that he had not guessed. 'He'd do likenesses for a little curio shop in London, near Burlington Arcade, and send them up by the railway. Well-known faces. Her Majesty. Prince Albert. Mr Disraeli. Mr Calcraft the hangman, even, and some of his clients. Mrs Manning was a good one. We often had our supper off Mrs Manning, poor soul. And he used to do a lot of *poses plastiques*.'

106

' "*Poses plastiques*"?'

'Oh, come on, Mr Swain. You know.' Had she been any closer she might have nudged him. 'All them goddesses that never had no clothes to wear. Diana with her bow and arrow. Venus and Master Cupid. And another of 'em stoopin' to draw water at the well. That sort of thing.'

'Yes,' Swain said thoughtfully, 'that sort of thing.'

'I tell you one thing,' Mrs Beresford said reflectively, 'we've often had our dinner off Venus and Cupid, too, that we'd never have had otherwise.'

The gaslight fell on the chintz of the mantelpiece and the table-spread, the plum-coloured sofa-velvet that was almost a match for the dress, and the stern marble clock with its white and gilded face, its little silver plaque from the Royal Humane Society recording the sacrifice of Constable Beresford. There was no photograph of Constable Beresford in the room, not even a black silhouette likeness from the Chain Pier at Brighton. Yet Alfred Swain always felt uncomfortable in the presence of the clock.

No doubt the photographs were in the bedroom. It might have seemed curious that though he and Mrs Beresford had for several months been lovers – a term that Swain found rather pretentious – he had never seen the bedroom. That remained somehow sacred to Mr Beresford. It was a condition of Mrs Beresford's treatment by the Commissioners of Metropolitan Police and the Royal Humane Society that she would forfeit pension and lodgings if she remarried or lived with a man as his wife. As Swain well knew, to live with another man as his wife would require only a single night's indiscretion, in the eyes of her benefactors. That an affectionate and passionate young woman of twenty-four, pretty if not beautiful, should be condemned to a form of death to the world seemed outrageous to Alfred Swain, the thinking man of the modern age. When Mr Bradlaugh and Mrs Besant had been tried for publishing a pamphlet that offered working people the means of love without fear, Swain had silently hoped for their acquittal as he had never done in any other criminal case.

Mrs Beresford stepped behind a candy-pink screen at the end of the room and Swain stood up to close the curtains. He caught a glimpse of himself in the mirror, an absurd clown-like figure in vest and long pants. Mrs Beresford appeared and the shoulders of the dress which had once hung upon her now held the garment on the divisions of the screen. She walked primly, nude as a ninepin, to the sitting-room door and turned the key in the lock, then moved quickly towards the sofa.

Swain eased himself down and Mrs Beresford ran her fingers through his hair.

'Your hair don't curl, do it, Mr Swain?'

'It never did,' said Swain truthfully, 'but then, I'm not sure I should want to be a detective with curly hair. Somehow, it would seem wrong.'

Mrs Beresford giggled. 'It's you being a detective that seems wrong, Mr Swain. I bet you wouldn't arrest me in a hurry.'

'I don't suppose I should, Mrs Beresford. Either in a hurry or slowly. If you don't mind, I shall just move this cushion.'

Later, in the quietness, Swain listened and heard not a sound in the house. Mrs Beresford stirred a bare leg against his.

'Mr Swain, do you ever think we might go somewhere? Somewhere on holiday?'

'I suppose we might. Somewhere that was all right.'

'When you get your week of summer leave, we could go to the sea. I'd like to go home again. Not that I know many folks now but it's nice down there.'

'I don't see why not.'

'Only, with you away, there'd just be Mr Hawkins and Mr Brewster. Sally, the little maid, could do for them.'

'It mustn't look as if we've gone together,' Swain said carefully. 'It mustn't look like that.'

'Oh no,' she said quickly, 'course not.'

The subject drifted into silence again. Swain lay contentedly against her. Amalia de Brahami with her constant neurotic questioning and stabbing jealousy, her self-doubts and avaricious passion could not compare with Mrs Beresford. Lord Byron's granddaughter had lost him to Constable Beresford's widow. Swain smiled to himself, recalling Amalia's interrogation.

'Mrs Beresford, what would you say if I asked you whether you liked me?'

She giggled and, being close enough this time, nudged him. 'Don't be soft, Mr Swain! Course I like you. I wouldn't be here otherwise, would I? And nor would you!'

18

Swain was still in his shirt-sleeves on the following morning, preparing for his return to Mondragon, when he heard the street doorbell jangle on its wire, Lumley's voice asking the maid for Mr Swain. Screwing a necktie into its wooden press, he went downstairs.

'This come for you, to the inspectors' office,' Lumley said. 'If it matters. Thought you'd better have it before you go down to Folly Ridge again. Could be important, I suppose. Anyway, I brought it round.'

Swain murmured his thanks and took the package, wrapped neatly in brown paper. There were postage stamps on it of a kind he had never seen. He broke the wax customs seals and opened the paper. There was a note inside. He caught gracefully penned words: . . . *and if your answer is not in these pages, it can be nowhere at all . . .* He saw the signature of Heinrich Schliemann.

A shabby volume, the red cover darkened by use. Not valuable. Not a choice volume from Heinrich Schliemann's library. It had the look of a cast-off school-book which might have ended its days on a street barrow, offered for a penny or twopence. Swain opened it and saw the flyleaf much signed and noted by previous owners. He turned to the title page. *The Agamemnon of Aeschylus.* edited by Professor Sidgwick. Published by the Clarendon Press for the use of schools, with notes. He turned again and saw page after page of verse in elegant Greek script. It was intimidating as a deep pool to one who had never swum a stroke.

If your answer is not in these pages . . .

Answer to what? The problem of learning Greek? The mystery of Mycenae? The choice of his future life? The truth of murder? He stood there a moment, shirt-sleeved and collarless. Schliemann was right, of course. Alfred Swain felt what he could not prove. Some pattern, some cycle in human events was working its way out. The pattern, recorded in the great drama, was repeating itself as patterns always do. There was no fluke in that. The fluke was that twice in the history of mankind it should have touched upon a few acres of rocky hillside above the plain of Argos, where a great power had once ruled the civilized world.

With all his powers of belief, he knew Schliemann was right.

But Swain longed to understand how he could be right.

Sergeant Lumley gave the snort of one whose good nature has been abused. "F I'd known it was just another book, Mr Swain, I'd 'a bloody left it where it was.'

3

MAJOR MONTGOMERY

1

Major Hugh Montgomery, European representative of the City of Chicago Loan Corporation, advanced towards his reflection in the gilt-columned mirror between pillars of raspberry-coloured marble. The carpets under his feet were soft as snow and the air about him stirred with the murmured conversations of the new Charing Cross Hotel. The Second Empire, though dead in France, had bequeathed a Parisian sense of luxury to the new London hotels. Outside, in the sparkling summer morning, the major thought that a man might almost expect to find the Champs-Elysées or at least the Quai d'Orléans.

He smiled at himself in the mirror, a dapper little figure in his cream linen suit, the moustache neat and the eyebrows trim. If he had had a cane just then, he would certainly have twirled it this time with exhilaration. The way he was prospering, Major Montgomery believed that he was going to be rich before the summer was over. Very rich indeed. His smile expanded a little at the thought. '*Enormément riche!*' he said to himself and laughed at the allusion to Mr Podsnap. Not rich in England, of course. That would scarcely be possible. But rich in Paris ... rich in Lisbon ... rich in New York ... rich in Rio de Janeiro ... rich where men of the world are rich. But not in London.

He executed something like a little dance step, in order to turn aside and tip his hat as he passed an elderly woman in black velvet walking forward with the aid of a stick. It was not quite an English politeness and, indeed, all Major Montgomery's education had been in France. He was not quite European, though. He looked and talked like a man who had seen a good deal of Australia, or

America, or even Brazil. Not quite English. Not quite anything else either. A man who had spent much of his life on the move, the quick dark eyes constantly measuring new horizons.

Major Montgomery stopped at the cashier's desk. 'I will, if you please, make my *adieux*,' he said, as if the humour was preposterous. 'My compliments to your manager, Mr Ferrers, and if the room can be kept for me, I shall return to England in a fortnight.'

The clerk was about to say something when his eyes stopped at the sight of the new five-hundred-pound note which Major Montgomery was holding.

'Is it not enough?' the major asked.

'Enough?' the clerk stammered a little. 'Oh, far more than enough, sir. The account is one hundred and fifty. Mr Ferrers himself will have to change the note for you.'

Major Montgomery looked disappointed. 'I regret inconveniencing him. I should have made arrangements before.'

But Mr Ferrers, with his cleanly bald head and his air of managerial efficiency, appeared and assured the major that it presented no difficulty. He led the way through into his office while Major Montgomery followed with a look of rather foolish gratitude. The manager unlocked a large safe, a fortress of polished steel in the corner of the room. From an inner set of metal drawers he drew out a tray and a package of notes, counting out three of a hundred each and one of fifty.

'How useful,' Major Montgomery said meekly, just before Mr Ferrers closed the safe again.

'I beg your pardon?'

'I was saying how very useful it must be to have a safe like that. In the ordinary way, I carry a good deal of money with me, though not as much as I find myself with now. The European response to the City of Chicago Loan has been quite beyond expectations. We are already placing funds with contractors for the raising of the Lakeshore Drives.'

Ferrers hesitated before closing the steel door.

'You could not, Mr Ferrers, keep some of the money for me until my return? Just personal funds, sir. Nothing to do with the corporation itself. You could not, I suppose?'

Ferrers relaxed. It was a small matter after all.

'If you wish. It can remain in the cash-box and I will give you a receipt for the sum.'

A tooth glinted moistly in Major Montgomery's smile. 'Thank you, sir,' he said with the same air of apologetic gratitude. From his pocket he took a roll of banknotes, all of the largest denomination. Ferrers watched with unease as the total grew from tens to hundreds of pounds and then passed a thousand. Presently it amounted to more than Ferrers himself would earn in two or three years. Before the major had finished counting, the hotel manager interrupted him.

'I'm sorry, sir. The hotel could not take responsibility for so large a sum. You really should leave it in the hands of a bank.'

Major Montgomery favoured him with another smile, wry and wistful, chosen as carefully as he chose his tie or his cravat.

'I have accounts with several European correspondents of First National Chicago, sir, but not one in London as yet.' He began to gather up the notes. 'I shall carry them with me. It really is no matter.'

'If you will allow me,' Ferrers said, and the major paused because he had known from previous encounters of this kind how it would be, 'I will give you an introduction to our bankers. The Western Branch of the Bank of England in Burlington Gardens. Your funds would be safe there.'

'Safe as the Bank of England,' the major said thoughtfully. 'But let me not impose on you now.'

'It is no imposition,' Ferrers said. He just managed not to swallow with eagerness. No, the major thought, it was no imposition. Mr Ferrers would cut himself a nice fat commission from this. Succulent as the tenderest carving off a whole roast. Ten minutes later, the two men got down outside a handsome town house off Piccadilly, once the home of Lord Uxbridge. Here the Bank of England, anxious that its patrician customers need not travel all the way east to Threadneedle Street, had opened a western branch.

A bank porter saluted Mr Ferrers and held the door open. Major Montgomery put on a performance of amiable surprise, gazing around him at the fine marble paving of the banking hall, which had once been Lord Uxbridge's banqueting room, which rose to the elegant curve of the Adam staircase and the high domes that patterned the area with sunlight. But the major was not truly surprised at all. His friend Mr Kurr had told him all about the place. Mr Kurr had seen it often, on those occasions when he followed and watched Mr Ferrers as the manager rode

113

with two stalwart employees to deposit the earnings of the Charing Cross Hotel at the Bank of England's Western Branch.

Mr Ferrers introduced the major to an assistant manager. Something was said of the new scheme to raise the lakeshore thoroughfares of Chicago above the flood level of Lake Michigan, whose waters filled the streets and ground floors with mud that had the consistency of treacle. The assistant manager hummed politely and thought he had heard something of the scheme. This was not surprising. Major Montgomery always took care to base his schemes on real problems and their solution. Ten minutes later, arrangements were made for the banknotes to be lodged in the safe of the Western Branch. The major insisted that he did this in a purely private capacity for his own money. He was not the City of Chicago Loan Corporation in person.

'When I return, sir,' Major Montgomery said to the banker, 'perhaps Mr Ferrers will accompany me and authorize the withdrawal of the sum.'

The banker spread out his hands. 'If you wish, sir. But you may do so for yourself. Now that this account is opened you may draw from the sum or add to it.'

Major Montgomery made a fluting sound of surprise and approval, as if he had never thought the opening of an account could be so easy. Nor had he, indeed. He was about to thank the assistant manager of the bank and take his leave when it seemed that he had an afterthought.

'I should prefer not to carry the money with me, sir. However, I confess it would not be inconvenient if I might draw upon a little of it while I am in France. If such a facility exists in your bank. Just in case of necessity.'

The banker shrugged. 'Of course. As much or as little as you like, provided it does not exceed the total deposit.'

Major Montgomery smiled in such a way as to show that the idea of exceeding the total was a very good joke. He left with a bill of exchange for five hundred pounds in his pocket. The summer air was soft to his face and the sun warmed the comfortable cream linen of his suit. The major had seen all that he needed. By the time the summer ended, he thought that he would be even richer than he had supposed an hour before. Rich enough to buy the Charing Cross Hotel and all the people inside it. But of course the hotel was the expensive item, Major Montgomery thought. He had bought people before and found that, by his own standards, they came rather cheap.

2

'I can't see why Handsome Palmer isn't doing this,' Lumley said with an air of portly grievance, 'I'm not on duty at the house.'

'You're doing it, Mr Lumley, because I want you and I don't want Mr Palmer. If this goes wrong – if I'm going to be made a fool of – I'd rather it was in your presence than in his.'

'I ought to be at Spider McBride's inquest.'

'Nonsense, Mr Lumley. That inquest stands adjourned until tomorrow morning. Do as you're told now and you may have something of interest to report to it. Something to your credit. Good God, man! You don't want to be a sergeant all your life, do you?'

'Yes,' Lumley said, sinking deeper into his sulk.

The sack of damp sand bumped and slithered on the narrow enclosed staircase of the octagon tower at Mondragon. Lumley was dragging it upwards, trying at the same time to keep the wet sacking from contact with his black regulation frock-coat and his polished constabulary boots. Swain, with a sense of rank, followed up the stairs, merely edging the tail of the sack over some ridge or stair-edge from time to time.

Lumley stopped, coughed, and spat into a red white-spotted handkerchief. 'What's this weigh?'

'Half a hundredweight, Mr Lumley, just like the others. Careful of the turning in the stair. You don't want to tear the sacking on the edge of the stonework or we shall both be covered in sand.'

A narrow eyelet window gave them a brief sunlit glimpse of fields and treetops below them.

'Put a foot against it!' Lumley panted. 'Stop it slithering down again.'

'I've got it, Mr Lumley. Easiest thing in the world.'

The dank and earth-smelling air of the narrow stairway was heavy with Lumley's sense of outrage.

'Almost there now, Mr Lumley. Mind the door behind you! Oh,

dear! Not hurt are you, old fellow? No real damage? Good. At least the sack remains intact. That's what counts.'

On the small platform of the octagon tower, eight bags of sand were now lined up, slouching corpse-like against the balustrade. The sky of the summer afternoon was faultless blue and in the stillness of the day the clouds scarcely moved.

'What now?' Lumley asked sulkily.

Alfred Swain dusted a little sand from his shoe and hand-brushed his neat grey suiting, just to be on the safe side.

'You remember Spider McBride, Mr Lumley. What sort of a man would you call him?'

'Stupid little tyke, he was. Always doing other people's work for 'em and always gettin' other people's kicks.'

'No, Mr Lumley. What sort of a man to look at?'

'To look at? He was a spiderman, Mr Swain. He was bigger than a child, of course, but not much bigger.'

Swain stood with his back against the balustrade and the infinite sky beyond.

'According to his post-mortem report, he was more or less nine stone. One hundred and twenty-eight pounds, to be precise. Five foot eight inches tall.'

'Was he so much?' Lumley seemed interested at last. 'He never looked it.'

Swain turned round and touched one of the sandbags with his boot.

'How far could you throw him, Mr Lumley? How far could you pick him up and throw him?'

Lumley stared back, getting the point but not believing it.

'You can't throw a person that far, Mr Swain, not unless there's a trick in it, like when they whirl 'em round and round at the circus.'

Swain squatted down and took a length of stout cord from beside the sandbags. He began to truss two of the bags together, roping them into a single bulk.

'A test for you, Mr Lumley. There's Spider McBride. How far can you throw him? Not a circus, remember. Just standing here on the platform of this tower. Standing in the dark, shall we say?'

Lumley stared at the trussed sacking and was unimpressed. 'Couple of feet, Mr Swain. And I'm not trying it either. This coat

116

and trousers got to do me the rest of the inquest.'

'All right, Mr Lumley, all right. Just give me a hand to help him up on the balustrade.'

'Him?'

'Spider McBride, in this case.'

Lumley planted his feet apart and took one side of the bundle. Together they heaved it on to the narrow balustrade of the octagon tower. Below them, as Swain looked down, the narrow strip of lawn against the wall of the house was edged by a path which separated it from the paved terrace beyond.

'Ready, Mr Lumley?'

Lumley nodded. No one needed to tell him what was coming next. The trussed sacks slithered against the stonework as he and Swain pushed forward. Then the weight was gone, turning through the summer air, diminishing below them. The bundle hit the grass below and burst in a scattering of wet sand across the turf.

'They'll be pleased with that mess,' the sergeant said with heavy irony. 'Really pleased.'

Swain put away the hunter watch, the legacy of his father, which he had drawn from his waistcoat pocket.

'Three seconds, Mr Lumley. He'd have been travelling at over ninety miles an hour by the time he hit the ground. That's supposing he fell from up here. Right, Mr Lumley?'

Lumley peered down at the remains of the two sandbags. 'You got it wrong, Mr Swain. He never fell there. Not on the grass. He was further out, on the paving. About six feet further out.'

Swain patted the waistcoat pocket of his neat suit, where the gold hunter now lay.

'Someone certainly got it wrong, Mr Lumley. Tell me how it could have been.'

Lumley looked uncertainly at the ground below. 'He must have fell backward from lower down, while he was climbing.'

Swain joined him at the parapet, gazing benevolently at the turf. 'But, Mr Lumley, if Spider McBride had fallen from lower down, he'd have had even less time or space in which to fall outwards. And even between us, we couldn't have thrown him far enough out from this balustrade for him to fall in the middle of the marble paving.'

Lumley turned to him with a distinct air of grievance. Swain placated him. 'I know, Mr Lumley. You see it all. Spider McBride jumped from the balustrade here. Jumped out as far as he could. He climbed all this way and found the door to the stairs barred. In an access of grief and frustration, the poor fellow decided to do away with himself. He stood on the balustrade and leapt out into thin air, determined to dash himself to pieces on the terrace paving. That it, Mr Lumley?'

The kindly suggestion was lost on Sergeant Lumley. 'For God's sake talk sense, Mr Swain.'

'Very well, Mr Lumley. Stand here, not on the balustrade. Just stand. Now, how far across this roof might you jump? Recall that McBride was fully dressed and wearing boots. How far, Mr Lumley? No run at it, just a standing jump. Three feet? Four? At any event, not far enough into empty air to fall in the middle of the terrace.'

Lumley folded his arms and stared at the treetops below them. 'How should I know, Mr Swain? P'raps when he hit the grass, he sort of bounced.'

'Did you see those two sackloads of sand bounce, Mr Lumley? Bounce six feet?'

Lumley breathed harder. 'He could have been alive when he hit the grass and then crawled a few feet to where he was found. According to you, he was alive for a few minutes after he hit his head. And if he landed on the grass, it would explain why he didn't have a lot of broken bones.'

Swain nodded sympathetically. 'Any trace of grass or earth on his clothing, Lumley? Or of gravel from that path he must have crawled across.'

'Not that anyone noticed.'

'No,' Swain said. 'Not even that Dr Stevenson the pathologist noticed. Spider McBride didn't land on the grass because he probably never fell, Mr Lumley. I'd stake my life on it. He climbed up here all right. But I reckon he was dead by the time that someone carried him down the stairs through the house and laid him out for a witness to find. Otherwise, he climbed down of his own accord and met his death down there. When you're arranging a trick like that and you've got to do it in a hurry, I imagine it's not always easy to guess by sight just where the body might fall.'

'Gammon!' Lumley said spiritedly. Swain sat down on the balustrade and sighed.

'That's what we're supposed to think, Mr Lumley. You just consider this. McBride, one of the best-known spidermen in the business, is found dead below a hundred-foot tower. His clothes have stone dust and fragments of stucco to show that he'd climbed it – bitumen on his knees to show that he got to the very top. The state of his skull suggests that he hit the ground head first. Now who's going to look any closer to see exactly how he died?'

'The inquest,' Lumley said, 'that's who.'

'But they haven't, Mr Lumley, until now. If he fell, he couldn't have landed on that paving. If he was pushed or thrown, he still couldn't have landed that far out. As for crawling, he was as good as dead the moment his skull was smashed. The last few minutes before he breathed his last, he wouldn't have crawled anywhere.'

Lumley surveyed the billowing landscape of leaves and hill-crests.

'Why would anyone have knocked his brains out on the tower and carried him down? Or waited down below and done 'im there? Why?'

'Perhaps, Mr Lumley, because Spider McBride had probably been sent to remove certain items from Mr Lerici's desk before anyone else got their hands on them. It was worth murder to stop him getting away with them. Let's just say that.'

'But who was in the house the night he was killed?'

'Signora Lerici and Signorina Amalia de Brahami, so far as I know. And two menservants and the kitchen maid and the Greek maid, Basileia.'

'Well,' said Lumley feebly, 'I don't see one old woman or one young girl – or both of them together – knocking the poor devil's brains out, then carrying him down all those steps and laying him out on the terrace to be found. And I don't see servants doing murder for their mistress.'

'No,' Swain said thoughtfully, 'nor do I, Mr Lumley. Nor do I.'

Lumley brushed damp sand from his shabby frock-coat. 'This is going to be another mess,' he said miserably. 'Bloody inquest might go on for weeks at this rate. When am I going to get home?'

'I shouldn't worry, Mr Lumley. Just tell the truth. That might be your quickest way home after all.'

A little before midnight, Alfred Swain closed his volume of *Saturn's Kingdom: or, The Feast of Blood*. To him, John Posthumous Lerici's imagination shared the diseased psychic miasma of Edgar Allan Poe but without the great American's plea of sickness and misfortune. Lerici had enjoyed money, privilege, and health. He was a natural son of Lord Byron, if the story was to be believed. Yet there was all the difference in the world, Swain thought, between the vigour, wit, poetry – above all the idealism – of the great Romantic genius, and the sickly sleep-walking sensuality of Lerici's tale. Swain had read more than enough of 'moonlit caresses on lithe bare flanks . . . the perfume of hair blown in a night-wind across the face of beauty's possessor . . . the urgent cry lost in the dark labyrinth like a night-owl fading in the distance'. Underneath it all, there was a shabby reality of abduction, grievous bodily harm, rape, murder, indecency, and a goodly number of other outrages which belonged to the provisions of the Offences Against the Person Act of 1861 rather than in a work of literature.

He snuffed out the candle between finger and thumb, lying with a single sheet over him and the window open to the summer night. It had rained a little during the evening, the moisture almost steaming from the warm ground. Now, under the tiles of the servants' rooms at Mondragon, the air was heavy and warm. Unlike Sergeant Lumley, who had been lodged with the landlord of the Cavendish Arms, Swain was employed by Mr Abrahams on behalf of the family, under the terms of Lerici's will. Therefore he slept like a servant at the house itself.

He sighed, drawing breath deeply and with difficulty in the low-ceilinged attic. Who was it that Lerici had feared and what was it that made him determine that a policeman should be first to see the papers in his desk? Was he party to the frauds of the Turf Insurance and the City of Paris Loan? Or was he a victim? He was certainly regarded as a thief who had stolen several pieces from the excavations at Mycenae with the aid of a dishonest workman. But there was more to him than this. And surely he feared that 'Poodle' Benson and Billy Kurr meant him harm. Were the papers in his desk not an assurance that foul play must be avenged? Small wonder that Benson and Kurr or someone of their kind had sent Spider McBride on his mission.

Swain turned restlessly in bed. As other men had nightmares after lobster mayonnaise, he suffered from a surfeit of gothic fiction. Lerici had been murdered in southern Greece by a rural bandit called Petrides who had become his servant. But that hardly concerned a pair of common swindlers like Benson and Kurr. They had merely sent McBride to remove compromising papers. And someone, it seemed, had brained McBride. Who? And why?

Alfred Swain turned the other way. The swindle of Iphigenia and the Portland Plate made no sense either. In his life, no less than in his fiction, John Posthumous Lerici appeared by nature as a man gangrened by fraud and dishonesty. He was corrupt by nature, a criminal type, which was something very different from a man convicted by the criminal courts. Corruption attracted him, like beauty, for its own sake.

Swain had encountered only one or two men of this moral disposition. They hated either the human race or at least the society in which they lived. They took an almost self-righteous pleasure in destroying whatever they could of the society whose rules and beliefs they despised. Such a man, it seemed, had John Posthumous Lerici been. The disease of his soul was profound and quite incurable.

Swain turned the other way with the slight groan of a man who feels the minutes of the night passing and sees sleep as far away as ever. With an effort he tried to put the whole thing from his mind. At six o'clock that evening he had sent his report on the afternoon's experiment to the coroner's office. No doubt it would cause delay and confusion at the inquest on Spider McBride. That, Swain thought, was not his fault. If the people concerned had done their work properly to begin with, the matter could have been settled at the outset.

He turned the other way again, closed his eyes, and tried to imagine being drawn down and down, round and round, into the dark vortex of sleep, deep into the underworld of dreamland. Thoughtless, he drifted down, threads of reason falling slack, memories clouded, purpose and resolution carried aimlessly in a semiconscious tide.

Vaguely, she came to him in sleep, outlined against the starlit sky of the window. She must have come in by one of the other windows, he thought, without opening his eyes. There was a narrow gully where rainwater ran, between the attic windows and the low stone battlements, faked like Lerici's prose, which topped the west front of Mondragon.

The dark hair was piled high, the blossom-scented hair of Lerici's preposterous romance. He sensed the tall brow and sharp young nose, the orient gold of her skin that suggested Provence or the Nile, the tight-lidded almond eyes that had an air of more distant enigmas and myths. There was something whitish about the lids of the eyes, as if they had been lined by cosmetics. Swain saw her outline in the arch of the open window, moving towards him. She was in naked silhouette but the starlight caught a gleam of gold at her throat, gold at her fingers, gold at her wrists, gold embracing the narrow waist – lithe, as Lerici would have called it in his fantasies.

Gold. The treasure of the tombs on warm-toned living flesh, as Schliemann had adorned his young Greek bride, Sophia. A necklace of petal-thin sunflower discs with a head or amphora hanging from each. A sleek gold bracelet that wound up her arm like a snake with jewelled eyes. Linked wafer-thin gold round the slim warm waist. A comb that held the dark piled hair had the dull pallor of ivory. The hand was held towards him now and he saw in the starlight the gold seal-rings, a pair of winged griffins, a goddess sitting beneath a tree, a procession of daemons that were half horses and half fish, standing almost on their tails.

'Mr Swain . . . Do you like me, Mr Swain?'

It was surely no dream. Amalia de Brahami, like a lovely ghost from *Saturn's Kingdom*, was her father's creation, if ever there was one. He heard the whisper of her bare skin against the curtain as she moved into the room.

'Do I please you, Mr Swain? Poor Mr Swain, it has been so difficult for you, has it not?'

He must keep his eyes shut and make no answer. They had opened too little for her to notice. Swain the practical man saw his way out of the difficulty. If he refused to wake, she would weary of this and go away. It was out of the question to argue with the girl when she was naked in his room and he wearing nothing but his nightshirt.

But she was gliding close now, starlight on skin that seemed like pale bronze satin. The curve and swell. The breasts under the crescent of the gold necklace. A sinuous passing of thighs and the movement of haunches.

'Would you die for me, Mr Swain . . .?'

For God's sake! Swain kept his eyes shut and felt his anger increase.

'Do you love me, Mr Swain? I think you do. I think you have loved me even before you knew I existed. There are women, Mr Swain, whom every man loves in his imagination. A sort of woman . . .'

She was lowering herself now. By God! She was going to sit on the bed! Perhaps even slide into it!

Alfred Swain was about to pull himself upright and, if necessary, tip the harpy on to the floor.

'I know you have sought me, Mr Swain . . . Your friends tell me so . . . And now you have found what you sought . . . Please, Mr Swain. I am the woman you have asked for and sought . . . The story of the true Iphigenia, Mr Swain . . . I can tell you that story . . .'

Swain sat bolt upright and tried to hold her. But the supple limbs escaped from his hands as easily as a bird in air. She was in the window arch and then she was gone.

He was fully awake now. Had he been so before? Was it all as he had seen and heard in the starlit room or was it in part his imagination? Had he been told a secret by Amalia de Brahami or by his own unconscious mind? Iphigenia. What had this girl to do with the true Iphigenia? The true Iphigenia was dead. By the laws of history, mythology, or the rules of the game she was dead. Murdered by her own father three thousand years ago. Sacrificed for a fair wind to Troy.

Alfred Swain was wide awake now. He lay in his bed and watched the sky grow pale. The inquest was to resume at ten o'clock. It would never do. He was going to feel bad by then. Very bad indeed.

4

In the pauses of Spider McBride's tragedy, a plain-faced municipal clock ticked time away in a quiet self-confident beat on the wall of the converted class-room. The room in its present state was one that might have come from Swain's childhood, with its tall and sloping master's desk at the front, the rows of benches and the aisles, the blackboard on its easel and the dust of chalk, the church-gothic of the windows at either end. Over such a room as this, in a small Dorset village, his schoolmaster father had presided until his death, when Alfred Swain was ten years old. A text in black letter at one end of the room commanded the witnesses: 'Remember thy Creator in the days of thy youth.' How about Spider McBride, Swain wondered? How much remembering had the little man had time for between the raised arm and the murderous blow?

The coroner, a kindly old man Swain thought him, occupied the master's desk. A clerk sat at a small table to one side. The two chairs of the schoolroom ushers, who kept order while the children were taught, now contained a sheriff's officer and a parish beadle.

So far as Swain could see, his report to the coroner had been without any effect on the proceedings. The benevolent old man peered over his glasses at Inspector William Palmer of Scotland Yard who was now describing how the body of Spider McBride had been found. Palmer stood at a lectern, a makeshift witness stand, and answered the coroner's questions. Palmer had what might be called 'presence'. He was noticed and he was listened to with a special attention. 'Handsome' Palmer, Swain thought, was not truly handsome at all. There was too much flesh and a sense of something animal about him. But he had solidity and the air of a man who can get things done. Women, young and old, gazed at him as he gave evidence. They were women who would have treated Alfred Swain with amusement or scepticism or curiosity for his apparent inexperience of life. They would allow that Alfred Swain was far the nicer man, but they would prefer Handsome Palmer. That was the answer, as Swain saw it.

'How was it, Mr Palmer, that you came to discover the body of James McBride?'

'In the absence of Inspector Swain, who was then on his way

back from Greece, I was detailed by Superintendent Toplady to deal with any matters referred to the division by the family of the late Mr Lerici. By that time, of course, Signora Lerici and her household had returned to England by train so that preparations for the late gentleman's funeral might be made. I was then on private-clothes duty, investigating a series of thefts in the Brunswick Town area of Brighton. Being so close, it was thought convenient that I should answer any summons from the family. The day previous to McBride's death being a Sunday, I was in London on Sunday leave. I left the police office in Whitehall Place just before seven on Monday morning and travelled to Brighton by the parliamentary train. I was met at Brighton by the station-master at 8.30 with an urgent message from the local division that I should proceed at once to Folly Ridge, which I did.'

'You went direct to Mondragon House?'

'I did, sir. I went direct to the house and was there about nine that morning.'

'And what was the state of affairs that you found there?'

'Considerable distress, sir. The occupants of the house were Signora Lerici, Signorina de Brahami, and four servants – a personal maid, a kitchen maid, a pantry boy, and an elderly factotum. Shortly before my arrival, one of the servants had gone out into the gardens and had found the body of the dead man lying below the tower.'

'And what did you do, Mr Palmer?'

Swain's heart quickened. The elderly coroner was holding a sheet of paper in his hand. Swain recognized it as his report.

'I went to the scene of the tragedy, sir, and saw that there was indeed a man lying there. I lifted him . . .'

'One moment, Mr Palmer. You lifted him? You moved his body from where he had fallen?'

Palmer looked surprised and Swain felt a rage of frustration in his heart.

'I did, sir. One of the ladies had said that he was dead but her state of mind was obviously confused. It was possible, sir, that the poor fellow was still alive. My first duty was to see whether he might yet be saved.'

'How far did you move him?'

125

Swain saw that the coroner was looking again at the sheet of paper in his hand.

'I would find it hard to say how far precisely, sir. His face was in the ground when I found him. I wanted to put him comfortable and see if there might be a pulse.'

'How far did you move him? Was it six feet? Or ten? Can you not help us on that?'

'It might be six feet, sir.'

Swain cursed under his breath.

'Six feet?'

'And then, sir, I tried to find a pulse. But there was none. He was cold.'

The coroner looked Palmer straight in the eye. 'As an officer of the law, did you not think that you did a very wrong thing in moving the body from where it had been found?'

'As a man, sir, I hoped to save him, as any man would. That was my first duty.'

They almost applauded him, the rows of onlookers. Swain ground his teeth.

'But the evidence, Mr Palmer . . .'

'As to that, sir, there was stone dust on his clothes. It was plain that he had met his death by falling from the tower below which he lay. So I believe. I made my report accordingly.'

'You do not in your report state that you moved his body.'

'I did not state, sir, that I first tried to see if he was alive. That is true. I did not state it because I believed it did not need stating. It is what any man would do.'

There was a murmur from the benches this time, approving 'Handsome' Palmer and rebuking the coroner.

'Can you explain, Mr Palmer, why it was that if he fell upon the grass by the wall of the tower, there was no mark of grass upon his clothes?'

'No, sir. I do not recall if he was precisely on the grass when I first found him. He might be, he might not be. The ground was dry, however, from lack of rain. I can only tell you what I know. I cannot account for what I do not know. Perhaps the grass being dry from lack of rain left no mark.'

'Not dry from lack of dew, however.' The coroner was shrewder than he looked, Swain thought.

'I had supposed he fell before the dew gathered, sir. When I examined him, the body was quite cold.'

The coroner was not, after all, more nimble-witted than Inspector Palmer.

Swain sat there until the lunch adjournment and heard the details of Palmer's account confirmed by other witnesses. Signora Lerici was glum and Amalia de Brahami frightened. The two servants had seen little but understood that Mr Palmer had first tried to see if the spiderman was dead.

Swain followed the officials and the witnesses out through the vestibule and into the schoolyard, the July sun striking warm through his suiting. Sergeant Lumley stood there in his shabby frock-coat and trousers, his face deep-coloured under the rim of his hat. He patted his moist cheeks with a handkerchief and tucked it away.

'You was sure, Mr Swain! You was so sure you was right! Lugging them bags of sand up that tower and tossing 'em down again. Well, they put you right this morning, I should say! Not 'alf they didn't! Next time you fancy a caper like that, Mr Swain, you do it on your own. As it is, I shouldn't like to be wearing your skin when Mr Toplady finishes with you!'

'I don't suppose Mr Toplady will ever know.'

'Won't he?' Lumley swelled with the majesty of indignation. 'He'll know all right. Handsome Palmer is odds-on to tell him somehow. And if he doesn't, then I probably shall. Just look at the state of my private-clothes coat!'

Swain drew himself up, the long features fastidious. 'I think, Mr Lumley, that you have betrayed a confidence. Before Mr Palmer gave his evidence this morning, someone told him about the impossibility of McBride having fallen from the tower on to the marble paving. He never moved the body! Nothing but a story made up to put the facts right!'

Lumley stared at him. 'You want to sniff about closer to home, Mr Swain. I never said nothing to no one.'

'Did you not?'

'No, Mr Swain, I did not! Anyone of that lot at Mondragon could have seen us and said.'

'We were not watched, Mr Lumley. Even had we been, they would have had no idea what we were doing. They had no reason to tell Mr Palmer and probably no chance to.'

'All right,' Lumley said, 'then you just think of this. You sent word to the coroner. What's the first thing he does? Doesn't know you from Adam. He wires Scotland Yard, Mr Swain. The division. Gets their confirmation, their opinion. And if Palmer was tipped off, that's where it come from.'

'From the division?'

'Of course it'd be from the division. If Palmer knew what was coming this morning, it was because someone give 'im the nod. Someone in Whitehall Place minding his back for him. Unless, of course, he was simply telling the truth at the inquest. And that's the most likely thing of all.'

'Mr Lumley,' said Swain quietly, 'I find it hard to believe that anyone in the division, in any circumstances, would warn Mr Palmer to perjure himself in a murder inquiry.'

'Do you?' said Lumley with a look of sympathy. 'Then you might find it easier if you just remember that no one else thinks there is a murder case. It's only you. The rest of the world reckons Spider McBride fell off that tower and Mr Palmer moved him to see if there was any sign of life.'

'And you think that, Mr Lumley?'

The sergeant paused a moment. 'It's a sight more likely, Mr Swain. All this song and dance of yours about someone dotting Spider on the boko and lugging him down the stairs!' A look of portly grievance reinforced the sergeant's protest. 'All I know is I been made to lug sack after sack of sand up those bloody stairs – and my private-clothes coat ain't fit to be seen. Next time you want to be ever so clever, Mr Swain, I'd appreciate it if you was clever on your own.'

It was more than Swain could endure. Of one thing he was sure. Palmer had lied to the coroner. An officer of the Metropolitan Police had lied upon oath as to facts of a man's death. But why? If Palmer had killed the little thief and wanted to make it seem as though Spider McBride had fallen from the tower, he could have put the body in the right place to begin with. But Palmer had been in London with witnesses to prove it. If he was lying, it was done to protect someone else.

The coroner's jury had no such misgivings as Alfred Swain. On the following day they found that James McBride had met his death through misadventure. That, it seemed, was the end of the matter.

5

The dull leaf-brown water of the canal mirrored the dapper little figure in his cream linen suit and wide-brimmed hat. He stood at the iron rail of the bridge with its tunnel-like openings through which the waters of the Oudezijds Achterburgwal seeped rather than flowed. Along the quays at either side of the canal, where the sailing barges were moored, the trees formed a summer canopy of horse-chestnut green.

When the little man looked up, there was a light crease of anxiety in the line of his brow and a drop or two of perspiration above the neat dark moustache. But it was impossible for anything to go wrong at this point in the plan. There might not be honour among thieves but at least there was a sense of discretion. A cloud of pigeons rose, apparently from the rooftop of the Dutch East India Company's headquarters, four-square in seventeenth-century brick and white facing-stone. The area had 'gone down' in the past two centuries. No doubt of it. The tall narrow buildings on either quay housed poorer families. Tailors and money-lenders, printers and seamstresses occupied the basements. He straightened up and realized that quite a few people had noticed him, a figure alone in the busy quarter of close streets and narrow waterways. Best not to be noticed. He strolled across the bridge and sauntered under the trees until he came level with a plain-gabled house at the centre of its row, the brick darkened by two centuries of soot. There was a coffee-shop on the ground floor approached by a steep flight of steps. An equally steep flight led down to a basement area. In its window, there were several cards with specimens of print upon them and a scattering of dead flies.

He could see through the glass that his friend William Kurr was talking to the printer, or rather a dumb show was in progress between them. He and Kurr had tried learning Dutch for safety's sake but had found it unexpectedly difficult. '*Dank u wel*,' he had told Billy Kurr. Gratitude oils the wheels between those who do not understand one another's languages. '*Dank u wel*,' at every opportunity. 'Thank you. Thank you. Thank you.'

Through the glass he could see that the printer had laid out his work for display next to the original. 'Royal Bank of London.' It really was very good. Billy Kurr in his check suiting was nodding his large head in emphatic praise. The printer was moving his hands about to suggest that he too thought it very good, though he said so himself. 'Bank of England.' That was, if anything, better. Perhaps it was unwise to display these works of art quite so close to the window. Not that anyone who was passing in the ordinary way would be suspicious. Still, he would have a word with Billy Kurr about that.

More nodding now. Appearance of great friendship and money changing hands. Billy Kurr counting out banknotes. The printer counting them and nodding to confirm that they were the very sum agreed. Dutch printing, the very best, the little man thought. The heirs of Elzevir and the finest typography in Europe. More dumb show in the printer's basement.

The dapper figure in the cream linen suit responded briefly to a shout behind him but when he turned round it was only a man on one of the barges that was easing away from the quay. There was an appetizing smell of ground coffee from the shop on the floor above. The melodious chimes sounded the quarter. It was over now. He walked back to the bridge and smiled at his reflection below the rail. The dull-toned water slapped the stone piers as the barge pulled further out. He saw from the corner of his eye the large check suiting of a racing man.

'Well, Mr Kurr?'

'Well, Mr Benson!' Billy Kurr patted the leather portfolio which he was carrying. 'He's a toy, he is. A real toy! You could do anything with him.'

'And his work, Mr Kurr? How does he work?'

'The best, Mr Benson. The very best. Our late friend steered us right about that. Printing that brings tears to our eyes. Like great music.'

'And he's not one for language, is he? Don't understand much and don't say nothing? That so, Mr Kurr?'

Billy Kurr began to laugh, deep in his large chest, at the richness of it all. 'He wouldn't understand if you let off the Royal Horse Artillery just behind him. And he couldn't tell you the time of day if you offered him a thousand pound for it. When our late friend said he wouldn't talk, he meant he couldn't talk. He's got an art that ought to be on museum walls. But, for the rest, the poor fellow is deaf and dumb.'

'He never is!' Harry Benson straightened up.

'As I stand here, Mr Benson.'

'Well, I'll be damned.'

'I'd say you will, Mr Benson. But I hope you'll drink the health of the late Mr Lerici first. He's found us a toy, Mr Benson. A toy you could play with for hours and never get tired.'

'Fine printing, our friend said.'

'And what finer than this, Mr B.? You could pass this before the Scrutiny Committee of the Bank of England with Mr Rothschild himself on it and they'd never lose a wink of sleep.'

'You wonder, Mr Kurr, why Lerici ever wasted his talents writing them sickly tales for young misses, when he'd got so much else in him! Still, as to Rothschild, I rather think we'll start to unpick them from the Paris end. They'll come to us easier that way.'

It was so exquisite that they laughed in sheer good humour. Then they turned about and walked arm-in-arm towards the central railway station, from which a convenient express ran through Brussels to Ostend and the Channel steamer.

As they took their places in the carriage which had been reserved for them, the major sensed a residue of unease in his companion.

'What if they twig it, Mr B.?'

The cream-suited dandy smiled. 'Banks are like marriage,' he said, 'all trust and confidence. Tell me, Mr Kurr. Suppose you was married, which you ain't. Suppose you found out that some nippy fellow had cuckolded you. What'd you do? Black your good lady's eye, I dare say. Wait for the fellow some dark night and break his head on the quiet. That about it, Mr Kurr?'

'About it, Mr B.'

'You wouldn't put on sandwich-boards and walk the Strand, telling the world you'd been made a fool of?'

'Wouldn't do it, Mr B.'

'The same with banks, Mr Kurr. There's the beauty of it. If we was to be greedy and cash all the paper in one place, or sting one of 'em too bad, they might squeal. But ask yourself this. If a bank finds that a bill in its name is cashed elsewhere and it's a dud, what does it do? It could kick up and refuse to pay. In which case it tells the other bank and the rest of the world what a fool it's been and that the world's money ain't safe with it. I don't say it wouldn't kick up for fifty thousand. But a bit here and a bit there, nine times out of ten they'll take their beating and bite their lip. I don't say they wouldn't get the money back if they could, nice and quiet. But not with the world laughing at them or when the money's gone anyway.'

'Then there's the tenth time,' Billy Kurr said thoughtfully.

'There is, Mr Kurr. There is the tenth time. But nine out of ten again they won't know anything's wrong until the dud bill gets returned to them along with the rest for payment at the end of three months' account. We'll be long gone, Mr Kurr.'

'There's the tenth time again,' said Kurr cautiously.

'There is, Mr Kurr. One chance in a hundred or more. The bill comes back quick for some reason, and they see it's a fake. They want revenge. What do they do?'

'Law,' said Kurr glumly.

'Law, Mr Kurr. The best law. Scotland Yard. And not just Scotland Yard but the Detective Division. Nowhere else to go. And what's the first thing the Detective Division does? It warns us that the fat's in the fire. There's a screw loose. At least one of our friends is going to see the information entered in the divisional log. Might even be one of our friends who opens the complaint from the bank, reads it, tears it up, and throws it away. Our friends in Whitehall Place got a lot more to lose than us, Mr Kurr. If we go down, they're bound to go down with us. And they know it. They'd want us away. They'd do anything in the world to get us away, so that the tale might never be told. So the worst that happens if something goes wrong is we have two or three days to get clean away with whatever's in the bag so far.'

Billy Kurr rubbed steam off the window with his gloved hand, staring at the flat fields and herds of cattle.

'Surprising it ain't been done before, Mr B., if it's that easy.'

'It has been done before in a modest way, Mr Kurr, only the banks don't tell the world about it. But it ain't been done good and proper before because a man's always fearful of getting caught. But if the people who do the catching happen to be your friends, you won't have much worry there!'

They sat in silence until Billy Kurr said suddenly, 'Handsome Palmer reckons Policeman Swain dug up that horse, Iphigenia.'

Major Montgomery beamed at him. 'So long as he thinks that's Iphigenia, Mr Kurr, he'll be well busy. P'raps, when he's at the end of his rope, he'll have to dig up Lerici and slap the cuffs on him. Silly bugger.'

But whether the last epithet was intended for Alfred Swain or John Posthumous Lerici or both was by no means clear.

6

'Mr Swain?' The head that peered round the door of the Document Room had a schoolmasterly air of enquiry in its arched eyebrows and wry mouth. Mr Messenger, on behalf of Her Majesty's Home Office, presided over the little room where the records of the Metropolitan Police Detective Division were kept.

'Mr Swain? The day-books, isn't it, Mr Swain?'

'If you please, Mr Messenger. The divisional day-books for March 1874 and May 1875.'

The barred windows looked out on to a basement area. The room itself was lined with shelves on which the day-books and ledgers stood. The earliest records dated from the 1830s but these had long been transferred to the confidential Home Office files. Only those for the past ten years were still held in the Document Room. There was no other furniture apart from the high counting-house desk with its tall wooden stool and a small chair on which Mr Messenger sat to keep watch over his visitors. Mr Messenger hummed to himself as his finger ran along a row of volumes. He pulled one out.

'March 1874.' He laid it on the high desk. 'One at a time, isn't it, Mr Swain?'

'Yes,' said Swain absently. He hoisted himself on to the tall stool and opened the ledger for the first quarter of 1874. The entries were set out like those of a financial statement, day by day. He ran his finger down and stopped at 27 March. The entry was there, sloping across the page in Meiklejohn's dame-school script. 'Complainant: Messrs Abrahams & Abrahams. Ex parte Comtesse de Goncourt.' He moved across to the next column. 'Alleged fraud.' Source of information was given as 'Complainants, confirmed Chef de Sûreté, Paris, by wire'. And then the notes. 'Society for Insuring Against Losses on the Turf.' Action was there too. 'Premises of Archer, Certified Bookmaker, Northumberland

Avenue, searched. Previously vacated by occupants.' The entry was initialled by Inspector George Clarke.

Swain stared at the pages of the ledger as it lay open before him. Northumberland Avenue was close enough for any officer of the division to warn the conspirators in a couple of minutes. But still it would take time to evacuate the premises. It must have been, Swain thought, that someone in authority had delayed the warrant or its execution. He studied the entries for the previous day. At first glance there was nothing exceptionable about them. One or two had been written in pencil by sergeants or constables and made good with ink after an inspector or chief inspector had approved them. From his pocket, Swain took a small magnifying glass and studied the previous day's inscriptions.

Four had been inked in at the end of the day. Looking closely, he saw that one pencil entry had been not so much inked in as rubbed out and written over. Now that was curious. As it stood in ink, it recorded that Samuel Milne of Great Queen Street had been robbed of his pocket-book and its contents, the victim of a pickpocket in the forecourt of the North-Western Station at Euston Square. Inspector Clarke had initialled the entry.

Swain put down the magnifying glass and sat upright on the tall stool. He had not the least doubt that the entry in ink had nothing whatever to do with the entry in pencil which it obscured. How, then, could those who altered it be sure that Samuel Milne of Great Queen Street would never contradict them? Swain thought he knew.

'Mr Messenger, if you please.'

'Mr Swain, sir.'

'The bound volumes of *The Times* newspaper for March 1874, Mr Messenger. Might they be to hand?'

Mr Messenger put on another droll schoolmasterly expression and hummed to himself as he mapped a line of volumes with his fingertip, along the lowest shelf. Presently, he slammed a heavy buckram-bound folio on the high desk. Alfred Swain opened it at the beginning of March 1874 and traced through the obituary columns, day by day. He reached 26 March and was disconcerted. Perhaps he had been wrong. But he persisted, passing 27 March, 28 March, and coming to 29 March. With exhilaration like the shock from a galvanic battery, he saw it.

MILNE, Samuel James Arbuthnot, on 27th inst. at his residence, Ebro House, Great Queen Street, in his 76th year. His sisters request that all enquiries be addressed to Morrison, Elam and Co., City Road.

It was perfect! Samuel Milne was a gift from the gods. He sounded like an elderly bachelor or, perhaps, a widower. Even his sisters might know little of him. Someone had picked him from the obituary column with care and inked in a complaint on his behalf. Mr Milne was truly in no position to contradict them. Whatever had been written in pencil was now effectively blotted out. Swain had not the least doubt that the wire from the Chef de Sûreté had been received on 26 March and held, while the occupants of 'Archer & Co., Northumberland Avenue', were given time to make their escape.

'Thank you, Mr Messenger. The letter-book for 26 March 1874, if you please.'

Mr Messenger returned the bound volume of newspapers and the ledger. He slapped down the day-book on the desk. Swain turned its pages. Every letter or wire that went out from Scotland Yard was copied in here, also every letter received. On 26 March, the Detective Division had received a wire from the Chef de Sûreté, complaining of 'Archer & Co.' On the following day, Mr Abrahams' letter was entered. According to Inspector Clarke's ledger entry, both had been received on 27 March. In other words, Swain thought, George Clarke had withheld the most urgent warning, wired from Paris, for twenty-four hours. Long enough.

'I must trouble you once more, Mr Messenger. The day-book for May 1875.' Mr Messenger obliged. Swain found the entry on 21 May, the wire to the Chef de Sûreté, forwarding complaints of a bogus City of Paris Guaranteed Loan stock, being sold from an address in the Rue Réaumur. The wire had been sent at 10 a.m. on 21 May. The letters of complaint began on 18 May. Why the delay? It would be impossible to show that a warning wire had been sent from a London post office to the Rue Réaumur in the mean time. Swain had not the least doubt that it had happened. The conspirators, who were not named, had been given two days' leisure to collect their winnings and disappear.

The entry was signed 'Nathaniel Druscovich'. Inspector

Druscovich spoke both French and German. He was the division's man for international business. Swain stared at the page. Of the fifteen members of the detective division, four were surely part of a conspiracy: Clarke, Meiklejohn, Druscovich, and Palmer. How many more?

He closed the day-book and thanked Mr Messenger. The time had come to begin again. George Clarke seemed the most likely prospect.

7

Swain sat alone at his desk in the inspectors' office, waiting with the patience of farm cat for a cornfield mouse. He wanted Clarke alone. The afternoon passed. Meiklejohn came and went. Druscovich was there for half an hour. 'Handsome' Palmer came in with a message. It was just after four o'clock when Clarke appeared, the white hair curly and the round face red. He nodded at Swain, hitched himself on to the stool, glanced at a sheet of paper and said, 'Bless us all!'

Swain waited a moment. 'Mr Clarke.'

'Yes, Mr Swain?'

'A name, Mr Clarke. Mr Samuel Milne of Great Queen Street who lost his pocket-book at Euston Square station in March 1874. Still in your memory, is it?'

Clarke looked up at him with an air of honest puzzlement. 'Can't say it is, Swain. A lot of pocket-books have gone the way of all good things since then.'

Swain nodded, as if he understood.

'The thing is, Mr Clarke, it seems unusual for a missing pocket-book to involve Scotland Yard rather than a local division. Important man, was he? Mr Milne?'

'You being funny, Swain? What's all this to you?'

'It concerns a case I happen to be employed upon, Mr Clarke. If you have any doubt as to Mr Milne, I imagine there will be an entry in your diary. With Mr Toplady's permission, I could verify the incident from that.'

There was a movement, as it seemed to Swain, somewhere deep behind Clarke's pale blue eyes. Uncertainty, perhaps. Alarm, possibly.

'All right, Swain. He was a wealthy old fellow living in Great Queen Street. He wanted Scotland Yard, so he got me.'

'And you went to see him on 26 March as the ledger entry says.'

'Something of that.'

Swain nodded, as if he was satisfied. He took up the cylindrical ruler and drew a line across a paper of his own.

'The difficulty is, Mr Clarke, that he was dead the next day.'

'So I heard,' Clarke said sharply, 'that ended the matter.'

'The day after you saw him, Mr Clarke.'

'So it may be.'

'Indeed, Mr Clarke, you were most remarkably lucky in being able to interview the gentleman. He was unconscious the entire day of your visit and never regained his senses before he died next morning.'

Swain knew nothing of this unconsciousness but it was worth trying. Clarke slammed the ruler on his desk. The round good-natured face was aflame with anger. 'You got something to say to me, Swain, you bloody out and say it. Either here or in front of Mr Toplady or anywhere else.'

'Just the late Mr Samuel Milne,' Swain said mildly, 'just him, Mr Clarke. I don't see how you could have interviewed him that day or how he was in any state to have his pocket picked at Euston Square. Perhaps you had an hour or two to yourself instead of going to interview him. Time off to sit and think, Mr Clarke.'

'If that's what you reckon, Swain.' Alfred Swain marvelled at the way that Clarke snatched at the lesser dishonesty, almost with gratitude. 'It might be the previous day or so I saw 'im. Play the game, my son! You never put something down in the diary to fill in an afternoon you spent otherwise? I dealt with the gentleman, even if I didn't recollect the occasion exactly.'

This jovial acknowledgement of minor dishonesty seemed worse to Swain than if Clarke had blurted out his guilt entirely. The rubicund face was smiling again, like a happy sun in a child's story.

'Come on, Mr Swain! Don't tell me you never put down an hour in your divisional diary for a job that never took you half that time! And what you did with the rest of that hour was nobody's business but your own.'

'But why should I want that half-hour, Mr Clarke?'

Clarke shrugged and beamed. 'How the mischief should I know, old fellow? Come on, don't tell me you never took five or ten minutes that you wasn't entitled to. There's not a man on the force ain't done that.'

Swain marvelled at him and at the energy Clarke showed to prevent him getting his hands on the individual diary. 'I can't speak for every man on the force, Mr Clarke. I've never found the need to fabricate an official diary.'

'Haven't you?' Clarke's face was tightening with anger again. 'Haven't you? Well, I suppose there's no arguing with someone as perfect as you, Swain! You think you are, don't you? Bloody perfect! Clever! Books and cleverness!'

'Stealing time,' Swain said, knowing that the moment had now come, 'taking money. You needn't be very clever to see where that must lead.'

Clarke was off his stool and half-way across the room. 'You watch your tongue, Swain! I'll take you before Toplady any day you like. And when I do, he might like to hear how you can never keep your hand out of madam's drawers five minutes together. Understand me, do you? That sort of thing in lodgings puts you out of the door here. Puts her out as well, so far as the force is concerned! You got that, 'ave you, clever Mr Swain?'

Swain shook his head. 'You don't see it, do you, Mr Clarke? What happens to me no longer matters. I may or may not be out of the door. But you have destroyed yourself. As for Mr Meiklejohn, Mr Druscovich, and the others, only you and they know what lies in store for them.'

Clarke blinked sharply, as if each of the names had been a blow. 'What you talking about, Swain?' he asked presently. 'Who's destroyed? And what others?'

'Is it only Mr Meiklejohn and Mr Druscovich, then?'

But the chink in the defence closed tight again. 'I don't know what you got in mind, Swain. You think otherwise, you know what you can do. There's no talking to you and there's no reasoning with you. Leave it at that.'

'Other people, Mr Clarke, will not leave it at that, whatever I may do.'

Before Clarke could reply, Druscovich came in and sat down at his desk. Clarke went back to his stool, sat there for a couple of minutes and then went out. Swain tried to work in the presence of the new arrival. It was hopeless. He could neither connect the

138

words of a simple sentence in his report nor bring himself to begin a conversation with the other man. Nathaniel Druscovich sat at his work, the dark hair swept back immaculately, the waxed moustache and the little triangle of hair on the lower lip that was not quite a beard giving him an air of sophistication and acuteness. He looked to Swain like the lover in a French play. Clarke, the longest-serving inspector, was a man of nearly sixty. Druscovich was in his middle thirties, intelligent and fluent. He was not long married but already the father of two children. How could he have been such a fool? Swain put down his pen.

'Mr Druscovich, if you please. The City of Paris Loan fraud, three years ago. You recall it?'

Druscovich looked up at him and the eyelids blinked slowly over eyes that were moist and expressionless as slate.

'Yes, Mr Swain. I recall it very well. Never was brought to justice.'

'The wire that was sent to Paris, you recall that?'

'I sent it to the Chef de Sûreté, Mr Swain.'

'And the complaint of the swindle that was received from Mr Abrahams the attorney.'

'That too, Mr Swain, I recall that very well. It was the letter which prompted the wire.'

'Between the time that the letter was received here and the wire sent to Paris, two days elapsed.'

'They did, Mr Swain. They did. Two days during which I was confined to my bed with influenza. And the worst of it was, Mr Swain, that during those two days the villains made their move. Left the office empty in the Rue Réaumur. Never were caught. A matter of great regret. A coup in that case might have led to a man's promotion.'

'Curious,' Swain said sceptically.

'No, Mr Swain. The truly curious thing is that Scotland Yard has only a single officer able to communicate in languages other than English on urgent matters of criminal intelligence.'

Swain waited a moment, letting Druscovich relax. Then there was no harm in trying a surprise. 'And what of the Society for Insuring Against Losses on the Turf?'

Druscovich looked up. This time he did not so much as blink. 'I was told of it, Mr Swain. At the time, however, I was employed

139

on the Hamburg Packet fraud. I fear you must ask someone else about the Turf Insurance case.'

'Yes,' Swain said thoughtfully, 'I suppose so.'

Druscovich studied his sheet of paper without writing anything or looking up from it. 'A pleasure to have been of service, Mr Swain.'

And that, Alfred Swain thought, was that.

8

Mrs Beresford stood before the mirror and frowned. She took a stray hair that was growing at her temple and snapped it from her head. Swain gazed at her and thought that in the white bodice and pantaloons she brought an air of the Paris music-hall to his Pimlico lodgings.

'Mr Swain,' she said thoughtfully, beginning to unfasten the bodice, 'if we was to go to Brighton for summer leave, Mr Swain, we could stay with Mr and Mrs Nokes. Nice little boarding-house off the London Road. You can walk to the pier in ten minutes.'

Alfred Swain began to unlace his boots. 'Appearances, Mrs Beresford. In our situation, we have to consider appearances.'

She turned a little towards him and his heart leapt to his throat as the white cotton slid free from a thigh whose tint was warm ivory.

'But that's just it, Mr Swain, dear,' the young widow said gently. 'You couldn't have a better appearance than Mr and Mrs Nokes. I've known them for years. If I was to stay there, no one could say boo. And if you was to stay as well, what's wrong with the appearance of the thing?'

She turned away to the mirror. Like some double-image of reality and reflection in a masterpiece of sixteenth-century painting, Swain saw the fine high-boned prettiness in the glass, the fair curls that left the neck bare and stately, the long inward curve of the back with its contoured vertebrae, the sleek firmness of hips and what he had been brought up to term politely as 'posteriors', the easy casual grace of thighs, calves, and feet. More than anything in the world he wanted to be in Brighton with Mrs Beresford, the sun sparkling on the summer tide and the band playing on the pier.

140

'I'm not sure it will do,' he said sadly, 'not for my sake so much as yours.'

The young woman turned, frowning again. 'Go on, Mr Swain,' she said. 'Go on with you! Where's the harm?'

'No harm,' he said softly, getting up and moving towards her. 'Only appearances.'

'Be damned to appearances!' she cried, impatient as a child.

He was standing close now and as his hand moved on the cool resilient swell of flesh he remembered a passage in Lerici's masterpiece where the master's hand was said to glide like a skate on ice over the bare flesh of his female slave. It was insinuatingly accurate. And then Swain cursed himself for letting Lerici enter his thoughts at a moment like this.

A little later, with her head pillowed upon him, Mrs Beresford said, rather indistinctly, 'Folk can't always be living for appearances, Mr Swain.'

'Only yours, Mrs Beresford, not mine. I really don't care about mine.'

She sat up smartly and patted his leg.

'That's it, then. You don't care about yours and I don't care about mine. Buy me a new pencil tomorrow, nice and sharp, and I'll write to Mrs Nokes.'

'If it's what you want.'

'Course it's what I want! I said that often enough! Is it what you want?'

'Oh, yes,' Swain said dreamily, 'it's what I want all right. I wonder if it's what Mr Beresford would want. I never knew him, you see, even though he was a policeman.'

She sat with her back to him. 'Yes,' she said solemnly, 'it's what he would want. If you'd known him, you'd know the last thing he'd want is for me to spend the rest of my life sitting alone and miserable. That's no better than them heathen places where widows have to throw themselves on the funeral fire.'

'Perhaps they do it for love,' Swain said helpfully.

She turned back towards him. 'Yes, Mr Swain. Well, I loved Mr Beresford all right. But I'm not a bloody fool.'

'No, Mrs Beresford, you're certainly not that.'

She bounced a little to give emphasis to her idea. 'Tell you what, Mr Swain. I won't need to write to Mrs Nokes. We could go down any day on the train. Brighton and back for three-and-six. Just for the day. Call on the Nokeses and ask if they'll have us for the summer leave. Make a nice day out. What about it, Mr Swain? Or wouldn't it suit appearances?' Her elbow made the point against his ribs.

'I think, Mrs Beresford' – a yawn overtook him before he could prevent it – 'I think it would suit appearances very well indeed.'

9

Major Hugh Montgomery turned from the wide Parisian avenue of the Boulevard Haussmann into the narrower Rue Lafitte with its northward stretch to the pillars of Notre-Dame de Lorette and the height of Montmartre beyond. It was better to approach on foot. While a carriage would have been more dignified, the major preferred time to study the surroundings of his quest.

The building itself was scarcely impressive in any respect for one that called itself the Maison Rothschild. But once inside the courtyard, its true character was revealed. Major Montgomery looked about him at the graceful enclosed world of sunlight on biscuit-coloured urns and tracery that was now the House of Rothschild.

Through the long elegant windows, he caught a glimpse of gilt-framed mirrors and polished furniture that had once graced the salons of the Bourbon kings. Shepherdesses in wall-tapestries looked on coyly, while ceiling gods and goddesses watched the sport of human greed. A door to one side of the courtyard was marked ENGLISH BUREAU. The major opened it and stepped into a small, more plainly furnished room. Several desks were set out, the largest at the centre, a clerk at each one and a leather chair for the visitor. On the mantelpiece of the far wall, an ormolu clock ticked time away and recorded the quarters with a delicate chime, like a hand stirring tiny silver spoons in a drawer.

Major Montgomery chose the largest desk with the senior clerk and introduced himself. The clerk was polite but hardly deferential. The major concealed his disappointment behind a smile and handed over a letter of introduction. It was signed by the manager of the Western Branch of the Bank of England and confirmed

142

that the major's deposits there were in excess of £2,000.

But the major was not asking for credit. From his pocket, he drew £500 in banknotes and asked for a bill of exchange in francs at three months' notice.

'I regret,' the clerk said coolly, 'that we cannot offer long paper on such a sum. Two months can be arranged, however.'

The major smiled again. 'Two months will do splendidly.'

The major and the clerk understood equally well that Rothschild's was the most select of all private European banks. The fact that a man had the money to buy a bill of exchange was nothing in itself. Reputation and character were all. But the reputation and the character of Major Montgomery were vouched for by his standing with the Bank of England, where one of the Rothschild brothers was a director. Had that not been so, he and his banknotes would have been courteously turned away from the Rue Lafitte. As it was, the letter proved him to be a fit and proper person to hold such a promissory note for 12,555 francs and 55 centimes, issued by the bank's English Bureau.

The senior clerk took the details and made the arrangement. Perhaps he did not notice a certain look of concern on the major's face as the pro forma of the bill was produced and made ready for the inscription. It was a distinctive cerulean blue. Major Montgomery was too well bred to reveal that he had never seen a bill of exchange from Rothschild's before. He had certainly not expected it to have this distinctive shade of blue.

In a deep devotional silence, the air of the exchange room stirred with the scratching of the pen on paper as the script of the bill was completed. The clerk went out and returned with the document signed. Major Montgomery smiled. He took out a leather pocket-book and folded the bill of exchange into it carefully. As he stood up, the clerk rose again and bowed. The major took his leave and walked out into the Napoleonic splendour of the palace courtyard.

Two months would not do splendidly but he would work within that limit by some means or other. The present bill was genuine and there would be no trouble over that. Even the imitations would be undetected for several weeks. Of course, if the entire conspiracy had to be wound up within two months, it would require speed. But that was not impossible to him.

143

He walked out through the gateway and into the sunshine of the Rue Lafitte. The large man at the corner of the Boulevard Haussmann came towards him.

'Well, Mr Benson?'

'Very well indeed, Mr Kurr. When they saw the money, they believed the letter of recommendation. Why should they not, when a fellow only wants what he's already paid for?'

They drew back a little as a horse-bus passed on its route from Montparnasse to Clichy. The man in the cream linen suit unfolded the blue paper and showed it to his friend.

'Very good, Mr Benson.' Billy Kurr was smiling broadly for no apparent reason.

'But the paper, Mr Kurr. I had not expected it to be quite this shade of blue.'

Billy Kurr laughed and took his friend by the arm. They walked almost to the end of the street, where a shop-front of varnished wood advertised *imprimerie* and *papeterie*. The interior smelt of resin, ink, and rubber.

'Look closely, Mr Benson. You see?'

Harry Benson saw. The very same forms for money bills, printed on the same blue paper, lay in boxes on the shelves.

'They are so careful about letters of recommendation and having their cash in advance,' Billy Kurr said quietly, 'but when it comes to stationery, they run down to the corner of the street and buy blank bill forms from a box, as if they were sending for a newspaper.'

Harry Benson's eyes moved as if tracing his thoughts in the air. 'Can it really be so easy, Mr Kurr?'

'See for yourself, Mr Benson. Compare the bill in your pocket with the bill forms in the box. They are the same. All that Rothschild's has filled in might be filled in by any man who could copy the writing.'

'With the right signatures, Mr Kurr, a man could cash them by the dozen.'

'By the score, Mr Benson.'

Benson shook his head, clearing his mind of the astonishment. 'I think, Mr Kurr, that the ground needs to be well prepared. Let them see the colour of the money. Two or three bills of exchange in the normal way, at regular intervals. Then a score of them

144

from our own stable, placed quickly but widely. Paid at least a month before the House of Rothschild knows that they are in existence.'

The wheels of a smart carriage flashed by beyond the stationer's window. There was a glimpse of piled furs, a young woman's face with lips parted and cheeks of a peach-like bloom. Harry Benson's eyes followed her progress into the Boulevard Haussmann.

'Make them comfortable first, Mr Kurr. Reassure them. Let them feel the quality of the money.'

The stationer was approaching them, enquiring.

'I think, Mr Kurr, two boxfuls of that pretty blue stationery with the handsome italic script.'

10

He was dreaming. He knew it but could not help it. Smoke-grey cloud drifted in a haze across the pale moon as it rose above the spruce plantation of Mondragon. Alfred Swain struggled in his sleep with a voice that asked, 'Do you like me, Mr Swain...? Would you die for me, Mr Swain...? Do you love me, Mr Swain...?'

Dream-light fell upon the little row of books by his bed in the attic room. Lyell's *Geology*, *Idylls of the King*, *Recent Advances in Physical Science*, *The Agamemnon of Aeschylus Transcribed by Robert Browning* ...

> myself did nurse
> The much-bewailed Iphigenia ...

What of her? The sweat ran now. 'Iphigenia, Mr Swain... Do you like me, Mr Swain...?' He tried to talk. His tongue lay dead in his mouth, like useless sinew. She was there, a gold Mycenaean necklace on her naked breast, the bulls' heads and amphora flasks. The gold circlet of the slim brown waist. The golden snake that climbed her bare arm. The hips that were palest copper by contrast with her warm gold waist. Her profile to the moon. The tall brow and sharp nose. The dark hair piled and the perfume of sandalwood. 'Do you love me, Mr Swain?'

> Iphigenia – with kindliness –
> His daughter – as the case requires,
> Facing him full, at the rapid-flowing
> Passage of Groans shall – both hands
>   throwing
> Around him – kiss that kindest of sires.

The man who sacrificed his child . . . All along, he should have known who the true criminal was . . . Swain had him now . . .

A huge lungful. It was fresh and sweet as sea air, on the pier at Brighton. He had never known air so sweet before. 'We could go on summer leave, Mr Swain.' He turned to smile at her and saw only the tall brow and the sharp nose, the dark hair piled high and the warm gold of her skin that was Greece, Provence, Egypt . . . The tight-lidded ellipse of the dark odalisque eyes.

Another heaving breath. He was drowning now, like Constable Beresford in the cold current off London Bridge wharf. The water was foul and opaque but he had hold of his prey. The man who sacrificed his child . . . Alfred Swain felt as though his head was rolling over and over. But he held fast to the scoundrel . . . There was no sense of balance at this depth, no fixed point in the dark and muddied world.

> He is borne away who bears away;
> And the killer has all to pay

Who said that? There was no voice this time, as if it was only a thought in the mind. But Alfred Swain held the killer, the lines promised him that, and he was carrying the murderer down to his death. A spluttering cough. That puzzled him. Can a man hear himself choke under water? Does a scream carry through water? He would not have thought so. Tait's *Recent Advances in Physical Science* might have a note on it. But of course, Swain thought, he would never read it because he too was going to die.

That spluttering cough again. And such pain from the water entering his lungs. It surprised him that anything as gentle as water could cause such pain. And blood. He could swear that he was bleeding. Somewhere in his chest. Very deep.

'Mr Swain! For God's sake, Mr Swain!'

Was that her voice? No. It was more like Sergeant Lumley's. What was Lumley doing in these dark man-smothering depths, as Aeschylus might have called them? Still, the killer has all to pay. Hold him tight. Draw him down, down to the infernal regions of night from which there is no return.

'Mr Swain! Let go!'

Lumley again. Let go of what? The killer? By no means! The killer has all to pay! Suspicions of Lumley floated in his mind. The villain was slipping away from him. Hold him, you fool. Arm round the throat. Draw him down. Deeper.

'For Christ's sake, Mr Swain!'

The killer was struggling hard again, making a real fight of it. Hold him! They were falling again now. That spluttering cough. Retching and vomiting. 'Oh, then methought what pain it was to drown...' Who said that? Not a voice, however. Something he had read or heard.

'You'll do for us both, Mr Swain!'

That was a voice, though. Talking under water. How? Tait's *Recent Advances* would tell him how.

Out of the darkness, something hit Alfred Swain, very hard. He broke away and drifted down, down into the silt and clay of the river bed, sinking through it to the very depths of the earth.

11

He woke on his back. Mondragon had gone. There was nothing above him but early morning sky, vaporous blue with a thin watery sun shining almost into his eyes. It must be very early, Swain thought. Hardly more than summer dawn. There was wetness under his hands. It was dew. Someone said, 'Thank God for that.'

It was Lumley's voice. Swain drew breath to reply and almost cried out at the pain in his lungs. And he felt sick, as if he had swallowed sludge from the river bed. Another voice said, 'Someone meant you some harm, chum.'

It was a uniformed officer whom he had never seen before. Swain was about to reprimand the fellow for calling his superior

147

officer 'chum'. The words lodged like a hard ball of cotton in his windpipe. He began to cough, the vomiting retching cough that he had last heard so far below the surface. Someone else lifted his head a little. It was the mild-mannered coroner from Spider McBride's inquest. Had they really thought he was dead? Would they hold an inquest like this in an open field?

'Don't worry,' the coroner said, 'I'm a doctor. You've had a bad accident but you'll be all right. Just lie still.'

'I'm not . . .' Swain got that far and then began the vomiting cough. Something black was coming from his lungs.

'Don't try to talk,' the doctor said, 'we'll give you milk to drink in a moment. You'll be all right.'

'What . . .' It was no good. Black vomiting again.

'Mr Lumley saved you,' the uniformed policeman said. Swain recognized him now as having been on duty at the inquest, though he had never known his name. And he now saw one of the estate workers who had helped to exhume the racehorse.

'Without Mr Lumley, you'd have been a goner,' the man said.

'Drowning . . .' The cough again but not quite so bad this time.

'Smoke,' the estate worker said, 'the room was full of it. You'd be dead b'now, if Mr Lumley hadn't found you.'

'Found . . .?'

'Seems they all thought you were in London still,' the uniformed man said firmly. 'When the alarm was raised, they thought your room was empty. Mr Lumley went through the smoke to look. He saved you.'

'Sally, the maid . . . Knew I was back . . . Late last night . . . She could have told you . . .'

'She might have done,' said the policeman confidently, 'but Miss Sally sleeps down the village with us. Family trouble.'

Swain eased his throat a little and they helped him to sit up. His skin was black, what he could see of it. He was wearing a blanket wrapped round his nightshirt. Lumley's face was marked by grime but he had wiped the worst of it off.

'If someone'll just get the glass of milk,' he said, 'I'll see to Mr Swain. I'm his sergeant.'

In that moment Swain felt ashamed of himself for ever doubting the honesty or decency of the plump port-wine face with its black moustaches and flattened hair. Lumley knew his duty, if ever a man did. Someone came with a glass of milk. Swain drank a little and managed to keep it down. Like the Brighton air, it was sweet and fresh after the nausea of the black flux from his lungs. The others walked off a little and Swain, sitting up properly, found that he was on a lawn just outside the main entrance of the house.

'It seems I owe you a debt, Mr Lumley.'

'Course you don't, Mr Swain. Anyone'd do the same.'

'I fear that may not be true, Mr Lumley. I am grateful, though. Did the house burn?'

Lumley shook his head. 'Everyone thought so at first. I thought it'd be on fire when I got here. One servant woke early and found the passage full of smoke on the attic floor. That made 'em think of fire as well. The old butler or whoever he is came running down the village and they rang the school-house hand-bell for an alarm. Me and some others heard the bell and asked. We was told the place was on fire so we come up here quick as we could. Ten minutes must have gone by then.'

'But no fire?'

'Smoke pouring from one of the top windows. And there would have been a fire before long, Mr Swain. In one of them tall chimneys. But the cause of the smoke was in the kitchens. Seems a rook's nest or something must have fell into a chimney from the top. Blocked it. Every flue that joined the main chimney filled with smoke from the kitchen. They'd banked the kitchen fire when they went to bed and kept it in for the night. The smoke hadn't spread so far down as the kitchen. But your room and another on the attic level, being the highest, got the back draught of the smoke first. They was full of it.'

'Which was the other room?'

'Empty, Mr Swain. They said yours was too until the girl came from the village. By then, I'd gone up to see. Never thought I'd get down that passageway. Still, I kept low and got to the door and opened it. Dear God, Mr Swain, I thought you was dead soon as look at you. There was this dark grey smoke pouring in clouds out of the grate and across the room, acid enough to take the skin off your throat the first breath. I got across and bashed the window open.'

'The window was closed?'

'Yes, Mr Swain. Very unwise that was. Then I took a deep breath

149

of the fresh air and tried to pull you off the bed and to the door. How you struggled!'

'I was drowning,' Swain said thoughtfully, 'drowning.'

'You'd bloody have drowned in there all right. Anyway, what with you fighting and me not able to breathe there was just one thing.'

'What?'

'I hit you, Mr Swain,' said Lumley with pride. 'Then you stopped wriggling about. I managed to get you over my shoulder and down to the hall.'

'Thank you, Mr Lumley,' said Swain mildly, 'I owe my life to you.'

'Anyway,' Lumley continued, 'no one could say if there mightn't be a fire somewhere in the house. So the doctor comes and by then we've got you out here in the fresh air. That was half an hour back.'

'No one else injured?'

'Servants accounted for, Mr Swain. The elderly lady and the young lady came out safe. And that's all about that.'

Swain lay back with a sigh. 'No, Mr Lumley. It's not quite all. I kept thinking as I was dreaming and there was something that came back. Let the killer pay the price.'

'What's that, Mr Swain?'

Swain used Lumley's shoulder to lever himself to his feet. 'It's a line from Mr Browning's translation of the *Agamemnon*, Mr Lumley.'

He felt Lumley stiffen with disapproval as they moved slowly towards the house. The plump sergeant tried to check his feelings without success.

'If you was to live sensible, Mr Swain, and not sit half the night reading story-books and such, you'd remember to open the window before you blew the candle out. And if you'd done that last night and had a 'olesome draught of air, you wouldn't be in the state you are now.'

'If I'd opened the window?'

'Yes,' said Lumley uneasily, as if guessing the sequel.

'That's what worries me.' Swain paused and drew breath again. 'I opened that window, Mr Lumley. I opened it last night to the full extent of the latch, as I have done every night I've slept in that room.'

150

Lumley stared at him. 'I knew it!' he said bitterly. 'I knew there was something rum about all this that I never been told. All that gammon about throwing sacks off the top of the tower! What the devil you done, Mr Swain? What the mischief's been going on here?'

12

That morning, sitting up in bed with Lumley in the chair beside him, Alfred Swain sipped his milk and told his story.

'I couldn't tell you before, Mr Lumley,' he said at last. 'If I had any sense I wouldn't bother you now. But if someone tried to suffocate me last night, it wasn't you. And if you saved my life, you could hardly be part of the conspiracy.'

Lumley stared from the attic window towards the trees, hands folded under the tails of his shabby frock-coat. Black cloth hung from him in ill-pressed folds. He looked from the rear like a mythical beast of a child's fantasy.

'I do hope, Mr Swain ... I just hope this smoke hasn't gone to your head.'

There was a sigh from the bed. 'No, Mr Lumley. There is a conspiracy in the division – a conspiracy to pervert the course of justice, to put it precisely. And there's evidence. I've seen it. Furthermore, I have confronted one of the conspirators, an inspector in the division, and twice been threatened with public disgrace if I proceed.'

But Lumley turned and shook his head. 'You've seen a betting book with everyone's name in it, including yours and mine. It wasn't even Lerici's caper. You never bet at all. I had a bet on the Portland Plate at an office in King Street, same as thousands of people. What's that prove?'

'Possession of the ledger was Lerici's safeguard,' Swain said, 'rather than trust a pair of scoundrels like his racing friends, Benson and Kurr ...'

'Poodle Benson and Billy Kurr? You reckon they're behind all this?'

'I'm sure of it.'

'I'll be smothered,' said Lumley, solemn faced.

'I very nearly was smothered last night, Mr Lumley. That concerns me. The betting book was Lerici's guarantee against two men he never trusted. I think he was their partner once but then, somehow, they turned the tables and used blackmail on him. That was all right as long as he was alive. Once he was dead, the evidence was against them.'

Lumley tightened his face in disbelief. 'That's nothing to do with the division, Mr Swain. No one could be so stupid . . .'

'You ever hear of anyone being arrested for the Turf Insurance fraud, Mr Lumley?'

'No.'

'Or the City of Paris Guaranteed Loan?'

'No.'

'The Egyptian Bond swindle?'

'No.'

'Then who looks stupid now? Benson and Kurr or the Metropolitan Police? Go to the Document Room and look up the letterbook and the day-book in those cases. Study the discrepancies. The Turf Insurance fraud was covered up for two days by Mr Clarke pretending to question a man who was certainly unconscious at that time and died of natural causes next day. Clarke admitted that much to me.'

'You got a witness when he said it?'

'No.'

'Some bloody use that is,' Lumley said, sitting down morosely. 'How many of 'em in it?'

'I can place Clarke, Druscovich, and Meiklejohn. And Palmer.'

'Palmer? He's being made up to bloody chief inspector!'

'He's acted on behalf of swindlers by delaying the investigation and suppressing information. Read the ledgers, Mr Lumley. See for yourself what's happened. But the biggest swindle is yet to come. I'm quite sure of that.'

'So there's four officers out of fifteen being paid by a couple of criminals, if you're right.'

'I'm right, Mr Lumley. Depend upon it. George Clarke threatened me twice. He will swear evidence against me of unprofessional conduct unless I let sleeping dogs lie.'

Lumley buried his head in his hands. 'Christ Almighty,' he said reverently, 'four of them! That's the end of Scotland Yard for all the use it's going to be! Mr Toplady's going to dance the polka when he hears this.'

Swain stretched his hand out and put it on Lumley's arm. 'I don't know where Mr Toplady stands in all this. He's to hear nothing. You understand? Nothing.'

Lumley blew up his moustaches with a puff of laughter at the absurdity of it. 'Toplady's not been bought! Just look at him! He's not human enough to be bought.' The sergeant's protest grew shrill with anguish. 'And you've got to tell someone higher up. If there's anything in this at all . . . You could end up looking as though you might have been part of it!'

'I've already told Mr Abrahams. He's solicitor for the Lerici estate and he acted for the Comtesse de Goncourt in the Turf Insurance fraud.'

'For God's sake, Mr Swain, you've got to tell one of ours. You're going after Palmer and he's your senior officer! Go to someone above him. Go to Toplady!'

Swain nodded. 'I'll go to someone all right. Someone above Toplady as well, if I have to.'

They sat in silence for several minutes. Lumley puffed and sighed but could contain himself no longer.

'Have you thought, Mr Swain . . . Have you thought what's going to happen to you if you're wrong about all this?'

Swain turned wistfully away from his contemplation of the Poet Laureate's *Idylls of the King*, standing in the row of books.

'Yes, Mr Lumley. I've thought of that. It seems to me that I haven't thought of much else for the past few weeks. I almost gave up. But then I tackled George Clarke. As soon as I got close to the subject, he blew up. He threatened me with such things that I should be destroyed unless I left the matter well alone. Innocent men don't do that.'

Lumley waited, then addressed the unspoken fear. 'And what happened last night was an accident, was it? That rook's nest fell down and blocked the chimney? It wasn't someone who shoved enough grass and debris up the chimney to block it and then shut your window for good measure?'

'It doesn't matter, Mr Lumley.'

'Doesn't matter?'

'No, Mr Lumley. I want it to be known that everything I have

153

discovered is written down and placed in the hands of an attorney. The document will name the names of the suspects. In the event of my sudden death, they will be called to account for their dishonesty. They may also be called to account for murder. Meantime, they might be well advised to pray for my long life and continued health. Mention it to Inspector Clarke, if you see him first.'

'Where'd you get an idea like that, Mr Swain?'

Alfred Swain smiled. 'From the late John Posthumous Lerici. I only hope it does me more good than it did him.'

He spoke slowly and his eyelids were heavy. Even the *Idylls of the King* would have been too much at that moment. What he wanted most of all was a deep and dreamless sleep. A sleep where there would be no fugitive murderers and no phantoms of Iphigenia. Lumley watched for a moment and then, getting to his feet, tiptoed from the room.

13

This time it was Major Montgomery who was saluted by the bank-porter in black and gold livery. The spruce figure in the summer linen suit strode up the steps and into the vestibule of the Western Branch in Burlington Gardens. No one kept him waiting in the banking-hall on this occasion. The appointment with Colonel Francis, manager of the Bank of England's Western Branch, was timed to the minute. That was a sure proof of the visitor's acceptance.

At first the major had been a little concerned that the colonel might seize upon their mutual military experience as a subject of small talk. He might even look for Major Hugh Montgomery in the Army List. Indeed, had he known of the manager's military rank, the client would have presented himself as plain Mr Montgomery. Happily the subject had been deflected on his first visit by a reference to the major's military service as that of a volunteer officer in the Union Army of General Grant. Colonel Francis was far too polite to indicate that he considered such an officer to be no proper officer at all. All the same, Major Montgomery sensed the opinion and was content. He played up the part of the outward-going transatlantic cousin, English by right but international by inclination, bringing with him an air of the cigar-stand, the spittoon, and the brass-railed mahogany bar.

The two men sat in leather chairs either side of the broad partners desk with its china-shaded lamps. Net curtains shielded Lord Uxbridge's drawing-room from the morning sun. The colonel took the bills of exchange which the major handed him from his portfolio, the blue paper of Rothschild's English Bureau on the top.

'Well,' said the major, nodding at the blue paper, expanding a little and talking like one who had crossed more oceans than he cared to count, 'I guess that article should be good enough for your Scrutiny Committee.'

Colonel Francis glanced at the Rothschild's bill and smiled. 'What have you in all, sir? What sum to deposit this time?'

'Six and a half thousand to add to the total,' the major said comfortably. 'From now on, the credits should come quite thick and fast. Spring is the time when Lake Michigan does its worst. We aim to start work in the fall, protecting Lakeshore Drive by building up a rampart for next season. Our European subscriptions will be called in during the next few weeks. What notice will you require precisely?'

The colonel, who had been studying the bills through a lorgnette, looked up. The glance he gave the major was pleasant enough but he was no longer smiling.

'Notice for what?'

'Why,' said the major amiably, 'the conversion and transfer.'

'In what sense?'

The major laughed outright at his own foolishness in not making the matter plain. 'My aim, Colonel Francis, is to have about a hundred thousand raised from European investment this summer. A part of that will be deposited here. When the time comes, it would be most convenient if that amount could be transferred into United States Bonds, the bulk of which might have to be transferred from these shores soon after that. In a month or two, the Chicago scheme will need to spend some of its capital.'

Colonel Francis seemed easier but he still spoke with a certain reserve. 'If you want United States Bonds, sir, the bank can obtain those for you at a few days' notice. Subject to the limit of the deposits credited to you here. As to the transfer, you may do that at any time afterwards.'

Major Montgomery's hands opened and closed again. 'Admirable,' he said.

The colonel still showed caution, as if he feared his visitor might misunderstand him but his manner grew more relaxed.

'If you choose to withdraw money in United States Bonds, and if at that time the sum of a hundred thousand in bills of exchange has been authorized by the Scrutiny Committee or the sum has been paid in specie, there will be no difficulty. A week's notice will suffice.'

Major Montgomery's silver-tarnished tooth glinted a little in his smile. At length he and Colonel Francis looked at one another like two men who are well pleased with their agreement, though each may allowably be more pleased for himself than for the other.

4

SUMMER LEAVE

1

Evening sun fell deep yellow as an apricot aslant the leaded panes
of Mondragon's western gallery. Upon its walls hung the treasures of the house, the art collected by John Posthumous Lerici. A
perfume of sun-warmed curtains and the oily scent of varnished
oil paint hung in the air. Alfred Swain, sitting at a little table of
inlaid walnut, drew a line under his diary entry, aware of Amalia
de Brahami straight-backed on the settee, picking at the stretched
linen of her embroidery hoop. Of Giovanna Lerici there was no
sign. The stalwart maid Basileia sat at a distance beyond her young
mistress, black as a nun, darning a basket of clothes. From time
to time, Swain met the servant's gaze accidentally. The dark eyes
were deep and expressionless as stone.

Swain dipped the pen in ink again. On the opposite wall, Dante
Gabriel Rossetti's *Venus Astarte*, a reworking of the artist's *Astarte
Syriaca*, hung in dark voluptuous menace. Was it from this that
Lerici drew inspiration for his romantic fiction? Or had the fiction
come first and the purchase of the painting afterwards? Swain
gazed at the billowing black hair, the heavy flesh under tight
translucent silk, eyes that looked through and beyond the viewer,
venomous lips, the sleek gloss of bare shoulders and arms, golden
girdles and tethers. The figure mingled abandon and menace.

He had reason to ponder the mind of the artist. A few years
before, Swain had stood at night by the light of flares in Highgate
Cemetery, behind canvas screens, and watched the coffin of Elizabeth Rossetti, formerly Lizzie Siddal the golden-haired bride,
brought to the surface in order that her husband's poems should
be retrieved. After six years, it was said, she had neither aged nor

decayed. That was not quite true, in Swain's recollection. The skin and hair had a waxy impression of the living woman but death had done its work beneath.

He put the memory of that earlier case from his mind. The sun was moving across Venus Astarte, brightening *The Beguiling of Merlin* by Sir Edward Burne-Jones. The temptress, ensnared among forest branches and bright flowers, lured her victim. Black hair swept across ivory flesh and the limbs were more suggestively concealed by a thin silk drawn tight enough for the flesh to shine through.

'A twist of gold was round about her hair' – the lines of the poem filled Swain's thoughts – 'A robe of samite without price, that more expressed than hid her, clung about her lissom limbs, in colour like the satin-shining palm . . .'

He sighed. The dream of Vivien and Merlin . . . 'Trample me, dear feet . . .' Alfred Swain tried to imagine Mrs Beresford asking him to trample her and failed to conjure up the image. Would it be more exciting that way, to trample or be trampled upon? In his prosaic constabulary way, Swain thought, he could not see the point of it. Amalia de Brahami, though . . . He could imagine Amalia de Brahami prostrating herself, golden nudity ornamented with barbaric treasure, so that her lover might trample her . . . or rising in the jewels of Mycenae to trample in her turn. The wheedling self-abasement of the beautiful Vivien echoed in his thoughts.

> 'O Merlin, do you love me?' and again
> 'O Merlin, do you love me?' and once more,
> 'Great Master, do you love me? . . .'

'Do you love me, Mr Swain . . .? Would you die for me, Mr Swain . . .?'

Was that where she had got it from? Out of a poem? She was looking away from him, staring down at her needlework. Unlike Vivien or Venus Astarte, the skin was warm as Greece or Egypt. By contrast, the tall brow and the sharp nose, the dark hair piled and coiled, showed Rossetti's demoness for what she was, a pale and pudding-faced middle-class English miss! Undress such pagan beauty as theirs and you would find the pink impress of a whalebone corset or the pattern of a Windsor chair upon the flesh.

158

Amalia de Brahami . . . Iphigenia . . . As he brought the names together, Alfred Swain knew that he had done so long ago in dreams and half-thoughts. How could he ever have been unaware?

From the depths of an ill-remembered dream the lines of the *Agamemnon* in Robert Browning's version floated into recollection, unbidden like a corpse to the surface of a lake.

> Some vice-devising miserable mood
> Of madness, and first woe of all the brood,
> The sacrificer of his daughter . . .

A bell rang, far off in the house. The old woman, Giovanna Lerici, impatient, dying . . . Presently it rang again. Basileia stood up, put her darning to one side, and went to answer it. Alone with the girl, Swain took his dangerous chance.

'Why did they call you Iphigenia?'

Though she did not start, the needle pricked her finger. Amalia de Brahami made a soft sound deep in her throat and sucked at a tiny welling of dark crimson blood. 'Like the vampire, she has been dead many times and known the secrets of the grave . . .' Where the devil had that come from? Walter Pater, in *The Renaissance*, writing of the *Mona Lisa*. A copy of the work was in Alfred Swain's shelf of books. The Pre-Raphaelite models were sham, not vampires but types of the plain English miss who sulks because she is sent to bed without supper. Amalia de Brahami, however, was another matter. Swain caught her eye and repeated the question.

'I asked you why they called you Iphigenia.'

She shifted her narrow hips and faced him on the settee, straight-backed. 'Who calls me Iphigenia, Mr Swain?'

'You walk at night,' Swain said quickly, 'naked in the gold of a Mycenaean princess. Gold that was stolen or trumpery that was bought from a market-stall in Athens. Who knows?'

'You dream of me, Mr Swain. That is all.' She frowned at her needlework. 'I like the idea of your dreaming of me. It pleases me. Do I send you pleasant dreams, Mr Swain?'

'It is no dream,' Swain said. 'Who first called you Iphigenia?'

'It was a joke,' she said wistfully. 'No, not a joke. Something private. It was nickname and when my father had a splendid horse

159

it was called Iphigenia after me. No, not after me but after the nickname. That second time it was a joke.'

'But where did it begin?' Swain asked patiently.

Amalia de Brahami sighed and turned to him again. 'Well, then, Mr Swain! If you will have it, so you shall. My father first called me Iphigenia. Does that satisfy you?'

Alfred Swain felt foolish, literal-minded and obtuse. 'No,' he said. 'Why should he call you Iphigenia? Evidently, he did not sacrifice you to the gods for a fair wind to Troy.'

She sighed, shook her head and covered her face with her hands. 'You thin-blooded fool,' she said, almost in a gasp, 'I was my father's willing sacrifice, two years ago. Is that too hard for you to understand?'

Alfred Swain sat in the evening sunlight through the gothic windows. Venus Astarte and the wily Vivien brooded over him, heavy-fleshed.

'As you put it, I do not understand.'

'A fisherman in Nauplia or a housewife in Corinth would know,' she said in a helpless murmur, having gone too far to draw back. 'John Posthumous Lerici was my lover.' She took her hands away and stared at him, tragic but dry-eyed.

'But was he not your father?'

Amalia de Brahami's ellipse of dark eyes studied him pityingly. 'He was my father and my lover. He was everything to me. There was no one else. Now do you understand?'

'Your father debauched you?' The word sounded ridiculous as soon as he had uttered it, a cry from stage melodrama. How else could he phrase it?

She gave an exclamation of contempt. 'You talk like an English clergyman, Mr Swain. Presently you will want to reform me.'

'Your grandmother,' Swain asked quickly, 'Signora Lerici. Does she know?'

The girl almost flew at him in her impatience. 'My grandmother is a foolish old woman who thinks it is still 1824 and that the world cares about Lord Byron. She has not lived for more than fifty years.'

Neither of them spoke for a moment. A shaft of late sun caught a universe of dust particles spinning like little worlds in its brilliance against the pattern of the mullions.

160

'There are questions that must be asked,' Swain said quietly. 'Your father forced you to obey his demands?'

She stared at him in amazement. 'Forced me? Forced me to obey? My father was a god to me, Mr Swain.'

'And your mother? Was she a goddess to you?'

'She was nothing to me. I was so young when she died that I remember nothing of her. My father was everything. Whatever I was to him, I was proud to be . . .'

'Very well. Then tell me, was a child born as a result of your pride?'

'No!'

He thought at first it was an answer to the question but it was Amalia's refusal.

'By what right do you ask such a thing? You wish to pry behind the curtains and peep through the keyhole at it all!'

Swain controlled his feelings. 'I wish to know the truth. Though I may have cause, I bear you no malice for whatever has happened here.'

'Malice?' She sneered at him now. 'You would find cause for malice against me because you saw a vision of me naked? My father despised the English for such hateful prudery as yours.'

Swain kept his eyes on her. 'I have no interest in visions nor prudery. Only in the laws of chemistry and combustion. I believe that someone tried, half-heartedly perhaps, to kill me by suffocation. If I was intended to die, I should at least like to know my crime. You have nothing to fear from me apart from that.'

At first Amalia de Brahami seemed surprised. Then she stood up, dropping her sewing on the chair.

'Whether you live or die is nothing to me, Mr Swain. What happened to you is nothing to do with me. I care so little for you that I would lift a finger neither to damn nor save you.'

She turned and walked rapidly from the room. Swain thought that he heard a first sob break from her as her skirts whispered on the stairs. He had stood up at the same time as the girl, an instinct of courtesy. Now he went across to the other chair and for the first time looked down at the needlework. It was far from complete but two names were stitched in round the edge of the design. One of his few accomplishments in Greek had been to learn the letters of the alphabet well enough to remember them

161

all. He made out the names of Procne, Philomela, and Tereus. The design itself showed three birds: a swallow, a nightingale, and a hoopoe.

At first glance, it was an entirely suitable design for a young lady's needlework. But Alfred Swain was a reading man of the modern world and knew the legend as the story of Itylus in Mr Swinburne's poem. The sister of a queen raped by a king and her tongue cut out to silence her. Her revelation of the deed by working a tapestry with the crime depicted upon it for her sister to see. The queen's revenge by slaughtering the son of her marriage and serving him in a stew to his father. The terrible discovery that the father had consumed his own children. The gods, taking pity at last, had transformed the king, the queen, and her sister into a hoopoe, a swallow, and a nightingale. Swain put the embroidery down again, the design of the father who consumes his child. Behind the ladylike delicacy of the needlework lay a horror in the human soul.

The light at the leaded windows of the Western Gallery was turning to a cool grey. The maidservant who lodged with the policeman's family in the village came in and lit the lamps, one by one. Venus Astarte in the shadows looked down at Alfred Swain with a vicious contempt. He thought it was the mouth. Why should anyone choose to paint a mouth like that? To please John Posthumous Lerici, perhaps, the consumer of his own child. Was it painted at his command?

And what of the Greek virgin who yielded to Lord Byron's son, gave birth to a beautiful daughter, and then died? Amalia de Brahami spoke almost with contempt of her. Who had taught her that? Was it not all a little too convenient? The neatness of it troubled Alfred Swain in his policeman's common sense.

'My father was a god to me, Mr Swain.' He could hear those words most clearly of all and he believed them. But of what world had John Posthumous Lerici been a god? Surely the dark Hades over which Venus Astarte and her sisters presided, not the fleshy virgins of Pre-Raphaelite dreams but the dark spirits of another world.

Alfred Swain gathered up his papers and climbed the stairs to his attic room. In a few days he would have seen the last of Mondragon. No one would dare to harm him now. He knew too

162

much, for all the good that would do him. In the low-ceilinged attic room he looked at the little row of his books and hesitated to make a choice. Not Mr Swinburne's perverse erotics tonight. Certainly not *The Idylls of the King*. Not even Mr Browning's *Agamemnon*. Particularly not Mr Browning's *Agamemnon*, for which at other times he had so great an admiration. Something to refresh his mind and challenge his brain, like a cold plunge. In a flood of sunlit reason he saw what his choice should be, taking up Tait's *Recent Advances in Physical Science*. For the next hour, Alfred Swain sat immersed in the problem of why a tin box in flame would turn red hot inside when by the laws of physics it should have turned blue hot. The answer escaped him but he felt a good deal better at the end of the chapter.

2

'Mr Allardyce the village constable did it,' Lumley said. 'Fished all that stuff out of the chimney. Took his time and did it careful. Nothing's ever going to be proved, Mr Swain. Never.'

They sat in a corner of the four-ale bar on a plain wooden bench. A murmur of conversation in the smoke-hazed air gave them privacy.

'I don't want revenge or anything like that,' Swain said, 'but if there's someone prepared to murder, it won't stop with me.'

Sergeant Lumley put his tankard down, wiped his lip, and shook his head. Drink turned his plump face a deeper plum-red.

'Allardyce don't know. The way that stuff was in the chimney, it could have been a rook's nest from last year that just fell in.'

Swain looked at him coldly and Lumley took refuge in another sip of beer.

'You don't see it, do you, Mr Lumley? Whatever was in the chimney was nothing in itself. Twigs, grass, earth whatever it was.'

'It was enough to bloody near cooper you,' Lumley said aggressively. He had not saved Alfred Swain in order to be spoken to like this.

'No, Mr Lumley!' Two men sitting by the dead inglenook looked round at the force of the exclamation and then turned away again. 'If anything had coopered me, as you put it, it would have been the window. The smoke might have come down the chimney and into the room, but if the window had been open it would have found its way out. The room might have smelt of burnt grass but it would have been full of oxygen not carbon dioxide.'

'There's no telling,' Lumley said sceptically.

'Listen to me, Mr Lumley. Someone closed that window. There was no point to that unless that same person knew about the blocked chimney. And no one would have known about it unless they'd actually blocked it or been told by the person who had. It was no accident. Is that plain enough for you now?'

There was convivial shouting and a clatter of glass from the buttery hatch.

'But your door was bolted, Mr Swain. I had to kick the bloody thing open!'

'No, Mr Lumley. No one came in at the door. That window was closed by someone on the outside, walking along the gully, on the leads behind the battlements.'

Lumley screwed his face up. 'But who?'

'A ghost,' Swain said thoughtfully, 'a ghost from an ancient city of gods and heroes.'

Lumley relaxed, chortled, and wiped his mouth.

'Get away, Mr Swain! You had me thinking all sorts then. Ghosts and such! The wind blew the window shut, that's what you meant. Ain't it?'

'Yes,' Swain said in the same subdued voice, 'I expect that's what I meant.'

3

Major Montgomery settled his linen jacket upon his shoulders and gazed appreciatively at the elegant seventeenth-century house which now contained the Bartolotti Bank. He smiled at the urns and busts, the stone foliage in all its Roman elegance. From the surface of the quiet Amsterdam canal, the image of architectural grace shimmered and redoubled in the dull browns and greens of a Rembrandt masterpiece. The major sighed.

'Now, Mr Kurr, let every man do his duty this afternoon and we shall not be in the slightest danger. Give me five minutes to

164

present myself. Remember the six banks on which the bills of credit are drawn. The Bank of England they won't query because we have a letter to them from Colonel Francis. They will probably send a messenger to the Amsterdam branch of Rothschild's because it's only a few minutes' walk. When they find those two are the genuine article, they won't query the rest. Why should they? The smaller houses have no correspondents here. But they insure, Mr Kurr. Bartolotti know someone will pay them, if it's only the bank insurers. We must watch they don't try to send a wire, however.'

'Right, Mr Benson,' said Billy Kurr firmly, 'I'll watch from here. There's a good enough view.'

'Five minutes or so after I've gone in, you will very probably see a clerk come out in a hurry. See if he's got something like the Rothschild bill in his hand. Follow him. If he goes to Rothschild's, there's no cause for alarm. If he goes anywhere else, anywhere to send a wire for instance, you know what to do.'

Billy Kurr beamed. 'I stop him and say he's to come back to Bartolotti this instant. There's been an accident. I run ahead to Bartolotti's, gasping for breath, and say that Madame Montgomery's carriage has overturned and her ladyship is trapped. That gets you out the door with the bills in your hand again as soon as the clerk comes back.'

The little man nodded. 'Right, Mr Kurr. Still, once they've taken the main bill to Rothschild's, they'll let the insurers worry over the rest. As soon as I'm out of that door again, for whatever reason, we'll be on our way. The Bank of England bill and the Rothschild bill are the genuine article. Three thousand. The others ain't. Five thousand. But they can't check that without telegraphing. We'll take all the money together as a bill addressed to the Banque des Pays-Bas in Brussels. Keep the tickets ready in case there's a hurry.'

Billy Kurr grinned and patted his pocket.

'Good,' the major said. 'Tomorrow, Mr Kurr, our three thousand may yield eight thousand in bills at Brussels. Two days more and that's drawn out in Paris from Rothschild and Baring. Four days and it goes into the Bank of England City Branch in Threadneedle Street, where they don't know your phiz nor mine. And there's the promise of another bill to follow from Rothschild. They'll put the first one before the Scrutiny Committee and they'll find it's the real article. They won't be so nosy over the second one. With luck, they won't know they've been stung until a month after we've gone. Even Rothschild's paper isn't called in again for a couple of months.'

Billy Kurr leant over the rail, hawked, and spat into the canal. 'Suppose the bank – our bank – was to send the bills back to the guarantors straight off, Mr Benson? How should we go on then?'

The little man chuckled. 'We should call on our friends, Mr Kurr. They've had enough out of us in all conscience. They'd give us time enough to get clear. It's their necks as well as ours now. But it won't happen.'

'You quite sure, Mr Benson?'

'Opening of the new accounting period today, Mr Kurr. Banks want the best price for the international bills they've accepted. They wait a bit to see how the rates go, how many francs or guilders to the pound. They might trade after a few weeks but not before then. One clear month, Mr Kurr. By the time they come sniffing, they won't smell us any more.'

The two men looked relaxed and good-natured. What they proposed would hurt no one greatly in the end. Several minutes later, the dapper linen-suited figure of Major Montgomery presented himself at the door of the Bartolotti Bank. The guardian of the door was courteous but powerfully built. He led the major into the lobby which retained its air of a grand mansion on the Herengracht.

Ten minutes later, Major Montgomery sat across the table from Wilhelm van Mander of the Bartolotti Bank in the elegant high-ceilinged room which East India traders had adorned with profits from ivory and spice. He felt more like a dinner guest than a customer. On the table, upside-down to him, lay the letter signed by Colonel Francis, the heading of the Bank of England Western Branch printed boldly. Even upside-down, Major Montgomery could recognize those phrases which opened the way to the vaults of European finance. 'A valued customer of ours, Major Hugh Montgomery . . . guarantor of the City of Chicago Loan . . . our circular letter of credit . . . pleasure in honouring any drafts which he may have occasion to draw . . .'

Van Mander looked up with an expression of concern.

'We could not, of course, honour drafts on the basis of this letter, sir. It is not addressed directly to the Bartolotti Bank.'

Major Montgomery smiled amiably at the misunderstanding. 'I should not for one moment expect it. I offer the letter as an introduction. The bills I wish to encash, principally that drawn on Messrs N. M. Rothschild of Paris, are guaranteed in themselves. Since you might wish to confirm that I am the authorized holder of the bills, I offer you this letter from my friend Colonel Francis of the Bank of England.'

Even as he said it, Major Montgomery knew that 'friend' was exactly the right word. Doubt and embarrassment left the banker's face. But Major Montgomery had not finished with him yet.

'The bill drawn upon Messrs Rothschild is for far the greatest amount. No doubt you will wish to present that to them. I can wait while it is done. It will be no inconvenience.'

Van Mander looked hard at the bill and then shook his head. 'I see no reason.'

Major Montgomery smiled gently, concealing a riot of exultation in his heart. Van Mander gathered the bills and stood up. He was about to turn away towards the cashier's office when he paused.

'I do not wish to be impertinent, Major Montgomery, but since the largest of the bills of exchange is drawn upon Rothschild's, would you not have done better to go to them?'

The smile on the major's face was still gentle and unfaltering. 'I hope not, sir. I was told that bills would be discounted more favourably here, a better rate of exchange, than Rothschild's might offer. I trust you will prove me right.'

The smile became a little wan and self-mocking at the end of this. The frock-coated figure walked away and Major Montgomery knew he was right. They would not even bother sending the largest of the bills of exchange to Rothschild's bank, ten minutes away, for confirmation. Why should they? It looked genuine and it was genuine. It would be paid in any case. Under no circumstances would Rothschild's risk their reputation by acknowledging a forgery for a comparatively small amount to other banks. Moreover, the circular letter of credit, already endorsed in Paris for 15,000 francs, showed beyond question that Major Montgomery was genuine as well. Harry Benson had almost begun to believe in the major's existence for himself. He could close his eyes and imagine

Shiloh and Fredericksburg, Vicksburg and Bull Run.

An hour and a half later, there was a hiss of steam, a hoarse panting, and a shudder as the Brussels express pulled out of the Amsterdam central station, past the wharves and the masts of the dockside, and began its crossing of the level green pasture with vast skies and long horizons. The ancient towns with their crowding gables slid past the window, Leiden, Delft, then the port of Rotterdam.

'Mr Benson, you hear anything more of trouble from Policeman Swain at all, do you?'

'I hear of him, Mr Kurr, occasionally. From one of the others. A prig, Mr Kurr. Prigs are always the easiest – and they don't need paying.'

'George Clarke thought he might make trouble, Mr Benson. Prigs can do that too. I'd feel easier if he could be bought, somehow.'

Harry Benson smiled. 'Taken care of, Mr Kurr. There's things could happen to Policeman Swain that would make him wish his old mother had stayed a virgin.'

And the two friends laughed at the richness of it all. Each thought the other a perfect match. Billy Kurr basked in the confidence of Harry Benson's technique. The dapper little figure was sure-footed as a tightrope dancer or a stage conjurer. Harry Benson felt safe with Billy Kurr. Violence was not part of the plan. Yet Billy Kurr was a man who could hurt without any true ill feelings or, indeed, without feelings of any kind. Harry Benson closed his eyes and multiplied three thousand by three and the result by three again. Multiply that by, say, five and it would be close to the end of the month. But it would also be close to one hundred and forty thousand pounds.

'Policeman Swain got a doxy, they reckon,' Billy Kurr said suddenly. 'Got a dolly that does him stunning.'

Harry Benson opened his eyes and smiled. 'Policeman Swain is likely to have more doxies than he knows what to do with. He may wish that he should never see another so long as he lives.'

Billy Kurr grinned and bit the end off a cigar.

Brighton and back for three-and-six. Swain had promised her and he had kept his word.

A bright green sea stretched glassily away in the languorous afternoon. Hardly a ripple seemed to break on the shingle below the promenade. Gulls hovered and dipped as if to frustrate the aim of young men in rowing-boats, whose guns popped and spat at them. But the wind was cool and most of the bathing machines were deserted. Yachts lay on the shingle like fish on a slab. Only the *Victoria and Albert* and the *Honeymoon* were afloat with their white sails hoisted and their groups of giggling passengers. A party of young women on grey and piebald hacks cantered along the firm sand below the shingle. Gold and silver beaded nets covered their shining hair with multi-coloured feathers in their jaunty little hats.

Along the promenade, the men in peg-top trousers and coloured coats seemed dowdy by comparison with their wives and sweethearts under full sail. The long suspension-work web of the Chain Pier stretched out into the white-capped waves.

'It's lovely, Mr Swain,' said Mrs Beresford simply, 'isn't it?' She tightened the pressure of her arm upon his, where they were linked.

'Yes,' said Alfred Swain absently, 'very.'

They had almost reached the pier, its little kiosks busy despite the cool breeze.

'I shouldn't think France was very far from here,' Mrs Beresford said.

'About four hours, I believe. And, of course, another four hours to get back.'

'Really? So a person could have breakfast here, lunch in Boulogne, and have dinner back in Brighton the same night?'

'So I believe.'

Mrs Beresford sighed with contentment at the thought. The band was playing on the end of the pier and the approach to its gates was busy with toffee-sellers, a man with a performing dog, and the little black tent of the beach photographer.

'This is where Papa used to cut silhouettes,' Mrs Beresford said wistfully. 'No one does it now. It's all photographs done the same day. Times change.'

'Indeed,' said Swain courteously, following her through the turn-stile and on to the planking of the pier deck.

'When we come down here on summer leave,' she went on, 'we could go to France, just for lunch.'

'We certainly could.'

She stopped, the wind from the sea ruffling the edges of her hair under the plain bonnet. 'Everything's all right, is it, Mr Swain? I mean there's nothing wrong, is there?'

He took her arm again, reassuringly. 'Nothing in the world, Mrs Beresford. I don't think I've quite recovered from the accident with the chimney. My mind seems a little slow. Preoccupied. There are so many things, so close, that I can't quite see.'

The band had stopped playing. Its red-coated musicians formed up at the pier gates and moved off smartly in formation, past the Royal York Hotel and the oriental domes of the Pavilion, back towards the barracks on the Lewes Road.

'That scoundrel who was killed in Greece,' Swain said. 'That man debauched his own daughter.'

'Mr Swain!' She pulled away and stared at him again, shocked by the very mention of such a thing.

'I'm sorry,' Swain said, 'but the young lady claims it was so.'

'But it's horrible!' Despite her tone, he was relieved to feel her arm back in his again. 'There's things I don't understand, Mr Swain, nor I don't want to. Things where hanging is too good.'

'And murder, Mrs Beresford? Would murder be too good for him?'

'I don't suppose her mother would think so,' Mrs Beresford said solemnly. 'Poor little mite.'

'Her mother was a Greek girl from Argos or Corinth who died a long time ago. Soon after the child was born, I believe. The man was murdered for gold.' They stood at the head of the pier looking out to sea. 'I don't understand,' Swain said. 'All this summer it seems as if a story that was told long ago has been coming to life again. A great king who sacrificed his daughter and was murdered in revenge. But it's not quite right. This man wasn't a great king, only a charlatan. And there are people missing from it. Yet somehow it seems true. And as for the place where it all happened, I can't get that out of my mind. It's like being haunted by a place rather than by a ghost.'

Mrs Beresford sighed again and reproached him as gently as she knew how. 'All those books, Mr Swain. They don't always do good to read. When we come down here on summer leave, you'll see the benefit from leaving them behind.'

Swain looked at her uneasily. 'I was hoping to read Professor Ruskin. *The Seven Lamps of Architecture*. It's a subject I'd like to know more about.'

Again she squeezed his arm gently with hers. 'No, Mr Swain, dear,' she said persuasively, 'I don't think so. I'm quite sure Professor Ruskin would rather you had a nice holiday.'

5

They walked back to keep their appointment with Mr and Mrs Nokes at the seaside lodgings. In the sunlit afternoon, the streets of tailors' shops and ironmongers, coffee grinders and caged-bird sellers beyond the Pavilion and the Dome seemed almost deserted. Here and there, on dummies outside the tailors' premises, were displayed wide-sleeved silks and taffetas with gold buckles. Mrs Beresford slowed her step appreciatively as the couple walked past them.

Alfred Swain, looking about him, noticed two boys, one fair and one dark, with their rubber ball. They were patting it as they ran. The summer afternoon echoed to the *plop-plop-plop* of their progress down the street of little shops. They were ten years old, perhaps twelve, dressed in the ragged suiting which was the familiar costume of children in the alleys and slum courts. The two boys trotted down the quiet street, still patting the ball, bouncing it before them. A hundred yards ahead of Swain and Mrs Beresford, almost at the corner of the road, was a cutler's with canteens of tableware, cast-off spoons and forks in trays on the pavement trestles.

The two boys bounced their ball level with the shop. Then the dark-haired child gave it a hard oblique slap. It rose in an arc and disappeared into the cutler's shop, the two boys running after it. Swain heard a cry, a slithering crash, and then a man's curse, shouted with all his strength. As if in answer to this, a crowd of a dozen ragged children came round the corner, descending on the cutler's pavement-trestles like rooks on a cornfield. Trays and canteens vanished as the two boys in the shop overturned tables, brought down shelves, and trapped the proprietor in the debris of his own premises. The children in the street snatched their booty and fled.

Bystanders watched them. As the youngsters took to their heels, they went in all directions. To pursue one was to lose the rest. While the onlookers hesitated, the two boys appeared from the shop. One of them had a canteen of cutlery under his arm and was sprinting like a champion. His companion paused just long enough to overturn the trestles of discarded knives and forks, which hit the pavement with a salvo like artillery fire. Another shopman, in pursuit, lost his footing on the scattered cutlery and sat down heavily with a yell of pain and frustration. He seemed unable to get up.

By this time, the boy with the canteen had dodged across the street and was pelting along the far pavement in the same direction as the rest. Swain measured the distance. The boy had sixty or seventy yards start by now. There was no point in trying to close such a gap and merely looking ridiculous. From behind him, however, he heard a sudden clatter and saw that a uniformed constable had sprung his rattle. The figure in heavy boots and serge was plodding unavailingly after the sprinting boy.

Swain thanked God that someone else was obliged to make a display of himself on this occasion. But just then a smartly dressed man in a dapper linen suit turned from perusing the display of prints in a curio shop on the far pavement. The boy was almost level with him. Indeed, he swerved into the roadway to avoid the man's reach. Without seeming to move his arm, the slightly built man in the expensive suit twirled his polished cane. It shot between the legs of the sprinting boy, tripping him decisively. It seemed, at a distance, as if his legs were tangled on the stick. He fell headlong, the canteen crashing, breaking open and filling the road with slithering cutlery.

The uniformed policeman pounded harder. But the boy was up again, performing an injured run that was partly a skip and a hop. Then he got into his stride again and vanished round the corner. The uniformed policeman stopped.

'All right,' he said confidently to the nearest bystanders. 'We

172

know 'im. We'll find 'im and his mob. Just so long as they ain't got away with the goods.'

The man in the cream linen suit was smiling with pleasure at his accomplishment. A larger man, his companion, stood behind him in a checked suit that suggested sporting pubs and betting offices. The cutler was thanking the first man and a shopboy was collecting the scattered cutlery. Swain had begun to turn away when the smaller man in the linen suit caught his eye and smiled.

'Mr Swain!' The hand grasped his own before he could avoid it. The pressure was firm and friendly. As if to emphasize his good faith, the little man clung to Swain's hand for somewhat longer than was necessary or agreeable. 'Mr Alfred Swain, I believe? Allow me. Henry Benson of Adelaide Crescent, Hove. And, if I may present him, Mr William Kurr, my adviser. Mr Swain, Billy, is a Scotland Yard man. One of the best! One of the very finest, by Josh. How fortunate you should be here as an extra witness, Mr Swain.'

'I don't suppose an extra witness will be necessary,' Swain said coolly.

Benson beamed at him, the mouth smiling and the eyes blank as stone. 'But who better than you, sir? And your charming companion. Won't you introduce us, Mr Swain?'

There were too many onlookers, Swain thought, to deal with the man as he deserved. He bridled his anger.

'Mrs Beresford. The late Mr Beresford was also an officer of the Metropolitan Police.'

The cream-suited man looked as though he had been cast into desolation by the reference to Beresford's loss.

'Ah, yes,' he said, woebegone, 'of course. Dear lady, words cannot express... The debt is beyond... What little I can, I contribute annually to the Police Benevolent Fund. It is a pleasure rather than a duty.'

'Mrs Beresford is a lady of independent means,' Swain said sharply.

'And glad I am to hear it, sir,' said Benson meekly. 'Yet if you would both care to honour me by a visit to Adelaide Crescent during your stay here, I should do my utmost to make you welcome as best I can.'

Billy Kurr grinned and spoke to no one in particular. 'I don't know where we should be if we hadn't Mr Swain to help us on our way. I really don't. What he's done for us can't be repaid by money alone. True as I stand here.'

'We are here only for the day to visit friends,' Mrs Beresford said with prim courtesy, 'and must be back in London this evening.'

From the tone of her voice, Swain thought, she was as repelled as he by Benson's oily and insinuating charm. Benson's dark moustache moved as the lips performed their practised smile.

'The loss is mine, dear young lady. Perhaps, however, you may be tempted to make another excursion before the season is over.'

The mouth smiled but the eyes swept the face of Alfred Swain with a glance of sullen menace. As he spoke, Benson's words echoed with falsity, like a tune played awry. Presently, to Swain's relief, he took the hat from his head and lowered it. Then he bowed his way past them down the street with the check-suited bully in tow.

'*Au revoir*, dear young lady . . . and Mr Swain.'

Alfred Swain felt from his contact with Mrs Beresford's arm that the young woman shivered abruptly with a revulsion she had controlled during the presence of the two men.

'Who were they?'

'A pair of tricksters whom I should not care you to see again,' he said quietly, 'I think it may not be possible to spend summer leave here – or anywhere else for that matter.'

'Mr Swain!' Mrs Beresford had had enough. 'Mr and Mrs Nokes expect us. We shall make the arrangements today and spend the summer leave here. I have no wish to set foot in that man's house but I will not be chased from this town by the likes of him. You, if you choose, may tell him so.'

'It might be imprudent.'

'Oh, yes,' she said with heavy irony, 'and so it might. But there's a world of difference between being imprudent and having a bad conscience. I sometimes think, Mr Swain, dear, that you ain't quite cottoned to that yet.'

6

Billy Kurr liked Adelaide Crescent. He would stand at the long and elegant window of the late-Georgian house, gazing across the gardens towards the mirror-dazzle of sunlight on waves. A long sweep of grass, forming the central gardens, stretched down to the promenade. Among its paths and flowerbeds stood a dozen lime trees, warped by the prevailing wind. The sun was at its height now and the waves had turned a deep bottle green. Billy Kurr smiled. Every other house in the road was occupied by an earl or a countess or the colonel of a smart cavalry regiment. But Mr Benson was unique. And Mr Benson could buy them all, coronets and military braid, or would very soon be able to.

'He's a toy,' Billy Kurr said, smiling good-naturedly at the marine view, 'you could do anything with him. Make him roll over. Make him sit up and beg and lick your hand.'

Benson looked up from his accounts. 'Who's he?'

'Policeman Swain,' said Kurr with a chuckle. 'Now he's got a doxy, I'd say you could beat him black and blue and he'd thank you for it. That's the effect that doxies have on men like him.'

Benson put down his pen. 'Hostages to fortune, Mr Kurr, is what they call it. When a man cares about someone else more than he cares about himself, there's no holding him. Policeman Swain is going to dance, Mr Kurr. He doesn't know it yet but he's going to dance neat enough to please the Queen. I had a report from my little spies. Swain and his trollop were talking this afternoon of coming down here for a week in the summer, staying with some people called Nokes and taking the boat to Boulogne. Nancy couldn't get the whole of the conversation but she heard that. She and Jane Rip followed them on to the pier and Bo-Peep followed them off. Policeman Swain was talking about that fool Lerici as well.'

'Mr Lerici!' Billy Kurr smiled at the sea and the promenaders in the sparkle of late sunlight. 'Woman-struck he was. Surprising really that none of them hot-blooded husbands in foreign parts got after him with the gelding knife.'

'Petrides did better than that,' Benson said impatiently, 'and I think Policeman Swain might find the reason why. He won't have time for us when that happens, Mr Kurr. He's been kept on the go nicely with Lerici and that slut of a daughter. Best he should be. You don't want him with his nose in your breech the rest of the season, Mr Kurr. Wouldn't you say, Mr Kurr.'

'True, Mr Benson.'

Harry Benson patted an envelope. 'Just a week or two, Mr Kurr. Bills of exchange into gold. Gold into United States Bonds. Bonds into notes at the Clydesdale Bank. They don't ask for names there. Not the same law in Scotland. Why should they bother when they're paid in gold or bonds? Then Clydesdale notes into gold, bonds, or any currency you choose in any name you choose. They won't know where we've gone, Mr Kurr, because they won't know we were ever here.'

Billy Kurr smiled affectionately at his friend. 'How much, Mr Benson?'

'Starting with five hundred in Lisbon, Mr Kurr, we doubled it eight times. There was the printer to pay in Amsterdam and one or two friends to be thanked. All the same, I'd be a liar if I said we won't have one hundred thousand pounds at the end. Fifty thousand each.'

'And Policeman Swain?'

'Oh,' said Benson casually, 'we won't keep him waiting two weeks. He'll be doing a dance much sooner than that.'

7

Warm summer rain drifted like the gauze of a transformation scene across the river, softening the outlines of wharves and warehouses, colliers' brigs and barges. It surprised Alfred Swain that he could think, standing smartly to attention in this moment of his greatest peril, how much the river scene from the upper windows of Scotland Yard resembled one of Mr Whistler's paintings.

Superintendent Toplady stood sharp collared and gnome headed behind his desk. He leant forward a little, his weight on his palms and nostrils flared, studying the inspector with careful scrutiny. Behind him stood another man, his junior, whom Swain had never seen before. Toplady's mood was uncharacteristically subdued. The tightening of the mouth in what seemed a ghastly smile was absent. There was no gloating. He did not, as Sergeant Lumley described it, dance the polka in front of his victim.

'Well, mister,' he said quietly, 'y'would have it so and now y'may see the result. Refresh me, if you please, with the rules governing the conduct of officers in approved lodgings.'

'I believe, sir, that I am as well aware of those rules as you are,' Swain said defensively.

Toplady danced round from behind the desk. 'Then, mister, you will be aware of the first regulation. An officer is to comport himself decently and with dignity. In other words, sir, he is not to debauch the woman who keeps such lodgings.'

'With respect, sir, no person of self-respect or dignity would suggest that Mrs Beresford is debauched. The allegation would be unworthy.'

'Would it, mister? Would it indeed?' Toplady glared and then glanced down at a paper in his hand. 'The maidservant, Sally Smith, reports the hours spent by you in Mrs Beresford's drawing-room. Hours of the night for the most part.'

'I have had the honour to be Mrs Beresford's guest on occasion, sir. In the evening, perhaps. Certainly not at a late hour. As for Smith, I understand she was dismissed a month ago for petty dishonesty.'

Toplady made a face as if swallowing bile and resumed a familiar sneer.

'Have you understood so, mister? And have you also had the honour to escort the young widow Beresford about London and to take her to a lodging house in Brighton for purposes best known to yourself? Were you not lodged there for several hours and then left for London? And what does a man want a lodging for during the day, mister, with a woman on his arm? Eh?'

'I have been with Mrs Beresford to Brighton on one occasion, sir. It was three days ago, when she went to visit Mr and Mrs Nokes, who have known her since she was a child. She spent several hours with them and was in London again the same day. I thought it fitting that she should not travel unaccompanied.'

Toplady's head went forward like a game-cock. 'Did you so, mister? And did this visit necessitate taking her on the pier like a dollymop and planning to spend a week there together in the summer and take a trip to France? And did you not, at the same time, divulge details of an official investigation, an irregularity which alone would be enough to have you dismissed from this force and prosecuted in the criminal courts?'

Swain stared at the impressionistic river scene beyond the widow, blind to it. How the devil could Toplady know so much about his conversation with Mrs Beresford? They had questioned her first. Surely. They had broken her resistance and she, poor soul, had confessed everything.

'With respect, sir, I have done nothing dishonourable, let alone illegal. I do not know who my accusers may be. If allegations are made against me, I require that they be proved by those who make them. If I am informed correctly, it is a principle of English law that statements made in the absence of the person about whom they are made can be evidence only against the person making them.'

Toplady, rolling his head on his neck as if in preparation for attack, came close and thrust his face up at Swain's. 'Box clever with me, mister! Would y'box clever with me? Eh?'

'I am entitled to require the proof of such allegations, sir.'

Toplady's grin was back now. He liked a man who would fight as he went down. 'Are you, mister? Are you indeed? Entitled, eh? Then you may see the proof.'

From the desk, he took a pile of cards. Like a gamester playing a winning hand, he laid them down one by one. They were not cards, after all, but photographs. Alfred Swain and Mrs Beresford, arm-in-arm on the way to Chelsea Bridge and the penny steamer. Alfred Swain and Mrs Beresford in the Strand, outside a music-hall. Alfred Swain and Mrs Beresford walking down the little Pimlico street from the lodging. Worst of all, there was Alfred Swain with Mrs Beresford, arm-in-arm on the Chain Pier at Brighton.

Swain stared at them for a moment, searching for any words which would not make the matter worse. Toplady worried at him.

'The man that thinks to make a fool of me, mister, shall drink a bitter broth!'

'These are nothing,' Swain said. 'They prove my innocence, sir.'

Toplady emitted a faint hooting laugh at the preposterous courage of the reply. 'Your innocence of what?'

There was nothing for it now, Swain thought. He must say what should have been said a long time before.

'You might prefer, sir, to hear in confidence what I have to tell you. It concerns the honour of this division.'

The large man standing behind Toplady showed not so much as the movement of a muscle in his face.

'Might I, mister?' Toplady grinned again, the nervous impulse of the jaw. 'Staff Inspector Ainsworth of the Home Office is here to see you off the premises when this enquiry is done. What you say shall be said in his presence and reported where necessary. Now, mister, of what do you say you are innocent?'

'Of a conspiracy, sir, to pervert the course of justice by alerting suspected criminals to the progress of investigations of the Metropolitan Police and the Sûreté. Several officers of this division appear to have been accomplices in the matter.'

'Is this some trick, mister? Is it?'

'No, sir. There was a list of officers who appear to have been paid money. It was among the papers of the late John Posthumous Lerici. It suggests that some of them and Lerici collaborated, possibly under pressure of blackmail, with two men suspected of the Turf Insurance fraud and the City of Paris Loan swindle. Henry Benson and William Kurr. Both had escaped justice. It seemed clear that all the officers on the list could not have been suborned. Your name was among them. My name was there.'

Toplady walked back behind his desk, leant forward on his fists with his face lowered and appeared to blink away unshed tears. He drew a long breath through clenched teeth.

'You are to be pitied, mister,' he said after a pause, softly as if he meant it. 'You are most truly to be pitied.' The head snapped up again. The eyes were bright but tearless. 'Report all this to your commander, did you, mister? Eh?'

'I could not report it to anyone whose name was on the list, sir. That was plain.'

'Convenient!' muttered Toplady. 'A man that tells the tale only when he is cornered! I shouldn't wonder if that wasn't convenient.'

'I confided in Mr Abrahams, sir. I took his advice. He, strictly speaking, was my employer just then.'

Toplady straightened up. 'So you and this gentleman, mister, suppressed the evidence? Well, I don't wonder that you did. The Law Society may see whether Attorney Abrahams should ever practise law again. As for you, mister, tell me, who is this?'

179

He held before Swain a folded piece of card, a photographic print. The dapper little man in the linen suit, the quick mobile eyes, and the neat moustache were unmistakable.

'Benson, sir. Harry Benson.'

Toplady stood like a man in the dawning of his life's triumph. He unfolded the card and Swain saw himself on the concealed half. The camera had caught him shaking hands with Benson in the Brighton streets.

'Y'are to be pitied indeed, mister,' Toplady murmured. 'Whatever this scoundrel may have done or not done, were you not the man who was to cover his tracks and pervert justice? Were you not to warn him off and give him time by false accusation against your brother officers here?'

'Who brings these charges, sir? Who makes these suggestions?'

Toplady turned over his papers. 'That shall be nothing to you, mister. The record speaks plain.'

Swain felt a sense of relief and snatched at the chance to attack. 'Then my accusers are anonymous, sir. That is evidence enough to show that the charges are fabricated.'

Toplady swayed from side to side a moment, meditating. 'And the money you had from 'em, mister? That fabricated too?'

'I have received no such money, sir, nor asked for it.'

'Sure, mister?' Toplady turned over another sheet of paper. 'Quite certain?'

'There is not a word of truth in such a story, sir.'

'Nor in these, mister! Nor in these, I dare say!' Toplady was holding up two signed papers. 'Y'have an account with the Pimlico and Vauxhall Friendly Society, do you not?'

Swain's heart sank and he saw how he had underestimated the simplest operations of those who would destroy him.

'I have, sir.'

'Receipts, mister' – Toplady shook the papers – 'for £30 and £50, paid on your instructions by a Major Montmorency.'

'With respect, sir, it means nothing. Anyone might pay . . .'

'With respect, mister, it means someone paid £80 and you received it.'

The rain had stopped and the streets gleamed with moisture. An instinct of survival told Swain that he could not win where he stood. He must fight the right battle, in the right place, and at the right time. This was none of them.

'If you would have the answers to all these things, sir, you must ask my accusers. I demand the right to be confronted by them. There is not a court in the land that would deny me.'

Toplady hesitated and Swain guessed that he was safe for the moment. He knew beyond question now that the accusations were anonymous. Had there been witnesses, Toplady would have had him taken into custody on the spot. What had happened was bad, but it was not the worst. Toplady twisted his mouth, as though he might spit with disgust.

'Well, mister,' he said sullenly, 'you shall have your day for that, be sure of it. For the present, you stand suspended from duty, unremunerated. You are not to be paid. You will hold yourself ready to answer such charges as may be brought and to answer such questions as the police commissioners may put to you. Staff Inspector Ainsworth will escort you to your desk. You will remove from it any personal possessions. Your diary and other divisional property will remain neatly ordered in the desk. Is that plain?'

'Sir.' Swain felt no anger, no fear, and nothing of any kind for Toplady. He had decided what must be done. So far as his future in the division was concerned, he had nothing to lose. Alfred Swain, the mild-mannered thinking man of the modern world, knew where he must attack. Ainsworth followed him closely as they went down to the inspectors' room. It was empty just then, as Swain had expected it to be. Clarke, Meiklejohn, and the others would be at muster with the watch for the next ten or fifteen minutes. With any luck, it would be Clarke's rest-day.

It was a gamble, of course, but not without hope. There were half a dozen tall desks with counting-house stools but nothing to distinguish their tenants. Ainsworth could not know every detail and was now plainly embarrassed by his disagreeable duty. Swain walked straight to George Clarke's desk and opened the lid. Ainsworth stood in the doorway, trying to avoid Swain's eye and saying nothing. Swain waited for a command or a rebuke. None came. Ainsworth had not the least idea of the position of the desks in the inspectors' room.

Swain found Clarke's diary and several official forms. He put them to one side. There was little in the way of personal possessions. A small bottle of white tablets and another containing linseed oil. Clarke, of course, suffered from piles. Swain slipped the bottles into his pocket. There was a pencil and an indiarubber.

He pocketed those. If he left them, Ainsworth would think it odd. But where was the evidence of Clarke's complicity? There must be something, it was Swain's article of faith. He let the pages of the diary ripple without effect. His fingernails ran along the crevices at the desk's edges. Then he saw it.

Even on close inspection it looked no more than a wedge of paper, no thicker than his nail. It had been slipped between the side and the base of the desk's hollow top. No one was likely to notice it. Even to pick it out was difficult. Teasing it with his nail, Swain raised one corner and then drew it free. It was not a single item but three plain cerulean-blue envelopes with a paper of some sort inside each. They had been bought from the Post Office, already embossed with a penny stamp, and were now sealed as if ready for the post. The same address was written on each, though certainly not in Clarke's writing. It had been written long enough for the black ink to tarnish a little. Swain read it and knew that he had struck gold. *Major Montmorency, Adelaide Crescent, Brighton.*

Under the pretext of tidying the desk, Swain slit open one of the envelopes with his nail. He drew out a soft oblong of blotting paper with not a mark on it. The scheme was simple. Someone, presumably 'Major Montmorency', had addressed and prepared the envelopes. Nothing about them would implicate Clarke if they were found. But in the event of danger, Clarke was to post one and the major would know what to do. The signal was simple and it was safe. Small wonder that there had been no trace of an alert to the thieves in the scandal of the Turf Insurance fraud or the Paris Loan.

Ainsworth shifted with a little sound of impatience. 'Right, Swain. Finished, 'ave you?'

'Yes,' Swain said quietly, 'thank you.'

There was an exchange of voices in the corridor and he saw Lumley carrying a paper. 'Mr Ainsworth. Mr Toplady's compliments.'

Then Lumley walked, uninvited, into the room. 'Mr Swain? What the 'ell's all this?'

Now there were more voices, Clarke and Meiklejohn among them. There was no indication that they knew what had happened. As Clarke went to his desk, Ainsworth barked him away.

'Leave that desk! It's just been cleared.'

'It's my desk.'

'Mr Swain cleared it.'

'Search him!' Clarke insisted. 'He could have robbed my things.'

Ainsworth faced Swain. 'If you please, Mr Swain.'

Swain let them search his pockets. Clarke's white pills and linseed oil were retrieved. A pencil and indiarubber. Swain's own pocket-book, comb, pencil, handkerchief, keys, and half a dozen coins. And then the envelopes, one of them opened, addressed to Major Montmorency in Adelaide Crescent, Brighton.

'What's this, then, Swain?'

Clarke was there first. 'You want to keep close hold on anything like that, Mr Ainsworth. Mr Swain got some very funny friends. And I want him charged for pilfering my desk. That's his desk there!'

Ainsworth looked at Swain. 'Put your things in your pockets again.' He looked round at the others and flourished the paper Lumley had brought. 'As for the rest, gentlemen, you'll have to wait. Mr Swain's going before the Home Office supervisor that's to be Director of Public Prosecutions when the bill's passed. He's to go straight away. And he probably ain't coming back again.'

<h2 style="text-align:center">8</h2>

They marched him across Whitehall, through an archway on to Horse Guards Parade, for all the world, Swain thought, as if he was being taken out to be shot. The windows facing the parade and the billowing green of the park trees had sunblinds pulled out, their candy-striped frivolity suggesting a Parisienne boulevard rather than the command of empire. Ainsworth marched beside him and two uniformed constables behind. Alfred Swain was a walking man, rather than a marching man, but they set the pace and gave him no choice. The men who passed by in their swallow-tailed coats, the pretty women under the pastel-coloured parasols gave him those looks of mingled curiosity and compassion reserved for a prisoner under escort.

No one had told him he was a prisoner. So far as he knew, Swain might have declined to accompany them further. But as the little party swung sharp to the right, towards Birdcage Walk and Queen Anne's Gate, he knew that the point of refusal was long in the past. As they turned under the trees, he acknowledged to himself that he knew less about the office of Director of Public Prosecutions than he had thought, only that the post had been newly proposed by the Prosecution of Offences Bill and that its incumbent was to be Sir John Maule, who had been a Queen's Counsel and was at present Home Office supervisor of constabulary. Men who attracted the attention of the new Director were to be passed on to the Treasury Solicitor and seldom seen at liberty again.

A porter pulled open a pair of glass doors and the party went up the steps of a handsome Georgian house and into a domed lobby. Someone shouted a syllable from above and they went up the circular staircase, the escort stamping hard but breaking time. At the top, red carpeting deadened their boots. Ainsworth knocked at the double door of white-painted panels and opened it. He went through and there was a murmur of voices, audible to those who waited outside.

Ainsworth reappeared and the two halves of the door swung open.

'Mr Swain! Quick march!'

Swain walked forward at what he hoped might be taken for a quick march. It was absurd, this military performance in a civilian's suit. They kept time with him, however, a secretary at his elbow and Ainsworth behind him, as if fearing that the culprit might turn and run. The room was long and elegant, bookshelves floor to ceiling along one wall and windows overlooking the park on the other. Swain felt he was walking the length of a cricket pitch towards a leather-inlaid map-table, behind which sat a slim curly-haired and bearded man reading from a sheet of paper.

The man looked up and put the paper down. 'Thank you, Mr Ainsworth. Thank you, Mr Phelp. You may leave us now. Mr Swain, be seated, if you please.'

Swain hesitated, feeling that the inlaid and bevelled chair indicated was really too valuable for mere sitting on.

'If you please, Mr Swain,' said Sir John Maule a little impatiently, waiting until the door had closed behind Ainsworth and the clerk. 'Now, why have you come to see me?'

'Why, sir?' Swain stared at him, uncomprehending. 'I was brought here. On Mr Toplady's instructions.'

'Quite so, Mr Swain.' Sunlight from the window glinted on the pince-nez and the fingertips were touched together in an attitude of prayer. 'But what have you to tell me? What is the reason that you should not be proceeded against as a police officer who has failed in his duty and is in breach of the law?'

He bowed his head patiently and Swain found himself speaking to the top of Sir John Maule's head. For a second time that morning, there was nothing for it but to plunge.

'I believe, sir, that there is a conspiracy to pervert the course of justice and that several officers of the Detective Division are implicated in it. I have reason to think that they have been suborned by known criminals, including Henry Benson and William Kurr. There may also be a connection with one who was not known as a criminal during his life, John Posthumous Lerici.'

Maule looked up and his eyebrows arched a little in scepticism.

'Indeed, Mr Swain? The author of gothic romance? The man whose estate employed you? That was very convenient for you, was it not?'

Despite the sunlight of the June day, Swain felt darkness all about him.

'My duties, sir, included an inventory of Mr Lerici's papers. Among these was evidence that he had entered a horse, Iphigenia, to win the Portland Plate of 1874 by a cheat. There were documents which linked him with Benson and Kurr, and with Scotland Yard officers. There also exist links between Benson and Kurr and the same officers.'

'And you went at once to Superintendent Toplady with this information?'

'No, sir.' Swain tried to look Maule in the eye but the glint of the pince-nez prevented him. 'Mr Toplady was on a list of names in Lerici's papers. So was I. I could not be sure which officers in the division might be implicated and which were not. At that time, because I was employed to supervise matters relating to Mr Lerici's estate, my responsibility was to his lawyers, Messrs Abrahams and Abrahams of King's Bench Walk. I confided the matter to Mr Abrahams junior.'

'And that was all?'

'No, sir.' Swain clung to the thread of logic. 'I decided that I should need proof, rather than evidence, before I could report the matter. I examined the ledgers and day-books in the Document Room at Scotland Yard. In March 1874, entries had been falsified to conceal the fact that officers of the Detective Division had withheld information for a couple of days in order that those who perpetrated the Turf Insurance fraud should have time to strip their premises and leave the country. The same tactics were used again in 1875 in the City of Paris Loan swindle. Mr Abrahams represented the Comtesse de Goncourt and was one of the first to bring the Turf Insurance fraud to light. I believed that I could trust him.'

Maule looked at him without changing his expression. 'The names of the officers, Mr Swain?'

'Inspector Clarke altered an entry concerning the fraud so that he appeared to have interviewed another man on another matter. But the evidence is that the man had died of natural causes before he could be interviewed. I believe his name was chosen from the obituary column of *The Times* newspaper so that he should not be able to disprove the story. Inspector Meiklejohn was also involved in that case. In 1875, Inspector Druscovich delayed the dispatch of a telegram to the Sûreté, in order that his own wire to the perpetrators of the loan fraud in the Rue Réaumur should reach them first. Chief Inspector Palmer was involved in the race-horse swindle and, I believe, in helping to conceal the murder of a burglar, James McBride.'

Maule held up his hand. 'Four officers, Mr Swain? Four officers out of a total of fifteen in the Detective Division? Almost one-third of the division involved in a conspiracy to pervert the course of justice? Is that what you say?'

'There may be more, sir. I cannot tell you that. But there are honest men too. I owe my life to Sergeant Lumley. By the time of the chimney fire at Mondragon, the men who were guilty knew that I suspected them. Mr Lumley pulled me to safety. That argues his loyalty and honesty.'

But Maule shook his head. 'No, Mr Swain, it does not. It argues only that Lumley did not wish to see you die. A man may not wish another to die but he may still take his *pourboire* for leaving a villain in peace.'

'However that may be, sir, I believe in Mr Lumley's honesty. And I believe that a conspiracy exists in respect of two swindlers. I believe that the murder of McBride has been concealed. There is also more to the murder and crimes of Lerici than has yet come to light. The man debauched his own daughter.'

Maule took this information without so much as blinking. He stood up and walked across to the window, staring out at the sunlit trees with his hands folded under the tails of his coat.

'Well, Mr Swain,' he said with his back to the inspector, 'you are not a man for doing things by halves.' He counted off the charges on his fingers. 'We have at least four officers of the Detective Division perverting the course of justice. We have swindlers beyond the reach of the law. We have a man who was murdered and Scotland Yard says he wasn't. We have a man murdered in Greece and it seems we don't know the truth of it. We have a young person debauched by her own father. Is that quite all?'

'No, sir,' said Swain glumly, 'you also have me, suspended from duty and likely to be prosecuted, if Mr Toplady has his way.'

Maule returned to the table and sat down. He looked at Swain and sniffed. 'You have Mr Toplady to thank that you are here talking to me and not in Newgate Gaol.'

'Sir?'

'You are here, Mr Swain, because your commander has too high an opinion of you to believe the slanders directed against you. You are here because Mr Toplady took the anonymous communications about you as the slanders they undoubtedly were . . .'

'With respect, sir, why am I suspended, in that case?'

Maule smiled and shook his head. 'Mr Swain! Suppose Mr Toplady had told you, in front of another officer, that he dismissed such photographs and allegations as slander. Suppose he had put complete confidence in you and believed all that you said about the dishonesty of other officers. Suppose you had not been suspended. What is the result? The alarm would have gone out to those whom you suspect of conspiracy and to their criminal confederates. By now they would be covering their tracks.'

'And this is the reason for Mr Toplady's allegations about Mrs Beresford?'

'No doubt it is. Mr Toplady regards your abilities highly, Mr Swain.'

'I should not have guessed it,' said Swain coldly.

Maule smiled at him for the first time. 'I do not suppose he intended you to guess it, Mr Swain. But he did you the greatest service by accusing you in front of other officers and by having you marched over here like a defaulter. Your enemies must think themselves safe.'

'No, sir,' said Swain quietly, 'I fear not.'

'How so, Mr Swain?'

'When I was taken to the inspectors' room, I emptied Clarke's desk instead of my own to see what I might find. There were three envelopes, stamped and sealed, each containing a blank sheet of paper. They were addressed to Adelaide Crescent, Hove. To Major Montmorency. Major Montmorency was a name used, I believe, by Henry Benson in the City of Paris Loan swindle. Benson also mentioned an address in Adelaide Crescent. They were written in that man's hand, I think, not Clarke's. I managed to open one and found only a sheet of blotting-paper. These envelopes were surely the means of warning Benson in the event of danger.'

Maule stared at him, the smile gone. 'I could wish your colleague did not know that you had found them, Mr Swain.'

'That could not be prevented,' Swain said quietly.

Maule took up a little bell that stood on his desk. 'Then we shall move at once, Mr Swain, and trust that we may still be in time. If what you say is true, I should imagine that a message went at once to Brighton from the confederates. Those four officers have more to lose from Benson's capture than the man himself. His first step would be to win favour by turning evidence against them. And that offer, Mr Swain, would be accepted.'

9

Half a dozen times in his life Alfred Swain had travelled to Brighton and back. Never before had he enjoyed the soft and expansive luxury of a first-class carriage. He was alone with Sir John Maule, discussing the fate of John Posthumous Lerici.

'I spoke to Herr Schliemann at Mycenae before I came away,' Swain said.

'Did you, indeed? I envy you that opportunity, Mr Swain. I was at one of his lectures at the Hanover Rooms, two years ago.'

'It seems that Lerici had stolen certain items discovered by the workmen excavating the grave-circle. Rings or necklaces perhaps. Herr Schliemann believes that the workmen were bribed. The servant Petrides was with Lerici at the tomb of Clytemnestra when the place was deserted. There was a quarrel, presumably over the booty, in which the servant stabbed his master. Petrides hid the body in deep undergrowth, where it might never have been discovered. When it was found, his master's death was brought home to him. He confessed it under questioning and admitted that it was a matter of the stolen treasures.'

Sir John Maule pursed his lips. 'Really? I should like to have seen this stolen treasure. Has none of it been recovered?'

'No, sir.' Swain took from his waistcoat pocket the small flat tin, an inch or two square, that had once held menthol pastilles. He took out several brittle fragments of sealing wax and some folded paper, laying the wax on his palm. 'These were the prints with which the desk at Mondragon was sealed. I believe they are the rings which I later saw worn by Amalia de Brahami, the natural daughter of Lerici.'

Maule gave an approving murmur. He took a small folding magnifying glass from his pocket, opened it, and laid the largest fragment of wax on his own palm. Then he let out a sceptical sigh, still peering through the convex glass.

'Well, Mr Swain, Lerici may have stolen these but not from Mycenae. Indeed, I cannot think this was worth stealing. It was certainly not worth killing for nor dying for.'

'Then it is not Mycenaean gold?'

Maule chuckled. 'In my leisure time, Mr Swain, I am a Fellow of the Society of Antiquaries. The design on this seal ring, the two griffins, is not Greek. It is Roman. You are not, perhaps, familiar with the discovery of Roman plate at Hildesheim, near Hanover, ten years ago. There was fine silver, now in the Berlin Museum. The two griffins on this design of yours, the heads reversed, form almost a copy of the design on the base of a silver cup found at that site. It is not Greek, let alone Mycenaean, Mr Swain. I would have thought that this was a copy of the design at Hildesheim. Probably made in the last ten years. Indeed, Mr Swain, look close and you will see it is. See through the glass. Do you see the little flecks of gold on the wax? That is not true gold, Mr Swain. Base metal plated with gold, perhaps. A technique known only in this form to the modern world. I fear that Mr Lerici's treasure was as gimcrack as the house he built for it and the fables that he wrote.'

Maule took the sketches.

'These were drawings, sir, which I made from memory as soon as possible after seeing the rings on a young woman's fingers, and the necklace about her throat. I believe they are tolerably accurate.'

Sir John Maule examined them and shook his head. 'I have no doubt that they are accurate, Mr Swain. You have a good eye for such things. But like the others, these are Hildesheim designs again. Not Greek.'

Swain stared at his companion. 'Then he had no Mycenaean gold?'

Maule shrugged. Steadying himself against the rocking of the train as the pale green downland came into view, he was examining the other fragments of wax through his glass.

'Nothing here was Mycenaean, Mr Swain. Nor true gold. You would find these ornaments in a street market for tourists. Venice or Rome, perhaps. Not Greece nor Mycenae.'

'Yet Petrides killed him.'

Maule looked up. 'There I cannot help you, Mr Swain. I should be surprised if he was killed for these.'

'Then for what?'

'The outrage to his daughter?'

'But why there and why Petrides? Petrides was not the girl's father, after all. That was Lerici himself. The grandmother would hardly kill her own son. The servant who had been the girl's nurse, Basileia, was nowhere near.'

'Basileia?'

'It is a name, sir.'

'It is also the grandeur that simple folk give their children, Mr Swain.'

'She, at least, cannot have been there when Petrides killed Lerici. She was a hundred miles away in Athens with the old lady.'

'Then, Mr Swain, we had best put away our Aeschylean tragedy and give our attention to the matter in hand.'

Swain looked from the window. 'Sometimes in the past few

months, sir, I could almost believe that the tragedy unfolds here and now.'

10

A cab was waiting at the station. It bore Swain and Sir John Maule down the slope of Queen's Road to the sparkle of the sea, along the mile of the esplanade towards Hove. Swain had a summer vision of the little yachts like butterflies on the glimmering horizon, the holiday strollers with their parasols and telescopes, the handsome cream-washed houses that stretched westward to Shoreham and the harbour.

The cab turned into Adelaide Crescent. When he had given Lumley the envelope, Swain had no idea which house in the crescent it was addressed to. Major Montmorency would surely be well enough known to the postman. There was no doubt now which house it might be. Outside the *porte-cochère* by the area railings, two uniformed officers and a private-clothes inspector were standing in readiness, forewarned by a telegraph from the Home Office. As the cab stopped, the inspector stepped forward and opened the door. Swain followed Sir John Maule.

'Flown the coop, sir,' the inspector was saying. 'Locksmith opened the door as soon as the message came but there's nothing except furniture sheeted over and the rent for the past month not paid. Seems Major Montmorency was expecting a legacy any day.'

Swain peered through the window and saw the ghostly shapes of chairs and tables, sideboards and settees in unlit rooms.

'Not long gone, sir,' the inspector was saying, 'still warmth in the stove, as if it went out this morning. I'd say they can't have got far yet but getting further every minute. Nothing to show which way they went nor how.'

11

'It's all right, Mrs Beresford, really it is,' Alfred Swain said encouragingly. His hand idled on the fair curls of the young woman's head as she sat with her back against his knees. The gas-lamp of the sitting-room glowed gently on the familiar prints of London Bridge and Windsor Castle, the silhouettes of the beloved dead whom her father had immortalized in black paper when she was still a child in Sussex. Her tears had stopped but she was still badly frightened by what had happened.

'It can't be all right, Mr Swain,' she said doubtfully, 'not until all this mess is cleared up.'

'It will be,' he said, 'and there's nothing to worry about. All that was said about you – about us – was based on nothing.'

'I never thought,' she said dismally.

Swain took her hand. 'It doesn't matter now, Mrs Beresford, not one way or another. They've gone, the pair of 'em.'

'But who were the men in the division, Mr Swain, to do such a thing?'

Swain evaded the names, thinking of innocent associations that the young woman might have had with them through the late Constable Beresford. As yet they thought themselves safe and Swain in disgrace. It was no time to give the game away.

'No one can say who they are, Mrs Beresford. That's the worst of it. It could have been me. Most of them probably think it was me.'

'I don't understand how it could happen,' she said simply, 'how all this money could have been stolen.'

Swain stared at the design of the Lass of Richmond Hill on the porcelain biscuit-barrel. The buhl clock chimed the half-hour softly and a ginger cat curled more tightly in its basket.

'Bills of exchange,' Swain said, 'easy as that. A man can buy a bill of exchange from his bank for any amount he chooses. He can buy an open letter of credit, asking other banks to advance him money. So long as he pays the money to begin with, there's no reason he shouldn't have any of these things. He's paid for them all and it's his money. So Benson and Kurr bought them. And then they found an artist who forged some more. They'd show the bank the genuine bill first of all. But they'd offer to go and get it endorsed by the agent of the bank that issued it. Back it comes ten minutes later and no one gives it a second look, having scrutinized it the first time and seeing the endorsement looks all right. But this time it's a different bill, a forgery.'

'But how?' she insisted. 'They'd be found out when the bills

192

came back to the banks that were supposed to have issued them.'

'Oh, yes,' Swain said, 'but bills of exchange are long paper. That's to say they don't usually have to be returned in less than three months from the bank that pays out cash to the bank that issued them. Rothschild's have their bills of exchange returned after two months but that's unusual. Of course, a bank can insist on confirmation or endorsement before it cashes a bill. Once it's cashed, that's an end of the matter. They've had it confirmed by the issuing bank – so they thought. So long as Poodle Benson and Billy Kurr could work the dodge to get cash in their hands, they had two clear months to pile up all the money they could. After two months or so they were bound to be found out. But they'd be far away before that. Chicago. California. Brazil. Anywhere in the world. And any name you could think of. If anything went wrong before that, if there was a warrant out or an alarm from the police in Paris or Amsterdam, one of their friends in the division would probably burn the message and send them a warning. It must have happened a dozen times in the last few weeks. And once a man does a single favour for men like that, they've got him. He daren't refuse them and he daren't confess. He just goes on with it, hoping he'll never be found out.'

'How could they hide so much money?'

'They brought the money back here from all over Europe,' Swain said, 'to an account at the Western Branch of the Bank of England in Burlington Gardens in the name of Major Hugh Montgomery and Lord William Kurr. Benson opened it by some trick or other, using the Charing Cross Hotel. Then, a few weeks ago, they began drawing it out in United States Bonds. Their story was that they were a couple of financiers arranging money for the City of Chicago Elevation Loan. Half a million pounds they said they wanted and quarter of a million they said they'd got. They hadn't got anything to begin with but they acted like millionaires and people believed them.'

'But what was the money for?'

'According to them, they were going to raise the level of the lake shore avenues in Chicago against flooding from Lake Michigan. They reckoned the city had invested half the money and they were getting investments in Europe for the other half. When they told the bank to buy United States Bonds for them, no one thought anything about it. Most natural thing in the world to convert the funds into dollars. So they could take the bonds to half a dozen banks, bit by bit over three weeks, and change them for banknotes. We think they'd approached the Clydesdale Bank. It's the only bank where you can draw fifty-pound notes without your name and the number of the note being entered. The Clydesdale Bank didn't mind. United States Bonds are safe as gold bricks. What they were doing then seemed perfectly legal and no one would trace where the money came from.'

'Ninety thousand pounds?' Mrs Beresford's features tried to encompass the size of the amount.

'They've had one hundred and two thousand pounds in the past two months, that we know of. It could be more but some of the banks in France and Holland won't even know whether they've been swindled until the three months is up. There's hell let loose in Paris and Amsterdam and it's taken a dozen officers two days to trace the route that the money went. No one knows where it is now. And no one's seen Benson nor Kurr for three days past. They could be in France or half-way to New York or on a boat for Rio de Janeiro. But so far as anyone knows at present, all the money is still in United States Bonds.'

Mrs Beresford took his other hand. 'And what about us? You sure it's all right for us here, Mr Swain, dear? After that nastinesss from Mr Toplady?' As she turned her face up to him, Alfred Swain smiled.

'It's all right, Mrs Beresford. Mr Toplady's got far too much on his mind to worry about us. I was paraded again this afternoon. I'm not suspended any more. Toplady wasn't his usual self at all. I think he's had a fright over what's happened with Clarke and the others and what might happen to him. Almost the only time I've known him when he spoke without sneering and snarling. He seemed quite grateful, in a way. So we'll go to Brighton when summer leave comes round. We'll stay with Mr and Mrs Nokes. And it'll be the best summer leave of all.'

They had both got up and Mrs Beresford was leading him barefoot to the sofa when there was a dolorous clanking of the doorbell from below. Swain snatched his trousers and his shirt. He was back in his room, the door slightly ajar, when the maid-servant came up the stairs. She spoke to Mrs Beresford. Swain heard the name 'Lumley' and groaned.

194

12

The large man moved with the midnight crowd towards the piazza. The theatres had come out and like most of those among whom he jostled, he had made his way through the flaring gaslight of the streets from the oyster-stands and coffee-stalls of the Haymarket. Joining a line of arrivals, he pushed through a low doorway under a white glare of light which illuminated 'The Cave of Harmony'.

Once inside, Billy Kurr paused in an anteroom, hung with paintings of racehorses and photographs of chorus-girls. It was a place of round marble-topped tables, gilt-framed wall-mirrors, and the air of a Parisienne café, lacking only the click of dominoes. Like most of the others, however, he pushed further through into the music-hall itself. It was the size of a church with its Corinthian columns in cream and gold, its gilded cornice and smoke-hazed ceiling-dome. The curtains of the stage at the far end were closed but a grand piano stood before them and the pianist was just taking his seat. The auditorium was filled by rows of the round marble-topped tables with four chairs at each.

Billy Kurr's weight carried him to the marble counter of the bar and he beckoned one of the young women as the opening chorus from the stage began.

How do you like London, how do you like town?
How'll you like the Strand, dear, with Temple Bar pulled down?
How do you like the lardi-da, the toothpick, and the crutch?
How did you get those trousers on, and did they hurt you much?

Devilled kidneys, Scotch ale, and crusty bread. Billy Kurr basked in the homely warmth and din, safe among so many hundreds of other people. He handed the girl his sovereign. She spun it on the counter and listened to see that it rang true. Billy Kurr received his change. One half-sovereign, eight shillings, and some coppers. He slipped the other coins into his pocket and handed the half-sovereign back. 'Let me have silver for the half-sov,' he said amiably, 'there's a good girl.' She took the coin back and counted ten shillings in silver.

Someone put a hand on Billy Kurr's shoulder from behind.

'We'll leave without fuss, if you please,' said Alfred Swain gently, 'quietly.'

To look at Swain was to know him for a private-clothes police-man. The girl behind the bar was standing still, watching them.

'It's all right, miss,' Swain said quietly, 'you've just been caught by the old twining dodge. Very neatly done. Perhaps you'd have the goodness to drop that half-sovereign on the counter.'

The girl dropped the little coin. It made a dull wooden sound. The look of alarm on her face suggested that she thought she was about to be taken for the culprit.

'It was a real one!' she cried. 'I know it was!'

Swain felt for his handcuffs. 'Course it was. It's the oldest dodge in the business. Our friend here comes in with a genuine sovereign and a dud half-sovereign in his hand. You give him change for the sovereign, including a half-sovereign. He hands you back your half-sovereign and asks for silver. You don't spin it because you only just gave it to him. Only, of course, it's not yours. It's the dud that he's had in his hand all the time. I dare say he could pass a dozen of 'em every night.'

Swain turned to Billy Kurr again. But the big man was unimpressed.

'You stand clear of me, Swain,' he said quietly, 'unless you want another buttonhole through your waistcoat.'

He brought his hand up a little and Swain saw what looked like a long pistol barrel. Whether it was or not, he dared not take the risk. A single shot fired in a crowd like this might cause multiple death and injury, followed by worse in the panic that would have been caused. Billy Kurr backed away through the crowd. The mass of people closed round him.

Swain turned to the girl behind the bar.

'Get a message to the duty superintendent at "A" Division, Whitehall Place, Scotland Yard. The man who was here was William Kurr and he had a gun. Tell them that. And Sergeant Lumley's on the back entrance. Tell him what's happened. At once, if you please!'

Then he pushed forward, trying to make his way through the current of men and women pressing towards the bar.

There was only six feet between them but in the density of the crowd it might as well have been six miles. Swain dared not shout to the men and women to stop the fugitive. If the large man had a gun and was prepared to use it, the result would be unthinkable.

196

The best hope was to keep Billy Kurr in sight until they were outside and then try to track him down.

Kurr was pushing through the low door into the piazza where the gaslight blazed the legend 'Evans's Supper Rooms'. He was about eight feet ahead of Swain now and the current of the crowd was still against them. By the time that the private-clothes inspector freed himself from the pressure of bodies in the open air, he saw only the shape of the large man running across the piazza.

All around him the great buildings of the market were closed, the long wall huge and dead, full of blind windows. Swain ran in its shadow where the storage sheds were securely gated and barred. Yet even in the night air he breathed the suffocating odour of second-hand fish, vegetables and fruit, potato sacks and coal dust, the sulphurous reek of chimneys. Surely someone would see which way he was going and report the information. Mr Toplady or his deputy would have the news in a few minutes more.

Swain guessed that Billy Kurr was on his own, separated from Harry Benson, heading for the criminal rookery of the Seven Dials, a warren of alleyways and courts where the gutters were still open sewers and where the houses were so close together that a man might have to squeeze sideways between them. The shops had ended now and the houses began. Children had chalked the little street for hopscotch and fly-the-garter, thread-the-needle and shove-halfpenny. Swain paused. The narrow way was unlit and a fetid moisture of some kind overlaid the paving. On either side, the alley was overhung by tall, rat-ridden tenements, a monument to centuries of decay and destitution. Behind the boarded windows and cracked walls, the sharper and the razorman, the cracksman and the footpad waited out the night with their women.

Swain thought he saw shadows move. He could hear the fugitive, he was sure of it, but he could not see him. The alleyway curved to the left and he was almost blinded by the light which streamed at him from a cobbled square, where ornate gas-lamps on iron brackets hung the length of a gin palace. There was noise from inside the building but no sign of anyone in the square. Alfred Swain stopped, his hand shielding his eyes from the worst of the glare. He was illuminated like a figure in a stage spotlight. At that moment there was a crash that made his heart jump and his ears ring. Someone had shot at him.

It was shock rather than fright that made him throw himself flat. He thought he heard the bullet crack against the stonework of one of the walls. Raising his head, he looked into the glare of light and tried to make out the shape of a man or any sign of movement. There was nothing. The din and the brightness streamed from the gin-palace windows, its occupants apparently unaware of what had happened. Where the devil was Lumley? And where were the others? Would they know where to find him? Surely they must have heard the shot. The cobbled square was at the very centre of the Seven Dials with seven alleys running into it. Kurr could get out by any of them unless they were blocked soon.

Swain cupped his hands round his mouth.

'Don't be a fool, Billy Kurr! There's a man in every one of the Dials. You haven't got enough bullets for us all! And if you had, you'd hang for murder.'

Silence.

'Don't be a fool, man! There's no way out! Benson's given up!'

Swain hoped this final lie carried more conviction than he felt.

'I'm waiting for you, Billy Kurr!'

Movement!

Someone was walking slowly towards him from the light. Swain got to his feet. He was a target anyway, standing up or lying on the ground. He must either meet the man or turn and run. After so much, how could he let it be known that he had turned and run away?

'There's no way out, Billy Kurr,' he said gently as the large man approached him. 'What you've done so far isn't the end of the world. A few years, perhaps, and not that many if you turned evidence. A life to look forward to afterwards. A gun won't do anything but put you on the gallows trap with the hemp round your neck on a cold and early morning. And you haven't got enough bullets to shoot us all.'

Billy Kurr stopped and they looked at one another. The large man in his suit of sporting check, the pride of the betting office and the turf. The thin policeman in his grey worsted with the look of an intelligent horse.

'It's no good, Billy,' Swain said gently, 'and if you can't get away with the twining dodge, how could you ever hope to do this?'

198

Billy Kurr stretched out his hand and Swain felt the chill of smooth tooled metal. It was an old-fashioned long-barrelled Manton duelling pistol, an antique from the age of honour. Two shots at most. No wonder that Billy Kurr had given up.

There were footsteps in the alley behind him now, boots that were running. Swain thought he recognized Lumley's thumping tread. He stood between them and his prisoner.

'It's the best way, Billy,' he said gently.

Billy Kurr sighed. 'Poodle Benson's got the money,' he said philosophically. 'He should have been over the Channel with it by now, waiting for me to join him. If you got him, where's the point for me?'

In that moment, as Lumley and the others came into the glare of the lamps, Alfred Swain felt a little ashamed of the lie that he had told to weaken Kurr's resolve, but also rather proud of the skill which he had shown in such deceit.

13

Swain thought, as he stood at attention in his casual way before the superintendent's desk, that it was the only time he had ever known Toplady to appear uneasy. The gnome-like figure shifted from foot to foot behind the desk, as if uncertain whether to dance out or remain behind its protection. The high starched collars rasped on the close-shaven face. But the eyes moved with a strange clockwork precision, side to side, avoiding direct contact with their victim. Swain, for the first time in his career, had the impression that Toplady was afraid. Yet Montague Toplady was no coward, not by accounts of his leadership as a young artillery officer during the combat with Russian mounted regiments at Inkerman. Perhaps, Swain thought, the superintendent was not afraid in the common sense. Rather, he seemed unnerved.

'Well, mister,' Toplady said hastily, 'let all this be a lesson. Not a cause for a swollen head and getting above yourself. Eh?'

'As you say, sir,' replied Swain blandly. He could afford to be generous now. The sun was shining again across the broad river and the coal wharves at Westminster. Clocks were striking the hour.

'Not to be taken up and pampered like a lapdog, eh?'

'No, sir.'

'Not to think because y'have ridden to Brighton with Sir John Maule that y'have friends in such offices, eh?'

'No, sir.'

Toplady seemed to feel better now. There was a familiar gleam in the rather protuberant eyes.

'And not to think that because y'have taken a villain like Kurr through pure good fortune and no skill of your own, that the rogue Benson may go free. Eh? With thousands of pounds in government bonds. Eh?'

'I shall have him in the end, sir.'

'In the end, sir!' Toplady appeared to twist saliva round his mouth. 'In the end, sir! What sort of ninny's answer is that, eh? See this, mister? See it, do ye?'

He held up a blue telegraphic form for Swain to read, immediately in front of the inspector's face.

ARRIVAL IN BOULOGNE FROM THE FOLKESTONE BOAT DETAINED THIS MORNING. CORRESPONDS TO DESCRIPTION OF HENRY BENSON. ADVISE.

Swain recognized it as being from the Chef de Gendarmerie at Boulogne, dated the previous morning.

'Has the man been brought over, sir?'

Toplady's mouth tightened in a grimace of contempt for the world.

'No, mister, he ain't been and he won't be. See this, if you please! Sent from this building.'

Swain read the confirmatory copy of the previous day's reply to Boulogne.

MAN YOU HAVE DETAINED IS NOT BENSON, WHO WAS ARRESTED HERE TODAY. HEREBY AUTHORIZE RELEASE OF MAN HELD. TOPLADY, SUPERINTENDENT, SCOTLAND YARD DETECTIVE DIVISION.

Swain frowned. Clearly something was wrong but Toplady gave no indication yet.

'I'm not sure I understand, sir.'

Toplady grinned without a vestige of good humour.

'By God y'don't, mister, nor ever would without my boot behind ye! Heard that Benson was arrested, eh?'

'No, sir.'

'No, sir!' cried Toplady tragically. 'Because he ain't arrested, nor never likely to be at this rate. Imagine I sent that telegraph to Boulogne?'

'Possibly not, sir.'

'Possibly not, sir! Look at the style, man. It is the most damnable forgery! Whether they had Benson or not we shall never know. One of your precious comrades in the inspectors' room embezzled their message and sent that reply in my name. God knows where the rogue Benson is now or whether he was ever in Boulogne at all.'

Swain tried to make sense of it all. 'But how did the forgery come to light?'

'Because, mister, the inspector in Boulogne sent last night to say they'd released the fellow on my instructions. And that message wasn't embezzled because at five o'clock last afternoon your friends Clarke and Meiklejohn and Druscovich and Palmer were taken into custody on charges of perverting the course of justice. By the time the confirmation came from Boulogne, the scoundrels were locked in separate cells.'

The sky across the river seemed darker to Swain. But Toplady had by no means finished.

'And you, mister, instead of playing toe-to-toe and knee-to-knee with 'em under the table like mimping virgins, might have brought this to an end long before.'

'With respect, sir . . .'

'With respect, sir!' said Toplady scornfully. 'Well, y'may have that inspectors' room pretty well to yourself now. Think yourself lucky not to be suspended still and pray that it mayn't happen again after the pretty mess y'have made of the fellow Lerici. His case was nothing until it fell into your hands. But now, I'm told, we don't know how or why he died any longer! There's a story that the scoundrel debauched his own child. And the rascal McBride that was given his death certificate for falling off a tower now pops up and tells us he was murdered after all. A pretty mess y'have there, mister.'

'I believe, sir, that Mr Lerici's household is returning to Italy or Greece in a few days. I have been told so.'

Toplady seized the opportunity. 'Then see to it, mister, that y'have the matters of McBride and Lerici himself clear before they go. If the fellow came by his wealth dishonestly, it ain't to leave these shores.'

Swain, about to be dismissed to his duties, felt a sense of limitless oppression on his spirits. But Toplady had not quite done.

'A word in the ear, mister.' To Swain's dismay, the superintendent fulfilled the promise literally, speaking so close that the inspector almost felt the breath of derision on his lobe. 'It seems y'have chosen to spend the past months reading nastiness from those parts. Tales of rascals that debauched their mothers and children, murdered their parents, ate their sons. Pederasts and cannibals, mister. Wanton wives and parricides. All dressed up pretty in poetry books. Eh?'

'I have read a little of the ancient world, sir. I thought it right.'

'Thought it right!' Toplady drew away from the inspector. 'And do y'wonder that it should have muddled and fouled the processes of your thoughts? Eh?'

'I believe, sir, that Aeschylus . . .'

'You believe, sir! You ain't here to believe but to do your duty!'

'Sir,' said Swain humbly. In a way, it was a relief that the superintendent had returned to his vituperative self. Swain felt that he knew where he was.

'Very well,' said Toplady with a flourish, 'then oblige me by clearing your mind of heathen nastiness, mister, and getting to your work!'

14

The gloom that Toplady had inspired was nothing to what Swain felt sitting alone in the inspectors' room. It was not the only room of its kind in the division and chance alone dictated that Swain had shared it with three of the four men now in custody. The other occupant, Burnaby, was on the night watch.

Whether the man held by the Gendarmerie in Boulogne was Benson would never be known. Wherever Benson might be, he was presumably carrying a hundred thousand pounds in United States Bonds. A man might live the rest of his life in comfort on that. On the other hand, Swain thought, the fugitive could hardly pay the milkman or the baker with a foreign bond for a thousand pounds. Sooner or later, Benson would have to cash the paper promises. Unless, of course, he had done that already and was on his way to California or Brazil as Major Montgomery or Count Montmorency.

Billy Kurr had said little, claiming that he had been instructed to wait until Benson contacted him. He had so little money on him meantime that even the twining dodge had been worth a try. Kurr had done little for the investigation beyond indicating a willingness to give evidence against the four police officers under arrest in exchange for unspecified favours.

Alfred Swain took out the gold hunter watch, consulted the time, and saw that he was entitled to his lunch. Glumly he munched his bread and cheese, with an apple that tasted strongly of its sack. He wiped his hands and took from his desk *The Agamemnon of Aeschylus*, edited by Sidgwick for the use of schools. He opened it and stared at the pattern of Greek script.

A man would get nowhere unless he tried. Swain worked his way down the first page, getting the pronunciation of words, few of which he could understand. One day he would get the hang of it because the great Schliemann had promised him it was so. Then he began to daydream a little of 'Golden Mycenae' and the plains of 'Horse-pasturing Argos'. Agamemnon butchered by his wife. Iphigenia avenged by her mother. Clytemnestra, wife and mother. Who had she been, after all?

There was a knock at the door and a head appeared. It was Oliver Lumley with his round red face a little moist from excitement. Swain slipped Aeschylus into his pocket, as though it had been a set of indecent prints.

'You seen the telegraph that come, Mr Swain?'

'Yes,' said Swain wearily, 'Mr Toplady showed them to me. The one from Boulogne, the reply that was concocted, and the last one from Boulogne.'

'Boulogne?' Lumley stared at him with an air of suspicion.

'Yesterday.'

Lumley pushed the door wider and entered the room. 'Not this

203

one. It come this morning from Brighton half an hour ago. When the town police got word there, I don't know.'

'Word of what?'

'Well,' Lumley said awkwardly, 'you know how they say there's no point in making a lot of money for money's sake, because you can't take it with you when you snuff it?'

Swain stared at him. 'Well?'

'Well,' Lumley said quietly, 'seems they been wrong all these years. Mr John Posthumous Lerici presented a bill of exchange for five hundred pound this morning to the branch of the London and Westminster Bank in Western Road in Brighton where he has an account.'

'It's Benson!' Swain got up from his stool and began to put his desk in order, ready for departure. 'But surely, Mr Lumley, enough people knew Lerici was dead for the bank to think it odd that the man should have an account with them.'

'I don't know, Mr Swain. He'd only got to say he was a cousin of the same name. After all, he's there. The same face they always seen. They could see he wasn't dead so they thought he must be what he said. Anyway, you sure Lerici was dead?'

'Of course I'm bloody well sure!' Alfred Swain said with uncharacteristic violence.

'Well, they recognized this cove as being the one that usually goes to the bank. You see the body, did you?'

Swain paused. 'Not at his best, Mr Lumley. He was bandaged up and ready to be nailed down in his cask of rum by the time I got there.'

'All right,' Lumley said cheerfully, 'only they seemed quite sure it was Lerici this morning. You want to hear the rest?'

'What rest?' It seemed to Swain that Lumley was enjoying the whole thing a little too much. 'Rest of what?'

'Reason this come to light, Mr Swain, was that the bill was drawn on B. W. Blydenstein and Company. In the City of London at 20 Great St Helen's. No one at the bank thought anything about it. Then they noticed that the issue date was wrong. It got tomorrow's date on it! Now, you could put tomorrow as the date when it's to be paid. But you can't issue tomorrow's bill until tomorrow comes.'

Alfred Swain's heart quickened. 'Right, Mr Lumley.'

'Anyway, they thought it was just a mistake at Blydenstein's. So the clerk says to the man that calls himself Lerici that there's an error in the issue date and they'll have to wire Blydenstein's for authority to pay. And he agrees to this, says he's sure it'll be all right because Blydenstein is his brother-in-law – which it proves he ain't. So he says he'll be back in an hour. And they've never seen him since. He's got an account there with almost nothing in it and a deed box.'

'And that's all?'

Lumley unfolded a piece of paper. 'No, Mr Swain, it ain't. They had a reply by wire from Blydenstein. "We have no record of this bill and can only assume it is a forgery." That's what puts the fox among the chickens.'

'My God!' said Swain reverently.

Lumley swelled a little. 'If he hadn't been on the run, Mr Swain, and hardly knowing the time of day, he'd have put the proper date and been paid. And no one the wiser for the next month or two.'

Swain stood up. 'More than that, Mr Lumley. If he had to try drawing on a bill of exchange like that, where's his hundred thousand pounds? Billy Kurr hasn't got any of it. It must still be in United States Bonds and he can't cash them anywhere in this country without being caught. He's carrying a hundred thousand pounds, Mr Lumley, and he can't spend it. And if he can't get ready money, he can't go anywhere. I think Poodle Benson might have trapped himself at last.'

'What comes of being clever,' said Lumley knowledgeably. 'You want to hurry and catch the next train? Or fetch your razor and towel from Mrs Beresford's and go down later?'

15

Alfred Swain sat once more in the cool and neutral summer light, filtered through the leaded panes of Mondragon's western gallery. Amalia de Brahami sat facing him straight-backed on the settee. Behind her stood Basileia, looking as if she would do nothing without an order. Signora Lerici sat to one side.

'I should like to speak to Signorina de Brahami alone,' Swain said gently to the old woman, 'if you will permit me. Sergeant Lumley will remain with us.'

Giovanna Lerici paused for as long as seemed prudent before she got to her feet and withdrew, Basileia walking in her wake. Swain waited for the door to close.

'Do you love me, Mr Swain?' As he looked at Amalia de Brahami, he knew that question would never be asked again. Yet Alfred Swain thought how easily he could imagine himself desiring that warm gold skin, the austere sensuality of the tall brow and the sharp nose, the dark sleekness of the piled hair, the energy of the straight back and the narrow hips. She perched on the settee and they faced one another a little awkwardly, like friends who meet as strangers for the first time. She did not wait for him to question her.

'I have nothing else to tell you, Mr Swain. We leave England in a day or two. I do not think I shall ever come back here. The house is to be emptied soon and sold, all that my father created here, all that is the legacy of Lord Byron, will be gone. It will be the home of a religious order. How they would both have laughed at that! If there is any justice, Mr Swain, the novices will have uneasy dreams.'

Swain watched her as she chattered on. It was as if she was postponing the moment when she must answer him.

'I shall not keep you long,' he said gently. 'If we proceed with the matter now, it will soon be over. I have a question to ask you about your father's finances. Did you know that he had an account with the London and Westminster Bank, a few miles from here, and that a bill of exchange was presented to that account this morning?'

'By whom?'

'It was drawn in your father's name.'

The thought shocked her more than he would have expected.

'You come here to tease me with this? You come here to make fun of me?'

Swain shook his head. 'I wish only to find out who is using your father's name and for what purpose. You know nothing of this account?'

'Of course not.'

'Nor of who may be using it?'

There was anger in her face now. 'Mr Swain, my father's affairs have been put in order. The probate has been granted and Mr Abrahams has seen to all such matters. The man who has that account is not my father. Is that all you wish to know?'

'Almost,' Swain said, pretending to look at something of importance in his notebook. 'However, if you are leaving the country, there is one more thing. John Posthumous Lerici was your father. Now he is dead, who is your next of kin? Who was your mother?'

She blushed a little. 'I have told you before. My mother died in giving birth to me. She was a young woman of the village of Brahami in the Argoloid. I was called Amalia de Brahami – Amalia from Brahami, you would say. I did not see my father very much until I was fifteen or sixteen. I lived with my grandmother and Basileia, the servant who was my nurse when I was little. Is that all, Mr Swain?'

Swain pretended to study the notebook again, as if ensuring that he had carried out his instructions.

'Yes,' he said presently, 'but you are heir to your father's estate and you have authority over it. You are quite sure that the account at the London and Westminster Bank was not your father's?'

'Mr Swain!' It came like a cry of despair. 'I have nothing to do with it. How can it have been my father's? How can it be now when it is still being used? I have never heard of it before.'

'Quite so,' Swain said gently. 'If the manager of the bank were to approach you, you would have no objection to that account being examined by the proper authorities?'

'Do as you wish with it!' she cried. 'It is nothing to me!'

Swain nodded and stood up. It did not surprise him that the door opened at once and that Signora Lerici and her servant, who had been listening outside, came in without ceremony. These two would see him to the door, Swain guessed. He turned to take Amalia de Brahami's hand for the last time but she had walked away, her head bowed, and now had her back to him. Swain thought that it was best not to make a fool of himself in front of Lumley. He followed Signora Lerici and Basileia to the door that opened on the terrace. But there was one thing he could not forget. He turned to the old woman.

'Signora, there were manuscripts of the greatest value in your son's possession. Works that have been published nowhere. If you will forgive me, they should not be left here with the other contents when you go. Let them be placed somewhere for safety, in a great library or a public collection. And they should be published.'

The old woman shrugged, as if such things now filled her with contempt. In that moment, Swain wondered whether she knew of her son's criminal debauchery with his own child. It was impossible to say but Swain, in his own mind, felt certain that she did.

16

It was on the following afternoon that Mr Abrahams, gravely bearded, joined Swain, Lumley, and Mr Rogerson, solicitor to the London and Westminster Bank, at the branch office in Western Road, Brighton. They sat round the desk in the manager's room, the black metal deed box on the desk itself, while Mr Abrahams drew the items from it like a good-natured uncle playing Santa Claus. Mr Rogerson watched gloomily. Whatever the outcome, it offered no comfort to the London and Westminster Bank.

'First,' said Mr Abrahams, holding up a document by its corner, 'whoever may have been the owner of this box and its contents, his writing is certainly not that of my client. This is not Mr Lerici's script. Quite clearly the man who opened the account did so in my client's name but without his knowledge.'

'Benson,' Swain said quietly, 'Henry Benson, otherwise known as "Poodle" Benson.'

Mr Rogerson intervened.

'Whoever he was, Mr Swain, he opened the account two years ago with the best references. Some time ago, he drew all but twenty pounds of the balance. Then he returned yesterday with the bill of exchange.'

'And never asked for his deed box,' Swain added, 'because everything in it is evidence against others rather than against himself.'

'He left in something of a hurry, Mr Swain.'

Mr Abrahams took a photograph from the deed box. Swain recognized it as the type of studio portrait taken in the hour of an author's fame for display in bookshop windows. He had seen Lord Tennyson, Mr Browning, and Professor Ruskin thus displayed in the windows of Hatchard's and its competitors. John Posthumous Lerici sat in Byronic profile, the line of it long and angular, eyes raised a little to some vision hidden from the onlooker. He wore a military cloak of some kind, fastened across his chest, and a buckled tunic underneath. He might have been his putative father setting out to die for Greece in 1824. There was another portrait of Amalia de Brahami against velvet curtains, hands exquisitely clasped and the look of her father about her.

'If Benson kept these,' Swain said, handing them back, 'I assure you it was not for sentiment.'

But Mr Abrahams had now produced a bundle of papers tied with legal ribbon.

'These, gentlemen, appear to be letters addressed to the owner of the deed box. I hardly think they were intended for the real Mr Lerici. Indeed, one of them is written by him. The first is dated two years ago from Tripolis in southern Greece, written by an Englishman and enclosing the transcript of a baptismal entry for Amalia de Brahami, born in 1859. I think, Mr Swain, that you and Mr Rogerson had both better read it. In Benson's hands, if it was he, it was the foundation of blackmail against the man who debauched his child.'

Swain let Rogerson read it out.

Sir—I could not at first find the entry you spoke of, believing it would be under the name of Lerici. I have traced it however and enclose an accurate transcription. Should you think I deserve anything for my trouble, I will leave you to decide what the sum should be. I was at considerable pains to find what you wanted. Jonathan Browne, MA.

Swain winced at the air of distressed gentility in the style, the travelling man short of funds. Rogerson glanced up and then turned to the second sheet of paper.

'The birth of the child is in the register here as Brahami. The custom is commonly to give the name of the place rather than that of the mother when the child is born out of wedlock. The name of the father is . . .'

'Petrides!' Swain said suddenly without quite knowing why. 'The man who was shot for killing Lerici!'

'Yes, Mr Swain,' said Rogerson, wondering at the trick, 'but why?'

'Because he loved the woman, though he was not the father of the child. I dare say he stood with her at the font while the true father sported himself in Pisa or Paris or London. Lerici claimed her as his daughter. She claims him as her father. A servant may stand proxy for his master's indiscretion, but not the master for his servant's. Take Lerici's photograph and see if there is not a resemblance in the height of the brow and the sharpness of the features. I spent an hour with Petrides before he was shot. There is nothing of him in the girl's appearance.'

Mr Abrahams shook his head. 'You take a lot upon you, Mr Swain.'

'The mother's name . . .' Rogerson began.

'Basileia,' Swain said, 'it can be no other. I confess, though, that I never supposed she was anything to Petrides. She was the girl's mother, not her nurse. Lerici's servant, twenty years old perhaps, who had a child by her master. He cared nothing for that, leaving her as servant in the family of his mother, Giovanna Lerici, where the child also lived. A commendable solution in its way. He returned from years of fame or infamy to find Amalia de Brahami as a beautiful girl of his kind. He treated her as he would have treated any other beautiful girl of that age. The law would do nothing to him, if it thought her father was Petrides. But Petrides was nothing to her. I have never heard the man's name cross her lips. She knew who her father was. She swears he was a god to her.'

There was a silence in the stuffy little room, only the rumble of wheels from the street outside. Abrahams frowned. 'Mr Swain, you make a curious accusation. Do you say that the woman Basileia killed him and that Petrides took the blame?'

Swain shook his head. 'No, sir. Petrides killed him and died for it before the firing-squad at Nauplia.'

'Killed him for the gold that was stolen from the grave-circle at Mycenae?'

Alfred Swain shook his head again. 'No, sir. I dare say golden ornaments were stolen from time to time. Herr Schliemann said as much. But Lerici's gold was sham. Sir John Maule has seen the designs. They are Roman, not Greek. Moreover they are modern plated metal. Like so much else about him, Lerici's treasure was a fraud.'

'Then why his death at Mycenae?' Abrahams asked quietly.

'The woman Basileia, sir. She watched, I dare say, while the girl was debauched by her own father. Only that woman could tell you, sir, whether she begged Petrides to put a stop to this with his knife or whether Petrides killed him in a quarrel for the contents of his purse.'

'Petrides was prepared to give his life for the girl's honour?'

Once more, Swain shook his head. 'No, sir. Petrides had no intention of dying for anyone. Lerici's body was hidden, carefully hidden, in the wild ground of the valley below the grave-circle. By all the laws of probability, it should have remained there a few months until the predators had left mere bone or nothing at all. It was Petrides' misfortune that it was found and the sounds of the quarrel remembered. The man knew he would die anyway. He shielded the woman and the girl. Lerici mocked her even as he debauched her. Iphigenia, he called her, the daughter whose own father sacrificed her. He named a horse after her when he planned the swindle at Goodwood. And as Petrides was shot he called out to me to find Iphigenia before all was destroyed.'

Abrahams hesitated. 'Surely he would have called out the name of Amalia, not Iphigenia.'

'I believe he protected her to the end, sir. To have hinted anything against Amalia would have been to disgrace the girl with his last breath. But if he called her by the name her father gave her, the name of a daughter who was foully wronged by her father, Petrides thought I would understand and guess something of Lerici's guilt.'

Abrahams stood silent but Rogerson was doubtful. 'There are laws against such debauchery, Mr Swain, even in Greece. A man need not be killed.'

'There are laws, sir,' Swain said sadly, 'but when the baptismal register showed the girl's father as Petrides, those laws might be of no avail. It would be mere slander by servants against their master.'

When Rogerson had withdrawn and Swain had dismissed Lumley, Abrahams closed the door.

'There is one more item, Mr Swain, which is for your eyes only.

It may prove you right but I cannot feel it will give you much satisfaction.'

The photograph had evidently been taken at night and Swain had no doubt what it represented.

The room was arched and vaulted in imitation of a castle chamber. Its ceiling was dark blue or black and painted with stars. At the centre of the floor was a dais and a strange scene created upon it. There was a dwarf palm tree, which might have been real or not. A girl of sixteen or eighteen, with bronze or coppery skin, lynx eyes, and a bold profile, posed by it, naked but for a funerary mask that appeared to be of thin beaten gold, a necklace of some kind, and a gold belt. She lay as if breathing quickly and greedily like a huntress after a chase. Lamps concealed in the foliage of the tableau had been angled in such a way as to shine upon various aspects of her figure. The entire display seemed designed to turn slowly, by some invisible mechanism. A grey-haired man sat in a red velvet chair, dressed in a nightgown. He was watching the girl calmly and contentedly, seeing her from the front, the side, and the back in succession. There was a wide bed with crisp linen, ready for them, and a fire in the grate.

'Mr Lerici,' said Abrahams gently, 'and the masked figure is too little disguised. The photograph must have been taken by a third member of the party. There alone, Mr Swain, you have sufficient for blackmail. Was it done by Benson or one of his minions for Lerici's pleasure? There is written in pencil on the back, *Eugénie de Franval*. You are not familiar with that?'

'No, sir,' said Swain, gazing at the print.

'A gothic novelette, Mr Swain, by the Comte de Sade. Its subject is the passion of a father for his daughter.'

Swain stood up and walked across to the mantelshelf. He took a match from the box and lit it. Then, while Abrahams made no attempt to stop him, he held the flame to the edge of the photograph, watched the glaze crack and darken, then dropped the black leaf of ash into the grate.

17

In the next low-ceilinged bedroom of Mr and Mrs Nokes's board-ing-house beyond the Steyne, Sergeant Lumley was snoring in a steady and self-indulgent rhythm. Across the lawns of the Steyne and the domes of the Pavilion, the clock of St Peter's church chimed midnight. Alfred Swain, sitting up in bed by the light of a single candle, frowned as he struggled with the elegant Greek script of his *Agamemnon*. He had started a dozen times, picking his way through the lines with the aid of the notes at the back. After an hour-long effort, he had completed the opening speech of the play, in which the watchman on his tower at Mycenae saw the beacon fires signalling the end of the ten years' war at Troy.

Swain was absorbed by it, thinking it far superior to Shakespeare in the way that the watchman appeared as a grumbling and exploited private soldier. Not dissimilar to Sergeant Lumley, he supposed, as another nocturnal snort announced the return of the vibrations from the next room.

Now the chorus appeared on stage, recalling the causes of the war, the rape of Helen by Paris, Agamemnon and Menelaus lead-ing their thousand black ships in vengeance on Troy and the court of King Priam. Alfred Swain's blood stirred with the thrill of the drama and the poetry, richer than ever after two thousand years and more. Now the great queen herself, Clytemnestra, wife of Agamemnon and mother of the sacrificed virgin, was called from her bed as the beacon fires blazed brighter on the long chain of hills, bringing news of the fleet's return. Swain read the words softly to himself, savouring even when he did not understand, as the chorus of Argos addressed the queen.

'*Soo day, Tyndareo* . . . But you, daughter of Tyndareus, Queen Clytemnestra . . . *Basileia Clytemnestra* . . .'

Basileia! He turned to the notes and it seemed that the expla-nation hit him like a bullet. How could he ever have doubted it? Or ignored it? Or simply not known it? The Greek word for a queen! Just as little English girls nowadays might be called Queenie! *Basileia Clytemnestra*, the sublime avenger of her daugh-ter's sacrifice! *Basileia Clytemnestra*, whose lover struck down with mortal steel the evil father. In the cramped bedroom of the Brighton boarding-house, some great wheel of history had come full circle and Alfred Swain of Pimlico swore to himself that he had lived through an heroic drama of the ancient world. It was ghostly and yet sublime. He had stood before the Lion Gate at Mycenae, the very spot where the catastrophe had taken place more than three thousand years before. And now it had happened again. And Aeschylus had foreseen it.

In his excitement, he scrambled out of bed, candle in one hand and book in the other, and opened the door of the next room.

'Mr Lumley! Wake up! I've got it!'

He was disconcerted but not deterred to find that Sergeant Lumley, whom he had never seen in bed before, wore his moustaches tied up at night in a cheese-cloth of some kind. The sergeant's face had a tragic look. 'God's sake, Mr Swain, it's the middle of the night!'

'I've got her, Mr Lumley! Here in this book! In the *Agamemnon*! Basileia! She's here!'

'You woke me up for a book?' There was a piteous tone to Lumley's words, as if he might cry at any moment. He heaved the bedclothes round himself again.

'It fits, Mr Lumley! It's all here! Basileia! Iphigenia!'

'And Poodle Benson?' said the self-pitying presence under the blankets. 'He's there waiting to be arrested, is he?'

'Don't be a fool, Mr Lumley! This is much more important than Benson!'

'Lovely job,' said Lumley miserably, 'you go back to Mr Toplady and tell 'im you got one of your poetry books that's more important than his case. He'll do more than dance the polka this time.'

'This is the case, Mr Lumley!'

Lumley put his face above the sheet again. 'It's the middle of the night, Mr Swain. What's so important about it all?'

'What's important, Mr Lumley, is that I have spent months following procedure, interviewing witnesses, travelling all over the place, being half-suffocated, lied to, led on. And all the time I should have been reading Aeschylus instead.'

'You tell Mr Toplady,' said the sergeant unhappily. 'When we get back to London, you tell him just that. Your backside won't touch a single stair until you land at the foot of 'em and out the door. Now for God's sake let me sleep!'

With an air of austere superiority, Alfred Swain returned to his room.

18

Two mornings later, Swain walked slowly under the first of the four cast-iron arches of the Chain Pier. Against the fresh sky of the cool summer morning, the suspension cables of the pier swooped and dipped in their elegant web. Each of the triumphal iron archways over which the cables passed was a model of regency elegance with its cornice and ornamental lamp, the base on either side wide enough to have a little kiosk selling refreshments or souvenirs. A silvery tide rattled and rushed on the shingle underfoot, then fell silent as the water deepened further out and the wind whipped the crest from green Channel surges. At the landing stage, the *Fleur-de-Lys* was moored for the crossing to Dieppe and the Paris express of the Chemin-de-Fer du Nord. With Lumley walking beside him, Swain followed the trail of passengers.

Three porters were carrying the baggage of Giovanna Lerici, Amalia de Brahami, and Basileia. Two had been the lovers of the dead brandy-soaked romantic. One had been daughter and lover, one the mother. All three women were dressed in black, mourning Byron's lost son, with whom their bodies had had such intimate yet various connection. Their mourning costumes had not struck Swain so forcibly at Mondragon. Here, among the blue and yellow summer dresses, the coloured ribbons flying from windblown hats, they seemed like women of ancient myth in their grief.

'Black stoled, black hooded, like a dream,' Lord Tennyson's lines came unbidden to the mind of Alfred Swain. 'Three Queens with crowns of gold – and from them rose a cry that shiver'd to the tingling stars.'

'What you on about, Mr Swain?'

Swain cursed to himself, thinking he had breathed the lines too softly for anyone to hear. 'Nothing, Mr Lumley.'

'Right,' Lumley said, 'I'll just stop here and get a hot pie from the stall. You go on, if you like.'

Swain went on. He stared at Amalia de Brahami. In her he saw the truth of Helen, bride of the House of Atreus, not in Mr Rossetti's pale English school-misses. The skin of warm gold, the odalisque slant of the dark eyes, the high brow and sharp profile, the narrow hips and thighs agile as a mountain goat.

'O Merlin, do you love me? Great Master do you love me ... Do you love me, Mr Swain?'

Had she asked him now, Swain would have confessed it. She was Iphigenia, part of the great and wonderful story. He had an instant's fantasy in which Amalia de Brahami turned, threw herself into his arms, and refused to go aboard the steamer with the others. They travelled together to the great adventure on which Herr Schliemann had already embarked. Alfred Swain toiled at Mycenae and came home each evening to the simple meal, the wine, the warm embraces . . . It was the fantasy he had indulged at Mycenae, of course, not knowing that the golden maiden would have an identity.

What about Mrs Beresford? Swain sighed and recalled himself to reality.

'I thank you, Mr Swain, for what you have done. It has not been easy.'

But it was the old woman's hand in his own as they stood on the landing stage, the smoke rising in a thin trail from the tall custard-yellow stack of the *Fleur-de-Lys*. Basileia ignored him, staring out to sea. Amalia de Brahami walked away without speaking, her head bowed as if in a sadness of some kind. They went down the gangway and on to the deck of the steamer among the piles of luggage.

Swain looked up. Amalia de Brahami was at the rail gazing at him. Their eyes met and never left one another for a moment that seemed to Swain longer than the drama of the *Agamemnon*, longer than the Anger of Achilles, longer than the *Odyssey*. 'Do you love me, Mr Swain?' Surely the eyes asked that question now, and Alfred Swain promised her silently that he did.

The gangway was drawn aboard and the ropes splashed down into the water from the pier's mooring bollards as the steamer's capstan began to haul them in. With a mighty effort, the finned paddles of the steamer made their first slow turn. The *Fleur-de-Lys* moved forward in an exchange of shouts and waves from passengers and friends. Only as Amalia turned away and Swain's eyes followed her did he discover that someone else had been regarding him with equal intensity of feeling. Briefly he met the eyes of the black-hooded Basileia and saw in them such hostility that she would have murdered him on the spot for his glances at the girl. Swain thought again of the nightmare in the smoke-filled room at Mondragon, the struggling and the drowning. How little reason he thought the woman had for harming him then. How great the reason seemed now as she bore away to safety the person she loved most in her life. Petrides had given his life, the lover of Basileia perhaps, to avenge the girl. And Basileia, faithful to her lover as to her child, had she struck the blow that brained Spider McBride who would have stolen the secrets of her child's shame? Had she, rather than the wind, shut the window as smoke filled Alfred Swain's room? The figure with whom he had grappled in his nightmare ... The phantom whose vengeance had fallen upon Lerici and Spider McBride ... One day, surely, the truth would be revealed to Amalia de Brahami ... Swain stared at the dwindling figure of the servant and thought again of the line from Robert Browning's translation of the *Agamemnon*, which had lingered in his nightmare. 'The killer has all to pay ...'

The steamer had turned beam on, squat as a duck with the width of its paddle-boxes. A beat of finned wheels carried across the water, as Amalia de Brahami was carried to Dieppe, Paris, Marseille, and a life of questionable chastity in the household of Giovanna Lerici at Venice. It was to be several years later when Alfred Swain heard that his goddess had entered a religious order.

As the *Fleur-de-Lys* merged with the yellow haze of the Channel horizon, he walked back slowly down the Chain Pier with Lumley. Swain was not in the mood for discussion and Lumley was too preoccupied by a second warm meat pie to care. At the gates of the pier, Swain saw Arthur Squires, a uniformed inspector of the Brighton force.

'Morning, Mr Swain,' said Squires cheerfully, handing over a blue form. 'Duty clerk said he thought you was down here, seeing the boat off. Message come for you from London. Mr Toplady, I shouldn't wonder.'

Swain took the blue telegraph form and read it. 'Yes,' he said, 'thank you, Mr Squires.'

As soon as he could do so without discourtesy, he led Lumley aside. The two men stood by the promenade rail in the struggling morning sun.

'Seems I shan't be going back to London with you, Mr Lumley.'

'You ain't been sacked, Mr Swain?' There was no mistaking the apprehension in the sergeant's voice on Swain's behalf.

'No, Mr Lumley, nothing like that. I start my leave on Monday, down here with Mr and Mrs Nokes. Being Thursday now and my rest day tomorrow, Mr Toplady is good enough to suggest that I need not report back until the end of leave.'

'Oh!' Lumley shouted at the mean-mindedness of it. 'Ho! That's generous, that is. What he give you, Mr Swain, must be about half an hour off actual duty. He got the meanness of a stoat, Mr Swain. And that's not insubordination neither. I'm not talking about him as senior officer, just as a man.'

'Well,' Swain said feebly, 'there it is.'

Lumley stuffed the rest of the meat pie into his well-fed face, wiped his fingers on the paper, and swallowed.

'That old girl, Mr Swain. So-called nurse with the funny name. The way she looked at you when the boat pulled out. If looks could 'a killed!'

'Really?'

'Oh, yes!' Lumley chuckled. 'She knew your little secret all right, Mr Swain. You was smart, you was. You twigged that it was her that stuffed up the chimney when she thought you might be a bit sweet on Miss Brahami. Which you could 'a been, after all! Most wouldn't say no to that.'

There was intense relief. Lumley had missed it but not by much.

'I dare say you're right, Mr Lumley.'

'On the other hand, Mr Swain, you was dead wrong over Spider McBride. "Handsome" Palmer still swears he moved that body out from the wall below the tower to see if the poor devil might have life in him. So you was wrong there. Sandbags and all. Old Spider missed his footing and fell off that tower, Mr Swain, only you not knowing about Palmer couldn't see it.'

Swain stared at the last faint smoke of the steamer on the Channel horizon. 'Yes, Mr Lumley,' he said, closing a door in his mind on the drama of the past, 'I expect it must have been that.'

The sergeant gave a superior snort. 'Course it was, Mr Swain. Still I'm surprised an officer of your experience never saw it somehow!'

19

With Mrs Beresford on his arm, Alfred Swain walked through the stalls and entertainments of the circus and hiring fair that accompanied the summer races. The sweep of downland was rich with the stirring of sheep bells and the high trilling of larks in an infinite vault of warm sky. To one side, the heat mist turned the sea to a dull and motionless mirror.

The week of Swain's leave was almost over. He felt again something which he had lost over the past few months, while scarcely noticing its departure. He had regained contentment. With the young woman beside him, her cheerful prettiness and easy manner, with his lodgings and his books, he felt that there was nothing else in the world he wanted. Amalia de Brahami had been a dream after all. If he could have wished her back, there beside him, he thought he would not have done it.

The races were on the far side of the road. Here, in the fairground, the steam-organ was pumping and blasting, the painted horses turning, and the entertainments of the canvas booths had begun. At the centre of the great ring of tents and chair-wheels, roundabouts and caravans, the auctioneers bawled and cajoled their audiences while sheep and calves and ponies from the Welsh hills or the western moors shifted, nuzzled, and tossed in the hurdled enclosures.

Swain and Mrs Beresford had found diversions of their own among Mrs Jarley's waxworks, the roundabouts, and the peep-shows that offered Sultan Omar's Harem, The Execution of Sam Hall, Beauty Bathing, The Last Stand at Gandamack, and Lady Godiva's Ride.

A slight frown gathered on Alfred Swain's face. He walked slowly through the babel of fire-eaters and jugglers, tight-rope walkers and grease-removers, cheap-jacks, mountebanks dressed like the King of Hearts, corn-curers, and fortune-tellers. Exponents of the three-card trick on an upturned bucket rivalled the hucksters of three-thimbles-and-a-pea.

Several of the faces were familiar to him here as in the streets of Hoxton or Lambeth. Pineapple Jem and Iron-Foot Poll, French Nellie and Dancing Dick, Joey Footfall and Rotten Jane. Tricks and promises were their stock in trade.

Beyond this arena of ordinary folk the turf of the downland stretched away to a vast horizon, broken only by dry-stone walls and a few wind-stunted trees. Upon this scene the smug regency crescents of Brighton turned their elegant backs. Where the town became woodland or downland, Lerici's folly, its Portuguese gothic pinnacles and lantern like extravagant architectural pastry against the flying clouds, marked the limit of sophistication and fashion.

It was the time of day when the booths were patronized by farmers and graziers who had come for the livestock auctions and the hiring. Here and there were nursemaids with children or families of industrious tradesfolk and craftsmen from the town.

'Mr Swain, dear.' There was a slight pressure on his arm, as if to remind him that his thoughts had wandered from her. 'You have enjoyed your leave, have you?'

'Oh, yes, Mrs Beresford. Very much indeed. I haven't felt so happy for a long time. And you, Mrs Beresford? Have you been happy?' The pressure on his arm increased.

'Oh, yes, Mr Swain. I haven't been so happy since – well, I don't know when.'

She meant, he thought, since the sacrifice of Constable Beresford in the chill current off London Bridge wharf. He was grateful to her for not referring to it – for not obliging him to say again how sorry he was for a man he had never known.

Beyond the shooting gallery where the metal pellets popped and rang on the tin targets, the amusements ended.

'I expect, Mrs Beresford, I expect you'd like to see some of the other sideshows.'

'That'd be nice,' she said eagerly.

'What would you like to see?'

She hugged his arm again. 'I don't know, Mr Swain. Perhaps it ought to be something improving.'

The last comment was made without conviction. Swain suspected that she would not have minded Lady Godiva. With a transient sense of guilt, he said, 'The camera obscura, perhaps? It's better than any magic lantern show.'

'Is it?' There was no mistaking a certain tone of disappointment. 'And then Lady Godiva?'

'Well,' she said eagerly, 'if you think that's best, Mr Swain, dear.'

They turned towards the entrance of the tent, where the mirrors and lenses of the camera obscura had been erected. The showman with a red-lettered board by the entrance flap was drumming up custom while a fair-haired child took the coins of the patrons. The proprietor was a lolloping giant with unruly curls and a fixed stare.

'Giambattista Della Porta was born of a noble and ancient family at Naples about the year 1543 ... In his book on natural magic, he describes how a small aperture in the shutter of a darkened room will produce upon the wall delightful images of all that passes outside ... The connoisseur may study at leisure the courtship of the innocent among the bushes and tall grass ... The lewd and sensual embrace of the guilty who believe themselves unobserved in their wickedness shall be brought into the 'olesome light of day ... Within this dome, ladies and gentlemen, may be seen all that passes in secret for miles around ... Reflected through a mirror in the centre of the roof, the image is displayed before you on a reflecting table ... You shall recognize figures upon the horizon as if they stood in the room with you ... This miracle of science and detection, this harmless yet diverting show ...'

'Afternoon, Jemmy Fashion.'

'Afternoon, Mr Swain. What you doing down here?'

'Summer leave, Mr Fashion. Lot of innocent courtship round here, is there? Many lewd and sensual embraces of the guilty been seen through your mirrors today?'

The fat man in the entrance of the tent huffed with pure good humour.

'Come on, Mr Swain! We just put two couples out there in the bushes. They don't do much. Just enough to make the clients think they're seeing something they shouldn't. An' the ones out there need the money, Mr Swain. Play fair.' The comfortably creased face looked up at Alfred Swain in apprehensive appeal.

'I'm not here to complain, Mr Fashion, just to buy two tickets.'

'You shall 'ave 'em, Mr Swain. My compliments.'

'Rather pay, if you don't mind, Mr Fashion.'

'Well, Mr Swain,' said the showman cheerfully, 'if you will have it so, you will.'

Swain led Mrs Beresford through the shabbily tented archway into the warm canvas space that served as the camera obscura. At the centre of the booth a black tent had been arranged about the mirrors and lenses. With Mrs Beresford beside him, Swain entered the darkness. Only once before, as a child at Salisbury horse fair, had Swain seen a camera obscura. This one was far more dramatic than the one he remembered. In the darkness, a beam of daylight reflected from the apex of the black tent produced a sharp panorama as if in a brilliantly silvered mirror on a table-top. By turning and adjusting the surface, it was possible to bring into view different parts of the landscape outside. By some use of a lens, the images were large and clear as if they were seen through a telescope.

It was a strange feeling, to be looking into bright, sharply delineated scenes, as if into a fortune-teller's globe. The innocent lovers and the guilty parties, caught abruptly doing nothing, busied themselves with one another on a signal of command from Jemmy Fashion. The panorama of tree-filled valleys with cottage roofs and the dovecotes of manor-houses swam across the mirrors. The trees were pale green and in generous leaf.

'Stop a bit, Mr Fashion, if you please,' Alfred Swain said presently. 'That's where I was, Mrs Beresford. Mondragon.'

The other patrons of the canvas booth leant forward to study the sunlit image of Mondragon's gothic tower.

'There, Mrs Beresford. Up there, behind the battlements. That's where I had my room. Down there, through the arch, that's the entrance hall, all hung with crimson velvet inside. That's the western gallery with paintings by Mr Rossetti and Mr Burne-Jones.'

Mrs Beresford squirmed a little with innocent pleasure at being linked, however indirectly, to such things.

'Made you quite knowledgeable about such finery, Mr Swain,' Jemmy Fashion said. 'You living there so long.'

'A little of it,' Swain said modestly.

'And what's to become of it now he's dead?'

'Sold, Mr Fashion. Personal effects moved out and the place taken on by a religious order.'

'Got the right sort of look for it,' Mrs Beresford said.

The other patrons of the booth were watching the three speakers intently, mouths gaping with delight at being admitted to the secrets of the great house.

'I read a funny book once,' a man said, 'about what they gets up to in places like that, all them monks and nuns!'

'No need for offence,' said Jemmy Fashion hastily.

'There,' said the man, 'there's one of 'em. They took the place over all right!'

A figure in soutane and biretta was making its way between the trees, along the path that led to the garden tomb of John Posthumous Lerici.

'That's the tomb down there,' Swain said. 'They buried Mr Lerici there after he was murdered abroad. He built it years before as his resting place.'

'He did himself all right then,' said the man who had once read a book. 'There's folk ain't got houses as good as his tomb is.'

'Turn the picture on, Mr Fashion,' someone else said.

'No,' Swain said, 'wait a minute, Jemmy. That fellow's gone into the tomb.'

'P'raps he's going to snatch the body,' said the book-reading man.

'He can't have an idea in the world that he's being watched,' the other man said.

'Hello,' Jemmy Fashion said, 'here he comes again, up the steps from the mausoleum. Looks as if he's got something that he didn't have when he went in there.'

'Well,' Mrs Beresford said, 'I've heard of people taking something to a tomb – flowers and such – but not bringing things away!'

The cassocked figure turned and began to walk back towards the house.

'He got a portfolio or something,' the reading man said.

Swain turned to the proprietor. 'Can you make this picture any bigger, Jem Fashion?'

'I could do, Mr Swain. But you won't see any more. He's walking away with his back to you now.'

'I'm not interested in the man, Mr Fashion. Can you focus this contraption on the octagon tower?'

'If the other ladies and gents don't mind, Mr Swain.'

'Police business, Mr Fashion.'

A cooing of approval broke out all round him when police business was mentioned. The landscape swirled across the glass of the table and the base of the octagon came into view with its arched doorway to the winding staircase.

'Now move up, Mr Fashion. One row of windows at a time, if you don't mind.'

'You sure this is all right, Mr Swain? Prying into people's windows?'

'Quite sure, Mr Fashion.'

The picture in the glass moved slowly up the grey architraves of sunlit stucco.

'Bit more, Mr Fashion. Where the tower rises clear of the roof of the main abbey building.'

The picture moved a little more and stopped. Swain saw that they were level with the so-called tower-room, the locked apartment sacred to Lerici's pleasures. The westerly sun was striking level into its interior, illuminating a shadowy view of vaulting and arched recesses. It was difficult to see much of the room but light was reflected on the yellow damask wall-hangings. The picture in the far recess, between velvet curtains, was large enough and so brightly painted as to be vivid at any time. Such was the masterpiece which the Flemish bohemian Félicien Rops had painted in Brussels for the Master of Mondragon. It showed a young woman who leant naked over a page of text on a lectern. Her back was to the viewer and she was completely naked, the thighs and buttocks fleshy and pale. A broomstick was clamped between her legs, its brush protruding backwards. Under the stand of the lectern, a baboon crouched in shadow. The young woman was smiling at the page of text as she read it.

'Mr Swain!' It was Mrs Beresford who was the first and only member of the party to utter such dismay. The man who had read a book, as if echoing Spider McBride's philosophy on seeing the same picture, assured the others that that was how 'the harristocrats hooks it'.

'Now, Jemmy Fashion,' said Swain quietly, 'what officers of the town police might be on duty up here today?'

'They got 'em from everywhere, Mr Swain, what with His Royal Highness himself being here for the races.'

'Even village constables?'

'Them too, Mr Swain. They don't get leave on a day like this.'

'Mr Allardyce, perhaps?'

'Seen him about an hour since, Mr Swain.'

Swain drew the proprietor of the camera obscura aside. 'Now, Jemmy Fashion. I can't promise you there's a reward in this case. But if there should be a reward, you'd kick yourself for missing it. Is that right?'

'Right, Mr Swain.'

'Very well. Get your boy to find Mr Allardyce and bring him to me here. And then get him to go to the superintendent of the town police with my compliments. That house and grounds is to be surrounded.'

Jemmy Fashion looked disconcerted. 'They ain't got men to do that, Mr Swain. Not today, of all days.'

Swain looked at him sadly. 'Mr Fashion, do you or don't you have the look of a man who knows a reward when he sees it?'

'I have, Mr Swain.'

'Then see to it, Jem,' said Swain gently, 'while I have another look in this contraption of yours. Just see to it.'

20

With the helmeted figure of Allardyce at his side, Swain stood once again at the turning of the country lane where the pillars marked the driveway of Mondragon.

'You don't want to wait, Mr Swain? Wait for the others?'

'I think not, Mr Allardyce. Whoever he is, he may be getting ready to leave.'

'Religious order, I was told, sir.'

'How many religious orders do you suppose, Mr Allardyce, hang pictures like *that* in their rooms? Even if the house was just being made ready, isn't that one of the first things they would get rid of?'

'Can't be many of 'em here yet, Mr Swain. Most not expected for a week or two. Some from France.'

The terrace and the crenellated outline of the house were still screened by the copses and spinneys. The sun fell as a faint dappling in the alleys and bridle paths.

'Where would you hide a leaf, Mr Allardyce?'

'A leaf, Mr Swain?'

'Policeman's litany, Mr Allardyce. Where would you hide a leaf? In a tree. Where would you hide a corpse? In a graveyard. So where would you hide a fugitive that could get his hands on a cassock?'

'Oh, said Allardyce thoughtfully, 'see what you mean, Mr Swain.'

They were near to the enclosure among the trees where Lerici had built his tomb beside the carriageway.

'This religious order, Mr Allardyce. Connections with France, you say? Pilgrimages abroad, I dare say? Travel of some kind?'

'Believe so, Mr Swain.'

'Yes, Mr Allardyce, you may well believe it. A crowd of folk in religious habits getting on the steamer for France. Who in his right mind would search that lot to the skin? Eh?' Swain paused, aware that he was beginning to sound like Toplady in his exasperation.

The gravelled track had opened out at the mausoleum.

'I'm not waiting, Mr Allardyce. We're going in there.'

'In there, Mr Swain?'

'Of course. Good God, man! He's been dead a few months! He's not going to do you any harm now!'

Allardyce hesitated.

'Stay here, then,' Swain said, 'and keep a look out.'

Leaving Allardyce to his uneasy duty, Swain crossed to the tomb. He walked between the stone lions, stepped over the iron chain between the posts, and went down the steps of York stone which led him to the iron latticework of its doors. At first he thought the doors were locked. Then he saw that only the bolt was across. He drew it back, turned the handle and stepped down into the sepulchre.

The stone catafalque stood squarely under the gothic obelisk. Upon it lay a heavy sealed coffin of bronze with a florid plaque bearing Lerici's name and title. Swain stood quite still and heard a slow drip of moisture somewhere in the shadows. A candle burnt fitfully in a shuttered lamp, giving off the faint odour of sandalwood.

If there was a place of concealment it must be near the coffin itself. Swain moved forward. There was a single step that ran round the catafalque. Despite his scorn of Allardyce, the menace of John Posthumous Lerici hung like a vapour in the air. Swain stepped reluctantly on to the raised surround. As he did so, a shape like a black wing passed across the far wall and his heart seemed to stop. It was not fright, he swore to himself, only shock. But it immobilized him for a second or two.

Someone who had been standing concealed by the catafalque and coffin went out through the door. Swain turned to follow and, in doing so, tripped. His hands met the tiled floor and he saved himself. Yet by the time he was on his feet again, the figure had gone. Now he understood why the mausolem gates had been unlocked. Whoever the fugitive might be had the keys to Mondragon, or at least had had ample opportunity in the past to copy certain keys.

Where the devil had he gone? Swain was out of the darkness and into the sunlit afternoon, the fantasies of the tomb dispersed by the air and brightness. Allardyce would have caught the suspect as he came out. But Constable Allardyce was standing in the middle of the gravelled carriageway, looking as if he had been turned to stone by a gorgon's eye. Swain had been startled. But Allardyce had been terrified by the black apparition which emerged from the tomb into which Swain had stepped.

'Mr Allardyce! Where is he? Where?'

Allardyce pointed towards the house. 'There, Mr Swain! All dressed in black! He ran for the house.'

'And thanks to you, Mr Allardyce, he may have got there by now!'

Swain began to run with Allardyce after him. It was two hundred yards or so to the western door of Mondragon, the octagon tower rising on their right and the great entrance arch opening into the western hall. They crossed the terrace of marble boxes, where Spider McBride had been found, and went up the flight of shallow steps to the main entrance.

Swain, his heart pounding from the sprint, looked about him for some implement that might be used to batter through the closed door. Then, to his astonishment, he tried the door and found it unlocked.

'Careful, Mr Allardyce. He could be armed. Billy Kurr was.'

Swain pushed the door wide and walked slowly through, half expecting someone behind the door to strike at him. There was no one. The western gallery with its mullioned windows had been denuded of its paintings and some of the furniture. It was in that curious state of a house that has been abandoned but not yet disposed of. Swain stopped.

'He didn't lock the outer door, Mr Allardyce. He must have locked himself in somewhere.'

Even as he spoke, Swain knew the answer, seeing in his mind the plain little room with its distempered walls, the chair and the desk. A man might offer evidence to mitigate a charge of forgery or theft. Blackmail was another matter. Blackmail would add fourteen years to any other sentence passed upon Harry Benson. Swain had been so preoccupied with the money that it only occurred to him now what Benson's true mission might be – to complete what Spider McBride had failed to do.

'This way, Mr Allardyce, if you please.'

They turned away from the western gallery, across the great hall and through a drawing-room whose windows looked out on the terrace. Swain paused before the door at the far end. He tried the handle and found it locked. From inside the room there was a sound of scampering and slithering. It might have been rats or mice. Swain knew it was neither.

'Mr Benson! Open this door, if you please! There is no way out of here. If necessary, the door will be broken in.'

There was no response beyond a resumption of the sound that suggested rats or mice scurrying through paper. Paper! Swain believed he saw it all.

'Mr Allardyce, we must have this door open. There is evidence in that room and the fellow may destroy it. We shan't be able to kick it down with panels like that. See what you can find outside. I will stay here and block his way out.'

Allardyce disappeared while Swain continued his unanswered entreaties to the fugitive. But Allardyce returned, carrying a hatchet and looking uneasy. 'There's smoke, Mr Swain, coming from one of the chimneys. I should think he's just about set fire to himself in there.'

Swain took the hatchet, swung and brought it down on the panel of the door. It bounced off like a rubber baton and there was such pain in his shoulder that he thought he must have broken his arm.

'Give it to me, Mr Swain,' said Allardyce encouragingly.

Swain handed over the hatchet. Allardyce stood back, breathed hard and struck four times at the lock. He burst it open and the door swung back.

The slightly built figure of Harry Benson stood at the centre of the room, bare-headed, his face smudged by smoke, dressed in a black soutane with a crimson border. His biretta was on the desk. The room was hot as a furnace, a gasping breath of flame sucked up the chimney from the leaded grate, a black drift of paper-ash spilling out of the grate and into the room. The desk was open and the drawers empty.

'Really, gentlemen,' the little man said with a surprised smile, 'I see no reason for such a violent entry. If there was anything that needed to be discussed, you had only to ask.'

Swain looked at him. 'Thank you, Mr Benson, I have been asking for the past fifteen minutes without avail. Take him, Mr Allardyce. Handcuff Mr Benson and lead him outside to await the others.'

Benson showed no alarm and no resentment. 'May I suggest, Mr Swain, that all this is unnecessary? Your business with me is to see that my evidence is taken against four men who have disgraced the name of Scotland Yard. That wipes out the charges against me. I can bring the house down, Mr Swain, or rather two houses. The house of finance and confidence would be destroyed if what I have accomplished in the past two months became common knowledge. And the house of the law will be in ruins after what I have had to say.'

Until that moment, Swain had not known how much he loathed the repellent creature.

'And after all that, Mr Benson, when you have saved yourself ten years in Newgate for forgery, you will serve fourteen more years for blackmail. Handcuff him, if you please, Mr Allardyce.'

Benson made a slight show of resistance, quickly suppressed by the uniformed policeman. The two men went out, leaving Swain alone. He sifted the leaves of ash, seeing here and there the ghosts of words and phrases. *United States Government . . . Issue Date . . . Place of Redemption . . . Title of Bondholder . . .*

Swain straightened up. After so much, after months of planning and execution, it had come to nothing but this. Harry Benson, cornered, had taken refuge in the deserted rooms of Mondragon. It did not surprise Swain that Benson had contrived to steal or copy keys while he was a guest in the house long before. It was a precaution he would have taken under any conditions of hospitality. Presumably the United States Bonds had been hidden in the mausoleum after Kurr's arrest. No one would intrude there and no one would search there. No doubt Benson had been removing them prior to his departure. Caught at that moment, he had no choice but to burn the evidence against him. Among the ashes, lay not only the money he had stolen but the money of his own with which he began. Justice had been self-fulfilling.

Somewhere, Swain thought, there was a sermon in all this on the fate of Mammon. He stared down at the leaves of blackened paper again and was held by a chilll thought. There was a page whose inked lines were just visible in their ghostliness. '. . . *n Juan in the New* . . .' Swain dropped to his knees, sifting with gentle fingers. Here and there was a phrase, an imperfect stanza, sometimes a line and even a fragment of soaring chords on musical staves.

It had never occurred to him that such treasures would have been left behind after all. Benson had destroyed the evidence against him, evidence of blackmail and evidence of forgery or theft. He had also destroyed gems of cultural history, including four books of unpublished cantos by the greatest poet of the past two centuries.

Alfred Swain had been prepared for a good deal but not for this. Allardyce was right. It would have been better to delay, to take Benson by weight of numbers before he could destroy so much.

With a sense of oppression, Swain turned his back on Mondragon for the last time, knowing there was nothing to be saved there. By the time he went out on to the sunlit terrace, several other officers had arrived from the fairground and the race course. Benson was still standing there, his hands cuffed behind his back and Allardyce holding him by the arm. Swain stood before him.

'In your concern for your own miserable skin, you have destroyed several of the most important manuscripts of our time, including Lord Byron's continuation of his great poem.'

To his dismay, Benson put back his head and laughed. 'Nonsense, old fellow, they ain't anything but jokes.'

'Jokes?'

'Lerici's jokes. When he and his guests wasn't doing things with that daughter of his, he'd drink them to sleep. And while they drank there was games. Clever games. Who could write this and who could write that. He was going to publish them one day and then tell the world it had been had.'

'I don't believe you.'

Benson grinned. 'I don't care if you do, my friend. But I can knock off as many stanzas of Lord Byron as you like. Nothing but a knack to be picked up in an evening or two. It's a sight easier than faking a bill on Rothschild or Baring.'

'I still don't believe you.'

Benson's smile never faltered. He beamed up at Swain, the tarnished tooth glistening. 'But you'll never know, will you, Swain? Never be sure. And you can't show them to anyone else now. The joke's on you, old fellow. It really is.'

Swain walked away, anywhere to be out of sight of the sickly little figure in his ruffled soutane. Fraud rose round 'Poodle' Benson like a stench. It enveloped 'Handsome Palmer', Clarke, Meiklejohn, and Druscovich, who would undergo a public martyr-dom at the Central Criminal Court in a few months' time. Billy Kurr and Benson himself would go to prison until they were grey-haired and broken by it. Amalia de Brahami would nurse the memory of a father who was a fraud in almost everything he did. The thought of it was more than Alfred Swain could endure. A uniformed inspector was arriving in a cab from Brighton. Let the town police have the man and take the credit.

He came to the clearing where the author of so much aimless depravity had built his own memorial, the gothic obelisk pointing its dark finger at the summer sky. Swain read the inscription again.

'My task is done – my song has ceased – my theme
Has died into an echo; it is fit
The spell should break of this protracted dream.'

As he read it, the spell broke for Alfred Swain. What did it matter, in the end, whether the lost manuscripts were real or fake? There was so much that was true. *Don Juan, Childe Harold, The Aga-memnon*, Mrs Beresford . . . On Monday his leave would end. But there was the rest of today and the whole of tomorrow. Across the valley and up the hill, as the light faded, there was a glimmer of illumination on the fairground. Swain thought he heard music and voices, chatter and laughter. There was the camera obscura with its views of the night sky, and Jemmy Fashion at the entrance arch, and Mrs Beresford waiting. Alfred Swain lengthened his stride and felt as if the summer leave were beginning all over again.

231